I0760307

A Bond in Blood

Blood Bound Duet
Book I

C.A. Blooming

Character Art by @avoccatt_art

Cover Art by @selkkiedesigns

Map by @studioallred

Editing by Wonder and Wander Publishing

Paperback ISBN 978-1-964087-08-5

Hardcover ISBN 978-1-964087-10-8

For all the *"rule-following, good girls"* who deserve the chance to hate-fuck the villains.

Author's Note

A Bond in Blood is intended for mature audiences only (18 years or older).

This book is a Dark Fantasy Romance, with an emphasis on the ***dark***. I'm talking morally ***dark*** men, not these "morally questionable for a little bit" kind of characters. Meaning, the contents of this book may be uncomfortable for some. While they may be absolutely delicious for others.

I won't yuck your yum if the thought of being kidnapped by a tattooed, shadow king and forced to sleep in his bed gets your blood pumping. Just remember, you're an **adult** choosing to read this deliciously dark novel. If suddenly your yums have been yucked—stop reading.

Enjoy the men.

Content Notice

This dark romance is full of themes that may make some uncomfortable. Please review the below content notice (if you want to) prior to reading.

Kidnapping
Violence
Death
Public beatings (whipping)
Sexual Content
Full sexual scenes
MFM sexual scenes
BDSM play
Attempted sexual assault

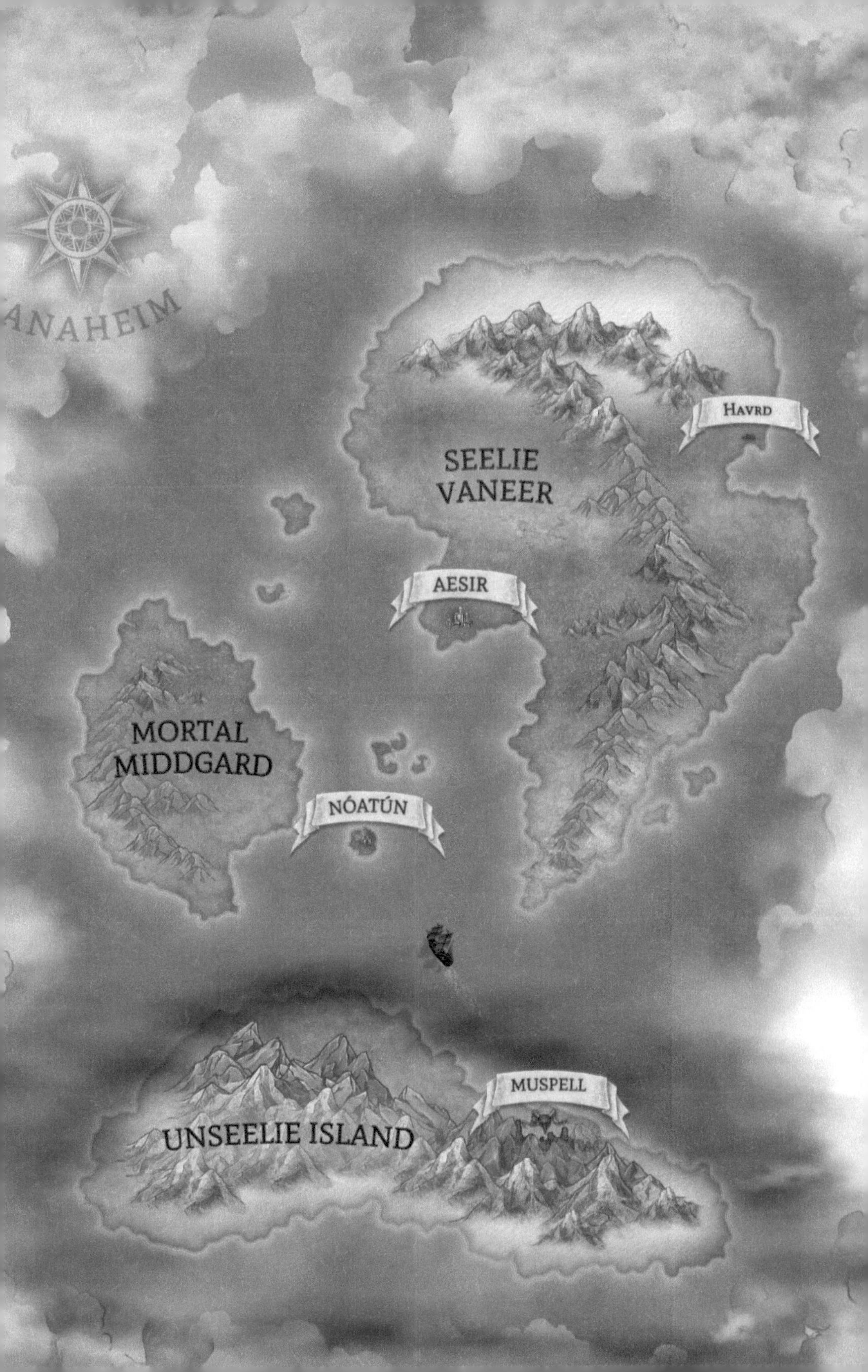

ANAHEIM

SEELIE
VANEER

HAVRD

AESIR

MORTAL
MIDDGARD

NÓATÚN

MUSPELL

UNSEELIE ISLAND

Chapter I

The Gods were whispering, beckoning for me to listen.

But my heart and mind were focused ahead of me, watching the fjord. Searching for the signs of my future approaching. The destiny I hadn't known to be an option.

Beside me my father, the king, fidgeted nervously. The movement was irritating, and while I would have usually questioned his disjointed shuffling, I held my tongue. It was my day.

One I'd waited for.

Three long years of patience for my betrothed to sail his ship to our secluded island in the sea. Years that should have been nothing for me as a half-fae woman, nearly immortal. Yet, the longing had almost killed me. Even with our letter-only communication, those years had moved as slowly as the glaciers that had formed my beloved fjord.

My hands twitched at my sides while I looked for him—Prince Leif of Havrd.

He'd surprised us all with that first letter. Addressing it only to my father, he made his intentions known that he'd heard of the beautiful, auburn-haired princess living in the mortal realms and he intended to make me his bride.

My father had objected at first.

Surprising no one.

But Leif was insistent, sending only letters to father at the beginning. Laying out his intentions. Sending portraits of not only himself, but his kingdom and family. Slowly breaking down my father's anxious heart until he allowed the letters to go to me.

My heart instantly latched onto the first two words.

My enaid.

Enaid—the silly word the Seelie fae used in their land. A word the mortals refused to use when describing their other halves. Previously, I would have scoffed at it. I wasn't one for fae customs, leaning more toward my mortal half.

But the word...

It had wrapped around my soul, dragging me to him instantly.

The wind picked up around me while my mind drifted along with it. I wondered if perhaps the Gods were blessing this first meeting. Perhaps Odynn was granting his approval for the joining of our kingdoms.

My family would be making history again by joining mortal and fae people together. Creating a new kingdom and potentially bringing additional change to this world as well.

My eyes lifted upward while I gave my thanks to the Gods for their love and blessings.

Then the rain fell.

Small patters at first which turned to a downpour, instantly soaking me to the bone.

Every warning bell inside of me went off, forcing my eyes back to the fjord. I scanned the water, now darkening with the sudden storm, and my blood ran cold.

The brilliant, blue skies from before were encompassed with threatening dark clouds, heading over my island at alarming speed. At the forefront of that storm was an ominous black ship.

Screams rang out along the deck behind me as my people scattered. They all knew, as well as I, only one being in our world had a ship so dark no sunlight shone on its surface. A moving casket in the water, traveling to lay wreckage on the unsuspecting mortal lands when its owner grew bored.

The Unseelie King's vessel was as brutal as the man himself.

I shook my head, stepping back in shock as the boat moved against the waters of the fjord. The speed—it was unnatural, unthinkable. Bringing a dark air of violence over myself and my small kingdom.

Only, I was frozen in my place. As though the ice from the hills beyond my home had held me still, commanding me to remain where I was.

Time slowed; it moved at an agonizing speed as the ship approached, cutting through the water with ease. It pulled the very air from my lungs the closer it grew.

I did not move.

Instead, my eyes moved back and forth, keeping track of the omen approaching the dock where my betrothed's vessel was intended to go.

My hands balled the skirts of my dress when it finally arrived. As I scanned the massive hull, my stomach sank. It was as terrifying as I'd heard.

My eyes tried and failed to take it in in its entirety, where it towered over me. Casting a dark shadow across what had been a bright morning. Looming over my little home like the bringer of death itself.

Ropes came from the sides and more screams echoed behind me at the monsters sliding down the tethers. They were horrible, grey, with tiny black horns on their heads. Even worse were their blood-red eyes that stared at us all as though we were their next meal before their claws dug into the wood of the ship and they climbed back up the hull.

When they'd disappeared over the edge, the gangplank slammed against the dock.

Thud.

I stepped back, heart racing when father's hand found mine, grasping it tightly.

In the haze, I'd forgotten he was beside me. I returned his grip and bit back my cry, horrified by the shining, black creature approaching us on all fours, ripping fear throughout my body.

It was like a bear, but so much worse. Broad, muscled shoulders, paws larger than mine and my father's clasped hands together, with claws dragging against the dock. Its face— Gods was it horrifying. The snout, more elongated than a bear's and thin, black lips at the end. It's head was massive, terrifying.

I lost my senses while I watched the creature, not realizing my people had all scattered. Or that my father had released my hand.

I could only focus on the beast. The shine of its fur catching the small amount of sunlight barely shining through the gray clouds. The dark red scar running down the upper half of its face. The sickening cold that grew closer with each of its steps.

The black eyes staring right into my soul.

"Why wait, king?" the creature asked.

The rasp in its deep voice startled me and my father remained silent.

I glanced at him, eyes widening at the fear splayed across his face. He appeared utterly unable to speak while his mouth opened and closed. Like something had taken the tongue right from his mouth.

With one step forward, I squared my shoulders. "We wait for my betrothed," I answered.

The beast's eyes flashed briefly with what appeared to be amusement.

"Hello, Brenna," it growled.

My skin pricked at the sound of my name on the beast's tongue. It was unnatural to hear it from a creature so terrifying.

Its eyes flashed with amusement again. Likely due to my silence before it turned its attention back to my father.

"I am Olen, the right hand of the Unseelie King. I come on his behalf."

To my shock, my father sank to his knees. "Please." His hands rose as though he were praying to the Gods. "I know of the *deal once made*, but please."

I bit back my disgust. My father was *begging?* What had overcome the usually stoic and unfaltering man?

Olen—the creature—grinned and brilliant white teeth shone through silky black. Long canines protruded over its lips while it replied, "A deal once made. A deal cannot be broken."

My father didn't move. His hands remained raised in pleading while his arms began to shake.

"Please," he repeated.

The creature only blinked in response while the wind and rain grew thicker.

Taking control, I stepped forward, pointing at the ship. "Sir Olen, I'm sure the Unseelie King has his reasons, but please, my betrothed will arrive soon. Can you not take your discussions with my father elsewhere while I wait?"

The creature's laugh boomed out and lightning cracked in the sky.

I stepped back, blinking away my shock when one of those smaller Unseelie monsters walked down the gangplank. Its clawed hand wrapped around a small sack. The creature passed the item to Olen, glancing at me once with a vile smile while it returned to the ship.

I turned my attention back to Olen who grinned that unsettling smile before throwing the sack my way.

"Your betrothed, princess."

It landed at my feet, splattering dark liquid up my green dress. My stomach lurched at the smell while time ceased the longer I stared at the liquid seeping from the fibers of the fabric. Slowly, I forced myself to kneel, peeling the tied edges open.

It wasn't possible.

It wasn't...

My scream ripped from my throat, echoing across the fjord. In the sack, a short length from my fingertips, was the bloodied head of a fae man.

Not any man.

The man I'd been waiting for. The man whose portrait I'd slept next to for years—Leif.

"You monster!" I cried, throwing the sack back to the creature who had infiltrated our shores.

Only, my effort to rid myself of the gore was useless. The liquid, Leif's blood, had stained my dress. The smell clung to every part of my skin.

"Please give us one hour," my father whispered beside me, startling me. "One hour to gather her things and say goodbye."

"What!" I cried. "I'm not leaving with *that*."

The creature at the dock laughed again, the sound forced my body to recoil with fear.

"A deal once made, princess."

"Father!" I protested with tears lining my eyes. "Father!"

I watched as the man I'd once believed would do anything to protect me rose from his knelt position, placing a single finger over his lips. He shook his head for me to remain silent.

He turned back to the Unseelie King's creature once more.

"One hour," he repeated as he gripped my wrist and pulled me toward our modest palace.

I tripped on my soiled dress while he wove through the crowds of our people gathering once more.

"Don't speak," he whispered, keeping his voice low.

My heart raced, my head swam, and my skin smelled of death as I followed. I had questions. More than I was able to form on my tongue.

But not one was more pressing than the one at the forefront of my mind. *What does the Unseelie King want from me?*

My father slammed my bedroom door closed behind us, keeping his voice at the whisper he'd had since the dock.

"We must make haste," he said with command.

His hands moved in an unnatural frenzy, ripping my wardrobe open and throwing my clothing onto my mattress.

"Papa," I protested, catching a gown before it landed on the comforter. "Papa," I repeated.

His eyes were glazed over when he turned my way, like he was terrified to his bones. He kept pulling the clothes out, not acknowledging my pleas. Not even blinking when I continued to call out to him.

My bedroom door opened, before slamming again. I glanced up, finding my grandmother.

"Will you two tell me what's happening?" I begged, falling against my mattress.

My grandmother shook her head. "No time to despair, child. Let's get this dress off you quickly."

I shook my head, flattening my hands against my thighs. Not caring that the tips of my fingers were resting against the rotted blood of the man I loved.

"I'm no child," I replied, "and I am not leaving this castle. I am certainly not going anywhere with that *monster* if neither of you answer my questions."

"A family secret," my father replied, not meeting my eyes.

I turned to my grandmother's pale blue gaze. "What is he speaking of?" I asked.

"Please, Bren, change and we'll tell you." Her crooked, aged fingers pointed to the dressing screen in the corner of the room.

I stared down at the blood-stained gown, trying to ignore the foul smell. With a slight nod, I pulled myself upward and silently made my way to the dressing screen.

The sounds of trunks unclasping and rustling fabric filled the room while I slipped off my gown.

I watched it fall to my feet in a sad, destroyed pile, biting back my grief.

The color—a dark, forest green—had been one I'd chosen just for Leif. After countless letters of him telling me his love of the color, specifically the rich color of the pine trees in the mortal lands. I had thought I'd picked the perfect gown for our first meeting. Now it was at my feet, covered in his blood from his cold, dead body.

Possibly as cold as my heart had begun to grow.

A thud against the screen startled me, and I forced my eyes up, finding a muted gray gown hanging over the side.

"For you to wear," my grandmother said before coughing. "For you to remind the Unseelie King that you're in mourning."

I scoffed at the words. My grandmother spoke as if I would have any idea what she was referring to. As if I were to accept this notion of me going with the beast outside to meet the most notorious monster of our world.

After throwing the gown over my head, I stepped out from the dressing screen, finding every trunk clasped and my wardrobe bare.

"How did you do that so quickly?" I asked, sinking against the chair at my vanity.

Hate boiled in my blood at how my father, a man who took ages to walk from one end of our small island to the other, could pack my things so rapidly. It made me wonder if he were glad to be rid of me, and if this *family secret* was feigned and I was being played a fool.

"Anxious hands work quickly," he replied behind me, and I watched through the mirror while he sat himself on the mattress behind me.

My grandmother groaned, pulling a small chair at my back. Holding her palm open, her fingers wiggled. The life-long sign I knew meant *hand me the brush.*

Reluctantly, I obeyed, passing her the whale-bone brush, staring back at my lifeless reflection while her hands worked the strands of my hair.

"The family secret," my father began, choking on his words. "I'm ashamed to have never taken it seriously."

My grandmother's eyes rolled. "Enok, tell the truth."

My father's eyes met mine in the reflection before he dropped his shoulders in shame.

"I was terrified from the moment you were born. Your mother—"

I jumped at the mention of my mother. My father rarely spoke of her. Even when I'd pried. Even when I'd begged, he'd remained silent. But now he sat behind me, speaking of the mother I'd never known, like it was a topic we discussed openly within our family.

My father cleared his throat, continuing his tale. "Your mother—she knew of the secret and when the midwife announced we'd had a daughter, well... I believe her heart gave out that night out of fear and despair."

I pulled away from my grandmother's hands, growing irritated. "Will you please get to the point?" I snapped, forgetting my controlled tongue.

"A deal once made," he whispered. "Generations ago, one of your great-grandfathers made a deal with the Unseelie King. It was almost laughable what the king asked for, but our ancestor... He agreed."

My stomach sank. I'd heard of these *deals*. Of the havoc they wrecked. Of the pain they inflicted upon those unsuspecting souls desperate to have their prayers answered by silent, inattentive Gods.

"He made a deal?" I asked, holding my fingers to my lips.

"Yes, the Unseelie King would convince Oberon to allow our ancestor to start his own kingdom in between the mortal and Seelie lands, taking a mortal as a wife in exchange for the first daughter of our bloodline born on the first day of the blood moon."

A confirmation, old and deep, settled over me. Unlocking something within me that had, apparently, been hidden inside throughout my life. A quiet nodding, accepting a secret my soul appeared to recall.

I'd heard the stories of my birth.

The rough torrential rains that morning. The dark skies that had lingered over our island as my mother had wailed through the hours of the day and into the night.

How the blood moon—an anomaly our world only experienced every millennia—had appeared early. Starting one hundred and fifty years of a fog of red every night. And how that night, the moon had risen over the island, brightening the fjord as though it had been filled with blood itself.

My father stood from the bed, approaching behind me.

"Our ancestor, he didn't think anything of the deal. The blood moon hadn't occurred in millennia, so he agreed."

"He sold me for a kingdom?"

"You didn't exist in his mind, my dear," my grandmother replied.

"But I exist *now*," I countered. "I was supposed to go to the Seelie lands! I was supposed to be married!" My tears fell while I covered my face with my palms. "And you both are going to just allow him to take me? With no questions? No protests?"

My father's hand landed on my shoulder. "I can't fight against the Unseelie King." He gave me what felt to be a reassuring squeeze. "There's more."

I shirked off his touch. "What?"

"It's only for a year," he replied.

I twisted in my chair, my brows crumpling with confusion. "A *year?*"

He nodded his head. "Thirteen months. That's all."

"Why?" I asked.

"That was the deal," my father responded. "All he required. Our family got their kingdom, and the Unseelie King would get the service of a daughter for one year."

My skin pricked. "Service?"

My grandmother let out a boisterous laugh. "Bren, my dear, I'm sure he didn't mean sexual service."

My cheeks warmed at her voicing the place my mind had gone to and my eyes went back to my father. He shuffled his feet, shaking his head.

"I—" He cleared his throat. "He didn't specify what service meant."

"So, I'm meant to be his whore?"

"Brenna!" my father yelled.

"What?" I shouted back. "Some *man* in our family sold a woman to a king. I can think of countless tales where that usually ends up as the woman whoring for said king."

"I will cut off his head if he makes you his whore," my father snapped.

I stared back at him, sitting straighter in my seat. "You should have cut off his head the moment you learned you had a daughter. You should have sailed to his kingdom and killed him on the spot. You should have protected me even if it were the last thing you had done."

He held my gaze, before his head dropped. "I know," he muttered.

"Why now?" I asked, turning my eyes out my bedroom window, tracking the white bears cresting over the hill.

"Because I disobeyed him," my father replied. "I allowed you to be betrothed. It was the last part of the deal. He would claim your year of service whenever he pleased."

My vision blurred with my tears. "You've spoken to him?" I whispered while betrayal ran through me.

"No!" my father yelled out. "When I say I disobeyed him, I mean he was disobeyed in general. This secret, Bren—it was passed to me on my Father's death bed as it was passed to him and so on. For generations. I didn't believe it. I thought it was an old myth."

I thought back on my life. Of the years walking through our small palace, never leaving. Always the dutiful daughter doing as I was told. Always at my father's side, nurturing our people like it was my life's purpose.

"Is this why you've kept me away?" I asked. "Why I've never been allowed to visit our Seelie family and Oberon's court without you there? Why I've always had to deny Titania's invitations to spend summers with the court?"

I turned to my father while my hands balled my dress at my thighs. I was sure my heart was breaking. Sure everything I knew and loved had been a lie.

"You may lean closer to your mother's mortal blood, but you know how superstitious the fae can be. I couldn't ignore the ominous warning of the secret. Even if I didn't fully believe it," my father replied.

"So now I'm supposed to board that moving casket and disappear for a year without fighting back?" I asked, meeting his dark brown eyes.

"Bren," he dropped to his knees before me, grasping my fisted hands. "If he doesn't get his full year, our kingdom is gone. Everyone and everything you love will be ripped apart by his monsters."

My disgust grew and I ripped my hands from his. There it was, the words he did and did not say. My *duty*. My expectations as this island's princess.

Even though I knew the stories and the horrors of what the Unseelie fae could do to mortal kingdoms, I didn't want the future of my kingdom to lay on my shoulders. Not when I hadn't asked for this. Not when I'd been given this knowledge so suddenly.

I stood, crossing the bedroom before turning back to my father.

"I agree, but when I return..." My eyes scanned my little room, out to the blue waters of the fjord lapping against the shore mere feet from my home. "I get to leave. I get freedom. I get to decide whether or not I will continue to live in this kingdom created by selling my soul to a demon."

My father's eyes grew wide, but I lifted my hand, stopping him from responding. My eyes darted to the small clock on my bedside table.

"We've wasted our time; the monster is expecting me."

CHAPTER 2

"You're late," Olen growled as my foot hit the dock.

I glared up at him, coiling back with disgust at the returning smile I received.

"I'm a princess, I arrive when I wish."

Olen laughed loudly; his silky fur shook with the movement. "I'm sure my king will appreciate your attitude."

"Usually, I'm told I'm a rather pleasant person. But that changes when I'm being *kidnapped*," I replied, glaring into its black eyes.

"Your father never told you?" Olen asked, his eyes darted to where my father stood at the edge of the dock.

Betrayal and anger burned on my tongue while my shoulders slumped with defeat. "Can we please go? If I'm forced to leave my home, I'd rather not elongate my goodbyes."

Olen stared back at me, one canine protruding from his lips before he nodded.

Turning my back, I made my way across the dock, heading straight for the gangplank. I couldn't have forced myself to look back if I had wanted to. Not when I knew what was behind me: A tearful grandmother and my handmaids, holding each other; people of our kingdom staring in shock at their princess leaving with an Unseelie monster, and my father with a blank expression to mask his shame and guilt.

I climbed over the threshold of the massive vessel, still in too much shock to process that I was truly leaving for a year. Every plan I'd thought I'd made was now a whisp in the breeze, heading toward the cruel amusement of the Gods. It mocked me with every step that Leif's arrival had only produced a feigned hope of control over my life.

But there was still that small kindling of fire deep inside of me, burning with hope at what awaited me at the end of this insane journey.

A year—and then I was free.

I would get to travel the world. See the courts freely on the Northern Seelie island. Possibly even explore the fellow small mortal islands littering our seas. I could travel to the West island, the main mortal island, and meet family I'd never had the chance to know.

The ability to put my long half-fae lifespan to use.

Yes, a year. It was nothing for a woman who had lived nearly one hundred and fifty years. If I could survive that long on my tiny island home, then I could survive a year in the depths of the Unseelie court.

Perhaps even less if I were able to complete the plan now circling in my mind.

I walked through the deck, avoiding the inquiring eyes surrounding me until my foot hit something wet. Glancing down, I bit back my cry when I spotted the sack from before, cast aside as if it were meager everyday trash. Like Leif's life had meant nothing.

My heart lurched while I tried to push aside the image of his dull gray eyes staring up at me when I'd pried that bag open. Of the stench of rot, evident the king had removed my betrothed's head at least several days before. Of the blood, now stained forever on the dress I'd left on my bedroom floor.

My stomach turned and I pulled my eyes away, staring off toward the fjord as the ship rocked forward.

If I were going to go to the Unseelie court, then I would go. It didn't mean I had to be there the full year.

Not when I planned to remove the king's head with my own bare hands.

My head pounded as the ship rocked beneath me. I hated sea travel. Ironic, considering my home was surrounded by water and I have always had a desire to travel my world.

It drove me mad of course, the contradictory circumstance I regularly found myself in. Most especially in our yearly travels to the Seelie lands to Oberon's court. Several days of agony on the ocean, locked away in a cabin cursing my body's negative reaction to the swaying waters.

I turned on the cot I laid on, staring out at the cabin I'd been given. Or more so locked in forcefully by the beast Olen and only after I'd emptied the contents of my stomach right onto the deck, in front of every beastly Unseelie on the crew.

Olen had laughed brashly before whisking me away to my traveling prison.

I just hadn't expected him to lead me to the Captains quarters. Or for him to claim his king wasn't on board and how much of a *shame* it was. Because, according to the monster, the king would have loved a body to warm his bed.

I swung for his face.

An action I instantly regretted when the beast had shoved me back and the clang of the door locking on the other side echoed down to my bones.

I wasn't sure how many days I'd been in there, swaying in that cot. Barely able to accept the meals shoved through the open door twice a day.

I don't know if it really mattered though. Every day the sun set and the red of the blood moon casted its light through the cabin's small window. I prayed to the Gods this journey would be a quick one. Even when my island had disappeared into the distance, I only wanted to complete whatever service my ancestor had assigned me to so I could begin my life the way I deemed fit.

My body rocked in the cot, and I turned my head back to the window, admiring the way the red moon lit the dark sea beneath it. I knew the Unseelie lands were south of my island, but given the several days the sun and moon had cycled, I began to wonder why the Unseelie island was kept so secretive.

My tutors had never divulged much—never saying how many days it would take to get to the island. Most teachings usually consisted of warnings to never make a deal with the king ruling the land.

If only my tutors were here to see the irony of their teachings.

Then there were the two pieces of information I knew of its landscape. One—it was large, very large. Two—it was surrounded by a thick mist.

Many said these islands were misted by Oberon as a way to protect the world from the evils of the Unseelie Court. Others said it was the Unseelie King himself, protecting his people from the world.

Whatever it was, few knew what lay beyond the mist and those who did, rarely spoke of it.

I had always wondered why the Seelie and Unseelie resided on different continents. A whole ocean lay between their lands with my and many other small islands scattered between them.

Once, when I was young and foolish, I had almost asked Oberon at our yearly visit. That was until my grandmother realized the question on my tongue and I'd been whisked away before I could *embarrass our family*.

Every mortal and fae knew of Oberon's distaste for the Unseelie King. So much so that to know or utter his name in Oberon's presence was considered treason. Why Oberon allowed this king to live and enact chaos on behalf of the entirety of the fae court, never ceased to amaze me.

Perhaps it would be another secret that I would learn. Perhaps this would be my new life. Learning secrets of others. Keeping them locked up inside to use to my advantage.

Eventually the boat stopped its rocking, waking me from the sleep I had fallen into. Hesitantly, I pulled myself from the bunk and the room spun around me.

I really hate the sea.

The door slammed open, and an unfamiliar man ducked under the frame, standing before me. He offered me an unsettling grin with teeth bright and menacing, and moved forward to approach.

I scrambled back to the cot. "Get away!" I screeched.

The man stopped, cocking his head to the side. "Excuse me?"

His voice was thick, heavy, and completely without the airy accent the fae were known to have.

"I don't know who you are sir, please leave," I replied, voice shaking.

The man's eyes gleamed and he glanced down at himself. "Don't recognize me?"

I focused my gaze, observing him from head to toe.

He was large, alarmingly so in both height and stature. His bronzed skin had a glow to it that matched the golden flecks in the braids of his long hair. His defined jaw tightened while my eyes took in his body, taking note of the light scar across his cheek. He was dressed in black leathers and matching long boots stopping at his knees.

He was attractive, yes, but I had no idea who he was.

"I'm sorry," I replied, allowing my royal formality to sneak through. "I do not know you."

A bright light filled the room in an instant, blinding me. I raised my hand to my eyes in a panic, trying to focus my vision once more. Then it was gone and the monster from the docks was before me. Now on all fours, grinning wildly with the same elongated canines peeking out from its black lips. The silk black fur glistened once more.

It was Olen.

I was blinded by bright light again and I watched in shock as Olen shifted from the beastly form back to the man who had entered moments before. Only, I realized he wasn't just a man—he was fae. Of course he was fae, at least Unseelie, with the abilities I'd just seen. It was evident now with his long ears I finally noticed poking out from his braids and the bright golden earrings that ran down only his right ear.

My hands instinctively went to my own pointed ears, though only slightly from my family's half-fae lineage.

Olen laughed at my shock. "Get up, princess. The king is waiting."

"I'm not going to that monster," I refused.

Olen's amused grin shifted to a tight expression of authority. "You will do as I say and go to your king—now."

I stared at the man before me, crossing my arms over my chest. Every tutoring of royal manners and respect fought against the stubbornness controlling me. I didn't have to follow the commands of this shifting monster. The king he referenced was not my king. I was a princess of another land, and I expected to be treated as such.

A foolish expectation considering these beasts were known for their debauchery and lack of manners. That was made even more evident when Olen crossed the cabin and threw me over his shoulders. As though I were nothing but a sack of flour.

"Let me go, you beast!" I yelled out, slamming my hands with all my strength against his back.

His responding laugh rumbled against my chest as my body bobbed against his. I was enraged, while also amazed by the strength of the man. He'd picked me up so effortlessly and there had been nothing I could have done to stop it.

He ducked under the doorframe and the light of the moon shone above, illuminating our path in blood.

"Welcome to the Unseelie Court, princess," Olen said.

My mouth hung open while he walked across the deck of the ship and onto the gangplank where an assortment of Unseelie fae kept their heads down while he passed. I stared at them, bewildered by their strange physical appearances.

I'd never seen anything like them. I'd of course heard the stories—but to see them with my own eyes?

The scales. The teeth. The wings.

Terrifying monsters that could easily sneak up to torture and terrifying you n the dark. Brutish creatures one would run from. They were awful.

And beautiful.

My head whipped back and forth, taking them all in while Olen continued walking. My desire to fight his hold on me was a distraction from the creatures that lined the dock of this strange king's land. Olen began to climb and as I looked down, finding stone steps, the reality of my future settled over me.

I didn't know what was waiting for me at the top of these steps. What cruelty I would be subjected to. What service was expected of me.

Would I even return to my home in a year as the same person I was when I left?

The creaking of a door told me Olen had reached the entrance to whatever building he'd been carrying me to, but I kept my eyes down. I didn't want to admire the king's home. I didn't want to know what the halls of his palace were.

So, I made myself familiar with the dark stone floors until Olen suddenly stopped and dropped me right onto the solid surface.

I exclaimed in shock, jumping to my feet while Olen pointed to the wood door before me.

"Get in there," he demanded.

"No," I replied, crossing my arms.

"Now, princess," Olen said with a wink.

"I'm going to request you stop calling me that."

Olen grinned. "Why? That's what you are. Your father is the king of that quaint little island. Making you a princess."

I glanced back at the door. "Then treat me like one."

Olen stared back at me, his smile unfaltering.

"That's the thing, princess." He stalked closer, forcing me to step back toward the door. "You aren't my fucking princess."

His hand moved and I jumped, expecting him to hit me but instead I fell onto the floor again as he flung the door open behind me.

"Get in there," he said again.

I refused to look back. "What's in there?"

"Attire appropriate for your king," he replied.

I huffed out my chest, pulling myself to my feet. "He's not my king."

"Yet." Olen grinned wider. "Go. Now."

He shoved against my shoulders, forcing me to turn into the room. I stumbled, my eyes bulging while I took in the grand space before me.

Bright candles lit the room, creating a semi-sensual glow cascading up the walls, turning into a path of light toward the middle of the room. There, the largest bed I'd ever seen sat covered in black sheets and a velvet blanket folded at the foot. It called to me, telling me to climb into its tempting comfort.

My eyes moved from the bed to the floor-to-ceiling windows, filling the room with additional red light from the blood moon.

It was a room that—for all intents and purposes—exuded sex.

I ignored the sensual design and walked forward, taking note of the two exits. The one I'd been rudely shoved through, and two double doors leading out to where I assumed was the rest of the king's palace.

"Is this my room?" I asked, trying not to sound too enamored.

Olen chuckled. "Yes. It's yours."

My eyes caught the sheer red dress hanging on the dressing screen across from me and I turned back to Olen.

"I am not wearing that," I exclaimed, pointing.

"You're wearing what the king demanded. Get dressed," he replied, setting himself in a chair near the window and folding his arms.

We held our gazes, and I realized he wasn't moving until I did as he said. For a moment I considered arguing, but relented, too tired to fight someone so godsdamn stubborn.

Scuffling to the screen, I slipped around it and shucked off my dress. I was suddenly disgusted that I hadn't once asked for my trunks on our journey. My own stench made me wince and I cursed myself.

"I stink!" I yelled over the screen.

"Welcome to sea travel. The king has smelled worse," Olen replied bluntly. "There's soap and a wash basin beside you. Hurry up."

I scoffed, taking note of the basin and soap. Unwilling to meet the wrath of the fae who shifted into a monster, I wiped myself as clean as I could before sliding the gown over my head.

How the king had known my exact size was beyond me, but the dress was a perfect fit.

I turned, finding a mirror behind me. I hadn't stared at my own reflection since the day in my bedroom and the woman staring back at me was alarming. The dark circles were evidence of my disdain for ships. The unruly waves of my hair, like the sea itself had whipped it into a frenzy atop my head.

I flipped my head back and quickly ran my fingers through the knots, wincing at the pain.

When I lifted myself again, I found I looked as wild as I felt.

Perhaps it was fitting if I were to meet a wild, unrelenting king.

My gaze caught the dress, and my eyes widened. The fabric was thin, so thin I was shocked every crevice and curve of my body wasn't on display. My eyes ran up my reflection and I realized, the outer fabric was sheer, with a lower layer covering my most private parts. I wasn't sure whether to be mad or amazed.

One thing was for certain: these fae dressed differently than the mortals.

Nervously, I came out from the dressing screen, scanning the room for my captor. A low whistle came from the double doors and I turned.

"Well, Gods, princess, you know how to clean up," Olen said.

"I'm not going out there dressed like some whore," I bit back.

Olen stepped forward, with one hand behind his back. "I can promise our whores show quite a bit more skin than that."

"Your king can come to me."

Olen shook his head. "No. He won't. Take this." His hand extended and I stared down at a dark red mask.

I shifted my gaze back to his, finding him adjusting a mask on the bridge of his nose. Only his was gold, matching his piercings and the gold braided into his hair.

"A mask?" I asked.

"The Unseelie Court," Olen smiled, "wears only masks when in the presence of the king. Haven't you heard the stories?"

"I've heard of the debauchery," I replied.

"Oh, we have that too." Olen opened the door, pointing out to the hallway. "After you, princess."

I tracked our movements while Olen led the way. I took note of which exits were closest to the double doors. Which stairways appeared to lead outside, or what hallways looked too dark to venture down.

Finally, Olen stopped grinning ear to ear.

"Ready?" he asked.

I stared at the white doors before me, gulping down my fear.

Olen's hand shoved me forward and deafening music flew at me, blocking any other sound. Just not blocking out the creatures before me.

Some appeared as the fae I was used to. But most were similar to the monsters on the ship and the dock. Half were dancing.

Half were—occupied.

My cheeks burned with the realization that these Unseelie indulged in their most carnal pleasures out in the open. As if they had no care in the world that everyone around them could see them lost in their lust and passion.

I forced my attention away from the moving bodies right as Olen shoved me forward. The movement caused me to stumble on the long hem of my gown.

The sound of my feet clashing against each other echoed around me. I glanced up, finding the room silent and the bodies unmoving. My eyes continued their observations, pausing when they connected with the gaze of a man seated on the throne across the room.

The Unseelie King.

Chapter 3

My whole life I'd been told of how vile the Unseelie King was. Of his predatory smile. His sickening, decaying skin.

He was the monster who stalked the dark. The creature you'd never want to find in the shadows.

But the man sitting on the throne before me was the exact opposite of what I'd been told.

He was breathtaking and terrifying. Despite the fact he had a black mask covering the upper half of his face, I was enamored by his presence. Or maybe it was his power. A cold that exuded over the entire space, taking control of everything inside of me. It silently demanded attention and obedience.

I stepped back, bumping into Olen's chest.

The king smiled across the room.

Instantly, I hated him. The amusement in that smile. The knowing behind it. The idea that he believed he had any control over me.

Olen's hands gripped my arm, holding me in place while the king stood and slowly approached.

I couldn't take my eyes off of him. His long, dirty blond hair and beard, all perfectly groomed. The way his tunic appeared to struggle to cover the muscles of his chest and broad shoulders. His stature was equal in height to the brute holding me in place. Yet, the most shocking part of his appearance was the ink on his skin.

There were black horns on either side of his neck, heads of beasts on his chest, peeking through his open tunic, and even more strange markings on his forearms, revealed by his rolled sleeves.

Every head in the room bowed while the king made his approach. Every head but my own. Because despite the cold of his power growing closer, I wouldn't bend my knee. I wouldn't allow this quiet call for obedience to take root inside of my heart.

I could admit he had a power about him, overwhelming and deadly. It forced my body to shake as if death were coming for my very soul, like the Gods were ready to claim me back to their realm at any moment.

But I would not kneel.

"Brenna," the king said when he completed his approach.

My body lit with rage at how casually he said my name. At the way his tongue licked across his lips, as though he were savoring the sound of it.

"I don't know how you know my name," I replied, holding myself confidently.

The king grinned, glancing back at Olen who released his hold on my arms.

"You'll come to find I know all when it comes to things that belong to me."

I stared in disbelief. *Owned? Things?* Was that all this creature viewed me as? Something to possess and control?

"*Belong?*" I held back my yell. "I belong to no one."

His grin widened and I narrowed my eyes, trying to see beyond the masking hiding the rest of his features. My eyes met his emerald green gaze and he cocked his head.

"Not used to masks?"

"I don't know why you would believe I am," I replied.

"You're half-fae, masks are a natural part of the fae customs," he replied blankly.

"I lean more toward my mortal side. In the years I've visited Oberon's Court, I've never been forced to wear a mask."

Hisses echoed out across the room at the mention of Oberon's name. I watched the king, waiting for his cool demeanor to slip. To my disappointment, he was the only being in the room who didn't react. Instead, he stood unphased, staring down at me.

"Oberon is a fool," he replied calmly.

Lifting his finger, he motioned forward while he turned on his heel.

"Come, Brenna."

Olen's hands hit my back, pushing me forward. Forcing me to follow the command like some animal on a leash. It instantly infuriated me.

The bowed heads surrounding us remained low while we crossed the crowded room. I kept my eyes forward, avoiding the scowls I'd caught glimpses of while also saving myself from gawking at the naked fae in the room.

The king sat on his throne, motioning to a small cushion beside it.

I stared at the seat, my stomach twisting with hate.

I may not have been completely familiar with the fae customs. I may have done everything I could have in my life to avoid them or know them. I did, however, know one thing from visiting the Seelie lands: the small cushions on the sides of the royal thrones were reserved for sexual playthings.

Their bedmates—their whores.

All of my composure unleashed.

"I am not your whore," I seethed, crossing my arms.

The king's eyes brightened with amusement. "I never said you were. Sit Brenna—now."

Olen pushed my back again and my cheeks heated with embarrassment. I was making a spectacle of myself. I wasn't holding the image of a composed princess who deserved respect. No, I was throwing tantrums.

My knees bent reluctantly while I lowered myself, keeping my head high.

"That's better." The king smiled.

With a clap of his hands, the music resumed. Along with the dancing and moving bodies returning to their activities.

My eyes darted to the ground, avoiding the sight before me.

"Uncomfortable?"

My body jolted at his voice. It was smooth, like an aged wine, begging to be indulged.

"No," I snapped. "How long must I sit here?"

"For having been raised a princess, you have almost no manners," he replied.

My eyes met his. "You killed the man I love. You kidnapped me. You know nothing about me. I am here to fulfill a duty I have no choice to fulfill. Excuse me if you are not meeting me at my best, *King.*"

His eyes narrowed with amusement while he leaned against his throne. With a cross of his legs, one finger flicked, and my eyes traveled to the direction he was pointing.

Just below the dais were two naked fae women, smiling hungrily up at the king I was being forced to sit beside. They moved eagerly at the flick of his finger, and I shook my head as they both took a seat on each of his knees.

The king's hands landed on their lower stomachs, and I shifted my eyes to the floor.

He was trying to shock me. He was trying to embarrass me.

To my dismay, it was working.

"Brenna," he taunted. "Brenna, look at me."

I pulled my gaze up, finding the women's hands on each other, lost in the lust of their lips moving together.

"These are whores, Brenna," the king said with a smile, running both hands over their naked bodies. "They do as they're told."

"You're disgusting," I replied.

The women on his lap both went still, their lips pulling apart. Their heads turned my way, and I almost laughed at the shock on their faces.

"You're excused, *Ursa*," the king replied.

I jumped from my seat, scowling. "You humiliate me in public and now you insult me by calling me a *bear?*"

His hands tightened around the naked bodies still on his lap, but I didn't care to be respectful any longer. If they wished to sit on him, allowing the world to see everything they had, that was their decision.

I would address the monster who was determined to play me a fool as the princess I was.

He smiled at me, waving his hand before slapping one of the bare bottoms of the women.

"I've excused you. Olen will escort you back to the room."

At the mention of his name, Olen appeared with a grin on his face, motioning to the doors we'd come through.

I turned on my heel, rage boiling before I snapped my body back to the king.

"If I'm being forced to stay here for a year, do me the courtesy of telling me your name."

His gaze shifted away from the women who had resumed their kissing. With a grin that turned my annoyance to pure hatred, he replied, "Ulrich, princess. My name is Ulrich."

My hands trembled while the words left his lips. *Ulrich.* It wasn't what I was expecting. Not that I knew what I had been expecting.

With a nod of acknowledgement, I squared my shoulders and followed Olen out the doors.

Ulrich—the Unseelie King.

I repeated the name in my head while we made our way through the palace. Ensuring I would never forget the name of the first life I planned to take.

Olen left me in the room, slamming the doors behind him. He clicked yet another lock outside of my access, reminding me I was a prisoner.

I surveyed the room once more, hating the beauty I found in it. Hating that my body begged me to sink onto the bed and sleep away my troubles.

Instead of listening to the demand to sleep, I explored. There wasn't much to the room once I had a chance to really take it in. Besides two side tables, plush chairs by the window, and the dressing screen, it was simple. The light of the windows and the candles pulled focus to the bed as if that had been intentional.

My feet moved while I walked the large space, guiding me to the doors Olen had first brought us through. Glancing back, I prayed to the Gods the brute had forgotten to lock this escape. That had been a foolish thought when my hand pulled at the handle and the deafening *clank* of the locked barrier mocked me and my misery.

I turned back on my heel, crossing the room to an open doorway I hadn't seen earlier. When my feet crossed the threshold, my steps echoed against the marble. It surprised me with all the stone I'd been walking across since arriving.

I looked across the new space and tears lined my eyes. It was a bathing room. A room that shouldn't have brought so much emotion. In the middle of the room, was a tub that appeared to have been carved from obsidian with pipes at the end.

Running water—this monster had running water. An uncommon commodity at home. Not even my personal bathing chamber had it. We had to rely on the pipes in our kitchens as our source of water in our small palace.

I rushed across the room, stripping the dress off while my hands turned the faucet. A prickling sensation ran across my skin at the sound and I let out a sob.

I could allow myself a few moments of reprieve in this insanity. Even if it only meant scrubbing my body of the shock of the last few days.

Settling into the tub, I let out a sigh, allowing the warm water to wrap around my body. I leaned back, dunking my head while my hands searched the surface for any soaps. Luckily, I found some quickly and lathered my hair.

The scent was magnificent. Smokey and earthy, with hints of something floral.

I rinsed myself before I forced my body out of the tub. Even with it begging me to stay where I had been, my eyes were drifting along with a weight of emotions in my heart.

It was all coming down over me. Reality. Pain. Anger.

I wrapped a towel around myself and walked back into the bedroom, finding a thin nightgown on the bed.

Stepping back, I put up my hands. It was a foolish belief that I could fight anyone naked and unprepared, but no one came. The room was as empty as it had been before I'd gone into the tub.

Hesitantly, I slipped the gown over my head before climbing into the lush blankets of the bed. With the heat and comfort warming me, I allowed the emotions to come out.

The sobs tumbled from me. Loud, echoing throughout the expansive room. My own song of melancholy and lament from the madness of my future.

The longer I cried the harder it became to control myself. I couldn't stop it. The hate in my heart. The hate for this king, my father, and mostly myself.

Why wasn't I fighting? Why wasn't I standing my ground and doing something?

I curled my body around myself, tears wetting the fabric against my knees.

Then I heard it—*click*—a door opening.

I sat up, wiping my tears and turning toward the sound. The hate grew hotter when my eyes found Ulrich at a hidden door behind a thick tapestry.

"Get out," I demanded, wiping my still-falling tears.

He smiled. "It's my room, *Ursa,* and you're my guest."

He shoved against the wall as he headed toward the bathing room.

"Get out!" I demanded.

His hand rose, catching the pillow I had thrown at his head. Shocking me with the reflexes and how he'd known I'd grabbed a pathetic weapon.

He turned on his heel, changing his approach to my direction. "Would you like to know the terms of your year of service?" he asked.

"I won't be your whore," I sniffled, covering myself with the blankets.

His brow rose above the upper rim of his mask while his eyes scanned me. I recoiled at the burn in his eyes. I would remove each one of his balls slowly and carefully if he ever attempted to put his hands on me.

"I don't expect you to be a whore, princess. You've clearly seen I have that available to me," he replied, setting himself on the edge of the bed. He set the pillow beside me. "But I will sleep next to you. Every night for the next thirteen months."

I stared back at him. He was likely the most insane being I'd ever encountered.

My mouth opened to respond but he held his hand up.

"I will sleep beside you," he continued. "In total darkness and you will not ask questions. You will not try to escape. And—" He paused, narrowing his eyes. "You will never look upon my face. Do you understand?"

I blinked at him, trying to find the words in my mind to leave my lips.

"Brenna?" he said, his expression turning menacing.

"This is the most bizarre set of *rules* I've ever been given," I forced myself to say.

"Do you understand?" he repeated.

I stared back at him. "What happens if I don't obey?"

The room went dark. The candlelight was gone in an instant. The bed shifted and before I could cry out, his hand gripped my jaw while he pulled my face against the rough hairs of his beard.

"I will destroy everything and everyone you have ever loved," he whispered.

My body went rigid with fear. But even more so—hate.

"I understand," I replied.

"Good." He dropped me back on the bed. "I'll return in a moment."

Chapter 4

The candlelight returned with his retreat but I remained on the bed, rubbing my jaw. Waiting for the monster to return from the closet I hadn't noticed beside the bathing room.

One year of laying at his side. One year of watching his depravities. A year of not questioning. Of obeying.

Once again living the life of duty and silence I'd always lived. *Was it worth it?* I wondered. Was my freedom worth being prisoner to someone with little regard to who I was and what I needed?

To someone who put his hands on me with little thoughts. Who had killed the only man I'd ever loved.

My mind reeled while I waited. I didn't know what to do. I was confused beyond words. I'd readied myself for the possibility of using my body for my freedom or scrubbing every corner of his home.

But to sleep next to him? Every single night?

I tucked my knees under my chin keeping my eyes on the doors he'd gone through, trying to gather the courage to enact my revenge.

I'd planned on waiting to watch his movements. To learn him and understand him. Now my hands were being forced. I couldn't allow him anywhere close to me. I wouldn't risk the chance of his skin touching mine.

While I thought, the air in the room shifted. I didn't have to look up to know he approached once more. The cold that encompassed him came at me, like a wall of evil.

To my surprise, the curtains shut and the candles went out again, layering the room in total darkness. I hadn't gotten a single glimpse at the face I was now forbidden to look upon. I cursed the mortal blood in my body for not giving me the keen fae eyesight in the dark.

The bed shifted with the weight of him and my skin crawled. I uncurled around myself, moving closer to the edge. Trying to create as much space between us as I possibly could.

"I'm going to sleep on the floor," I finally said, grabbing the pillows behind me.

His body moved in an instant, ripping the pillow from my hand. "That's not part of the deal, Brenna. You must sleep *beside* me for the entirety of your service," he whispered.

"Fuck the Gods," I muttered.

"What?"

"Nothing," I snapped, leaning back against the headboard.

"Are you scared?" he asked with a laugh.

"No," I replied with a squeak.

His laugh chilled my bones, and the bed shifted once more. "Go to sleep, princess." His voice lowered to an order.

I turned my head, trying to find an outline of the curtains covering the windows I'd been admiring before. My eyes became heavy with the shifting of his breathing, the sound of rest and exhaustion tugging at my tired body. I couldn't sleep, though. I refused to do as he ordered; that hadn't been listed on his requirements for my service.

I only had to stay where I was until I was sure his large body was asleep beside me.

My hands fidgeted in my lap, wringing against the nightgown I now realized was far too thin to be wearing with him beside me.

His breathing grew heavier, at an agonizing speed. As if my fear were calming this madman.

Eventually, however, I became confident he was indeed asleep. Slowly, I slipped off the bed, creeping through the dark room with my hands out to guide me.

To some miracle graced by the Gods, I made it to the bathing room.

I closed the door behind me and scanned the dark space, realizing he hadn't covered the frosted skylight above. My eyes quickly took in the room. If this was his room, this meant his personal belongings would be in the washroom.

All I had to do was find them and hopefully—a razor.

I couldn't logically remove his head with one like he'd removed Leif's, but it would slit his throat.

I searched through the cupboards, trying to be as silent as I could, cursing when I found each one lacking a sharp weapon. My eyes lined with frustrated tears and I'd almost given up when my eyes laid upon a high shelf above the sink.

Sitting just out of my line of sight was a glass cup, with a razor sticking out of the top.

I pulled the small stool beside the tub to the vanity, climbing on top as quietly as I could. My hands shook while I pulled my weapon down, careful not to slice myself. Once my hand was grasped around the handle, I let out a breath of relief and held it to my chest.

"You can do this," I whispered to myself.

I hadn't taken a life before. Gods, I hadn't thought about doing anything this violent. But desperate times called for desperate measures, and I would end this deal even if it resulted in death.

I just hoped it wouldn't be my own.

While keeping the razor clasped in my palm, I made my way back to the room. I nearly tripped when I returned to the pitch-black space, so dark I couldn't have adjusted my eyes if I'd tried.

Holding out a hand again, I blindly felt the space, hoping I wouldn't knock my shins against the bed frame. Or fall and slice my own neck in an unfortunate accident.

By another miracle gifted by the Gods, I made it back to the bed. I held the razor close while I peeled back the blankets and slipped under the covers once more.

My stomach dropped as my mind accepted I was about to take a life. The only reprieve I had was this wasn't *any* life. This was the monster who had plagued the mortal lands for centuries, possibly even millennia.

He was the villain in every folktale I'd ever heard.

A tyrant.

A murderer.

If anything, I was doing this world a service by ending his reign of terror.

I moved closer to his sleeping body and pulled the razor forward, hands trembling with cowardice.

"For Leif," I whispered.

My hand came down, moving to slice his neck. To my shock, his palm wrapped around my wrist, and his booming voice flooded through my body.

"The violent creature's true nature has been revealed," he sneered.

The grip on my wrist forced the razor to fall and before I knew what was happening, he was flipping me on my back. His body pressed me against the bed, pushing me into the soft mattress.

My hands shook as his grip on me tightened.

His long hair brushed against my face. "If you wanted to play, you could have asked," he whispered with a laugh.

"Unhand me!" I demanded.

His chest rumbled against mine with his laugh and his grip somehow grew tighter. "You just tried to slit my throat in my own bed. What makes you think I'm going to *unhand you*?"

"You killed him," I whispered, holding back my angry tears.

To my surprise, his grip loosened. "You were not his to have."

"I was never going to be his property! He promised me."

Ulrich's body tensed against mine. "Promises mean nothing."

I wiggled under the weight of him, hating the heat growing across my body with him against me.

"I can't be worried about my throat being slit while I sleep," he said calmly.

One hand released me while the other brought both of my wrists above my head. I could barely fathom the size of his palm and how easily he held me still. With his now free hand, a snap echoed across the room.

My eyes searched the darkness, and I yelled out in rage when his hand suddenly clasped over my eyes, blocking my sight.

"The terms of your service," he chuckled. "No looking upon my face."

"You're twisted," I seethed, wiggling against the hold he had on me.

"Brenna, if you keep moving under me like that then I may change your terms to something more pleasurable."

I froze and my body went rigid with his warning leaving his lips.

"I won't be your bedmate."

"Then stop moving like one," he demanded.

Shuffling feet filled the room, followed by a bellowing laugh. "Looks like the princess isn't so prim and proper."

My teeth gritted at the sound of Olen's amusement.

Ulrich pressed his body against mine, an obvious tease to bring me discomfort.

"She tried to slit my throat," he replied with little emotion.

Olen's voice shifted from amusement to rage. "Excuse me?"

Ulrich's hands on my wrists and the one covering both of my eyes tightened. "She likely needs to spend the night in the dungeons."

"So, I am to be your prisoner," I yelled out, struggling to slip from his hold.

"Stop moving like that. I've warned you."

Olen laughed again. "Gods, this is going to be entertaining."

Ulrich's beard brushed against my cheek and his voice lowered with his whisper. "We can play if you want. Get lost in the pleasure of our hate. Maybe even invite my right hand to join us. What do you say?"

In all my years of royal training for how to interact with a king—what to say and how to say it—I had not once imagined the way I'd reacted as his whisper left a mark on my skin.

Spit flew from my mouth, and I prayed to the Gods it had landed right on his face.

Ulrich's grip turned from tight to searing pain, burning into my skin.

"Do that again, and you'll regret it," he sneered.

My mouth opened to disobey, and a hand clamped around my lips.

"Usually I'm the one spitting," he seethed, and his fingers dug into my cheeks.

He was disgusting. He was as much of a monster as I had been warned.

Unable to speak or see, but realizing he'd released my hands, I started to claw. My nails hit his skin, scraping down the corded muscles along his arms. Tearing at his flesh. With my other hand, my fingers brushed against his long hair and I tugged. As hard as I could.

Ulrich inhaled loudly but he didn't move. As if he were possibly enjoying my rampage. Enraging me even more, fueling the scream that ripped from my throat. Like a feral animal fighting for its release.

"Gods, you beast!" Olen's voice echoed.

Ulrich only laughed. "Take her to the dungeon. Let her brood over her actions."

His hands remained on my eyes and lips as hands slipped under my body, lifting me up. I yelled out, shaking my head, trying to fight him off of me. Fabric replaced his hands and was secured tightly at the back of my head.

"You're really blindfolding me?" I asked, unable to hold back my laugh.

"I told you the terms. Don't think I've forgotten them so quickly," Ulrich replied.

"What happens if I look upon your face? I melt from your beauty?" I snapped.

Olen's chest rumbled against me with his laugh. "Fuck," he whispered.

Ulrich's amusement wasn't easy to miss, even if I couldn't see him as he replied, "Amusing to hear you think I'm beautiful." My cheeks flushed while he continued. “Or perhaps my full image will stop your heart, filling you with terror.”

Olen’s grip on my body shifted and I cried out when he threw me over his shoulder—again.

“Would you stop throwing me around like a sack!” I yelled, kicking my feet.

“That nightgown is all kinds of indecent,” Ulrich’s voice echoed behind me.

Rage burned my blood, and my kicking turned more violent. Yet Olen didn’t react. No grunts, no shifting. His hands only tightened around my legs.

“I thought you’d appreciate it,” he laughed.

“Get her to the dungeon,” Ulrich’s voice echoed behind me.

“I’m going to kill you!” I promised, slamming my hands against Olen’s back.

“Will you calm down you wild thing?” he grunted.

I didn’t stop. I kept screaming and fighting while Olen walked us away. My wails echoed throughout the Unseelie palace as he made his trek to wherever the demon king’s dungeons resided, and I was determined to be as loud as I could.

Making sure this entire fucked up court knew I was here unwillingly.

The temperature dropped and I barely registered the sound of dripping water. My eyes strained to see through the thick fabric when creaking metal echoed in front of me, followed by Olen stepping forward.

Then he dropped me right on the ground.

Breathtaking pain shot up my back from my tailbone and I whimpered. I tried to regain my breaths, and I blinked when his hands suddenly removed the cover and light flooded back to my sight.

The stench hit me immediately. Rot, mold, and death. It filled the air. Seeping into my pores.

I glanced up, finding Olen grinning down at me.

"I'll behave," I finally said.

He shook his head, stepping backward toward the bars I now realized were behind him. I moved to scramble to my feet, determined to chase after him, but cried out in pain. Agonizing jolts ran down my legs, forcing my body to stay down.

I stared back at the man who shifted to a beast. "Please." I clasped my hands together. "Please, I'm begging you."

Olen only grinned wide, slamming the dark gray bars closed. Sealing me in yet another prison.

"You should have thought of what would happen when you tried to kill the king."

Hot tears ran down my cheeks. "He took me! You took me!"

"A deal was made, princess. You have to accept that," Olen replied with a wink.

My hands slammed down on the rotted, soiled surface while the brute sauntered away. Not before I let out my scream, returning to the wild noises I had been making earlier. Filling this king's halls with my protests.

Olen's laugh echoed over my yells before I heard his voice snapping at some unseen being to keep an eye on me.

My tears ran down my cheeks while I listened to his footsteps retreat and the scream scalded my throat. Burning the flesh with my rage.

I screamed until nothing would escape my lips. Until my body could no longer hold me up and my bones protested in pain. Until

I was forced to curl around myself, cradling my knees while the pain continued to rush through my body.

As my cheek lay against the rotted surface, I prayed to the Gods for warmth. I prayed for safety, for release and rescue.

The prayers left my lips while I silently muttered them, watching water drip in the corner of my cell.

Drip.

Drip.

Drip.

It drove me mad with each echo they left in its wake.

It was how he was going to punish me. Ulrich's ultimate plan to make me go crazy. For me to lose my mind and make me as insane as the fae blood that rang through my veins.

I stared at the water, wishing he would have just snapped my neck. That he would have taken the razor and plunged it into my heart, saving me from this insanity.

Chapter 5

"Get up," a rough voice growled over me, moments before freezing water was dumped on my body.

I shrieked in shock, pulling myself upward. My eyes scanned the cell, finding Olen in his beastly form. He stood on all fours, glaring at me with a small Unseelie creature beside him. A creature who held the bucket I assumed the water had come from.

At least I hoped it had been water.

"I said get up," Olen growled again.

I glared back at him. "No."

"Now."

"No. If I'm going to be his prisoner then I will spend my days in the cell he's assigned me to," I replied.

Olen's laugh bounced off the gray stone walls, chilling my blood. "The king has made you my duty while he runs this court. I have things to do and you're coming with me."

"Why are you in your beast form?" I asked, trying to distract him.

The creature beside Olen gulped loudly. Olen's head snapped down at the little being. "You are excused. Run to the king. See if he has any tasks for you."

The creature, keeping its eyes on me, nodded before rushing out the open cell.

"Are we going to do this the fun way or the easy way?" Olen asked again.

I watched while he spoke, realizing his lips weren't moving. Instead, the sound of his voice vibrated from his chest.

"The fun way?" I asked.

That was a stupid question.

I screamed, flailing my arms when his elongated snout gripped the hem of my now-filthy nightgown, dragging me across the cell. Right through the rot and slime that layered over the disgusting surface.

I choked down my gag, yelling curses as he dragged me through the long corridor. I was amazed my gown wasn't ripped, but irritated as it pulled down the further he dragged, almost exposing my breasts to the unsanitary surface.

"Stop it!" I yelled, kicking my legs.

To my shock, one foot slammed into something warm—his face.

The dragging stopped, giving me enough time to scramble to my feet. I groaned as I stood from the pain still vibrating in my tailbone.

Olen whipped around slowly, his body heaving with the slow breaths he took.

"You kicked me," he snarled.

"You dragged me through filth!" I countered.

He stalked closer and his menacing paws dragged against the stone. "Do you not wish to be?"

My head shook with annoyance. "What makes you believe anyone would enjoy that?"

"The mortal lands must not be any fun," he replied.

His creature form twisted away from me. "Well, follow me. You're not decent enough to go out while I complete my duties."

"I'm not going back to that room," I said, crossing my arms.

He twisted to meet my eyes, and a canine peeked through his lips. "Yes you are. It's where you're staying, princess. Your trunks are waiting for you."

My feet planted against the prison surface while I held his stare. I was ready to challenge him. To claim my royal privilege to be treated with even a sliver of respect. The only flaw in my plan was the beast I glared at didn't seem to care.

No, his eyes were lit with amusement at my determination.

His paws moved, pulling my gaze down then his voice echoed across the space. Somehow quiet but commanding all at the same time.

"Upstairs, princess."

My body went rigid and reluctantly, I followed, refusing to allow him to drag me again. I picked up my feet, forcing my body to move. The limp was evident in my walk, but I continued forward, holding back my groans of pain.

"Something wrong?" he asked, walking ahead of me.

"You injured me last night," I replied roughly.

He was silent while he continued guiding the way. Behind him, I was studying the halls. Taking note of the length of the prison and the stairway we now climbed up. My hands were stiff at my sides as my mind made a map of the exit the further he walked.

When we'd reached the top of the stairs with sweat running down my back from the physical strain, Olen finally spoke once more.

"You almost killed my king." His body twisted as his black eyes met mine. "You're lucky I wasn't given permission to end your life for the stupidity."

I let out an irritated sigh. "I know the fae aren't well known for logic, preferring to live lives of amusement and frolicking, but do you really not understand *why* I would try to end his life?"

My hands twitched at my side as my mind reminded me I should also be trying to end the life of the beast before me.

Olen's body moved and an odd noise rumbled from inside of him. A noise, I quickly realized, must have been a deep laugh.

"The *fae* do enjoy being carefree as they wish. I understand, princess. It doesn't mean I agree."

I narrowed my eyes. "I could petition Oberon. I could write to one of his wives. Mab or perhaps Titania. Titania has always shown me preference when I visit. She's also well known for sympathizing with helpless women."

I could barely register my surprise when I was suddenly thrown across the hall. Olen slammed my body against the opposite wall, his snout inches from my face with his canines bared.

"Do not utter those names in this place," he growled.

His claws dug into my forearms and my lips trembled. I couldn't form the words to reply.

"Do you understand?" his deep voice vibrated from his throat.

Slowly, I nodded my head while a tear ran down my cheek. Not able to process my fear, disgust quickly replaced it when a long black tongue licked my cheek.

"You're an animal!" I yelled, staring into his black eyes.

"Of course I am," he replied.

His claws released my arm, leaving a trail of blood in their wake. "Go," he demanded, hitting my legs with his snout.

I held my wound, forcing my tears to dry while I followed him down the hall. Back to the bedroom. Unsure of what a day with the king's right hand would entail.

I bit back the bile in my throat when Olen's jaw wrapped around the creature, tearing its head from its shoulder.

Black blood covered the grass we stood upon, and my stomach weakened.

Olen had forced me to dress quickly. He nearly shoved me down the stairs the moment I'd stepped out from the dressing screen, telling me of his duties and his responsibility to enact on behalf of the king.

He hadn't taken the time to explain that meant ripping heads from shoulders.

From what I could gather, the still twitching creature before me had made a deal with Ulrich. But they had failed to uphold their end of the bargain. So, as Olen had explained, there were two choices. One—submit fealty to the king and do his bidding for the rest of their days. Or two—die.

This creature chose death.

Shocking me.

Olen had repeated the options twice, his voice booming across the small town we'd traveled to. The spectators in the courtyard had kept their heads bowed low while the now dead creature had stood defiantly. Staring into Olen's eyes, calling the Unseelie King a *coward*. Claiming, *he could come and get me himself.*

It brought shocked gasps from everyone in attendance.

So, when Olen gave the option for the second time, and the creature sneered *death*, he hadn't hesitated pulling its head from its shoulders.

My eyes continued to stare at the body on the ground, with the head rolling off to the side. I'd never seen this much depravity in my life. First Leif's rotted head. Then the fae openly engaging in carnal lust. Now this, a twitching body and head rolling out in the open with no one moving to stop it.

The thoughts ran through my body and finally, my stomach failed me.

I threw my hands over my mouth and ran to the nearest corner, bending at the waist.

The light of the sun shone above me while I embarrassed myself once again. Emptying my stomach in the open, repainting myself as a woman unable to hold in her disgust instead of the calm royal I should have been seen as.

My body stopped heaving and I stood, staring up at the sky. I leaned against the building I'd run behind, wiping my mouth when Olen's voice filled the courtyard.

"Find her!" he bellowed.

Shaking my head, I shoved from the wall and stepped out from my hidden spot. "No need. I haven't run off."

He whipped around, black blood dripping from his jaw, his teeth coated in the gore. His snarl turned to an unsettling smile.

"The king would be displeased if you had."

I rolled my eyes, wrapping my arms around myself. "Are you done with your duties?"

"Was that not entertaining?" he asked, cocking his monstrous head.

"Disgusting is how I would describe what that was," I replied.

His laugh boomed out across the courtyard and the remaining fae scattered in response.

"You've been here for a day, princess. There's still so much more to see."

I glanced around the small town, taking in the little buildings, realizing I'd run behind what appeared to be an inn. It was quaint and well taken care of. Only, I couldn't fathom why they all lived under the rule of such a gruesome king.

"What does Ulrich do for them?" I asked, turning back to Olen.

His fur rippled down his back before his low voice replied, "He does his duty."

I let out an annoyed breath. "You didn't answer my question."

Olen's body turned in my direction, his menacing canines still dripping with blood. "The king's duty is not of your concern. You are here to complete the deal your ancestor made. You are not here to ask questions."

Olen walked away and I stared off in the distance, where Ulrich's city and palace lay barely within my eye's sight.

The people in the courtyard began to return, along with their muttering, pointing at me. The spectacle in the middle of the town. Standing beside the corpse of a creature they'd likely viewed as a friend.

With a scoff, I picked up my feet and walked as fast as my injured body could take me. When I caught up to Olen, I sneered at him.

"I'm sure Ulrich would be displeased to know you are leaving me alone."

Olen's shoulders shifted slightly while his paws hit the ground below.

"Trust me, princess. He'd find you in an instant if you tried to run."

The words were a warning but also thrilling in some way and I glanced back at the town, wondering if I should have tried. Maybe get the monster to come for me. Force him to meet me where I could attempt to end his life alone, with no prying eyes around.

And no one to haul me off to the dungeon later.

"Don't think about it," Olen replied.

My eyes turned back to him. "I wasn't."

"Princess, you're easy to read. Try and run, I dare you. I haven't had enough blood tonight. I could use some hearty, mortal blood in my veins."

"That's foul," I replied.

"That's life," he snickered. "Keep walking. We have to be back before the moon rises."

I turned my eyes back to the sky, watching the sun lower further in the sky.

"What happens if we don't return? Will Lokii turn you into a serpent?"

Olen stopped. His body twisted while what I believed to be his brow rose.

"You mortals put some much trust and belief in these *Gods*. Tell me, princess, have they ever answered one of your prayers? Have they ever heard your wailing and cries?"

I blinked at him, my hands falling to my side.

"No," I admitted, casting my eyes to the ground.

"You asked what Ulrich's duty was," Olen continued. "That's his duty. He's the one listening in the shadows. He's the voice answering the cries. It's not his fault if people don't hold up their end."

"But—" I began to protest.

He cut me off. "Why do you think the Gods stopped answering, Brenna?"

Olen stalked away and I watched in shock, unable to process what he'd said. Was he right? Was there something else behind this monster his people appeared to adore? Or was I being made a fool—again?

Chapter 6

The weeks of my service *dragged* on. When I wasn't being forced to follow Olen around, watching him fulfill brutal punishments on behalf of Ulrich, I was forced to lay on the cold rotted floor of the dungeon.

That was until Ulrich called me back to his bedroom each night, or day.

I'd barely begun to get used to the change in how these fae lived their lives. Waking before the sunset, living their normal lives under the light of the moon, and then falling into their beds right before sunrise. At least this was how Ulrich ran his court, given the towns and cities the palace surrounded were always awake and bustling when Olen and I ventured out.

Still, week after week, I ended up back in the dungeon after only a short time beside Ulrich. Due to my continued attempts to end his life. Slowly, to my amusement, his room was emptying of its furniture and any potential weapons.

The war was growing tiresome though. With each failed attempt, I was reminded of my uselessness. My lack of strength, magic and skill. The painful reality I'd lived my entire life.

It was one of the many reasons I preferred the company of mortals over fae. The mortals never expected more than kindness from their princess.

I shifted through the haze of the past weeks, of the events missed in my life at home. The celebrations. Moments in my life with my loved ones that I would never get back. Hours of sobbing on the prison floor in my mourning. Days of trying to predict when Ulrich's notoriously cruel hand would finally come down on me. When he would finally punish me for my attempts, instead of laughing in my face each time.

The dungeon door slammed open, and I jumped. When I turned around, my eyes widened when I found Ulrich at the caged entrance.

He was, as always, in that damned mask.

"Where's Olen?" I asked, jumping to my feet.

Ulrich's head tilted down as his eyes scanned me from head to toe before an amused smile graced his lips.

"Preoccupied."

"What do you want?" I asked.

The king glanced around the cell before running one finger against the damp walls. I couldn't see his eyes from a distance, but the grimace on his lips wasn't hard to miss.

"It's rather disgusting in here," he said.

"I wasn't aware," I replied, taking a step back.

He mimicked the motion, pointing out the open cell door. "Time for your service, *Ursa*."

I shook my head in defiance. "No. I'd rather stay in here tonight."

An alluring laugh echoed around the cell before he was crossing the space, pinning me to the wall.

"Get out there now," he demanded.

My knees buckled in fear while I stared into his eyes.

"No," I managed to squeak out.

"You make everything so difficult," he replied as his hand wrapped around my wrist. "I have something fun planned tonight."

He yanked on me, pulling a pained cry from my lips.

"Now, Brenna."

My feet stumbled as he pulled me through the dungeon, passing the previously sleeping guard, now sitting alert.

"Stop!" I cried out, trying to rip my wrist from his strong grip. "Stop!"

Ulrich paused and he whirled around, his green eyes swirling with amusement.

"No."

He pulled again and I stumbled once more, my feet catching the dirtied hem of my gown. As he guided me through the palace, I realized we weren't heading to the bedroom. No, he was leading me back to that damned ballroom. Where the fae played and fucked in the open.

My stomach dropped. He'd said he had something *fun* planned. Was I part of that plan?

My eyes drifted down to my gown, now stinking with the prison rot. No, I realized, he wasn't going to defile me. He was going to humiliate me.

His hands slammed a door open and I jerked, finding us entering the ballroom from a hidden passageway.

"Too many prying eyes at the main entrance," he winked.

I was almost relieved when I was suddenly, and violently, thrown out in the open. The sound of my body hitting the dais halted the previously deafening noise.

Hisses rang out followed by laughs and sneers. I kept my eyes down, refusing to meet the masked eyes of his deprived people.

Hands gripped the back of my head, ripping my hair slightly.

"This princess thinks she's better than us!" Ulrich yelled out.

I bit my lip, fisting my gown while Olen approached in beast form with a sick glee in his eyes while his teeth held a mask.

He approached and Ulrich kneeled, grasping the mask before he placed it on the bridge of my nose. "Masks, every single night, princess. Don't forget."

Ulrich dropped my head after tying the ribbons at the back and I fell against the hard floor again. His footsteps rang behind me while he sauntered toward the middle of the ballroom.

"Each night we celebrate!" His voice took command of the room. "Each night we enjoy ourselves. We welcome lust and liquor. We fall into our darkest fantasies."

His eyes barreled into my gaze with his last sentence, latching onto my hate.

"But there's one among us who doesn't deserve such freedoms."

My stomach dropped and hushes filled the ballroom. I moved to run, when my body hit a solid wall of muscle and fur.

"Keep watching, princess," Olen ordered, keeping me in place with his paws holding my gown against the dais.

Ulrich crossed the room in a flash, the blond of his hair like a streak of dark gold in the wind. His arms reached behind a large column and a shriek echoed across the space. He yanked the body of a fae man out of the shadows. A completely nude fae man, one who had obviously been too occupied to realize the king was speaking.

"Hello, *Tristan*," Ulrich sneered.

Olen's claws dug into the fabric of my gown, but even if I had wanted to, I couldn't look away. Ulrich pulled the man upward to meet his eyes.

"My grace," the man choked out.

My eyes stayed on his face but briefly, I glanced, watching the fae around Ulrich gawk and point at the man's erection quickly disappearing.

Not surprising but still shocking that he'd been in the height of pleasure and was now a public spectacle.

Cold infiltrated the room while Ulrich kept the man in the air. I couldn't stop myself from staring at the muscles in the king's arm and wondered how in the Gods he kept a full man's weight up for so long.

"How long?" Ulrich's voice boomed.

"Your grace?" the man cried out.

"Do not lie to me," Ulrich replied, somehow lifting the man's body higher for the entirety of his court to see.

"My king," Olen growled behind me. "Would you enlighten the court on this beast's crimes?"

Ulrich's gaze snapped to our direction and my body chilled. His expression, even behind the mask, was one of death. An emotionless predator determined to make his kill.

"Traitor," was all that Ulrich snarled. The word warming the cold of the room.

Tristan struggled in Ulrich's hand, his legs kicking frantically. "Please—" he choked out.

"It's a shame you were caught," Ulrich replied.

Tristan's eyes filled with terror, sending me into a frenzy of equal terror. The man lost control of himself and my heart ached in empathy when he relieved himself on the ballroom floor. Disgusted screams and gags filled the room, but Ulrich only laughed.

My eyes turned back to Ulrich who was now whispering something to the whimpering man. Something that caused the fae to relieve himself once more before the *snap* of his neck rang out across the ballroom. Instantly silencing the noises of disgust from Ulrich's people.

The king tossed the body into his own filth before snapping his fingers and the music began again. Like it was all nothing. Like these monsters were so used to these kinds of acts of violence.

My body shook in place while the smaller creatures I now knew to be attendants gathered around the body, cleaning up the mess. Another followed beside Ulrich, offering him a bowl with what I assumed to be water and a towel to dry his hands.

Olen released his hold on me and I glanced down, realizing he'd somehow been dragging me to the seat beside Ulrich's throne. Placing me near it like the object they both believed I was.

"How was that?" Ulrich asked.

I blinked, sitting slowly to try and prevent myself from falling down. He was speaking to me, but I couldn't form the words to reply.

"Not entertaining?" Olen laughed.

My eyes darted between the two men. One staring at me with his elbow leaning on his throne, the other, a beast, admiring what I assumed to be people lost in their lust once more.

"We're speaking to you," Olen said without turning his eyes from the ballroom behind me.

"That was awful," I managed to respond.

Ulrich's amused smile turned vile, and he straightened in his seat. My eyes shifted when one of his naked fae women approached the throne, bending as though she intended for me to see all the Gods had given her. Only Ulrich didn't welcome her to his lap, instead I watched him grip her cheeks roughly, pulling her face up to his.

"Go," he snarled, throwing her away from him.

Her gasp made me feel for the humiliation he'd put her through before she ran off to the side.

"That was brutal," Olen said. "I could have had her."

"Then go and claim her," Ulrich replied while he scanned the ballroom.

My eyes went down again, praying he would release me from this spot soon. That he would grow tired of whatever game he was playing.

"I would," Olen paused. "But I can't leave you alone with a murderous princess."

I snapped my head up, eyes widening. "I could kill you both."

Ulrich's laugh echoed around me. "Brenna, you are as terrifying as a mouse. Perhaps even less. You're only alive because you've become entertaining to me. I wonder when you'll finally give up."

I sat straighter. "I'll keep trying. For the remaining twelve months. I won't stop."

"Thirteen," Ulrich countered.

My feet were pulling me up before I realized what I was doing. My voice rose and I pointed at him.

"Thirteen? No!" I yelled. "It's been thirty-one days. Three days past a full month. I have completed the first month of my service."

Ulrich sneered at me, his hair brushing past the black mask covering half of his face. "You have attempted to kill me each night for thirty-one days. Do you really expect me to not punish you?"

"That wasn't part of the terms you gave me!" I protested.

"Well, neither was your determination to kill me," he replied. "Sit back down, Brenna."

I crossed my hands over my chest. "No."

His eyes glared back at me, and I swore black flecks rushed past the green. "Sit down. My court is now staring."

"Let them stare," I challenged.

Olen's eyes widened beside Ulrich.

Slowly, Ulrich stood from his throne. I braced myself for his wrath but gasped in shock when shadows appeared from behind him, climbing up his body as though they were part of him.

The lights in the room dimmed while whispers filled the space.

"My guest!" Ulrich yelled, not meeting my gaze. "Did you all know she's tried to kill me each night?"

"Traitor!" voices chimed together.

"What should I do about that?" he laughed.

"Remove her head!" one voice yelled out.

"Force her into courtesan servitude!" another laughed.

Ulrich's smile coursed through my body as he approached. His shadows wrapped around my legs, holding me in place. After flipping me to face his people, his hands wrapped around my body, but I could do nothing to fight him off.

His hand crawled past my stomach, traveling between the plains of my breasts, stopping at the base of my neck.

"Should I give them a show?" he whispered into my ear.

"I hate you," I replied.

The hand on my neck gripped me, not enough to choke the air from my lungs but enough to bring out a shocked gasp from my lips.

"I hate you, Brenna," he muttered. "I hate your presence in my home. I hate your useless attempts to end my life. *Me*—a God of Millennia—a beast who could wipe out everything and everyone you love with a snap of my fingers."

His hand released my neck, and his shadows climbed higher, forcing my hands to my side.

"I hate that I am duty bound to keep you here for the next year," he continued as his shadows moved me from the dais and toward the middle of the room. "You think you *hate me*?"

I was forced to my knees, his shadows holding my chin up while he approached me. "You don't hate me yet," he laughed.

His fingers snapped and the bodies surrounding me scattered. Heavy footsteps approached behind him and my eyes laid on Olen.

"Yes, your grace?" the beast snarled.

Ulrich grinned. "I think one for each day she's attempted to end my life."

My mouth opened to cry out, trying to decipher what he was referring to, but his shadows went down my throat, choking out my ability to reply.

Tears sprang from my eyes with the shock of his attack and the cold of the shadows. My hands went to my throat, a useless attempt to fill my lungs once more.

Olen cleared his throat. "Yes, your grace."

"Prepare her," Ulrich said with little emotion.

His shadows were gone as quickly as their attack and I fell against the floor, gulping in fresh air. I braced myself, ready for him to enact the revenge I'd been waiting for. Waiting for him to allow whatever he planned to defile me. Only I didn't expect Olen's sharp teeth to rip my dress, exposing my back to the crowd.

"Lashes," Ulrich sang out. "Traitors get lashes."

More tears fell from my eyes along with the cheering cries of his court.

I tracked him while he held me in place and his shadows lifted my arms above my head. My dress slipped, barely stopping before my breasts would be exposed to the monsters before me. He circled me, his hand brushing against my hair.

"Thirty-one lashes, Brenna," he whispered and his hands ripped the front of my dress down, exposing me. "Then you will truly hate me."

I held in my cry from the cold of my exposed skin, ignoring the hungry eyes gawking at my body.

The first lash hit. Cold, hard, biting.

My body jolted in pain, but I didn't cry.

Then the next one.

Three.

Four.

Five.

I counted each one, my arms shaking in his shadows, tears lining my eyes, refusing to let out the cry he was attempting to force from my lips. The sixth lash pulled a whimper from my throat, and I shook further.

"Kill me," I whispered.

He leaned over me, pausing his beating. Gripping my neck once, he pulled me against him.

"That's the easy way out," he replied before licking the tears running down my cheeks.

I screamed in response, jerking against his shadows when another lash hit my back.

"Show no mercy!" a voice from the crowd yelled out, encouraging the show of depravity that I had become.

I focused my ears, trying to figure out where the voice had come from but laughed in shock and disgust when I realized people had resumed their fucking.

"I hate you all!" I screamed, hoping they would hear me over their moans.

"And we hate you," Ulrich responded.

The next lash hit my back, harder, deeper, the blood instantly running down my skin, warming me from the cold. The pain—my head spun from it. I would have collapsed onto the ground if his shadows hadn't held me in place.

"I hate you," I whispered again as the next lash hit, in the same spot as before. The sound of my flesh breaking turned my stomach in knots while my eyes rolled to the back of my head.

I fell into darkness, allowing the pain to take over. Repeating my hate for him as I drifted away to the sounds of my flesh tearing, sending me right toward newfound vengeance poisoning my soul.

Chapter 7

I woke with my face in a soft pillow, the burn on my back somehow not as severe.

"Don't move," a gruff voice said beside me.

I turned my head, the stiffness in my neck making me groan. When I forced my eyes open, I found the room dark.

Fuck the Gods.

The last place I wanted to be taken after my torture was his bed. He must have been beyond sanity to believe I would have willingly stayed beside him. Near him. Following his *terms.*

"I said don't move," he repeated, shoving me back against the bed.

I bit down on the pillow from the shock of his touch, unable to hold back the tears falling from the pain.

"Why?" I asked quietly.

He was silent while his hand pulled away from me. His sigh filled the room. "Haven't you heard of my violence, Brenna?"

I shook my head against the pillow, gripping the sheets below me. "Why?" I repeated, lost in the haze of hate, pain, and shock.

A creaking sound told me he'd leaned back on whatever chair he sat upon. "You're going to learn, *Ursa*, the kind of monster I am. To have order in my court, I must rule with fear. I must punish those who deserve punishment. I must ensure my people know to never cross me."

"I'm not one of your people," I snapped.

"You are during the term of your service," he replied.

I closed my eyes, burying my face in the pillow. "Please kill me," I cried, unsure if he could hear my muffled plea.

He was silent beside me, but the air had shifted. I could only assume he'd left his spot beside me, understanding now the cold that emitted from him was due to the shadows he could recall in an instant. I strained my neck, trying to track him in the dark but yelled out in pain when the bed shifted beside me with the weight of his body.

"Get away from me!" I cried, unable to move from my spot.

His voice became low, predatory, a warning.

"Go to sleep, Brenna."

I was too tired to fight. I was in too much pain to shift away from his body settling into the covers beside me. My tears fell against the pillow while the burn of my wounds served as a reminder of my plan.

He hadn't done anything to deter me from my conviction to end his life. If anything, he'd solidified it. Made is stronger. Turned it into a monster of my own.

I would end his life. Even if it was the last thing I did.

My legs trembled while the quiet attendant helped me from the bed, allowing me to drape my arms over her slender shoulders. Tears lined my eyes from the pain as we walked toward the bathroom. But even more, the tears were brought on by the fear coursing through me.

I'd been in Ulrich's bed for days. How many? I didn't know.

It had been a fever dream. Laying there, jolting every now and then by the rough, callused hands rubbing freezing salve over my wounds. Hands I wasn't sure were his or Olen's.

Making me hate both of them even more.

Ulrich had been the one to mark me, to shame me publicly, and Olen had been his willing accomplice. Yet one of them believed they could care for me? Tend to my wounds?

What kind of monsters was I imprisoned with?

To my relief, Ulrich hadn't demanded to stay in the room when he ordered me to bathe. Claiming I *smelled like death*.

Part of me had wanted to refuse. Because the thought of sickening him with my stench gave me disgusting satisfaction, but he'd picked up on my intentions. That had resulted in him quietly informing me I could bathe willingly, or he would carry me to the tub himself and force me to bathe with him.

Nude.

Horrified, I relented and allowed him to call the attendant.

I cursed him and his vile nature while the attendant, a quiet young woman, lowered me onto the stool in the bathing room. I watched her, taking note of her bronzed skin, the freckles across her cheeks, her elongated ears, and the twisting braids running down her back.

"What's your name?" I asked.

She jumped, her head jerking from her attention on the tub. Nervously, she glanced through the bathing room doors.

I laughed, followed by a loud wince at the pain shooting down my back from the movement. The girl scrambled to her feet, rushing to me, but I held up my hand.

"Don't fuss over me. Would you tell me your name?"

"Adalie," she whispered.

I nodded my head. "That's a beautiful name. Are you Seelie or Unseelie Fae?"

Adalie startled, her eyes widening before she shook her head. "I—"

A booming laugh cut off the girl's words and my head turned to the sound. The lights in the room vanished with the movement but I was able to catch Ulrich's frame leaning against the doorway before the dark took over the space.

"Stop asking my people personal questions," he said coldly.

I leaned back, using my hands to feel for the wall behind me. "I'm just trying to get to know people. Do you expect me to live in solitude for my remaining twelve months?"

"Thirteen," he replied.

I cried out. "Not this again. Please! I have completed my first month."

Ulrich's commanding presence filled the room, but due to the lack of light, I could only assume he'd crossed the threshold. My pulse quickened while my hands gripped the thin nightgown I wore.

"Are you scared?" his voice whispered above me.

I swallowed, not sure how I hadn't felt him approach so closely. But now that he was before me in the dark, it was hard to ignore the cold, sickening power coming from him. Like a darkness, determined to pull life from any living thing near him.

"To answer your plea," he said calmly, "I've already told you the other evening that your time has added an additional month. This wouldn't have happened if you hadn't misbehaved."

Tears lined my eyes while I calculated the time that gave me. "That means my time ends when the blood moon ends."

"What?" Ulrich's cold grew more frigid.

"My..." I snapped my mouth shut. "Nothing."

The room grew silent before his voice echoed around me again. "Technically you are right. Your service will end on the last day of the blood moon. Did you have plans, Brenna? A blood moon rite you were hoping to make it to?"

My tears fell without my control, and I shook my head, unsure if he could see me.

"You aren't answering my questions," Ulrich spoke with the same blank command I'd heard my father use countless times before.

My tears fell heavier at the thought of my father. In all the days I'd been gone I hadn't received any word from him. No letters. No armies coming my way.

I'd expected—I'd hoped that he would have written to Oberon and begged for help. Or that he would have rallied our allied islands in the seas to come to my aide. But he hadn't come for me. He'd left me here, to be tortured and tormented by this awful king.

"Adie, you may leave. I'll assist my guest."

Ulrich's voice pulled me from my despair.

"Wha—"

My protests were cut off when his palm wrapped around my lips. His mouth brushed against my neck. "You're in my home." His hands trailed down my forearm. "By my bath." He continued his trek, freezing me in place, stopping only when his fingers touched my hands in my lap. "You will obey *my* rules."

His hand gripped the hem of my nightgown, pulling it upward. I threw myself out of my haze and held his hand still.

"Get your hands off me," I warned.

"Baths are usually better with nothing on," he replied with a laugh.

"Get out," I demanded.

"Get in the bath, Brenna," he whispered, lowering his lips against my neck again.

I shook my head in shock. How he believed I would undress in front of him was equal parts confusing and intriguing. I couldn't though, I couldn't give him the satisfaction of making myself any more vulnerable than I already had.

His palm released my face, and I stared into the darkness.

"I don't give you my permission," I said.

He laughed. "I can easily toss you in that tub. I don't need your permission. I just need your stench gone so I can enjoy my bedroom again."

"You wouldn't dare," I replied.

You're a godsdamn fool.

The moment the words left my lips, his hands gripped my waist. In one fell swoop, he had me over his shoulders.

I screamed but couldn't fight due to the heat burning through my body.

"Please!" I cried while my hands fell limp against his chest. "Please, my wounds—the pain. I'm going to be sick."

He set me in the tub, more gently than I'd expected, but the shock of the water pulled another scream from my lips.

"Fuck the Gods!" I yelled out.

His laugh filled the room. "That's quite the curse."

Shivering from the cold water, I rolled my eyes. "Why is it frigid?"

The water moved around my feet, while I assumed he waved his fingers to test the temperature. "I wouldn't describe that as *frigid.* It's warm. Heat isn't good for your wounds."

"This is freezing," I replied through chattering teeth. "And I wouldn't have any *wounds* to worry about if you hadn't been such a monster."

Silence layered over the room, as though he possibly felt a sliver of guilt for what he'd done to me. Biting back an additional response, I laid my head against the cool edge of the tub. I began slowly lowering my body down, allowing the water to flow over my shoulders.

The wounds beneath my soaked nightgown burned in response, but the temperature, to my annoyance, was soothing.

I lowered myself further into the tub, losing myself in the weightlessness. Not caring if the man above was possibly watching. Even knowing the white gown was likely sheer now, revealing my most intimate places.

The hem of the gown floated around my thighs, dancing against the water. It lapped against my skin while I stared up at the void of the room, realizing he'd somehow blocked the skylight above.

I chose to ignore it, releasing a relaxed breath. That was until the water moved, and to my horror, Ulrich was climbing into the tub on the other end.

I scrambled upward, covering my body. Suddenly caring how thin that gown was.

"You looked comfortable," he said casually while the water level rose as he lowered himself down.

"You can't see me," I replied, crossing my arms over my chest.

"Yes I can. You're looking less like a wild beast."

I moved to stand but his legs wrapped around mine, holding me in my place.

"Release me!" I demanded.

He let out a content sigh. "No. I'm rather comfortable."

My legs thrashed beneath his, making the water around us lap over the edge of the tub. The sound of the liquid hit the floor, echoing around the room. Yet he didn't release me. Instead, his hold tightened.

How in the Gods are his legs this strong?

I tried to fight but each movement sent jolting shocks of pain down my back. Reminding me once again of the wounds he'd inflicted on my skin. I knew I had to stop. I had to allow the water to cool my wounds, but I didn't care. I leaned forward, reaching through the darkness, trying to aim at his face.

His hands gripped mine, stopping me instantly. His hold grew tight, painful and controlling. "No," he said calmly.

I twisted my wrists, burning my skin against his, trying to break from his hold. To my frustration, he responded by plunging my hands into the water, away from my target.

"Calm down," he said.

I yelled again, flailing my legs under his. Trying to get his unbreaking calm to crack. Trying to get him to react to my wild movements.

"Let me go!" I commanded.

"Gods, you're an animal," he laughed.

My fingers moved under the water, searching for anything to claw. To hurt him like he had me. My nail brushed against skin and I froze.

"Well," his voice dropped, "I didn't realize you wanted to *play*."

I threw my head back with a scream, somehow surprised the king had shucked every last shred of clothing on his body.

"You're completely nude!"

"I am in a bath," he replied.

I shook, trying to find a thread of strength in my body. Anything that could overpower his unnaturally large body.

A thought, simple and fleeting, crossed my mind. Just enough to slow my frantic heart.

I cursed the lack of light but smiled a sweet, sultry smile. I knew what men, both mortal and fae preferred. Gods, I'd used my body to get my way plenty of times in my life.

I relaxed my shoulders, dropping my voice like he'd dropped his. "I didn't realize playing was an option."

It was silent on the other end of the tub, and I was sure I had perhaps failed. He let out a heavy breath.

"Come here," he replied.

His hands released me, and his legs unwrapped from around mine.

Freedom.

I could have run then. I could have sprinted out of the room. But I was too focused on my goal. Too ready to enact revenge.

Slowly, I crawled through the water, running my hands across his bare legs to guide me toward him. The feeling of his muscled legs beneath my fingers brought an annoying ache low in my belly, but I focused on my need for another kind of satisfaction.

The rough hairs of his beard brushed against my cheek when I reached his face and I gasped, not realizing I'd gotten so close.

"Sit," he said.

I shook at the command in his voice, the ache in my belly begged me to allow some physical reprieve. To let the hate turn to passion. To let pleasure replace the burn of my flesh crying out from the air now whipping past my healing wounds.

A release from the madness I was living.

But I threw it aside, regaining my control.

His hands wrapped around my waist, lifting me with ease.

"I said sit," he repeated gruffly, placing me on his lap.

The end of my gown slipped between my legs, creating the only barrier between my flesh and his. With a steady breath, I leaned forward, running my hands down his torso.

"What do you want?" he asked.

I tried to reply with any kind of smart response, but the way his fingers circled my lower back nearly brought me to insanity. His palm flattened against me, pressing my chest to his and a pulse grew between my legs. Thumping against the fabric of my dress.

A pulse of arousal that wasn't my own.

"What do you want?" he asked again.

I closed my eyes before placing my hands on his shoulders. Trying to keep control of myself, I leaned into him further, brushing my lips against his ear.

"I want—" I paused, positioning myself above his hardening arousal. "I want you to fucking die."

An animal took over as the words left my mouth and my teeth clamped down on his ear, pulling as hard as I could. My nails moved as well, clawing at his skin. I bore down, with both my teeth and hands, internally screaming at the breaking of his flesh under my nails and the taste of his blood in my mouth.

I jumped up and ran. As fast as my injured body could take me.

His bellows of rage filled the room, and I slipped on the slick floor, heading to where I thought the doors were. Praying to the Gods he wouldn't catch me.

Chapter 8

Gods, he was going to kill me. I could feel it in my bones as I ran through the dark, somehow not colliding with any walls in the room.

"Brenna!" his voice rang behind me, sending a chill through my body.

I slipped on the stone of his bedroom, stopping for just a moment, trying to determine which door to take. I remembered the hidden door he'd come down, and hoped I had disoriented him enough that he wouldn't consider something so simple.

I moved through the dark room, trying to find the wall beside the bed and the tapestry the door was hidden behind. My hand wrapped around a circular handle and my pulse picked up. Glancing back in the direction I came, I couldn't help but wonder what was taking him so long. I pulled the door open, relishing in the candle-lit hallway that greeted me.

"Brenna!" his voice sang behind me. "I suggest you start running."

My wet nightgown stuck to my body, but I picked up my feet and obeyed him willingly. I threw my body down the hallway, skirting around the corner with no idea where I was going.

I only knew he was approaching by the smell of smoke from candles extinguishing behind me and his overpowering cold at my heels.

My tears fell while I continued to propel down the hallway, cursing the constant twists and turns. Most importantly, cursing the lack of any doors to make my escape.

Maybe he had planned this along. Maybe he'd only allowed me to see this door countless times because only he knew where it led.

"Run little beast," his voice bellowed—too close for my comfort. "Because I will destroy you when I catch you."

I rounded another corner, letting out a sob of relief when my eyes spotted a door at the end of the long hallway. My logic tried to warn me I was running right into a trap, but I didn't care. The door was a light at the end of the darkness encroaching around me and I needed an escape.

My legs moved faster while my back grew slick, with either my sweat or blood from my lashes, I wasn't sure.

My hands connected with the door, and I shoved as hard as my body physically could. I stumbled through the threshold where screams and grunts of surprise welcomed me.

I glanced back, watching the darkness grow closer before turning my attention to the occupants of the room I'd barged through.

"What the fuck, princess?" Olen's voice yelled out.

I blinked, focusing on a fully naked Olen with a woman beside him. Not any woman I realized, it was the woman Ulrich had sent away days before. And she was staring at me with pure hate in her eyes.

"I—" I began, then paused when the hairs on my body rose. Ulrich was approaching, just beyond the door.

Olen's eyes snapped to the threshold then the woman beside him.

"Leave," he ordered.

She let out an offended scoff but didn't protest. With the blanket still wrapped around her, she ran out the doors on the other side of the room.

"Come here," Olen said briskly, pointing beside him.

My eyes widened, landing on his muscled naked body.

"I'm alright."

His white teeth shone through the candle-lit room. "Come here, princess. My king is about to enter this room, and you will be completely defenseless in the dark. Unless this is a game you're playing, being chased until you're alone with two men."

I couldn't argue when the door shook behind me. I clambered to my feet, running to Olen and landing on the bed next to him, curling around myself.

The lights in the room went out the moment my chin touched my knees. The mattress shifted with Olen's weight and his voice echoed in the dark.

"Your grace."

Ulrich's power permeated the space with a frigid, burning cold. Searching for life.

Searching for me.

The king didn't speak while his presence took over. I could hear it though—the rage in his breaths. The determination to *punish* me.

"She attacked me—again," Ulrich spoke, addressing Olen.

Olen laughed. "Gods, I bury myself in one woman and you two can't stop your fighting long enough for me to finish."

My mouth opened to counter, but I slammed my lips shut. It wasn't the time to provide the beast-man with a quip. It was the time to pay attention and save my own foolish hide.

"Based on the way your heart is beating and the stench of her bleeding wounds, I'm going to assume something happened, more than her attacking you," Olen continued.

Both Ulrich and I were silent. My hand rose, touching the wet nightgown and I brought my slick finger back to my nose.

Blood—definitely blood.

"He's mad I didn't ride him in the tub." The words left my lips, and my eyes widened in the dark.

Olen's laugh boomed throughout the room. "Fuck the Gods. Really, Ulrich?"

"Brenna, get off the bed," Ulrich replied, not answering his right hand.

"I'd rather not," I muttered.

"Wrong choice," Ulrich sneered.

Cold wrapped around my ankles, pulling me across the mattress. Smearing my blood on the sheets while I was dragged. My body hit the floor in a crash, as I fought the invisible hold on me. Enraged, I cursed the darkness around me and the unexpected attack.

My body rose suddenly, and the brush of Ulrich's beard scratched my cheek. My hands moved but then they were slammed to my side.

"We're in a predicament," he seethed. "I'm stuck with you in my palace. I'm forced by my duties and responsibilities to uphold every single deal I make, landing you in my lap. A defenseless, wild creature, determined to kill me."

My head reared back while I swirled the liquid in my mouth but the same cold holding the lower half of my body, gripped my cheeks. Stopping my plan.

"If you spit on me," Ulrich's voice dropped, "I will pry your mouth open and spit back."

He released his hold on me, and I turned my head, spitting at his feet.

"You disgust me."

"And you disgust me. Are we even?" he replied.

Olen's chuckle reminded me he was still in the room. Likely still very much naked as well. The sound appeared to have distracted Ulrich, who dropped me to the ground. My knees hit the stone, and I cried out.

Tears sprang from my eyes, and I laid on the cold stone, wincing at the shock against my back. My eyes stared up at the dark ceiling, unsure if either monster stood above me.

"Please," I said quietly. "Please."

My heart cracked with my sobs, fracturing the resolve I'd been holding for weeks. My hand landed on my chest and I flattened my palm against my heart beating beneath my skin. My reminder of my life. One I had once valued.

"Please what?" Olen responded.

"Please stop this."

Ulrich's laugh echoed around us, and I jumped when his toes bumped into my legs. "You are the one who will not obey. You are the one who is refusing to accept this deal. *I* am not making this difficult."

"Fine," I replied with tears running down my cheeks.

The heat of his body hovered over mine and his rough hand brushed away my tears. "Fine what, *Ursa?*"

"I give up."

"That was fast," Olen said off to the side.

Ulrich's finger continued to wipe away my tears. "I agree with Olen. I was expecting a longer fight. I was enjoying our little games."

I scoffed, turning my face away from his touch.

"What do you want from me?" I whispered.

"It's simple." His heat lifted away. "Obey, Brenna. Do as you're told. Allow this court and island to become your home for the next thirteen months."

"That wasn't part of your terms."

"Always so difficult," Olen groaned.

Ulrich chuckled. "You will sleep beside me, without fighting. You will not try to escape. And—"

"I will never look upon your face," I finished his terms for him.

"Get her cleaned up and take her into one of the spare bedrooms," Ulrich whispered.

"What?" Olen replied

I kept my eyes forward, staring at the darkness above. Uttering a word could have meant Ulrich's sudden kindness would be revoked and I wouldn't risk a night of solitude.

"She's injured, she's bleeding, and she made a sopping mess of my bedroom and bathing room. Give her a room until those wounds heal and then..." The heat from before appeared above me once more and his hand brushed my cheek. "Then she'll warm *my* bed.

In an instant the candlelight in the room returned and Ulrich's soul-chilling presence was gone. I blinked through the shock of sudden light, turning my head. Following immediately was my surprised scream when I found myself staring right at Olen's full erection.

"Oh my gods!" I yelled, covering my eyes.

"Like what you see?" he asked with a teasing little lilt to his question.

"How can you still be aroused?" I cried out, shaking my head.

"Well, I wasn't until Ulrich left and I remembered I have a naked woman in this palace somewhere whose forgiveness I have to beg for."

"Then go!" I replied, keeping my eyes closed while my hands motioned to the doors I'd seen her run out of.

He groaned and I allowed myself to glance over, finding his bare buttocks while he reached for a towel.

"I would, but my king has given me an order. Get up. Let's go find you a room."

My cheeks burned with annoyance that I was alone with a naked man. After I'd just run away from another naked man. What kind of fucked up palace was this where I didn't have the autonomy to deny being surrounded by uncovered cocks?

"Something on your mind?" Olen asked, turning to me with a smile on his face.

I scoffed then moved to pull myself off the floor. Only my skin stuck to the stone and tears sprang from my eyes again.

"I'm going to be sick!" I cried, falling back against the stone.

Olen rushed to me, his hand wrapping around mine. "Gods," he whispered. "Stay here."

As if I could have attempted to move, I nodded my head, staring up at the ceiling. I listened as Olen's footsteps ran across the room and his door swung open with a *bang*. Then they retreated down whatever hall his rooms were located in, leaving me in silence with only the iron smell of my blood to keep company.

My eyes rolled as I waited, accepting my new Fate. Unknown to Ulrich, this newest battle between us may have been the one that took me from this *game*. He'd successfully rid himself of his opponent. Even if he hadn't meant to.

My head tilted to the side as my hands went lax against my body.

I was losing blood. At least I thought I was. Calloused hands gently lifted me from the ground. I turned my head, expecting to find Ulrich but to my shock, my gaze landed on an older gentleman. His stature was about the same size as Ulrich and Olen but his eyes—they were kind and surrounded by aged wrinkles.

My vision grew black when it dawned on me; Ulrich had a mortal healer.

Chapter 9

"There are limits to cruelty!" an unfamiliar voice yelled out in the haze fogging my mind.

"There are laws and rules I must abide by!" a second voice shouted back.

My body went cold, and I kept my eyes shut. I may not have known who the first voice was, but the second voice had been haunting my nightmares. The king who found pleasure in my pain and suffering.

"My king," the first voice said quietly.

Silence layered over the room. My breaths quickened in my chest while I hoped whatever room I'd been carried to would empty soon. I needed nothing more than the solitude I'd hoped for when Ulrich had left me in Olen's room, allowing me a space to myself.

"Frode," Ulrich's voice rose with command. "Do what you must. I expect her to be healed and back on her feet in two days."

"Yes, my King," the unfamiliar voice replied, which I had just learned belonged to someone named *Frode.*

The room warmed but I kept my eyes sealed, trying to slow my breaths.

"You can open them now," Frode's voice said above me.

I remained unmoving, squeezing my lids tighter.

"Princess, do what the healer said." Olen's beastly voice came from another part of the room.

I gripped the blankets, forcing myself to welcome in the light. Fear coursed through my body, but to my relief, the pain that had knocked me unconscious was gone.

As I let out a breath, I turned my head to find the same older gentleman who had carried me out of Olen's rooms.

Frode smiled down at me and my body instantly warmed with comfort and safety. His brown eyes, surrounded by the aged wrinkles on his skin, sparkled with kindness. My eyes took him in, desperate to memorize the face of the first genuinely kind man I'd met on this island.

Atop his head was grey and white peppered hair, combed back, but he had a full head of hair. Surprising given he appeared nearly my grandmother's age. He stood confidently, smiling at me while I stared at his towering, solid body.

"You're handsome," I muttered, then gasped, covering my lips.

"Well, those tonics are working." Olen's laugh boomed out.

Frode's smile rose, and he nodded his head. "I'm glad to see you're feeling no pain, princess."

I was nearly brought to tears when the healer bowed his head in respect. A gesture I hadn't received since being taken from my home.

"I'm so sorry," I apologized, shaking my head. "My manners have left me."

Frode lifted his head then chuckled. "No apologies, your highness. Your inability to hold your tongue only means I've done my duty."

I pressed my head against the pillow, trying to hide my embarrassment. My mind clouded as I stared up at a dark grey canopy.

"Where am I?" I asked.

"In the room my king instructed me to put you in," Olen replied.

"My back no longer hurts," I noted, moving my shoulders as the place where my wounds had been rubbed against the sheets beneath me.

"Yes, your highness. The pain shouldn't come back."

I turned my eyes from the canopy and met Frode's kind gaze again.

"You're mortal."

He smiled. "Half-fae, highness."

My eyes widened. "I rarely meet half-fae outside of my own home."

Frode sat on the edge of the bed. Pulling myself up, I watched the elder gentleman admire the room.

"Nóatún is an island gifted to us by Fate."

My body jolted at the name of my home. "What?" I asked, taken aback by how familiar Frode was with where I'd come from.

The healer turned back to me, grasping my hand. "How is Hilde?"

I darted my gaze to Olen, who sat unmoving on all fours, near the hearth. My pulse raced while I considered my response.

"My grandmother is fine," I said quietly.

Olen cleared his throat and Frode released my hand. The healer stood from the bed, addressing the beast who'd been made my keeper.

"Tonics, several times a day even when she leaves this room in two days. I will return to apply salve twice more today and three times each day after."

Olen nodded in acknowledgement and my heart sank as I watched the only tether I had to my home walk away. Once alone, Olen turned to me, his canines shining against his black lips.

"Sleep well?"

I laid back down, waving him away.

"Your king allowed me this privacy. I request you respect it."

"Can't do that," he replied roughly.

"Why not," I asked, glancing back at him.

"Ulrich only gave you these chambers until you were healed. He never said you were to be left alone."

Frustrated tears ran down the corner of my eyes while I refused to look back at the fae.

"How does that healer know my grandmother?"

His clawed paws clicked against the floor, but I kept my eyes on the canopy. The bed shifted, and I jumped as Olen crawled into the bed beside me. Like he was some large pet searching for warmth and soft caresses.

"Not sure," he sighed, laying his head on his paws.

"Get off this bed," I demanded.

"Can't, have to stay close," he growled.

I cried out, hitting a soft pad of fur near his shoulder. "Please!"

His monstrous head snapped up. "I am not the king," he snarled. "I will bite that hand off if you hit me again."

I pulled it back to my chest, turning on my side to get away from him.

"Your king hates me."

"Yes, but he doesn't kill or hurt without reason," the beast replied sleepily.

I laughed. "He killed that man in the ballroom. He beat me until I lost consciousness. He chased me down the halls, determined to end me."

Olen yawned and laid his head on his paw again. "The man was a *traitor. You* keep trying to *kill him.* And he chased you because you attacked him. From my understanding, the poor man was only trying to bathe."

I huffed out an annoyed breath, twisting myself to get further from the beast. The blankets tugged with the weight of him.

"Did you have to lay beside me?" I groaned.

"This bed is more comfortable than the hearth."

"Why are you in your beast form?" I asked.

His head moved up again and his black eyes studied me. His large mouth opened with a yawn and he laid his head down again.

"It's more comfortable to sleep as a beast, princess."

"I don't believe that."

The bed shook along with his body while that same unsettling laugh sounded from within him. "You'd never know."

His breathing turned heavy, and I observed my temporary room of safety. It was simple, one window overlooking Ulrich's city, that I suddenly realized I'd never learned the name of. In one corner was a bathing room door, and in the other, a modest hearth warming the space.

The simplicity instantly reminded me of my room at home, bringing me unexpected comfort.

Once I settled into the covers further, I laid my hands over my chest. An attempt to guard myself from the sleeping creature beside me. I watched the sun complete its crest over the city and listened while Ulrich's palace quieted for their day-sleeping.

And to my surprise, my body drifted back to sleep. Seemingly adjusting to life living under the blood moon.

Chapter 10

My hands fidgeted at the vanity while Adalie's hands brushed my hair gently. The reflection staring back at me was unrecognizable. Nothing like the woman who had been taken just weeks before. Instead, something lifeless, something more similar to the monsters that stalked the court I was captive in, met my eyes.

The auburn hair I adored appeared a muted brown, the life and rich reds gone along with the fire in my heart. And my eyes... Usually brilliantly blue were a pale, and an almost opaque, greying color.

"Your highness," Adalie whispered.

I met her eyes in the mirror and smiled.

Gods she was young, but she'd been kind since she'd entered my room an hour before. Bringing me gowns from my trunks and offering to help me pick the ones that wouldn't bother my healing wounds.

"Yes?" I replied.

"He's expecting you."

I blinked before nodding and returning my eyes back to my reflection.

The two days had gone by in a flash. Ripped from me far too quickly and now I was being readied as a presentation for the tyrant.

Thankfully, he'd left me alone as he'd promised. Not entering my bed. Not pestering me.

No, it had been two days of blissful silence. Minus having had Olen's irritating presence the entire time.

When the sun had begun to set and the red of the moon had brightened my small room, Olen finally excused himself, leaving me only for only a few moments before Adalie entered the room.

I squared my shoulders, choosing to finally present myself as the trained princess I was.

Adalie stepped back when I stood quickly and walked out of the bathing room, right to the door leading out to the palace. Before I gripped the handle, I turned back to the young girl.

"What is the name of your city?" I asked.

She stared back at me, her face blank. "Muspell, your highness," she muttered.

"After the fire God?"

Adalie offered me a knowing smile before jumping back when the door before me slammed open.

"Gods!" I yelled out, stepping back to find Olen grinning at me.

"I've said it before," his eyes scanned me, "but you clean up *very* nicely."

"Uncle!" Adalie yelled behind me.

I turned on my heel, eyes widening at the word.

"Uncle?" I exclaimed.

Olen laughed, moving me to the side gently before sauntering into the room.

"Adie, you've blown our cover."

My eyes watered with tears of betrayal. I'd thought—hoped—Adalie would become a safe person to lean on and learn to trust. Between hers and Frode's kindness, my heart had come to believe I would have friends on this island. Now? Now, my heart was building its cage back up, determined to keep out anyone I came to meet.

Adalie's head shook. "Don't listen to him. Please, your highness." Her plea sounded genuine, but I couldn't be sure. The girl continued, shooting a warning glare at her uncle. "There was no cover. No intended betrayal."

"If you're the niece of the king's right hand, why do you work as a handmaiden?" I replied.

"Because my *uncle* is my guardian, and he believes I must learn from the experience of *manual labor*," Adalie responded, her eyes rolling.

I bit my lip at the snark of her adolescence, turning my eyes back to Olen.

The man only gave me a wide grin while the gold earrings in his right ear rang with the shaking of his head.

"Now that we've gotten that out of the way," he said, pulling his hands from his back.

I groaned, catching the gold of the mask in his hands.

"Again?"

Olen nodded. "The more you fight it, the worse it'll be."

I stepped back into the bathing room, eyeing the dark blue gown Adalie had helped me pick. Annoyingly, the gold suited it perfectly.

I returned to the bedroom and ripped the mask from Olen's hand, finding him with his own black mask situated on his face. His hands moved to help, but I held up my palm.

"I'm capable of placing a mask on myself."

I tied it against my head tightly, then turned on my heel again, right out the open bedroom door. Olen let out a startled sound behind me and the sound of his brisk stride to catch up with me ignited petty glee in my heart.

"Where are we going?" I asked, holding my hands at my front, keeping my shoulders straight. Like the future queen I'd been trained to be.

"Dinner," he responded.

I allowed him to move ahead of me, leading the way from this foreign section of the palace. But during the entirety of our walk, I observed my surroundings. I allowed myself to take in its unique beauty for the first time since being locked within its wall.

The grey stone-floors, ones I'd already become intimately familiar with, had a shine to them. A glistening as though they were possibly made up of remnants of the stars above. And the walls, stone as well, lined with candles lighting the way.

Only, these candles didn't drip wax like the ones I had in my home. These burned brilliantly, never melting. Likely from a magically gifted fae.

I tried to recount the different houses of magic the Unseelie fae possessed and cursed my lack of teachings around the people who made up one-third of our world.

Olen stopped before me while I picked through my tutors' instructions, startling me.

Blinking, I glanced up, finding a solid wood door with an odd, winged creature carved into the surface.

"What is this?" I asked.

"Where you're dining," he replied with an emotionless expression.

My mouth opened to question further when the door creaked open, and my eyes laid on an intimate room with a table in the middle. A table set for only two.

"No," I gasped, stepping back against Olen's towering body at the same moment Ulrich appeared from behind the door.

"No," I repeated, shaking my head. Wincing at the ribbon from the mask tugging at my hair.

"My, *Ursa*, that color *suits* you," Ulrich said with a smirk.

"Don't call me that," I replied, stepping away from Olen.

My body slipped back into the stance of an unphased queen, and I stalked past the Unseelie King. I'd barely made it beyond his reach when his hand wrapped around my bicep.

"Confident tonight," he sneered.

"King Ulrich," I stated, pulling my arm away, "I am the princess of the Kingdom of Nóatún. I will walk into the room with the confidence my people would expect of me."

Ulrich stepped back, his face deadpan. His hand rose and I held back my flinch, expecting some kind of pain for my words. I blinked, finding his hand pointing to the table instead.

"You're excused," he said, keeping his eyes on me.

"Yes, your grace," Olen muttered.

I walked around the king, holding my gaze on the table. Ignoring the black ink climbing up the forearm pointing the way.

A black horned creature appeared from the shadows and pulled my chair out as I approached. I nodded my appreciation, keeping my words to myself. To my surprise, the creature offered a tilted bow of respect before turning on its heel and leaving the room.

The door closed behind it and I steadied my gaze, watching Ulrich sink into the chair across from me.

His shoulder length, blond hair was half pulled up into a bun barely visible at the crown of his head. His beard, still as perfectly groomed as I'd previously seen it, masked the lower half of his face while his black mask covered the upper half. Behind the mask, his emerald green eyes stared back at me and an irritating smile crept across his lips.

"Admiring me, Brenna?" he asked.

I scowled, laying my hands on my lap.

"Can't admire any man who hides himself behind a mask and facial hair."

His brow rose barely above his mask, but his smile didn't falter.

"How's your back?"

"You're demented," I snorted unintentionally. "What would make you believe I'd answer that question?"

Ulrich leaned back in his seat; the motion caused his dipped neckline to strain against his muscle while his arms crossed over his chest. The dark ink on his skin poked through, but I avoided staring.

"Olen tells me you were *behaving* the last several days."

I mimicked his movement, leaning back with as much ease and lack of emotion. My arms crossed over my own chest.

"Hard to do anything when your healer had me inhibited by tonics for the majority of that time," I replied.

Ulrich's grin widened.

We were playing a game. Two royals, daring each other silently. Testing to see who would break their trained composure first.

Who would throw the first blow.

My shoulders tightened when the door opened once more, but I refused to glance at who joined us. Ulrich kept his eyes on me, holding himself as still as I was.

"Our meal is here," he said calmly before pulling his gaze away.

I held myself. I didn't care to see what meal he'd decided to feed me. I'd decided to best this king at his game. And as far as I was concerned, I was winning.

Platters clattered on the table before me and the scent of rich meats filtered throughout the room. The attendant creatures, beings

I hadn't taken the time to learn the names of, lifted the lids before ducking away.

"Hungry?" Ulrich asked, reaching across to the platter closest to him.

The cracking of him breaking off the leg of whatever fowl laid on the plate turned my stomach. I bit the inside of my cheek and shook my head.

His eyes gleamed in the light of the candles surrounding the room while he slowly took a bite. I grimaced while his tongue lapped at the grease falling from the meat and anguished over the painfully slow pace he chose to pull the meat away from the bone. Then, just when I didn't think he could disgust me further, he looked me dead in the eye while he licked his fingers clean.

I lost the game instantly.

I jumped to my feet, yelling out angry, disgusted sighs.

"Are you finished?" I demanded.

"No," he grinned, taking another horribly slow bite.

"Stop doing that!"

"I." Another bite. "Am." Then another. "Eating."

"Is there no other way to eat something? Must you make it so—" I tried to come up with the correct word when his voice broke through my thoughts.

"Sensual?"

I snorted—loudly—with full intent.

"That is not sensual."

His responding laugh startled me, and I watched as he threw his half-eaten meal back onto his plate. "You're right. That wasn't. Please sit, Brenna."

My hands shook at my sides. I'd already lost, too quickly. So frustratingly fast and here he was, offering me another chance.

"Why am I here?" I asked, ignoring his request.

"We're having a meal in my private dining room."

I observed the room while he spoke, finding a door to the side of the hearth.

"Where does that lead?" I inquired, pointing.

My head turned back to him, finding an amused smile on his face.

"That hallway you ran down."

My eyes widened and my mouth opened. "No, it does not."

"Yes, it does."

"No," I pushed. "The only other door in that hallway was the one that led to Olen's room."

"How was it, finding him nude and enjoying some carnal pleasure?" Ulrich asked, trying to get beneath my skin again.

"Absolutely fine," I replied. "Your right hand is *well* endowed."

A noise thumped beneath the table, and I jumped. "Did I hit a nerve?"

Ulrich's hands rose and he grinned again. "Absolutely not. Enjoy him if you'd like. He's rather rowdy in the bedroom."

I chose not to ask how in the Gods he knew that and instead turned my heel, heading for the door.

"Where are you going?" Ulrich asked.

"Back to my room," I replied.

He was in front of me before I could take my next breath. Towering over me like a terrifying vyking.

"I didn't excuse you," he said, leaning close.

"Get out of my way." I smiled sweetly. "Please."

He leaned closer, forcing me to take a step back. "We have a predicament, princess. One we must discuss like the trained royals we both are."

I stared up at him, wishing I had the courage to rip the mask off his face. To get under his skin. To prove he didn't have as much power as he believed himself to have.

"If you were half the kind of royal I'd expect you to be, you would remove your face from my personal boundaries."

To my surprise, he stepped back, gesturing to the table once more.

"I will be on my best behavior." He grinned.

I scoffed. "I doubt that."

But I relented and returned to my seat. He did the same, sitting slowly with his shoulders straight. His face returned to that kingly expression of disinterest.

"Your grace," I said with a sneer. "You said we have a predicament."

"Yes, your *highness,*" he replied. "I'm not sure what to do with you."

I straightened in my seat. "That sounds like a personal predicament, your *grace.*"

He smiled. "I don't argue, but it does put me at a loss of what I'm to allow you to do."

The stiff position I held began to ache down my back and my resolve slipped slightly while my shoulders slumped. I leaned back, hoping he hadn't caught my weakness peeking through. Instead, I hoped he saw a princess acting as casually as a king.

"I do not see how it's my duty to help you come up with a plan."

"I've whipped you publicly," he replied.

My hands fisted the skirt of my gown. "I know," I said through gritted teeth.

"My people can't see me allowing a punished traitor freedoms. Not this soon."

The realization that I truly had no knowledge of how many days it had been since that public humiliation dawned on me. Instantly enraging me.

"How soon has it been?" I decided to ask.

His unphased expression faltered for a moment before he cleared his throat.

"Just less than a fortnight."

"How?"

I was shocked, not understanding how nearly fourteen days had passed. There was no possibility that I'd been in my haze for that long.

"You were in my bed, stinking up my space for nearly seven days. Today marked the third day since you've been in the bedroom I graciously allowed you to rest in. Ten days, just less than a fortnight."

I stood, my heart racing. "You're a monster," I said calmly. "You laid your hands on me so brutally that I've lost close to fourteen days of my life. Days I will never get back."

"Brenna do not insult me by acting as though you don't understand that hand I was forced to enact."

"Excuse me?" My voice rose. "Is this how you believe kings behave? How I would act if I decide to take the queendom of my island?"

Ulrich said nothing.

"I've seen a just king. I've seen *queens* rule their people with love and kindness. I could write to them. Tell them you've injured their subject. Watch the wrath of Oberon, Mab, and Titania come down on this fucked palace."

The room shook and whatever magical wall he'd had holding back his power unleashed. His shadows crawled up his shoulders, creeping toward me, covering the walls of the space.

The candles faltered then extinguished and the red of the blood moon replaced the light. Layering a gruesome filter over us.

I shook in my place watching Ulrich stand, his hands went lax against his thighs.

"Write to them and see what they say," he said calmly. "Write to your father. Beg, Brenna. Beg for help."

His shadows moved him across the room. The unnatural magic crawled toward me as though it were trying to suck the life right from my lungs.

One tendril of the demonic power gripped my cheeks, pulling me toward him. Placing my face inches from his.

"No one will answer," he sneered.

He dropped me, allowing my barely healing body to crash to the ground.

"I hate you," I cried.

"Since you claim I've *taken* almost fourteen days of your life, I'll give you fourteen back," he replied, not responding to my decree of hate. "Return to that little room, princess, and pray to your useless Gods to come and save you."

He walked away, with his shadows trailing behind while he walked through the door I'd noted earlier. Alone, I let out a sob, thankful Frode had healed me with his salves and tonics. Leaving only sensitive pink scars littering my back.

My tears wetted my cheeks then I wiped them away, pulling myself to my feet. I glanced back at the door Olen had led me through and turned in that direction.

I wouldn't let this king break me. I would, however, take full advantage of my gifted freedom.

Chapter 11

I walked the halls of the palace with Olen in beast form at my side. It had been five days since my dinner with Ulrich. Five days of silence from the king.

And five days of exploration.

With my keeper always at my side.

In that time, I'd learned the attendant creatures were called *troll,* whose life purpose was to serve. At least from what I'd observed. I'd also learned Ulrich's palace was surprisingly not just laid with stone but was carved into a mountain. A towering giant that overlooked the city of Muspell.

I'd discovered this when Olen had guided me to the library and the jagged edges of the mountain wall, making up the back of the room, had startled me. As Olen explained, the mountain was believed to have been the previous home of Muspell, the God the city was named after. Other tales claimed the mountain was Muspell himself, turned to solid stone when his fire had grown too hot and melted him to the island floor.

A shocking tale I'd never been told, despite my tutors' determination for me to learn everything I could about the Gods the mortals bowed to.

My hands ran along the stone wall as we walked down the hall I'd come to call *the looking glass,* and I admired the windows running the length of the space. Brilliant glass panes that overlooked the city.

I found the beauty best at night. When the blood moon that had ushered in my birth shone through, painting the halls with a red no one in this world could mimic.

"Something on your mind?" Olen growled beside me.

"I was born under the blood moon," I said airily.

"I'm aware," he grunted.

I stopped my walking and turned to one of the many benches on the wall opposite to the windows. My gown shifted as I crossed one leg over the other and leaned back against the cold stone.

"My one hundred and fiftieth birthday is the last day of the blood moon."

Olen settled before me, letting out a groan. "I'm also aware. It's the last day of your service."

"The service I'm not currently fulfilling?" I asked.

His black eyes met mine and then they rolled with annoyance. "Don't question the king's logic. He's doing you a favor. He could have forced you into another kind of servitude."

My stomach tightened but I grinned through my fear. "It has been some time..." I eyed the beast before me, watching the fur on his back ripple with my words.

"Ulrich says you're rowdy."

Olen was on all fours once more in an instant, his snout barely touching my nose while his voice rumbled. "Want to find out?"

I smiled, shoving him away. "Perhaps another time, beast."

He laughed that unsettling laugh I hadn't yet grown accustomed to before laying back on the stone.

"What are we doing?" he asked.

"You follow me around each day," I stated. "What happened to performing the king's duties? What happened to forcing me to watch failed deals being claimed?"

Olen's shoulders rose. "I've been tasked to stand guard. Ulrich can't have people believing he's given you *total* freedom."

"I want to write a letter," I replied, forcing the request I'd been braving to ask out of my mouth.

"That's not a request I can grant," he replied.

"You could ask..." I stopped my words as the beast's head rose once more.

"Princess, if you want the king to do *anything* you ask, you must meet his demands first."

I groaned and sank against the stone behind me. "It's been five days," I said.

"You're rather full of statements this afternoon." Olen yawned.

"Tell him I'm returning him the other nine."

Olen sat up, his eyes studying me. "Why?" he asked, the question echoing down the hall.

"Because I'm a diplomat," I said calmly, standing from my seat. "I'll meet his demands if he meets mine."

The music boomed out from behind the ballroom doors, and I fidgeted in my place. It'd only been hours since my conversation with Olen, but Ulrich had responded quickly, alerting his right hand to have Adalie prep me for that evening's ball.

The first I'd attended since he'd murdered a man ruthlessly and humiliated me. Marking my body for eternity.

The doors groaned open, and I held my breath, flattening my palms against my thighs. I expected the music to stop, like it had before, but it continued on. To my surprise, not one eye tracked me while I entered the room.

No, it was as though I didn't exist in the sea of moving bodies. As though I were invisible amongst the music and moans harmonizing together.

How these fae managed to celebrate and hump one another night after night was almost admirable. Almost like they had nothing more to live for.

I made my way to the throne, where Ulrich sat with two naked women kissing his neck.

"Your grace," I said, dipping into a bow.

The women didn't stop their kissing. Also behaving like no words had been uttered. Ulrich grinned back, however, wide and bright. His silver mask illuminated his green eyes.

"Sit," he ordered.

My jaw clenched but I bit the inside of my cheek. We were playing our game again. Dancing around each other, trying to crack the other.

I tilted my chin down and took my seat on the rounded settee beside his throne, crossing my legs gently.

"So obedient this evening," he laughed.

I met his eyes, ignoring the tongue licking up his throat.

"I'm only trying to mend the fissures in our two kingdoms' relationship."

"Olen said you called yourself a diplomat. I'm impressed."

The king leaned forward, brushing away the women. "What do you want, Brenna?" he asked, his gaze holding mine.

"I wish to make a request."

"No," he leaned back.

"You haven't heard my terms, your grace," I countered.

His laugh was loud, drowning out the music. "Your terms, *Ursa*? Who said you were in a position to make terms?"

"I'm a princess."

"And I'm the king. But please, tell me another fact everyone in this room already knows."

"I want to make a deal," I replied.

I hadn't thought the words had come out louder than him being able to hear. I was proven wrong when the music stopped and gasped filled the room.

Ulrich's body turned my way, his eyes wide.

"What?" he snapped.

"A deal? That's what you're known for, is it not?"

The king's eyes went to his right hand silently gawking at me at the back of the dais.

"Olen."

Olen stepped forward, tucking his chin down. "I swear, your grace. I did not know."

The silence in the room was telling and I gazed out to find every eye on me and their king. Not one mouth moved. Not one body fidgeted. Even those that had been lost in their lust, were still fused together, but unmoving.

Ulrich stood, his command chilling the room instantly.

"You're here because of a deal," he said, not meeting my gaze.

"I'm here because of a deal a long-dead *man* made on my behalf."

Olen cleared his throat, and Ulrich turned his attention to his right hand.

"She wants to make a deal."

Olen nodded. "It would appear so, your grace."

Ulrich's laugh turned maddening, blood-chilling. The room darkened with his shadows appearing around him.

"Do you understand what you've just started?" he asked, turning to meet my eyes.

"No," I replied honestly. "But I've been told you're bound by your duty."

Ulrich dropped to my level, his hand pulling my chin up. "I'm bound by *blood*, princess."

"What is it you want?" he taunted.

"I want you to fulfill whatever request I make of you if I concede to your terms for another eleven months."

Ulrich laughed. "Twelve months, Brenna."

"Almost eleven months, your grace," I replied. "You added my additional month. I will no longer fight you on that. I only ask that you allow me to do my best to obey my original servitude. If I do—you allow me one request. Whatever I wish. No protests."

Ulrich's eyes flared and I watched the same wisps of black I'd seen before flash in his gaze. He turned his attention to the people silently watching us. Making me wonder if he was considering their thoughts on the matter.

"Fine," he replied.

I yelled out, not expecting the sharp sting of his shadows slicing across my wrist.

"What in the Gods?" I grunted, holding my hand over the now bleeding wound.

"A deal," voices whispered across the room.

The whispers grew—like a chant. An old, soul-gripping sound. Shifting to something else other than the simple words.

A deal.

A deal.

A deal.

It didn't stop, making my head turn while the blood flowed beneath my hand, seeping onto the stone floor through my fingers.

A drumbeat picked up, somehow thumping at the same beat as my heart.

What have I done?

I was terrified. Wondering if I shouldn't have uttered those words. If I were a total fool to fall into the exact trap I'd been warned to avoid my entire life.

Ulrich sauntered around the dais, my blood dripping from his shadow blade. Then, to my horror, he licked it. With a smile that should have sent my soul straight to the Gods.

"Blood, Brenna. A deal is bound in *blood*."

Without my control, I was standing and moving toward him.

"Open your mouth," he commanded.

My hand fell to my side, allowing my blood to fall freely from my wrist once more. And I obeyed. I do not know why, but I did. I tilted my head back, opening my mouth for the Unseelie King.

"I control you after this, Brenna," he whispered against my ear.

"Or I control you," I replied back, letting something quiet and commanding inside of me to respond.

I kept my eyes open and my shoulders stiff, watching him slice his own blade against his palm. Not closing my mouth when he dropped three drops of his black blood onto my tongue.

My body jolted when the liquid ran through my body. A shock of pure power radiated through me. Igniting my soul.

Then it was gone. As quickly as it had come.

"A deal made!" his people's voices screamed while he raised my bleeding arm into the air.

"A deal bound in blood," Ulrich yelled back.

The ballroom picked up with the same sounds of debauchery while the attention of his people quickly resumed to their most natural instincts. Ulrich held me though, flipping my body to watch the moving bodies. Pressing my back against his chest.

His hand tucked a piece of hair behind my ear and his rough beard scratched my cheek.

"You do not know what you've just done, *Ursa.*"

I bit my lip, holding my hand to my bleeding wrist again, not replying. Because he was right.

I had no idea what I'd just set in motion.

The party raged around us, but I remained in my seat beside the king. I held my hands in my lap and my shoulders straight while I watched the bodies move.

A burn lingered on my tongue from the drops of his blood, and I glanced at him, my eyes following the trail of his hands running down the two bodies on his lap. The women he'd called back after our deal had been sealed.

One of them let out a laugh, biting the edge of his ear while the other pulled the tie holding his hair at the top of his head. The gold locks fell, landing on his shoulders.

His eyes met mine while their hands continued to explore him. There was a fire burning behind the green, determined to burn me with it.

I turned my head, finding Olen in the center of the room, throwing back a mug of ale while bodies circled him.

My patience had simmered to nothing.

I stood quickly, turning my body toward Ulrich.

"Your grace," I said, forcing myself to bow before him.

His guests shifted their bodies, twisting to reveal Ulrich's face and chest. A chest I hadn't realized was bared by these women who'd spent the evening running their hands across his body.

My eyes shifted to the ink on his skin, my brows crumpling at the beasts on either side. Their elongated snouts almost met at the center of his chest, with their necks disappearing back toward his shoulders.

Ulrich cleared his throat.

I turned my gaze to his, cheeks burning, that he'd caught me staring at the strange markings.

"Not used to inked skin?" he asked.

The women on his lap laughed, one throwing her head back as she flipped her hair over her shoulder. A power-play to expose her breasts to me.

"I've seen inked skin," I replied. "Just not markings like yours."

Ulrich's palms slapped the bare skin of the women on his lap, a silent command for them to leave. Both offered me an annoyed scowl, then ran off behind me. Likely to find another to fulfill whatever needs they'd hoped their king would have offered.

"I'm assuming it's time for sleep?" Ulrich grinned.

I turned my eyes, finding the moon high and full in the sky.

"I don't believe the sun will rise for several hours, your grace. Your court does not sleep before sunrise."

Ulrich offered me a wink. "They do retire to their rooms far before the sun rises."

I scowled. "I am tired. I'm still healing. If you remember correctly."

His smile dropped and he nodded his head. His voice echoed throughout the chamber, halting the sounds behind me.

"Disperse," he ordered.

There were no protests and no groans. The feet shuffled out quickly and the music ceased. Not one soul in the room dared to object to their king's demand.

Footsteps approached behind me, and I turned my head, finding Olen with a fae woman and man. One armed wrapped around each body.

"My duties, your grace?" the towering man asked.

Ulrich smiled at him, then turned his body to face me. "I think you can disperse with your found bedmates, Olen. Have fun."

The king kept his eyes on me while he addressed his right hand. Emphasizing the last sentence of his response.

Olen let out a laugh, pulling my gaze from the game Ulrich and I had begun again.

"If you try and kill him—" Olen unwrapped his arms from his companions and leaned forward. I let out a yelp when his palm gripped the neckline of my gown, pulling me toward his face. "I will cut off those delicate hands of yours."

He dropped me, winking once then strutting away with his arms wrapped around the two silent beings who'd approached with him.

My skin warmed with rage. I was getting tired of being man-handled by these two. Tired of keeping my mouth clamped shut.

But I'd made a deal. A promise to do as I was told with a reward waiting for me at the end of it all.

I kept my back turned away from the door, holding Ulrich's gaze once more while Olen's footsteps retreated. The echo of the door slamming shut rang through my body, but I didn't flinch.

"Bed, *Ursa*?" the king asked.

I allowed myself to turn and look out across the now empty chamber. Noting the stone columns spaced throughout the room. The skylight, high above. The many corners hidden by shadows.

Places of darkness that appeared to have been deliberate for aching bodies to find their release.

"Do you like my palace?" His breath was hot against my neck.

I held still, only nodding my head once. "It's sufficient."

"That's an understatement," he replied, flipping me to face him.

His body towered over mine and I strained my neck to meet his eyes. We hadn't stood so close. Not when I could easily stare into his eyes.

"We made a deal tonight," he muttered.

I gulped. "Yes."

His smile lifted. "You have no idea what's in store for you."

I stepped away, pushing him as I went. "I have eleven months to do what I'm told. To follow your terms. I know what I just agreed to."

He was before me again, his hand hovering next to my cheek. I bit my lip, staring into his shifting eyes.

"You." He stroked my skin. "Are." Fingers trailed down, stopping at the base of my neck. "Foolish."

Our war was on now. His words a warning cry on the field of our battle. An approval to ready my determination to best him.

"I can accept the worst you can do is ruin me," I replied, wrapping my hand around his wrist.

"*Ursa*," his fingers tightened around my neck, offering just enough pressure to force out a gasp, "you may just ruin *me*."

Chapter 12

Three months.

Eighty-four days.

I wasn't sure how it had happened so fast. How the last month of my imprisonment had flashed past my eyes. Skirting around me while I played my role in this war between myself and the Unseelie King.

Neither of us bending. The fights had stopped though. With my attempts to end his life halting.

For now.

I walked the streets of Muspell, with Olen stalking beside me. His claws clinked against the cobbled roads of the city.

"This way," he snarled.

My body went stiff at the command. We were heading to another poor soul who'd failed in their ability to uphold Ulrich's deals. One name among a long list of the bodies I'd already witnessed lose their life.

A penance I suppose. Reminding me of my own foolish deal.

Ulrich's sick upper hand in our silent battle.

The cloak on my back slowed me down compared to the beast I followed. Yet I couldn't remove it. The most unexpected change in the last month had been the sudden drop in temperature throughout Ulrich's island. In one day, it had gone from brisk but comfortable autumn breezes to frigid cold and frost.

Ulrich had joked one night that perhaps Ymir was waking from his sleep in the far Mountains of Vaneer, forcing the world to celebrate his cold.

I told him Gods of only ice and snow were the most insignificant of all but if the giant had awoken, it was likely with Bestla's approval.

"Men do fall to their knees at a woman's command," he'd replied before turning on his side and falling into a deep sleep.

"How's sleeping beside the king?" Olen's question threw me from my thoughts.

"How did...?" I stopped my response. "It's *fine*," I replied.

"Are you keeping one another warm and snug?" His white teeth peeked out over his black lip.

I rolled my eyes. "I am following my rules, Olen. I sleep beside him. Unmoving like a stone. Me on one side of that monstrous bed and him on the other. Then each day I wake alone with his side of the bed empty."

"That's no fun," he grunted, rounding the corner of the cobbled road.

"Not all of us require an unending river of bodies each night."

His head threw back and his laugh rumbled, the fur on his body shook along with the sound.

"Princess, if you're ever interested, you know where to find me."

With a scoff, I walked around him, picking up on the panicked fae and creatures now running from the harbingers of death.

I'd been gifted a fitting new title in the court and city: *Ulrich's Wraith Whore.*

Me at Olen's side while I watched, unmoving, frozen in my obedience as Olen ripped apart body after body.

The title had begun its whisper just days after our public deal. Filtering through the halls I was finally allowed to venture down alone. Following me when I passed doors and alleyways in the city.

Even the trees seemed to whisper on the occasional journey when Olen would take me down the dirt roads leading out to the outlying villages.

Like this entire island had heard of me. And they all feared me.

I didn't understand why when I had about as much strength and power as a toddling. Perhaps even less.

Olen entered a courtyard surrounded by trees and I stopped. In the middle of the space stood Ulrich, his mask fitted against his face. It was a skeletal mask. One I was sure had been made from the bones of an actual victim.

Olen's head dipped, his snout touching the cobbled road.

His paw hit my foot, but I couldn't mimic the motion. Even when every head bowed to their king, I was rigid with shock.

Ulrich hadn't appeared at any of these reapings. Until that moment, he had always sent his right hand to do his dirty work.

Yet, here he was, staring at me with his hair tied half-up and his torso completely bare.

My eyes took him in. His ink—it covered nearly half of the bare skin. I first stared at the horns on his neck. Menacing, a warning to stay clear. Replicas of the horns he regularly wore on his masks. As my eyes traveled down his neck, I studied the piece on his chest, finding the snouts of the creatures I'd seen before were identical pieces on either side. Their heads making up his chest, their necks traveling across his shoulders and as he twisted his body, I found their bodies, both with large fanned out wings at the back. With their limbs wrapped around his sides and long tails wrapping down his arms, stopping at his wrists.

Monsters.

He had monsters inked into his skin.

A fitting piece of art for a monster himself.

My hands stared at the tails wrapping around his forearms, and the strange letters along the end. I didn't recognize the words, but they appeared old. Perhaps older than this world itself.

His hands clapped, pulling me from my daze.

"Enjoying yourself?" the king's amused voice asked.

I met his eyes then glanced to find his people peering up at me.

"Citizens bow, Brenna," he stated.

"Citizens of Muspell," I replied. "I am still a citizen of Nóatún."

His hands clapped together once more, and he turned away from me, giving me a clear view of his muscled back and the bodies of the creatures wrapping around his own.

"My deals are claimed each day," he said. "Surprising to see *so* many of you failing in your basic responsibilities."

He turned to face me again then his eyes traveled past my head and his hand rose with a pointed finger.

"Today's deal is special."

A shocked cry filled the courtyard, and I blinked, realizing Olen had left my side and was now dragging a woman through the crowd.

"Oh my gods," I exclaimed, covering my mouth.

I knew her, perhaps not intimately, but she was a Seelie Fae, a member of Oberon's court.

"Please!" the woman cried out, grabbing my forearm while Olen continued dragging her by the hem of her gown. "Please, princess! He's a madman!"

I stepped forward, addressing the king.

"Your grace," I lowered my head. "Please."

Ulrich was before me in an instant, his eyes staring into mine. "Please, what?"

"Spare her," I begged.

His head threw back with a laugh. "As much as you'd want to believe, I'm not the one who called for her deal to be claimed." He turned on his heel, addressing the woman. "Your *king* has informed me you've failed him."

My eyes widened while my mind attempted to remember the name of the woman cowering before the Unseelie King. She was familiar, a face I'd seen countless times in the crowd. Her laugh—one of her distinguishable features—rang in my mind.

Who was she?

A question plaguing my mind.

"My king," she sobbed. "Please."

Ulrich lifted her chin, and her dark curls fell around her face. "I'm not your king."

I rubbed my temple, praying the Gods would stop whatever this madness was.

What was her name?

Frustrated tears lined my eyes and then I jumped.

"Sigrun!" I cried out.

The woman's head snapped in my direction and her shoulders sagged.

Ulrich turned back to me, a vile smile across his lips. "You are familiar?"

I stepped forward, holding my hands out in a plea. "She's a member of one of the queens' personal courts. I've met her when spending time with Titania."

Ulrich's body went stiff, and hisses echoed throughout the courtyard. I chose to ignore them, keeping my eyes on the woman.

"Sigrun, why would Oberon call for your deal to be called? What was your deal?" I asked, dropping beside her.

The fae woman shook her head, tears lining her eyes.

"I cannot, princess. I cannot," she sobbed.

"Look, the woman can't even admit to her crimes," Ulrich laughed.

I jumped to my feet, pointing at him. "Do you know?" I demanded.

"Of course I know," he replied.

"Why would Oberon require this of you?" I asked. My hand landed on Sigrun's shoulder, giving her a reassuring squeeze.

"*Sigrun* failed in the duties the Seelie King assigned her to. When he'd found out her deal with me, to become one of those *personal members of Titania's court*, he was enraged."

"But you don't bow to the Seelie King," I countered, digging through the miniscule information I knew about their relationship and dynamic.

Olen snarled beside me. Ulrich gripped the neck of my gown, pulling me toward his face and dropping his voice. "I'm bound by duty and Fate, Brenna. Oberon unfortunately falls into that binding."

He dropped me and I fell back. Olen's body caught me, keeping me from falling against the hard cobbled street.

"Keep quiet," he snarled.

I moved to reach for the king, but Olen's mouth grabbed my cloak, yanking me backward.

"Stop!" I cried out.

"Brenna, just watch," Olen muttered.

Ulrich circled Sigrun, his eyes flashing with those brief wisps of black I'd seen before.

"Care to be truthful yet?"

Sigrun was silent for a moment then her head threw back and I screamed as her skin cracked across her face. In an instant, the beautiful woman that had been begging on her knees was shifting before my eyes. Her tanned skin now turning a decayed grey and her dark hair cascading to pure white locks down her back.

"Ulrich," she sneered, her voice now high and bone chilling. She stood, nearly meeting his height. Her fingers, now long and pointed, stroked his cheek.

"Oberon was angry," she snarled. "So, so, angry."

Her finger ran down Ulrich's bare chest and I wondered if he would allow her to continue her descent when his hand grabbed her wrist.

The creature let out a hiss. "So angry."

"You failed," he replied.

"Yes, my *King*." Her eyes met mine and she grinned. Her black teeth peeked through her thin lips and her grey tongue lapped while she held my gaze.

"You've got such a pretty princess here, my King. Tell me, *when* did you collect her from that quaint island her family rules?"

Olen let out a low growl, chilling my blood instantly. The cold that embodied him when he was in his beast form filtered over me.

Ulrich smiled at the woman.

"Do you know what she is, Brenna?"

I startled, not expecting him to address me.

"Well?" he asked, his forehead wrinkling with the brows I couldn't see raised under his death mask.

"I—" I stared at the creature. I had no idea what she was. Despite that, I knew she was awful. A monster I would never want to meet in the night.

"She does not know, my master," Sigrun cooed.

"Sigrun is—or was—a changeling," Ulrich answered, not allowing me to admit my lack of knowledge. "We made a deal, centuries ago. She received beauty and a new life with a Seelie fae family, replacing their child. When she had grown to accept Seelie adulthood, she would work for *me*, providing me details of the Seelie fae court. She's failed in her duties."

"Oh my poor king," Sigrun laughed. "Upset I didn't get you what you wanted?"

Ulrich's hand gripped her face, and I shuddered at the crunching sound of her jaw beneath his hold. "*Sigrun*," he sneered. "I was content to allow you to fail in your duties for centuries more. I knew you would fail the moment you left my sight all those years ago."

He threw her down to the ground, circling her while she laid curled around herself.

"You were *caught*." He put emphasis on the last word as it echoed around us all.

"It was not my fault, master," the creature cried out. "Oberon is on a tyrant's path now. Determined to find us all."

"Us?" I whispered then yelped when Olen softly bit the tips of my fingers. "What in the Gods?" I muttered.

"Shut your mouth," he ordered.

I straightened, holding my pulsating fingertips to my chest.

"How many?" Ulrich asked, his eyes moving to Olen beside me.

I turned my gaze back to the beast, watching his body rise and fall with slow breaths. When I raised my eyes back up, I found Sigrun sneering at me once more.

"Oh, my master," she hissed. "I'm one of many. He will require the demise of us all. Placing your duty before your people once—"

Shocked screams filled the courtyard when Olen suddenly lunged, ripping Sigrun's head off. Stopping her from finishing her biting statement.

He stayed above her, his body heaving while he appeared to consume the gore of her insides.

I stepped back, holding a hand to my mouth. Not understanding what I'd just witnessed.

Oberon? Deals? *People?*

I met Ulrich's emotionless gaze, finding Sigrun's greyed blood splattered up his bare torso. He didn't move as he stared back, his chest barely moving with his breaths.

I turned back to Olen, still consuming the body, sure I had seen a trick of light while his fur lit with silver for only a moment. Then he stood, grey blood dripping from his jaw, dipping his head to Ulrich's feet.

"A deal has been claimed," he snarled.

"Yes," Ulrich replied, patting Olen's shoulder. "Yes it has."

He addressed his right hand but his eyes staring into mine told me all I needed to know.

He was warning me of my future. Of the demise I was fated to receive if I did not hold up my end of our bargain.

Chapter 13

I laid in the dark room, listening to the sound of running water from the bathing chamber. My hand reached for the empty space in the bed beside me.

I still hadn't gotten used to it, after a month of lying beside his large frame.

So, any moment when I was under those heavy covers alone, was a gift given directly from the Gods.

The water stopped and my hand returned to my chest.

Blinking through the darkness, my breaths grew heavy while the sounds of the king's footsteps filled the chamber. The bed shifted with his weight, and he let out a content sigh.

"Was the public execution exhausting?" I asked.

The bed shook with his laugh. "My, someone has words tonight."

"I've followed your rules for a month, your grace. Do not forget that. I only asked a question."

The bed shifted again, and I shuffled to move away from him but his hand gripped my thigh.

My eyes widened and my head snapped in his direction, trying to make out his features in the dark.

"I am exhausted," he said as his finger circled my skin. "But not enough to not enjoy myself."

I jumped off the bed, gasping out my disapproval. "*That* was not on your list of terms."

"Get back in bed, Brenna," he demanded.

"No."

The air grew heavy with his cold when his chest was suddenly against mine, his hand gripping my wrist.

"There is a deal. You will obey."

"I will not be your plaything!" I yelled, shoving him away.

He was silent before he let out a chuckle. "Brenna, fall to your knees."

My eyes grew larger, and I reached around me, searching for anything to throw at him.

"Brenna," he repeated. "On. Your. Knees."

"You're a fucking animal," I bit back.

His laugh went deeper, like it was coming from his very soul. "Well, this is an interesting twist I was not expecting."

I backed up, my knees hitting the edge of the table beside the bed. "What were you not expecting?" My hands went behind me, wrapping around one of the solid bronze candlesticks that had been extinguished when he'd entered the room earlier.

"You're not obeying." He laughed again.

"I have three rules," I reminded him. "Sleep beside you. Do not try to escape. Never look upon your face. Being forced to ride your likely boil-covered cock, is not one of them."

"You watch your—" He started his warning but I cut him off by throwing the candlestick, hoping I had aimed it right at his face.

"Sorry," I whispered, running in a frenzy toward the hidden door.

"She wants to play," his voice echoed behind me.

In the month I'd been in his bed, I'd learned how to navigate through the dark and this time I found the hidden exit with zero struggle. I ripped it open, heading for the threshold when cold wrapped around my ankle, pulling me back into the room.

"Olen!" I screamed down the hall.

Ulrich's shadows dragged me back to him, shackling me while his heavy body pressed me against the floor.

"You like to be chased," he taunted. "Don't you?"

My eyes grew wide while his hips dug into mine.

"Get off of me," I squeaked.

"What was that noise?" he whispered, his mouth brushing against my ear.

I slammed my head against the floor, angry I'd allowed my insane curiosity to slip out.

"Your grace," I tried to reason with him. "You are not a beast that takes women with no regard to their consent."

His body went stiff against me, his shadows grew colder. "What did you say?"

"Please, Ulrich." I held a firm tone. "Do not do anything you would regret later."

His shadows released me the same time the hidden door creaked open.

Olen's laugh brought me instant annoyance.

"Oh thank the Gods." The sound of fabric rustling brought a protesting cry from my lips.

"Don't you dare!" I cried out.

Olen's disappointed sigh was almost amusing as a palm wrapped around my own. I stumbled when Ulrich pulled me to my feet, steadying me in the darkness.

"Olen, I will be removing myself for the morning," he said, clearing his throat.

I was shocked, completely unaware of what had happened. Before I could question anything, Ulrich's fogging power had lifted from the room and the curtains were thrown open, welcoming the sunlight.

I turned, mouth agape, finding Olen with an identical expression.

"What just happened?" I asked.

Olen blinked, running his hand through his unbraided hair. "I have the same question."

I sank against the bed, finding the candlestick slick with black blood.

"Was that you?" Olen asked, kicking it away.

"My blood or my attack?" I asked.

"Well, I know your blood isn't black, princess." Olen replied.

"I don't know what came over him," I sighed. "It was like every night since our deal. Me on my end. Him on his. We talked about the courtyard, then..."

"Stop," Olen cut in. "You spoke of Sigrun?"

I nodded.

Olen leaned back on his palms, letting out a sigh.

"Talk of Oberon and his court does things to Ulrich. Brings out a side of him few rarely see."

"That sounds like an excuse."

"Princess," Olen turned to meet my gaze. "We may be fucked and make jests we shouldn't regarding women and their bodies, but not one man in this court would lay his hand on an unwilling bedmate."

I blinked at him, not believing his words.

"Both you and Ulrich have alluded to bedding me without my permission."

Olen's shoulders rose with his shrug. "I said we're fucked."

"Good Gods," I sighed, laying back on the bed.

Olen's body lifted from the bed and I sat up, watching him head toward the hidden door.

"Got to sleep, princess," he said.

"I can't," I admitted.

His eyes went to the open windows. "Go enjoy the morning sun. You rarely get to see it since you've been here."

He left me alone, giving me permission to leave with no companion.

My heart raced and I jumped to my feet, rushing to the closet. My hands ripped through my trunks for the outfit I was searching for. Finally finding it, I held it before me, my heart swelling with a longing for home.

Once dressed, I ripped the door open and ran down the hall.

After a fast stop at the library, I moved through the palace, finding the towering fortress halls empty. I fisted the scroll in my cloak, almost making it to the front doors when a voice cleared from the shadows.

I turned on my heel, startled to find an Unseelie man smiling at me.

"My, my, my." He grinned.

I stepped back, glancing around the grand foyer of the palace. The stone stairs leading upward were now like a trap when they'd been my pathway to freedom just moments before.

"Where are you going?" he sneered.

"I don't know why that's any of your concern," I replied.

The man grinned and I bit the inside of my cheek to hold in my gasp at the elongated teeth dragging against his lips.

"I think you're lying," he said.

"Bjorn, why are you loitering for unsuspecting victims?"

I turned, finding Frode standing in the shadows, a look of disdain tight across his face.

The fae whose name I'd now learned let out a disturbing laugh. "Frode, you know I must feed. My kind cannot go long without it."

I stepped back, retreating toward Frode when the man's hands reached for me, ripping off my cloak.

"My, what an outfit." His tongue licked his lips. "Who gets to see you like this, princess?"

My hands covered the sealskin suit I'd changed into, grateful for the long trousers I'd slipped over myself. But my bust, there was barely a way to cover the curve of it through the suit.

Frode appeared beside me, wrapping his own cloak over my shoulders.

"The princess is from Nóatún, an island gifted in the sea. An island with a frigid fjord and filled with insane habitants who swim in its waters."

Bjorn grey eyes peered at me while his fingers pinched my cloak together. He brought it to his nose, inhaling loudly.

"You smell amazing. Can't I just have a taste?"

"I suggest you stop taunting the king's guest, fool. Unless you want his wrath to come down upon you," Frode replied.

Even with my suit covering my arms, and Frode's cloak wrapped around me, my body grew cold at the hate in the man's eyes while he stared back at the healer.

"Ulrich is starving himself," he laughed. "Many of us don't wish to do so."

"Leave," Frode commanded.

My hands gripped Frode's cloak tighter, trying to conceal more of myself while the man studied me.

We were in a standoff. The monster taunting his prey. Only, I was his believed prey. The predator before me had no sway in my ability to fight for myself.

I stepped forward, ripping my cloak from him. “I’m a princess. You will respect me, or I will use my Gods-given-right to request you be thrown in the dungeon.”

Bjorn laughed, throwing his head back. “You believe yourself to have power in the Unseelie court?”

I mimicked his laugh, allowing my voice to lift in the high squeal that his kind had.

“You fool.” I grinned. “I am half Seelie fae. I am the daughter of a king whose island was granted to his lineage under Oberon’s just hand.”

The man shrank while my words left my lips.

“I am a favored guest of not just Queen Mab, but Queen Titania. Have you heard the wreckage Oberon’s wives lay upon men?”

Bjorn's eyes darted behind me and Frode let out a breath.

“I will call upon them. I will use whatever power I have, and you will leave this island to rot in the dungeon of the Seelie. Did you know they drug you with their wine in those dungeons? Altering your senses, making you believe you are no longer attached to your own body. It drives the mind mad. Until one day—” I snapped my fingers and Bjorn jumped. “That mind collapses.”

The creature lifted his lips, barring his canines at me. “You use words of *war*, princess. Words I’m sure my king would gladly remove your head for.”

Frode stepped forward. “I’m sure our king would remove your cock and then your head for attempting to make this woman your victim.”

The Unseelie hissed then shrank back into the shadows, not uttering another word as he left.

My shoulders slumped once alone with Frode.

The healer bowed his head, and I pulled his cloak off then returned mine to my shoulders.

"Where are you headed, princess?" he asked.

Nervously, I glanced at the doors. "A swim," I admitted.

Frode's lips turned with a smile. "The king's docks are rather filthy. Where did you intend to swim?"

My hands shook when I pulled the scroll from my cloak pocket, unrolling it and pointing. "I've been in the library," I began. "I love history, especially maps."

Frode laughed. "You've been learning about our island."

I nodded. "It's what I do when I'm not following Olen as *Ulrich's Wraith Whore.*"

"What have you learned?"

I gulped. "There's a hidden passage here." I pointed to a dark spot just beyond the palace gates. "You can access it by a door near the gates. From my understanding, it leads to this hidden cove."

My finger traced the map and the barely visible markings. I didn't really need it any longer. Not after weeks of studying and committing it to my memory.

At first I'd thought I was mistaken when I noticed the lines, but the more I studied the map, I'd grown more confident in my observation. Whomever had drawn it had meant to keep the passage and cove hidden, at least to those without a knowing mind for cartography.

"Where did you learn to decipher maps?" Frode asked, looking up from the markings.

I rolled it once more, placing it into the safety of my pocket.

"My tutors. Growing up on that secluded Island, I developed a yearning to see the world. But my father only allowed trips to Aesir once a year during the harvest moon."

"Your birthday is near the harvest moon," Frode replied.

I casted my eyes down. "I'm aware. It's my favorite celebration. The harvest blood moon is a shade of orange-red that I see in my dreams every single night until I can look upon it again."

Returning my eyes to meet the healer's, I cocked my head. "How did you know that?"

Frode lifted his shoulders. "I may have already been Ulrich's healer the day you were born, but we all knew the stories. Anyone from Nóatún mourned the loss of a great queen while we celebrated a new queen born under the strength of such a powerful force of nature."

I blinked at him, my hands trembling at my sides.

"Did you?" I stopped the question. I never asked about her. I'd learned to keep those questions locked inside of me at a very young age.

Frode's hands grabbed mine. "Frey was beauty personified, and kindness was the blood that ran through her veins."

My tears lined my eyes. "Thank you," I whispered.

Frode grinned. "Enjoy your swim, princess. Just don't freeze. That cove is frigid."

He pushed the door open for me, gesturing to the empty courtyard. "Don't get caught." He winked.

"I don't plan to," I replied, rushing past him and out into the brilliance of a high winter sun.

The sun hit my skin while my feet landed on the gravel of the courtyard. I stopped, for only a minute, admiring the subtle beauty that was Ulrich's fortress. My eyes went across the yard, finding the gates at the other end.

I could not stop the pace at which I moved. I could not prevent the hope in my heart while I flew through the gates, startling the sleeping guards. I turned, finding the wall covered in the thick green leaves barely depicted in the map in my cloak. My hands ran across the leaves as I pulled it back, revealing the hidden passage.

The tunnel was dark at first, barely lit with the light peeking through the hidden door quickly disappearing the further I walked. I almost turned around when light filled the space. I glanced up, gasping at the clear ceiling above and the moving feet, seemingly unaware of the tunnel below them.

I stared ahead, blinking back my admiration at the beauty of this tunnel. The stone walls and the green leaves lining every surface. With the light above, it was breathtaking, almost to the point of unexplainable emotions.

Why was it hidden?

The tunnel was not long but it was also not as short as I had anticipated. When I was sure my feet were going to grow tired, the smell welcomed me.

Water, home, the sea.

I walked briskly until my feet hit the sand, and I let out a breath. Before me was a secluded beach with high sandy hills blocking it from anyone's view or access. I walked through the tunnel threshold, turning back to admire the only entrance to this secluded wonderland.

When I had reached the middle of the small oasis, I spun in my spot. In my unintentional prying, I had found a place my soul could breathe in.

A place away from the creatures determined to make me lose my mind. Somewhere I could wash myself with the cold of my beloved water, ignoring all the darkness on this island.

My cloak fell to the ground, crumpling in the sand and I threw myself into the water, letting out a gleeful cry as the liquid enveloped me.

As I moved onto my back, I allowed myself to become weightless while I stared up at the winter sun above. My hands moved slowly and I let out a breath, losing myself in the ecstasy of my first moments of true peace in months.

Chapter 14

My arms cut through the freezing waters, slicing it like my fingertips were the tips of the glaciers I longed to see again. My feet kicked ahead of me, and I stared up at the late-afternoon sun.

I'd been out in the water for the entirety of the day, swimming and lounging on the sand. Soaking in the small reminders of who I was.

Because I'd quickly been forgetting everything that made me—me.

The small habits that kept me grounded. Kept me tethered to that mortal side of myself. The side I preferred.

Not the wild beast I was becoming.

The sun continued to set, and I knew I had to leave. I had to get inside. Even with my suit, made to cover my body from the tops of my toes to the tips of my fingers, my exhaustion would soon surprise me. I chose to ignore my mind's warning though, continuing while my arms and hands moved me through the water, and I smiled. Likely too soon when my head hit a solid, yet soft surface.

Flailing, I jumped up, moving my feet under the water to keep me afloat. The sun finished its descent, and I glanced up.

"Fuck," I muttered, finding Ulrich. I laughed, covering my mouth at the black mask on his face.

"Even out here?" I chuckled. "In a hidden cove?"

He blinked at me then smiled. "Your rules, Brenna."

I rolled my eyes. "It's fascinating you're keeping it up. The commitment is impressive."

I moved my arms behind me, shoving myself away, but his hand went under the water, wrapping around the top of my covered foot.

"Let go!" I yelled, kicking out.

His hand released me, and I scowled.

"I was going to come back."

"When?" he asked.

"When I felt like it."

"You would have frozen to death."

I laid on my back once more. "Wouldn't that be convenient for you? We would have made it three months. Likely your shortest deal to have failed."

"Actually," his voice was muffled now with my ears under the water, "the shortest deal lasted one hour."

I propped myself back up, kicking my legs underneath me. "An hour?"

He laughed and I held in my gasp when I realized he had no suit to keep his body warm.

"You're going to freeze to death!"

His bare shoulders shrugged. "I like the cold."

"You're insane," I replied.

"But yes, to answer your question. It was only an hour. They wanted to be able to bed anyone they wanted for the rest of their life. A stupid request, but my only rule was that their bedmates would be willing." His eyes glanced at me from behind his mask. "They attempted to rape their second bedmate, and I cut them right in half as punishment."

"When you say...?" My eyes widened with disgust.

"I lifted their cock and sliced upward until they were split in half," he replied blankly.

I shook my head. "Fuck the Gods that's disgusting."

"So is assault," he replied.

"You've assaulted me," I replied, shoving further from him, heading toward the shore.

He followed me. "When?"

My hands hit the sand while the shore grew closer and I flipped onto my stomach, slowly crawling through the water.

"Is that a jest?"

"No," his voice was blank, emotionless.

I twisted back, my brow tight. "Ulrich, are you serious?"

He leaned back while we reached the water's edge.

"Will I admit that I was responsible for the scars now lining your back? Yes."

"You—" I interrupted.

His hand rose. "I am not done speaking."

My mouth closed.

"Was I too brash in inviting myself into your bath? Yes."

A cold hit my lungs while his gaze went out to the blue water before us. "Did I allow a part of myself that I fight to keep caged out this morning?" He turned back to face me, and I startled at the regret in his eyes. "Yes. But I have never forced myself into you. I would never."

I stood, holding up my own hand. "Stop. Now."

"Brenna."

My angry tears fell while I turned away from him, scooping my trousers and cloak into my arms.

"Brenna!" he yelled after me, but I picked up my pace, heading down the path that had led me to what I'd thought could have become my oasis.

His hand grabbed the back of my arm, but I screamed causing him to stumble backward.

"You have done nothing but assault my head, heart, and mind!" I cried. My clothes dropped while I slammed my fist against my chest. "You killed *him*. You took my *only* chance of freedom. For what? A fucking deal! A deal I did not even make!"

My anguish tumbled from me, a storm I could not stop. Words that had been building in my heart. Hate that was changing everything that had once been good about me.

"I have never wanted to kill until that day on the dock," I admitted, my voice shaking. "But I saw his lifeless eyes and there was nothing more that I wanted."

I pulled my gaze from the sand beneath my feet, finding Ulrich unmoving.

"I've been a pawn in your game, Ulrich, and the insult to know you don't believe you've assaulted me might just push me over the edge."

"Brenna," he reached for me, and I laughed.

"You hate me, remember? Do not ever forget that I hate you too."

Bending, I picked up my trousers and wrapped my cloak around my shoulders. I left the Unseelie King speechless at the opening of the frigid passage I was now forced to forget existed.

Dried and dressed, I ran my fingers along the lines of maps in the corner of the library. The table before me was littered with my project. The red of the blood moon came through the one expansive window facing toward the water in the distance.

I stood, groaning with my hand on my back, gazing out at the water. The sounds of the nightly party boomed the floors beneath me.

Ulrich hadn't followed me back to the palace. He hadn't interrupted my bath or barged in when Adalie had braided my hair back for me.

I had worried at first, hesitant over when he would bring down that hand of punishment.

But when he hadn't even sent Olen to fetch me for that evening's festivities, I determined that I'd made the feared Unseelie King tuck his tail between his legs.

Proving me the current victor of our battle.

I moved from the table, settling onto the ottoman leaned against the back wall. I observed the library. The dusty books, the barely available seating.

The room needed a desperate redecoration. Some places to sit and read, to fill one's mind and heart with unending knowledge.

It was evident in the smell and the color of the majority of the books I'd found that this room held Millennia of history. Stories and tales most of our world likely didn't know exist. Pages filled with names of people long forgotten.

I leaned against the jagged wall of the mountain, my fingers tapping on my knee.

The music floors below me was irritating, beating in repetition. Mocking me in my silence and solitude.

I turned my head, staring out at the water turned red under the moon.

The hours I'd spent out in that frigid blue had been the most restful hours I'd had since leaving my home. With the water cascading over me while my body moved through it. Weightless. Carefree.

Only to have it ripped away in moments by an ignorant tyrant's proclamations of innocence.

Did he really believe it? That he'd done nothing wrong? That no harm had come to me throughout the last three months?

I rubbed my fingers against my temple. I wasn't innocent, I knew this. I was acting out of character. A beast in his palace, screeching and demanding freedom. While acting like a wild animal determined to rip his soul from his body.

I was also not innocent, but I knew this. He, however, did not appear to be aware enough to realize his crimes as well.

I sighed. I needed the months to grow quicker. I needed the time to fly faster.

My eyes turned to the parchment and ink on the table.

I hadn't done it yet... Penning my request.

But the rage in my heart—how it pestered me to pick up the quill. To write like I'd never written before.

I stood, hands slick with sweat, seating myself on the creaking chair at the table.

My dearest queen,

I write, begging for your aid. . .

Despite my initial hesitancy, the words moved onto the parchment, the ink like my own work of spells. Magic by a hand lacking that very gift.

By the time I'd finished transcribing my plea, my hands were stained in black liquid with crumpled paper sitting to the side of the table. Each of them a draft of the request I was determined to send out.

When that day came.

The library door slammed open, and I jolted in my seat, my hands shoving the crumpled paper in one pocket and the completed letter in the other.

Footsteps echoed across the expansive room, and I began scribbling on the blank parchment before me. Pretending I was working on my own map.

"Your highness?"

I pulled my head up as Adalie came from around one of the towering bookshelves.

"Yes?" I asked, clearing my throat and wiping my stained hands on my lap.

"Your dress!" she exclaimed, rushing to me.

"Adalie, I'm fine." I motioned her away. "You called for me?"

"Uncle sent me," she whispered.

"What does your charming uncle want?" I asked with a wink.

Adalie laughed, covering her lips.

"I want you to pull your ass out of your head and come join the party," Olen's rough, beastly voice came from behind the shelves.

I groaned, standing from my seat. "I'd rather retire to bed."

Olen grinned, his slick dark lips moving along his monstrous face. "I'll tell his grace."

"Stop!" I held up my hands. "Why are you determined to bring me irritation?"

Adalie gasped beside me.

"I've been told I'm rather amusing."

"Annoying," I countered.

I walked forward, heading toward the exit when Olen stepped in front of me.

"You threatened Bjorn today."

My stomach sank. I stared into Olen's dark eyes.

"I did."

Olen grinned. "He reported you."

"I should have reported him," I snapped.

"Yes." Olen stepped out of my way, his wide beast form barely giving me room to move past him. "You should have. Instead, you disappeared for hours. Ulrich thought you'd run away."

I scoffed. "Running means I put the very people I'm trying to get back to in danger."

"Attempting to kill the king didn't do that?"

I paused my steps. "Fair point."

Olen appeared beside me, keeping a casual pace while I made my way through the library. He yelled back at Adalie to get into her rooms and bed before we exited the room. When we arrived in the hall, I turned right, heading toward *the looking glass* instead of straight to the stairs leading to the bedrooms below.

"How well do you know Oberon, his court, and his wives?" Olen asked.

"Why does that matter?" I asked, meeting his gaze.

Olen's fur stood slightly before his shoulders shrugged. "It matters because you're residing in the home of Oberon's most notorious rival."

My hands went to my pocket, protectively grasping the letter. I kept a blank expression on my face until we'd reached my hall of windows.

The light of the blood moon came through the glass. The red—brilliant, sensual, dark. Tempting and dangerous.

I sank onto a bench, propping my feet out before me. Olen grunted then lowered himself by my feet.

"To answer your previous question," I said, "my family is distantly related to Oberon. I knew our island had been a gift. One that required there to always be a full-blooded fae on our throne." I turned to meet Olen's gaze. "I just wasn't aware of the underlying conditions behind that gift."

Olen remained quiet, his fur-lined body moving with the breaths he took. I held in my laugh. The beast appeared as though he were listening intently.

I leaned back against the stone wall. "I've lived over a century and for as long as I can remember, we have done our duty to visit our homeland during the harvest moon. Titania—"

I bit my lip, unsure if I could continue opening up. My eyes drifted to the beast, still silent and staring at me.

"She and Oberon had no children. Not like he did with Mab. She saw me, a motherless half-fae with no magic in her bones and took an interest in me."

"Is she a motherly figure?" Olen asked.

"Yes and no," I replied. "More of a friend. Someone whose face was familiar and kind in a world I barely knew."

Olen let out a loud sigh. "Were you hoping to be in Aesir this harvest moon?"

I stared out the windows, my heart pulling at the red giant in the sky.

"I wanted to be in one of the most beautiful cities I've ever seen the night I saw the dark blue night sky for the first time."

"Muspell is beautiful," Olen yawned.

I laughed. "I've barely seen it. I didn't even get the chance to see its beauty on the shore when we sailed in."

Olen laughed, his paws stretched out before him. "You were sick in a cabin. That's no one's fault but your own."

I shook my head with a smile while silence filled the hall. Eventually, I settled onto the floor beside Olen, using his body as a cushion for warmth with the cold coming from the mountain walls.

Then I fell asleep, unsure how I'd become so comfortable with a beast.

Chapter 15

Ulrich and I didn't speak for five days after our encounter in the water. Uncomfortable given I was still expected to sleep beside him. But he stayed on his side of the bed, and I stayed on mine.

One night while I readied myself in the bathing room, the lights had extinguished, and his presence was suddenly chilling the room.

I set my brush down with a sigh.

"Yes?" I asked.

"I apologize," he said.

I turned on my heel, hoping to see him in the dark but as quickly as he'd slipped into the room, he was gone and the red light from the moon above was filling the room once more.

Twisting back to the mirror, I stared at my reflection. He'd apologized, even if it had been odd and abrupt, it had been an apology.

It made me hate him more.

Another five days passed. Not one word uttered between us.

I laid in the bed, staring at the ceiling, twisting my fingers against each other.

His body was as unmoving as mine.

I sighed.

"Something on your mind?" he asked.

I shifted to my side, propping myself on my arm. "Do you have a winter festival?"

He was silent.

"Forget I asked," I groaned.

"I didn't realize we were on speaking terms again," he replied.

I laughed, pressing my head into the pillow. "Were we ever on speaking terms?"

"A valid question."

I smirked at the amusement in his tone.

"To answer your question, yes, we do have a winter celebration."

"When?" I asked, my heart racing.

He was silent once more. The bed shifted and the heat of him right before me, startled me.

"Soon," he whispered.

"What happens at this festival?" I asked.

"Things."

"Do I only get one-word responses?"

"That depends, *Ursa.* What is the reasoning behind the questions?"

A tear fell from my eye, streaking down my cheek.

"I wanted—" My heart thumped in my chest. "I wanted to write my father a letter."

"This is your request?"

"No!" I exclaimed. "No, not *that* request tied to our deal. But yes, it is a request."

"I haven't prevented you from writing any letters, Brenna."

He shifted again, the weight of his body moving back to the other side of the bed. I stared through the darkness, trying to burn a fire of irritation through his scalp.

"Tell me about him," Ulrich said quietly.

I startled. "My father?"

He laughed again and the bed shook with the movement. "Not him. The other man in your life."

"Oh." My heart grew heavy. "I don't wish to speak of him."

"Are you not mourning?" he asked.

"You know, Ulrich," I scoffed. "I was just beginning to believe we were having a rather pleasant and cordial conversation."

I flipped onto my side, throwing my hair over my shoulder and pulling the covers over my head. My tears fell silently while I thought back on Leif's words. His promises. The hope he'd offered me.

The meeting we'd longed for that had been taken from us.

"What did he do to die so brutally?" I whispered.

"I'm bound by my duties," was all the monster beside me said before silence encroached over the room once more. Leaving me to wet my pillow while my grief threatened to drown me.

Four months.

One hundred and twelve days.

The number close to the age I was in years. Making me feel like an old woman.

I sat on the settee beside Ulrich's throne, watching the bodies move, bored beyond belief. Above me was the king, with his lap surprisingly empty.

I yawned, throwing my head back.

"Should we retire?" Ulrich's voice whispered.

I pulled my eyes up to meet his. "You speak as though we are some couple sneaking off into the night."

His eyes gleamed with amusement. "Could we not be?"

I shook my head. "No. We cannot."

Twisting back to the dancing members of Ulrich's court, my eyes found Olen in the crowd. Once again surrounded by bodies determined to gain his attention.

Without allowing myself to reconsider, I hopped to my feet.

"Where are you going?" Ulrich asked.

"To have fun," I replied.

I rushed down the dais and the people eyed me nervously, parting like the sea before a water nymph. When I reached the giant that was the king's right hand, I tapped him on the back.

"Get in line," he laughed, while he spun a naked courtesan in her spot.

"Do I have to?"

Olen's body twisted my way immediately and he offered a wide grin.

"You're off your seat."

"I'm no pet ordered to stay in my spot," I replied.

Olen's eyes traveled beyond my head to where the king's throne lay.

"That's debatable."

"Olen," I stated. "You have practically begged me to *play* with you for the last four months. You either dance with me now or lose the chance."

His braided hair clinked with the gold rings tied into the plaits while he shook his head.

"What kind of dancing are you thinking about?"

I fluttered my eyelashes up at him while I grinned. "Why don't we find out?"

My scream of surprise drowned out the music when his hands wrapped around my waist, swinging me around in a circle.

"Gods! Stop!" I laughed.

"That's a good sound," his voice boomed.

"I need a drink!" I yelled over the music.

Olen winked, rushing us across the room toward the table lined with every kind of liquor one could think of.

"There's no faerie wine here, is there?" I asked, trying to determine which dark liquid would numb my senses the best.

Olen shook his head. "Ulrich has that poison banned. It's not allowed past the mist."

I moved my head to the throne, finding Ulrich straight as a statue. His eyes wide and watching me.

"Is he jealous?" I asked while Olen passed me a full cup of golden liquor.

"Maybe jealous he can't join," Olen laughed.

I threw back the drink, setting it down on the table. "You two?"

Olen winked. "Your highness, where is that mind traveling to this evening?"

"Wouldn't you like to know?" I replied.

The liquor instantly warmed my blood, and Olen was swinging me around the room again, pulling uncontrollable laughs from my lips.

The music shifted. Something sensual, tempting. A beat pulsing through my blood. Begging me to move.

Olen stared down at me and I moved around him, my hand trailing down his chest.

"Princess," he grunted at my touch.

"Could you make me forget?" I asked, pressing myself against him, moving my hips with the beat.

Olen's dark eyes stared back at me, an unfamiliar concern flashing across his gaze.

"Forget what?" he asked. His finger brushed my lip.

"Everything," I whispered.

His hands landed on my hips holding tightly while I moved in circles. Then he was lifting me, placing me on his leg.

"This is not very proper, princess," he chuckled.

I breathed in, wrapping my arms around his neck. "Olen, I am not a pure virgin. I am a woman with *needs* and both you and Ulrich have continually claimed I should partake in the nightly activities."

Olen's eyes glistened and a smile graced the corner of his lip. He dipped closer, placing his lips against my neck.

"Dance," he ordered.

"Thank you," I replied, grateful for the control he was allowing me.

The tips of my toes barely reached the floor being raised on his leg, but I did as he said. I moved. Circling my hips on his thigh. Bringing a quick ache tight in my belly. A plea for release.

"Are we becoming friends?" I asked, shouting over the music.

"Are we?" he replied with a grin.

I returned the grin, throwing my head back while I moved. His hands held my hips in place. The size of his palms was maddening while his fingers rested against my soft, lower stomach.

"Your curves," he groaned. "Gods."

"They are magnificent."

My eyes snapped open, and I stopped moving. Olen didn't move, but he winked as his eyes traveled behind my head.

"Your grace," he said, tilting down his chin.

I turned my head, finding the king I was trying to forget standing right behind me.

"Ulrich," I said coldly.

"Oh, don't stop on my account," he grinned. "I was rather enjoying the show."

Olen's hands tightened around me. "Well, princess."

"No!" I protested. "No, I'm not your entertainment."

I scrambled off Olen's leg, straightening my dress. Ulrich leaned down, his beard tickling my ear as he dropped his voice.

"*Ursa*, the obvious arousal you left on my right hand's knee says you are."

My hand connected with his cheek, slightly knocking his mask to the side before I could stop myself.

Gasps rang out around me and Olen's arms gripped my shoulders.

"You are so stupid," he groaned, holding me back as Ulrich straightened his mask.

"I hit a nerve," the king laughed.

"You speak to me as if I were anything other than a princess. A princess who deserves respect! Even a sliver of it!"

"I have yet to see a princess dancing—grinding—on a knee so publicly," he shot back.

Snickers came from all the sneering faces surrounding me. I turned my nose up, scowling at him.

"Are you jealous, Ulrich? Upset I was enjoying myself with Olen? That I won't allow you to touch a single curve of my body even when I'm always but a fingers-length from you?"

The king smiled, snapping his fingers instead of responding. Three naked women appeared, their hands instantly eager and moving across his chest.

"Is this jealousy?" he asked. His hand grasped the back of one woman's head, and he pulled her face to his, kissing her hard.

"Yes," I replied blankly.

Olen snorted beside me.

Ulrich pulled away from the kiss, his eyes burning with hate.

"Do you want to watch me fuck them, Brenna?"

I raised a brow. "*Them*? Do they not have names, your grace? Are they not your subjects?"

The women all threw nasty scowls at me and Ulrich grinned. His hand grabbed the breast of the woman he'd just kissed, his fingers tugging at her nipple.

"This is Liv."

She groaned, offering me a smirk.

He pulled his hand away and I bit the inside of my cheek when his fingers entered the next woman. His eyes staring straight into mine.

"This is Ola."

The woman rolled her hips against his fingers, throwing her head back with her groans.

He pulled from her, standing and ran his thumb across the third woman's lips. They parted willingly and he slowly slid the fingers he'd had inside the previous woman into her mouth.

She moaned while her lips wrapped around his fingers, and I scowled.

"And this is Sylvi," he sneered.

I took a step back, bumping into Olen.

"Congratulations, you know the names of the women you bed. Do you want a prize?"

His green eyes lit behind his black mask.

"Olen, have your way with her."

His hand waved and I smiled with triumph then yelped at Olen throwing me over his shoulder.

"Gods," I grunted. "Not this again."

His hand slapped my backside, pulling a rageful yell from my lips.

"Don't worry, princess," He laughed. "You only get my cock tonight if you ask for it."

I had a perfect view of Ulrich as Olen carried me away. He was stoic in his place, his face emotionless as the women before him all fell to their knees, pulling at his clothing. Lowering his trousers.

Yet he kept his gaze on me.

I returned the hate back to him. Cursing his name while Olen carried me away. Holding my rage until we'd rounded the corner, and the man dropped me to the ground.

"I guess you're my bedmate tonight," he groaned, running his hand over his jaw.

"Sorry I'm a disappointment," I replied.

Olen leaned down, pulling me up by the wrist.

"Stop baiting him, Brenna. Stop trying to get under his skin."

I stared up at Olen then lifted myself onto my toes. "Kiss me," I begged.

His gaze was blank, his mouth unmoving while he stared back at me.

"Princess."

"Please," I asked, pulling at his shirt. "Please give me control over something."

Olen's head turned back as though he were checking for any prying eyes. His calloused hand brushed my cheek.

"I thought we were friends," he chuckled.

"Friends do favors for one another," I countered.

He tugged on the end of my hair, eliciting a gasp from me. "Not those kinds of favors."

He released his hold on my hair and turned on his heel. My pulse raced while I stared after him walking away, leaving me in the hallway alone with loud screams and moans of pleasure coming from the ballroom.

"Olen!" I yelled.

"Try becoming friends with him, princess!" he shouted over his shoulder. "You may actually like him!"

I turned back to the ballroom, determined to knock the doors down. To ruin Ulrich's night of pleasure. Only, when I arrived at the doors, throwing them open with a *thud,* he was no longer in the middle of the room. The women were still there, but each of them were being pleasured by their own man. And the throne?

Well... the throne was empty.

I didn't miss, however, the hidden door—still slightly open just beyond the dais.

No—I couldn't miss it at all.

Chapter 16

My utensils dragged across the ceramic plate, a melody alongside the others in the room. I pulled my gaze up, studying Ulrich across from me and Olen to my right.

Ulrich's hand rose while he set his fork on his tongue. His eyes sparkled, holding my gaze. My back went stiff in my chair.

"Do I need to give you two privacy?" Olen said, with a mouth full of food.

I turned my eyes from the king, glaring at his right hand.

"Do you not have manners?"

Olen grinned and his chewed meal appeared between his lips. "Not where I'm from."

A thump sounded under the table and Olen jumped. I twisted back to Ulrich, head cocking at his attack on Olen's shin.

"What did he say that you didn't want uttered?"

Ulrich sipped from his glass, a dark whiskey this evening. "Nothing that concerns a mortal woman."

"Half-fae," Olen grumbled.

"Thank you, Olen," I replied, scowling at the king.

I leaned back in my chair, eyes traveling across the dining room. "May I be excused?"

Ulrich's lips sipped from his whiskey slowly. He set the glass down, thrumming his fingers against the table top. "Such manners for a princess who grinds on a man's legs out in the open."

My hand tightened around the knife in my grasp. "Respect, your grace. It's all I am asking for."

"I'm not bound by your requests."

"Technically..." Olen cut in.

"Quiet," Ulrich snapped.

Olen went silent.

My hand held the knife firmly. "Sexual frustration does you no good, your grace."

Olen choked beside me, and I glanced over, finding him wiping whiskey from his mouth.

Ulrich's laugh echoed throughout the space. "I have no idea what you're referring to."

I sat straighter, choosing my next words for our battle.

"If I'm taking up space in your bed," I began, "just tell me. I can disappear for a few hours to allow you to find your release."

Olen coughed again. "Fuck the Gods."

"Silence," Ulrich growled, his eyes pulled from my gaze to scowl at his right hand. Then the green emeralds were back to my blue.

"I'm not the one publicly humping legs. Do I need to leave you alone in the room for a few hours, *princess?*"

"Maybe," I taunted. "Not sure who I would invite though."

Ulrich's hand pointed to the man beside me. "He'll do."

Olen's hands rose defensively. "I am not part of this game."

"I disagree," I replied. "You started this all. Taking me from my home."

Olen's eyes traveled to Ulrich for a moment, some silent conversation occurring before me between the two.

"I do as I'm told," he finally replied.

"Like the good little pet you are."

Olen's fist thumped against the table. "Princess, keep going. I'll give you more hate in your heart."

I turned back to Ulrich, spinning the edge of the knife on the arm of my chair.

"Well, your grace. Do I need to find a way to entertain myself to give you peace from my presence?"

Ulrich picked his glass up again. "Olen, I bet she squeals when she's humped."

I glared.

He sipped his liquor. "I bet she begs the Gods for release when she's taken from behind."

My hands shook, causing the knife to tremble just below the table.

Olen was silent but a vile smile was spreading across his lips.

Ulrich crossed one leg over the other, his eyes staring into my soul. "Yes, I bet this little *whore* makes the most delicious noises."

My knife was flying through the air in an instant.

Olen stood, shouting at me but the sounds all drowned out when Ulrich caught the blade, his black blood dripped onto the table as it sliced open his palm.

Those unnatural shadows of his whipped around him, crawling up the walls while he stood.

"Do you not like being called a *whore*, Brenna?" he asked with a smile.

My ears rang as I tracked the beast. He stalked around the table, shoving the chairs between myself and him to the side. His eyes swirled with black behind the horned mask over his brow. A fitting disguise for the creature preparing to attack.

Olen may have been shouting still, but I couldn't hear him. Not when my hand had wrapped around my fork, ready to stab it into Ulrich's neck.

His shadows grew around me, creating a wall. Blocking his right hand from reaching us.

"Do it," the king taunted. "Please, *Ursa*. I have missed our little game."

My hands shook while I stared into his eyes. "You're a monster."

"I'm a *beast*," he sneered. His tendrils of shadows shot out, wrapping around my wrist, lifting it from my lap. "I'm *despicable*." The shadows pulled and I was lifted to my feet, the pathetic weapon in my grip now placed at the pulse on his neck.

"I'm a *demon*."

He released his hold on me, tilting his head, providing the perfect target for my attack. But my hands shook, unable to press hard enough to break his skin.

"Can't do it?" he sneered, wrapping his massive palms around my wrist. He shoved down, forcing my trembling hands to break the skin, his dark blood now trickling down his neck.

"Let go," I demanded.

"Do it, Brenna," he replied. "Do it and see what happens. See what horrors unleash upon this world without me in it."

"You're a monster."

"I am *Death*." He pressed harder and the fork plunged further into his neck. "You *cannot* kill me."

The shadows around us disappeared in an instant. Olen's hands wrapped around my arms as he pulled me away. His shouts were loud but still muffled behind the ringing in my ears.

Ulrich stood, ripping the fork from his neck and throwing it onto the table. He turned to his red-faced, yelling right hand.

The ringing stopped at the clearing of his throat and Olen's shouting silenced.

"I want her at the docks tomorrow," the king addressed his most trusted confidant. "She sleeps in the dungeon. A shame, Brenna. We were just beginning to get along."

Ulrich left the room with his shadows trailing at his feet as Olen twisted me around, leading me out of the main doors. When we reached the hall, I shirked away his hands.

"I know the way to the dungeons!" I cried out, picking up my pace.

"You chose to ignore my advice the other night," Olen said beside me.

I refused to glance at him. "You're as demented as he is. Your friendship with him is not surprising. I, however, could never be close to such a monster."

"You don't know that," Olen replied.

I stopped my steps, turning on my heel to gaze up at him. "You have no idea what you're talking about."

He grinned back at me. "Neither do you."

"I hate you."

His smile grew larger. "I didn't know we were making proclamations of love. I would have prepared myself for the moment if I'd known."

I let out an annoyed breath, shoving him away while I made my trek down the stairs to the dungeon. My skin crawled the further I climbed with the sickening smell of mold and rot poisoning my senses.

When I reached the cells, Olen walked in front of me, opening my assigned prison.

With my head high I walked through the bars, pulling them shut myself.

"Sleep well, princess." He laughed.

"I hope you all die," I replied, watching him saunter down the hall with his braids dancing against his back as he went.

The late afternoon sun came through the small crack in the cell window above and I stared, waiting for the crimson of the moon to illuminate the space.

I hadn't slept. Even though my body had grown exhausted, I was too perturbed by that beast of a king to allow my mind to rest.

Footsteps came down the hall. Not footsteps, clinking paws against the stone floor.

I sat up, my dress sticking to the damp beneath me.

"Princess," Olen growled.

"Olen," I replied.

A grey-skinned Unseelie with small wings at their back appeared, unlocking the cage. The beast pulled the bars open with one paw, pointing down the hall with his snout.

"Is Ulrich planning on throwing me in the freezing water as punishment?"

Olen was silent, only snarling in response.

"Do I get to change?" I asked.

"No," he replied. "You get to walk these streets as Ulrich's *Stinking Wraith Whore.*"

I turned on my heel, my eyes burning with rage. "Do not call me that."

His canines dragged against his lips. "Touchy, princess. What? Will you throw a knife at me as well?"

I scanned the dungeons. "Unfortunately for you, I have no weapons within reach."

Olen grunted, the sound deep in his chest. His snout tapped against my legs, forcing me to return my walk down the hall. Toward whatever depraved activity Ulrich had in store for me.

We wove through the city streets. Streets that were eerily empty. Despite noting the lack of bodies, I allowed myself to actually gaze upon the city of Muspell, instead of walking through the pathways with my eyes focused on my steps.

There were a myriad of buildings. Some three to four stories high, some only one story in height. All built in rows beside each other with the occasional single building on its own plot of land.

Vastly different from the small handful of stone buildings at home and the humble wood homes that made up our unpaved streets.

I moved my eyes to the cobbled road, my heart aching for the feeling of gravel beneath my feet. For the sound of it when my boots crunched against the snow. Longing for home over these bumpy roads that hurt my soles.

I knew we were approaching the docks before Olen announced it.

The smell was a familiar one. Fish and game lined the market stalls that all faced out toward the water where the black mist lay in the distance.

I watched the water, my body longing to swim again. To allow the cold to lap around me and wash away my laments.

"Princess." I stopped, meeting Ulrich's gaze. My heart sank when I found the same skeletal mask from that day in the courtyard fitted across the upper half of his face.

"Your grace," I replied.

He stepped away, pointing to the end of the dock where I found a crowd of people.

"What is this?" I asked.

"Just watch."

Olen appeared before me, the warmth of his fur leaning against the skirts of my soiled dress. My hands rested against him, absent-mindedly using his fur to bring heat to my hands.

I made sure I was aware of Ulrich's place, and did as I was instructed. I watched. My eyes darted back and forth, searching the water for whatever we had all gathered for.

Hisses rang out around me when the black mist in the distance parted and the same black ship I'd sailed to this island cut through the veil.

It was as terrifying as it had been before.

"What is going on?"

"Quiet," Olen snapped.

I tightened my hold on the black fur beneath my fingers. Trembling where I stood while the omen of a vessel approached at that same horrifying speed.

Ulrich didn't move. He didn't speak. He remained unmoving and silent, even as the gangplank hit the dock.

But his people behind me? They all hissed again.

Towering black creatures walked down the gangplank, their crimson eyes filling my body with fear. Their long limbs dragged against the dock as they approached, and I instantly promised myself to never be left alone with one of them.

I thought Ulrich's people had been hissing at these strange creatures.

But I had been so painfully wrong.

The scream—it ripped into my soul. One of terror, anguish, and regret.

My eyes snapped back to the boat, watching as more of the creatures dragged a fae man down toward the dock.

There was something familiar about this man. His cut jaw, his brown copper hair. The straight nose. Yet, I couldn't place it.

Ulrich turned back to me, grinning.

"Prince Harold," the king bowed mockingly before the trembling prisoner. "I thought my warnings had been clear," Ulrich continued.

"Sire," the man sobbed. "Your grace."

Ulrich's hand rose and black shadows crept from his palm, heading down the throat of the man before us.

"Harry," Ulrich laughed. "I didn't give you permission to speak."

Tears fell from the man's eyes and my stomach turned. I pulled my hands from Olen's fur, holding them to my chest.

"How is Havrd?" Ulrich asked.

My hands fell to my side and my head twisted so quickly my neck groaned as I met the eyes of the man now shackled with Ulrich's shadows.

My younger brother, Harold, he's a fool. But he does his best to learn what needs to be done for our kingdom.

My eyes lined with blinding tears while one of Leif's last letters ran through my mind.

"Do not speak," Olen ordered.

I glanced at him, realizing I had stepped forward in my daze. Too blinded by my shock to detect my own movement.

Olen's teeth ripped at the sleeve of my gown, pulling me back.

Ulrich's eyes glistened behind his death mask.

He circled Leif's brother, gripping the back of the man's hair, pulling his head back. Humiliating the prince before us all.

"Your family is such a disappointment," the king sneered.

Harold's jaw tightened. "We understand he did not do his duty."

My heart stopped when Ulrich pointed Harold's body in my direction. "Recognize her?"

Harold stared at me, his face unmoving. Expressionless. No recognition in his eyes.

"I have never seen that woman before in my life," the prince grunted.

Ulrich shoved Harold to the ground, stepping on his palm while he approached me. His wrist wrapped around mine, pulling me toward the prince.

"Stop!" I protested.

"Watch, Brenna," he whispered.

My knees hit the dock and pain shot through my body as Ulrich threw me before the fae.

"Harold," I whispered.

"Lady," the prince eyed Ulrich hesitantly. "I do not know you."

"She was *betrothed* to Leif, Harold."

The man blinked in shock, shaking his head. "Impossible."

My heart sank.

"Tell him who you are," Ulrich commanded above me.

"I—" My mouth closed. Was it possible? Did Leif not say anything?

Shadows wrapped up my body, tilting my head back. Ulrich leaned down, his hand caressed the length of my neck.

"Speak, princess."

Tears lined my eyes, but my words remained in my heart.

The king gave me a disappointed scowl then dropped me, circling around me and Harold.

"This is Brenna of Nóatún, Harold. She's been writing to your brother for the last three years. Or—" Ulrich winked at me. "Was."

Harold kept his eyes on me. "Nóatún? That pathetic mingled island of half-fae miscreations?"

The words bit into me, stinging my soul.

"Excuse me?" I replied. "How dare you?"

Harold turned his eyes to Ulrich. "Your grace, what is this game?"

"Leif wrote to her, at my behest."

My mind separated from my body while the king spoke. I was weightless, a spectator watching, while my body slumped with defeat, collapsing into the dock. My tears began to fall without my control.

"It was part of our agreement," Ulrich went on. "My creatures here," a finger pointed at the black, limber beasts standing silently by the boat, "well they got rid of your father for him. In return, Leif had to write to a lonely princess on an island."

"No," I muttered.

Harold laughed loudly. "Leif would have never written to a half-fae. He was as disgusted by them as we all are in Vaneer. We all know of *her* island. Of her ancestor begging like a slave for Oberon to allow him to marry a pathetic mortal."

Ulrich knelt beside me while my tears continued, his finger wiping my cheek.

"Oh, but Harold, he did."

The king's gaze was burning into me while he addressed the prince behind him.

"He wrote to her. But he disobeyed me when he made her fall in love with him. When he promised to come to her aid, bringing her to Vaneer to marry and produce more of..." His voice trailed off and he turned his head back to Harold. "What did you call them? Miscreations?"

"I hate you," I cried, choking on my sobs.

Ulrich turned his head back to me, grinning. "He claimed something that was not his to claim."

Harold's laugh was wicked. Evil. A sickening sound as he replied, "She's pathetic. Look at her, covered in filth, crying like a babe. Making a show of herself before us all. Why would Leif have ever loved her?"

Ulrich's hand grasped mine and I glanced down, finding a shadow blade in my palm. His eyes were on fire, a hidden request.

"Look at her!" Harold laughed again. "Likely no better than a common *whore*."

My lips trembled while my grip on the knife went tighter. Harold did not stop. His insults hit me, one after another. Digging apart who I was and who I had longed to be. Tearing away the fantasy I had created of my future with Leif.

"Rage," Ulrich whispered above me. "It's addictive."

"My king!" Harold shouted. "Speak to *me*, not that filthy bitch on her knees."

My eyes met Ulrich's for just a brief moment before my rage came out of me, blinding me with hate as I ran. My scream echoed around the dock, a wraith's call, claiming her victim.

I landed on Harold's lap and the fae choked back his laughter. His eyes were wide, but I did not see his face staring back in fear. No, I saw Ulrich's, his vile grin, his masked eyes, and that stupid knowing he always had in his gaze. I lifted my hand then brought it down, plunging the blade right down Harold's throat. I let out a scream that ripped from my soul.

His gasp of shock was choked with his blood now spilling out around my fingers. His eyes stared back, and my vision cleared from my mind's imagination of Ulrich's emerald gaze. I stared down at the same grey Leif's had been when his head was presented to me all those months ago.

"Wraith."

The word echoed around me while I gazed into the fear forever frozen on Harold's face.

"Wraith," they repeated. All of the silent bodies that had been watching this show, chanting together.

I fell back, staring at the red blood on my shaking hands.

What have I done?

Ulrich was before me, pulling me from the ground and pressing his face against the side of mine.

"What a good *beast*," he whispered before leaving me at the dock with Harold's bleeding body at my feet.

Chapter 17

Five Months.

One hundred and forty days.

Nearly two weeks since I'd taken a life on the dock. Even with the days growing away from the moment that had marked my soul for eternity, I continued to scrub my hands raw each morning and night.

I could still see the blood—a damned spot staining my skin.

I sat in the library, staring at those hands in front of me, my chest heaving.

Olen snored on the ground before me, filling the spacious room with echoes of his comfort. All while I sat there, fixated on my palms.

My eyes closed and Harold's dead eyes stared back at me, the fear on his face marking my memories. The sounds of his mocking laughter and his fear-choked gasps.

The image of the blade shoved down his throat.

I stood, the chair beneath me clattering to the ground.

Then I ran.

Trying to force my mind from its own torment.

Olen let out a bellow of shock but, to my surprise, I was faster than him while he was pulling himself from his state of sleep.

My hands slammed the library open and I ran faster, heading toward the stairs. I didn't dare to look back. Not when I needed to rid my body of these stains, to wash away this shame I was carrying.

Troll laid themselves against the walls of the palace while I passed, all of them whispering in shock at the feral woman with the hair of fire whipping behind her back.

Somehow, by the grace of the Gods, I made it to the grand foyer without Olen catching me. My hands shoved the doors open, finding more strength than I'd ever believed I had.

My eyes went across the courtyard while my feet continued to propel me forward. Determined to get to one place and one place only.

I raced through the gravel and to the palace gates. I turned, my eyes catching the green leaves barely blocking the dark pathway to the tunnels I'd ventured down before.

I glanced back once, still finding no beast following before I tucked under the thick foliage and back down the tunnel.

It was dark, darker than it had been when I'd first explored it in the daylight. I pulled my eyes to the ceiling watching the barely visible footsteps above while red moonlight filled my hidden walkway.

My hands trembled at my sides, reminding me of why I'd fled, and I ran again. Until my feet hit the crunching sound of sand.

My sobs left my lips when the water came into view. It was peaceful, even with the red of the moon turning it crimson. Like the stains of blood on my hands and heart.

Without a care, I walked forward, right into the water.

The cold grasped my breath from my lungs.

Then I sank. Letting my body go weightless in the cold. Allowing the water I knew was not red to stain my entire being with my sins.

My limbs went numb under the cold, with my hair out behind me, floating on the water.

I kept my eyes closed, holding my breath.

I wasn't determined to die. No, that hadn't been my intent. I just needed to feel *clean*.

My body began to reground itself, to return to normal while my pulse slowed. Until hands were wrapping under my arms, lifting me like a child's plaything.

"What," a voice muffled by the water in my ears grunted, "in Fate's name are you doing?"

My eyes lifted and I tilted my head back, watching while Ulrich dragged me back to shore, depositing me onto the sand like a sailor's fresh catch.

The air hitting my skin instantly brought my teeth together in uncontrollable chatters.

"Fuck it all," he groaned while rushing to me, wrapping the cloak he'd ripped from his shoulders around my body.

"I needed to be clean," I cried.

"From what?" he sighed, lifting me against him. "The ink you leave splattered all over that desk in the library?"

My tears fell, warming then cooling in the wind on my cheeks. "Of course that's what you think this is."

I turned my cheek trying to get away but instead it rested against his chest, soaking his shirt.

"Why did you try to drown yourself, *Ursa?*" he asked more gently.

I hated the softness of his voice. The care hidden in the question. This feigned desire to soothe my black soul.

"You made me kill him," I cried.

Ulrich's body shook beneath me with his laugh. His hand brushed the hair from my face. A strangely affectionate touch.

"I didn't force you to do anything."

My mind cleared while my body warmed against him and I stood. "Why?" I cried. "Why?"

I pulled my eyes from the sand, letting out a shout of anger when I found a mask on his face. I ran for him, my hands, determined to rip that stupid fucking mask from him. In his lowered position on the ground, he didn't have time to clamor away but his hands caught my wrists right as my fingers gripped the edge of the black barrier.

"Brenna," his voice became a warning.

"What are you so scared of, Ulrich?" I seethed, and my fingers wiggled beneath the ends of the mask.

His grip went firm, attempting to pull my hands off. But I held firm, lowering my body onto his lap, holding him in place. Unintentionally straddling him while I tried to keep control.

"Do not consider it," he growled.

"Growling like the monster he is," I replied. "What are you going to do?" I teased, rolling my hips against him. "Kill me?"

My body hit the sand. My gasp was quiet with the shock of the collision, and he pressed his hips back into mine, lifting my hands above my head.

"You think you've bested me," he laughed. "I'm always one step before you, Brenna."

I could only come up with one response—spitting in his face.

"I've warned you enough fucking times," he grunted.

His hands were replaced with his shadows licking up my body, holding me in place.

"Stop!" I screamed, horrified at the smile across his lips.

He sat up, now straddling me like I had been him.

"No, Brenna," he said with a laugh, rolling up the sleeves of his shirt and revealing the ink on his forearms. "I am tired of you not listening."

I struggled against the shadows, flailing my legs under him. I was a fool, Gods I was stupid for thinking he wouldn't punish me for my fit.

"That's enough," he said calmly, and his shadows clamped down on my limbs, covering the rest of my body.

His long hair brushed against my cheeks when he leaned over me again. "Is this what you enjoy? Does this get your blood pumping? Does it warm that body in all the right places?"

His hand grasped my jaw, tightening at the bottom.

I kept my lips tight, my cries of protest muffled in my attempt to fight back. But he was too strong.

"You." He smiled, the strength of his fingers forced my jaw to open. "Will." He leaned forward, the amusement in his eyes burning. "Listen."

Then he spit—right into my mouth.

I was in too much shock to respond. To cry out from the pain of him holding my jaw. To stop my body from swallowing out of reflex.

Disgusting me to my core.

In an instant he released me, standing calmly like nothing had happened. His shadows crawled back to him. Strings returning to their puppet master.

I was silent as I sat up. Rubbing my jaw then spitting into the sand. Repeatedly. Until I was sure his own saliva had left my body. At least that's what I'd wanted to believe.

"Are you done?" he replied.

My eyes went back to his, watching while he rolled his sleeves back to his wrist. I threw off his cloak, standing quickly.

He turned, directing his body back to the entrance of the tunnel. Only I didn't follow.

I ran right back to the water.

My feet had almost hit the water's edge when his hands wrapped around my waist, ripping me back.

"Let go of me!" I screeched, slamming my hands backward. My fists connected with his solid body.

"No!" he yelled back, shoving me to the sand again.

"I hate you!" I cried, burying my face in my knees. "I hate you."

My words grew quiet as I repeated myself and my tears fell onto my already dripping gown.

"Get up before you freeze out here," the king ordered.

"I hate you."

He leaned forward and his hair hung over me, covering my face. "Tell me something new and I might actually tell you why I brought that sniveling coward to my home."

I stared up at him, silent.

He grinned, before standing again.

"Just like I thought."

"You're a coward."

Somehow the wind caught my words, wrapping them around us.

Ulrich's shoulders went stiff.

I stood, squaring my shoulders with my determined attack.

"You torment and torture to amuse yourself. To distract yourself from the coward that lives beneath that mask. The man who makes *deals,* forcing people to bow to him because not one body on this island follows you out of respect."

His shoulders moved with heavy breaths, and I continued.

"They follow out of fear. What a sad life it must be for a king to lack the respect of his own people. I doubt you could even protect them if the need ever arose."

The sand beneath my feet began to shake, lifting into the air while an unseen hum surrounded the secluded beach. My eyes snapped to Ulrich, whose shoulders were slumped. His shadows circled his body, creating a cyclone of sand and black around him.

"Gods," I exclaimed, stepping back.

His head shifted toward me after my proclamation and his eyes—they were pitch black. I stared back, sure a shimmering crown of shadows appeared above his head.

"You know nothing. His voice was low, terrifying, and unrecognizable.

I lifted my hands in defeat, bowing my head, retreating from this battle between us. Allowing the king to be the victor.

But I wasn't sure the being before me was the king I loathed.

His hands moved like he was painting something in the wind. My eyes went to his limbs, noticing the skin turning grey. Almost translucent with his bones becoming visible beneath.

The red of the moon made him all the more horrible. Layering red over the shadows and his body. Painting the Unseelie King as though he were dripping in blood.

I continued my backward retreat, cursing the high hills blocking this place of solitude from the rest of the city. Trapping me with the monster I'd awoken.

"*Fear*," Ulrich laughed. "It always smells the best right before death. When the soul is most alive. Fighting to stay attached to the body it lives within."

My heart dropped.

"Please," I whispered

His head threw back and I blinked in shock as his mask clattered at his feet. When I brought my gaze up, I found his shadows had replaced it, whipping around his features. A living, dark force blocking everything but his eyes. His laugh was just as low and dangerous as his voice, a warning to run.

But I couldn't. I was frozen in fear, trembling in the sand with my dress dripping around my feet.

"I rarely hear the begging." He continued his approach. "Rarely take the moment to allow that fear to build before I consume my victim. A shame when the most fearful are the most delicious."

His shadows bit at my ankles, dancing around the lower half of my body as he stalked closer.

His hand, greyed and almost decayed in appearance, gripped my face. "You've broken your deal, Brenna," he sneered.

"No!" I protested.

His shadows encompassed his body, turning him to a being of black. Licking up his arms, replacing his limb with the darkness.

"You *ran*. Attempted escape."

I shook against his hold, my tears falling onto the shadows. "No, I wasn't running. I wasn't."

"You are not obeying your rules, *Ursa*. Broken deals must be claimed."

He leaned forward and my body jolted. Pain swirled in my mind and throughout my entire being.

"I'm obeying!" I protested. "I just needed to be clean!"

He leaned closer and my mouth opened without my control. I couldn't understand what was happening. Why my body convulsed. Why suddenly, the pain was retreating and something else, something frigid, cold and horrible, was taking over.

"Your soul was marked before you took your first breath, *Ursa*."

The words branded me, coiling around me, tightening over my heart. I couldn't find the strength to refute them. To deny his claim.

Because what if he wasn't wrong?

Then I was flying into the sand hill behind me, my head hit it with force. My vision blurred and I watched as Olen ran across the sand, and attacked Ulrich, tackling him to the ground.

The king's shadows wrapped around the two men, blocking me from seeing what occurred. I could hear it, though. The bellows of rage. The shouts.

And, alarmingly, two different animalistic snarls.

"Ulrich!" Olen's voice shouted. "Ulrich return!"

Ulrich's shadows climbed higher, a dome of black blocking the fight he was tangled in.

"Don't allow it to take control!" Olen yelled louder. "Don't let *her* win."

Her?

A rage-filled scream replied, and the earth shook from the force.

"Brenna, get the fuck back to the palace!" Olen ordered.

I nodded, despite the beast not being able to see my silent acknowledgement and I ran. Faster than I had run to the beach, tripping on my dripping gown as I went. Tears heavier than before.

The red moon guided me on my journey, a protection for the woman born under its magic.

When I reached the palace, I stood in the foyer, unsure of where to go. Who to run to.

My mind reeled and my chest burned when I made my decision. Picking up my skirts, I rushed through the palace toward the stairs at the back. Hoping to the Gods I wasn't a fool for my plan.

My feet slipped on the damp stairs leading to the dungeons and I flew down the hall, startling the guard asleep in his chair.

"What in the Gods?" they groaned.

"He's coming," I sobbed.

The guard was on his feet but instead of helping me, he ran back up the stairs. Leaving me in the dark prison.

I scoffed, running to my assigned cell. To my relief it was open when I reached it. To my dismay, I realized I did not have the keys to lock myself in.

The palace shook and the lights went out. Turning the room black instantly.

Then it approached.

His cold.

His power.

So much more terrifying than it had ever been.

"Brenna," his voice sang in the darkness. "We were not done."

"Please!" I replied, my voice echoing throughout the dungeons. "Please."

I pressed my back against the cell wall, jumping at the sound of the metal gate slamming open.

The energy of his might took the air from my lungs, the wall behind me cracked with the force of his shadows pressing against me.

"I will not kill you." His voice was so close but I could see nothing through the thick fog of darkness. "Not tonight."

My body dropped and the red moon returned through the window. I sobbed, watching the mass of shadows retreating, leaving me in the cell with the gate now mangled at the side.

The dungeon grew silent around me while my body curled into itself, attempting to warm the freeze taking over.

My eyes closed and my tears fell. I would freeze in that spot, but I didn't care.

Arms lifted me into the air, pressing me against a broad and warm chest. I leaned into Olen, gripping his shirt. Not having to look up to know it as him with his braids tickling my face.

"Princess," he muttered. "What happened?"

"I just wanted to be clean," I muttered. "I just wanted to be clean."

Chapter 18

I woke in a strange bed, not recognizing the red comforter covering me.

Until I turned my head and found Olen. Snoring like a beast.

My tears fell from my eyes, and I pulled the blanket up to my chin, startling the body beside me.

"Morning," Olen grunted.

"Evening," I replied.

The bed shook with his laugh. "Fine, evening. My morning."

I shifted, watching him hop from the bed, his earrings jingling with the movement.

"Will you help me get home?" I whispered.

His shoulders stiffened and he shook his head. "No, princess. I will not."

"Why?" I cried.

He crossed the room again and placed himself on the mattress near my feet.

"I'm going to tell you something I should not utter."

My breath hitched in my lungs, and I nodded my head.

"Ulrich is *not* the monster you're experiencing."

I shoved Olen away, scrambling from the bed. My hand went to my hip and my eyes widened, realizing I was completely nude.

Olen grinned at me, his eyes tracking my body.

"Stop!" I yelled, covering myself as best as I could while I rushed back to the bed.

"What in the Gods were you thinking? Where are my clothes?" I demanded.

"Burning in the kitchens. You were dripping wet and covered in sand and rot from the dungeons. None of that was getting in my bed."

I shook my head. "My undergarments? My chemise? None of it could have been kept *on* my body?"

Olen shrugged. "I've got a sensitive sense of smell, princess."

He stood, crossing the room and opening a door, revealing a small wardrobe. His hand reached forward, then a shirt was flying through the air, and I grasped it. He didn't turn until I stood and slipped it over my head.

"It's insulting for you to proclaim Ulrich is not a monster."

His smile was irritating but amusing at the same time as he replied, "I didn't say he wasn't a monster. I said he isn't *the* monster you've encountered."

"That makes no sense."

"It does. Just not to you," Olen responded as he sat back down on the mattress.

I shifted my gaze, finding the narrow door leading to the hallway to Ulrich's room.

"What did you say to him?" Olen asked.

"I—" I held my tongue, shaking my head. "It doesn't matter."

"That's where you're wrong." Olen was standing again, his eyes narrowed with determination. "It very much matters. Ulrich has not had power that uncontrollable in millennia."

Olen stood before me, glaring into my eyes. "What did you say?" he asked slowly.

"I called him a coward."

"I tell him that daily," he laughed. "What else did you say?"

I kept my mouth closed, taunting the beast before me with my silence. My words, yes they had been cutting, but observant enough to send Ulrich into that rage. Confirming he was as much of a coward as I believed him to be. Attacking me all because I'd *hurt his feelings.*

"Princess," Olen sang, snapping his fingers in my face.

I slapped his hand away, turning from him.

His hand gripped my arm, pulling my body against him and forcing me to crane my neck to meet his eyes. "What did you say?" he repeated.

His hand landed on my lower back, pressing me closer.

"I—" The heat of him was shocking. It took my response from me.

Olen leaned down, his scarred face nearly touching my own. "We could make a deal," he whispered.

The word snapped me out of my daze. With a scoff, I shoved him against the chest.

"Stop!" I demanded, running my hand through my knotted hair. "I'll tell you."

Olen's eyes ran up and down my body, causing my knees to go weak. "But we were just about to have fun."

"You were teasing me, trying to gain some self-satisfaction," I replied.

I sat on the bed, pulling my knees against my chest and repeated what I'd told the king on the beach hours before. When I finished my recount, I met Olen's eyes, finding a gaze that was wide with both shock and rage.

"Why in the Gods would you say that to him?" he grumbled.

"I'm not wrong," I countered.

"You could never be more wrong," Olen groaned and rubbed his hand across his jaw. "Fuck, princess you really must have a death wish."

"I wish for him to die," I replied coldly.

Olen had my back plastered against the bed with his hand around my throat before I could take my next breath.

"Do not," he warned.

"Get your hands off me," I choked out.

"You will stop threatening my king. Do you understand?"

Olen released me, then leaned against the window by the bed. His arms crossed over him while he stared, waiting for my response.

"Stop speaking to me like I am a child," I snarled.

The hidden door slammed open, and Ulrich's presence filtered through the room. My head snapped in his direction, scowling at the death mask on his face again.

"You are a child, Brenna," the king chuckled.

"Spying?" I snapped.

Olen stood straighter, nodding his head. Once again becoming the unflinching pet at Ulrich's side.

"I require your assistance," Ulrich said.

"No," I replied, standing from the bed.

The king smiled. "Brenna, you do not have a choice."

His voice trailed off and his eyes went to my body, stopping where Olen's large shirt ended just above my knees.

"My," the king chuckled. "Did I interrupt?"

I opened my mouth to protest, but gasped when Olen was suddenly behind me, with his hands wrapping around my waist. His lips brushed my neck, and I froze. My hands went rigid at my side.

"Perhaps," Olen hissed. "Or perhaps you arrived at just the right time."

Ulrich approached, a burning heat in his gaze. He gripped my chin, tilting my face upward. "I think I may have."

Olen pressed further against me, tightening his hold around my waist. The size of his arms and palms made me feel so much smaller than my body actually was.

"What do you say, princess?" he whispered into my ear.

Ulrich's grip on my chin tightened but I couldn't have looked away if I had tried. Not with what swam in his eyes. The heat of it all made me forget the death mask covering his features.

The king's thumb brushed my lips.

"My right hand requires an answer, *Ursa*."

I startled at his touch, unintentionally pressing further into Olen.

The man behind me began to move one hand, circling his thumb on my bare skin at the edge of his own shirt hanging from my body. The touch was maddening. Even more so when Ulrich pressed himself against the front of me, trapping me between the two of them.

My head went back against Olen's chest without my control and my lip quivered.

"Just some fun, princess," Olen whispered into my ear. His finger trailed up higher on my thigh, climbing until he was nearly brushing my pelvis.

My body begged for it, loudly, forcing my knees to shake the faster Olen circled my skin. A haze of need fogged my mind, blocking out my hate for the two of them. It drowned me in a quiet plea for release.

And I'd almost fallen into the trap, allowing the waves of ecstasy to envelope me. Ulrich's death mask grew closer, his beard brushed my chin, and his lip hovered just above mine.

My breaths stopped as he leaned down to claim my lips. There was no time to react, no time to think—so I bit down, drawing his black blood.

The king's body snapped up and Olen let out a loud laugh.

"I guess that's a no."

They both stepped away and I scowled. "Do not touch me."

Olen grinned then shrugged. "You seemed to be enjoying it."

I let out a yell, throwing my hands up in the air as I rushed out of the room using the door Ulrich had come through.

Two sets of footsteps followed close behind, building my rage.

"Leave me alone!" I cried. "Please!"

"Can't do that!" Olen yelled back.

Ulrich was silent though, his commanding presence right at my heels.

I picked up my pace, heading right down the hall, hoping I could move faster than them.

A foolish hope, really.

To my relief, the door to Ulrich's bedroom was open. But to my dismay, every single candle was lit, and the red moon was shining through the window, creating that frustratingly sensual light across the room.

"Look, a mood already set," Olen jested behind me.

I screamed out my rage again, rushing to the bathing room and slamming the door shut as I went.

I placed my back against it, gripping my head in an attempt to block out my senses.

"Leave me alone!" I shouted.

“Can’t do that,” Olen repeated.

I hit my head against the door and repeated my plea to the silent Gods above me. Begging them to end the lives of my tormentors.

“Being interested in sexual release is not a sin,” Ulrich finally said.

The amusement in his tone turned my body cold. I threw the door open, glaring at him with all of my might.

“I am a woman, Ulrich. A woman who has lived a very long time. I hope you realize I am not an innocent, inexperienced *virgin.*”

“I’d be very disappointed to hear if you were,” Ulrich grinned.

“Get out,” I demanded, pointing to the three different exits out of the room.

Ulrich stepped back, that grin still a mocking image across his face. He turned back to glance at Olen lounging on the bed with one leg up and one hand behind his head.

“That bed is large enough for all three of us,” Ulrich said.

“Get out!” I screamed.

Ulrich rushed to me, pinning me against the door frame. “Olen will escort you to the library. You have mere minutes to get some proper clothes on.”

The bedroom door had opened and closed before I could let out my breath. I snapped my head to Olen, who had turned onto his side, offering me a wild grin.

“That was fun.”

“Get out.”

“You heard what he said,” Olen sighed as he hopped to his feet.

“Yes and I will get dressed in private. You stay outside that door for all I care.” I pointed to the door Ulrich had closed behind him.

“I’ve seen *everything* you have to offer now, princess.” Olen smiled. “No need to be shy.”

"Olen," I replied calmly. "If you do not give me privacy I will sneak into your room one of these evenings and cut you from your balls to the top of your head."

His eyes went wide, and he let out a booming laugh. "Gods, Brenna, you may just be spending too much time with Ulrich." His hands rose in relent as he went back toward the door. "Get dressed quickly."

I slipped on my most basic gown and threw the bedroom door open, groaning when I found Ulrich leaning against the wall beside the door.

His hand moved upward, and I flinched.

"What was that?" he asked, the light in his eyes dimming.

I shook my head. "Your attacks have created an involuntary reaction, your grace. What did you expect?" I placed myself two arms-lengths from him. "Why the library?" I asked.

Something clattered at my feet, pulling my gaze away from him.

A mask. Another fucking mask.

"Every evening, Brenna. You have been given too many leniencies," Ulrich said coldly.

I tied the ribbons at my head, staring the king down once more. "You did not answer my question."

Ulrich held his head high, motioning for me to follow. Still irritatingly silent.

I shuffled my feet, keeping a few paces behind him while we walked through his quiet palace. The booming of music was not shaking the walls like they had each evening.

We climbed the stairs and when we reached the long hallway with the library doors at the end, I stopped.

"Answer my question," I demanded.

Shadows ran past my feet, climbing the walls around me and Ulrich grinned. "I'm the king. Answers will not be demanded of me."

"Then I'm not following," I replied.

"Are we about to have another delicious battle?" Ulrich laughed. "Did the last one not fulfill your needs for violence?"

My mouth opened in shock. "I'm not the violent one!" I protested.

Ulrich's head threw back with his next laugh. "You tried to kill me for over a month and repeatedly attacked me. Yet you claim not to be violent." He turned on his heel heading back down the halls with his shadows running beside him. "You may want to consider some self-reflection, *Ursa,*" he yelled out behind his shoulder.

I stood at the end of the hall, staring at him in disbelief.

"Come, Brenna," his voice called down the hall.

I held my firm stance, determined to best him in this new battle. Hands shoved against my back, throwing me forward.

"Come now," Olen whispered. "Don't anger his grace."

I wiggled away from Olen, grumbling while I stomped down the halls. Like the child they were both determined to believe I was.

Ulrich waited at the library doors, holding them open with a fire in his eyes. I passed him, turning to sit on one of the few chairs in the room, but he cleared his throat.

"To the back of the library, please."

He hissed out the last word with something knowing on his tongue. My stomach dropped. Had he found my letters? The small pile I was collecting at the bottom of my trunk?

My hands trembled while I followed him with Olen close at my heels. We wove through the tall shelves until the table I spent most days at came into view.

Ulrich stepped forward, circling the table and picking up a few of the ink-stained maps.

"Who taught you cartography?" he asked, studying my scribblings.

I was shocked. Sure the king had found my hidden secret, but instead he was admiring the rough pieces I worked on at random.

"My tutors," I replied quietly.

Ulrich held up the map in his hands. The map I'd been drawing of his city.

"This isn't half-bad for a pampered princess."

I bit my tongue, forcing myself not to fight back.

"I have a project for you," he announced as he approached me.

"What?" I replied, blinking when I found him before me, his chest nearly touching mine.

He smiled down at me. "Do you want to continue following Olen around, claiming my deals? Or would you like to take me up on my offer?"

"I get one hour each day to swim—alone," I responded foolishly.

Ulrich stepped back and Olen let out a laugh behind me.

"I was not aware we were negotiating," Ulrich sneered.

I held my shoulders tight. "You're asking something of me, your grace. I believe requesting some form of payment is only just."

Ulrich opened his mouth to reply but I held up my hand. "And I request the ability to write to my father with no prying eyes on my letters."

"That's two requests," Ulrich replied. "If I'm to give you two payments then I must receive a fair reward."

I gulped, cursing my fast tongue.

"Dinner with me, each night—alone," Ulrich continued. "And my first request you rudely interrupted—mapping out the hidden passageways of my palace."

Olen choked behind me and the towering man appeared at my side "Ulrich," he snarled.

Ulrich only held his hand up, silencing his pet.

"I'm already forced to sleep beside you, your *grace*," I replied.

"And I've not once stopped you from writing to your father, *Ursa*," he snapped.

Our battle ignited between us while he held our stubborn gaze. Neither moving. Neither speaking.

Olen shuffled beside us, obviously irritated.

"Well?" Ulrich finally broke the silence.

"Explain," I replied.

Ulrich returned to the table, setting my scribbles back down. "Your craftsmanship is admirable, Brenna. The simple fact you found the hidden passage to my beach caught my attention. And as I've looked at your maps each day, I notice you have a keen eye for noting the dark and hidden spaces throughout my city."

My pulse thumped in my ears, hating he'd picked up on what I'd actually been drawing. That I had found those dark spaces when Olen marched us through Muspell, noting the areas I was sure I could disappear down.

"My palace is filled with hidden walkways. Gods, even ones I've come to forget in the years I've resided here." He met my eyes with a grin. "I want *you* to mark them all down. For me."

"Why?" I countered. "This feels like a trap."

Ulrich shrugged. "I'm *old*, Brenna. I may forget how to get around my home one day."

Olen chuckled quietly.

The jest was shocking but I held back my responding smile.

"You won't read my letters?" I asked.

Ulrich nodded. "I cannot promise your father will reply, but yes your words will be private."

"Why wouldn't he reply?"

"Brenna, it's been five months. I have yet to receive a letter or declaration of war from the man."

Ulrich's smile returned to the vile one that fueled my hatred. His eyes burning with some knowledge he knew would break my heart in two.

"He will," I cried. "He will reply to me."

Ulrich threw his hand up, walking past me. "Whatever you say, *Ursa*. I will begin escorting you through each passage beginning tomorrow."

I stepped forward, shock widening my eyes. "What? You did not mention this before."

Ulrich turned on his heel with a wide grin. "Did I not? Oh, well it appears we will have the opportunity to get to know one another twice a day now. Enjoy your swims, Brenna."

Olen fell back into the chair, holding his chest while he laughed. "You're a fool, princess. A godsdamn fool."

My hands balled at my side while I watched the king saunter away. His muscled back was stiff with his hair just brushing his shoulders. Even turned away from me, I could see the triumph on his face.

He'd tricked me, allowing my desperation for freedom to loosen my tongue and agree to something before asking more questions.

Leaving him the victor of our most recent battle.

Chapter 19

I met Ulrich in the library the next day. My hands trembled when I met his eyes.

"The princess and the beast alone," he snarled. "I'm sure there are countless tales recounting this story."

"Usually that princess is killed," I snapped back with a glare.

He stepped forward, his horned mask making him appear even more like the demon he was. "I believe I've read the opposite. Usually, they fuck and fall in love by the end."

"Likely a story written by a man," I countered, stepping away from his hand reaching toward me.

He smiled, pulling his hand back to his side then gestured to the table with my ink and parchment. "Grab blank parchment, Brenna. Then we'll begin."

I shook my head. "I need koal. Something I can wipe away if I make a mistake. The ink is what's been available to me."

Ulrich's smile dropped. "You said nothing about this yesterday."

I crossed my arms over my chest. "And you failed to mention you'd be giving me personal tours of your home."

"Fair," he replied, then sat on the chair, his eyes traveling out the window where the red moon sat high in the sky.

"I'll have my *troll* gather koal and whatever you need. We can begin the mapping tomorrow."

I nodded my head, stepping back slowly.

His head turned in my direction. "Where are you going?"

My heart sank. "Am I required to keep you company, your grace?"

"Drop the formalities, Brenna. Call me whatever you wish. We're alone."

"Alright," I grinned. "Demented Demon, am I required to stay with you?"

Ulrich's face cracked with a large smile and his hand slammed against the table. "What did you just call me?"

My cheeks warmed with embarrassment. "The first insult that came to my mind," I admitted.

"Do it again," Ulrich laughed. "Gods, that was hilarious."

"I'm not your personal jester," I grumbled.

He leaned back in his chair. "Maybe I should make you one."

"Ulrich," I sighed. "May I please go?"

"No," he replied. "Sit."

His hand pointed to the bench against the wall. With a frown, I did as I was told. I leaned my back against the wall while my eyes traveled around the red moon lit room.

"This is the saddest library I've ever seen," I whispered.

"Why?" Ulrich replied, turning his gaze away from the window.

My hands moved out around me. "The history on these shelves should be treated with respect. The stories should be cared for. But each shelf is covered in a thick layer of dust. There's almost no place to sit. It's heartbreaking."

"Are you a lover of tales and fables?"

I shook my head. "While I do read, I view myself as more of a historian, Ulrich. A lover of history and tales of our world. History is the most valuable weapon we have at our fingertips. You're making a mockery of our future by allowing all of this history to fall into ruin."

"Is this why you learned mapping?"

I rolled my eyes. "Why do you wish to know? What advantage does this provide you to hold over me later?"

Ulrich shrugged. "You've lived under my roof for five months. I should at least learn more about you."

"I thought you knew *everything* about the things you owned?" I bit back.

Ulrich's smile grew wide. "You love to load your tongue with fighting words, princess. Impressive for someone who allowed herself to live a life alone on that little island."

I went silent, turning my head away from him.

"Why did my ancestor come to you?" I whispered my question. "Harold said Oberon gifted my island to my ancestor, a false tale I was told my entire life. But you and I both know that's not true."

"It is," Ulrich replied.

"Explain it to me."

"It wasn't your deal," Ulrich replied coldly.

"I am here because of that deal. I deserve to understand the workings of it."

Ulrich glanced at me then placed his feet on to the table before him, leaning back on his chair.

"Your ancestor was a fool," he began. "A fool who had fallen in love with a mortal. Despite his king forbidding him from doing so."

Ulrich sighed.

"He called for me. Meeting me at a crossroads near Aesir and the small kingdom Oberon allowed him to rule."

"Called for you?" I asked.

Ulrich smiled. "There are many ways to enact a deal with me. Requesting it outright when in my presence, as you did." He winked. "Requesting it through a desperate letter—my least favored way.

And then my *favorite*—burying your blood deep into the soil of the earth at a crossroads in Vaneer, requesting my presence."

The air stilled while the king talked, and his hands tapped against the arm of his chair.

"Your ancestor fell to his knees when I appeared through my shadows. Lifting his hands, he begged me to convince Oberon to allow him to marry the woman he loved."

"I'd almost said no. Almost denied the pathetic request, but I had a moment of weakness that evening. So, I offered him my terms—he gets the woman, and I get the service of the first daughter of his bloodline born on the first day of the blood moon."

"Why?" I interjected.

"Why not?"

I stood from my bench, placing myself right before him.

"Why offer such an odd term? The blood moons are long, they take millennia to appear again."

"Well, that was the most entertaining part of it. I wasn't even sure it would happen. My deals do not have to make sense, Brenna."

"You're sick," I groaned. "Tricking innocent souls into deals they may never be able to fulfill."

He shrugged. "They could always wait for their Gods to respond. I do not force them to take my blood and agree."

"How does Oberon fall into this?"

Ulrich held my gaze, his chest moving slowly. "Unknown to you, and most of this world, I meet with Oberon yearly. In secret. We discuss the current conditions of our courts and every now and then, I will follow through with any deals that involve him. Your ancestor only wanted to marry this mortal. Oberon thought it was disgusting to have fae and mortal blood mixed. He came up with granting an island as long as your family paid him a yearly visit to acknowledge his rightful place as your true king."

"You also managed to place Sigrun in Titania's personal court."

Ulrich's hands gripped his chair. "Yes," he hissed. "And you saw how that worked out."

"How many spies do you have in Oberon's court?"

The words left my lips and Ulrich's chair clattered to the ground. He was before me, his hands wrapping around my wrists.

"Quiet your tongue," he sneered.

"No!" I pulled from his grasp. "I'm not stupid, Ulrich. She all but said it! How many? How many more deals will Oberon force you to claim? How many more lives of people *you* tricked?"

"Brenna," his voice dropped low. "You do not know what you speak of, and I suggest you stop immediately."

"Or what?" I countered. "You're going to attack me again? You're going to kill me in a fit of rage? Or will you whip me until I bleed again and mark the rest of my body with your violence?"

"Get out," Ulrich snapped. His hands landed on my shoulders, and he spun me toward the door. "Leave my sight now before you regret it."

I scoffed. "Still a coward."

Ulrich let out an angry breath and I expected his hands to grip me, but he kept away. I gave him another scoff, picking up my skirts as I walked towards the door.

"Don't forget you're a pawn in this game!" Ulrich yelled after me.

"And don't forget that I hate you!" I replied.

I made my way out of the library, hate heating my blood, and turned toward my *looking glass* hall. I didn't want to return to the bedroom. Not when I knew he would eventually lay beside me in bed. Sleeping like a peaceful brute while I spent the night fidgeting in my spot.

I saw the red moonlight before I crossed the threshold and relief flooded through me. I couldn't usually stay angry the moment I entered this room. Not with the beauty and simplicity of the space.

I approached the glass, laying my cheek against the cool surface while I drew scribbles in the fog left by my breath.

The city below was alive and bright. A population of people living under the moon of my blood. Oddly fitting when I came to ponder it, that I would find myself trapped on an island living under the moon that had ushered in my birth.

My hands continued to scribble while my breath fogged the glass, absently drawing the markings I'd seen across the king's forearms. The letters I didn't recognize running up the tails of the strange beasts on his body.

"Did he have you mesmerized?"

I pulled my head from the glass, finding Olen in his beast form. The red of the moon lightened the dark scar across his face.

"What's that from?" I asked, pointing to the scar.

Olen growled.

I glared in response. "It is only a question."

Olen laid before me, resting his head on my feet. Trapping me in place. His chest rumbled just below the tops of my shoes as he spoke. "A deadly creature marked me, leaving me with the shame of it for the rest of my life."

I shrugged, leaning back on my arms while I studied the scar. "I think it's handsome."

His chest rumbled and that strange laugh sound came from his throat. "Handsome? I have yet to be told that."

I smiled at him. "It's odd when I see it on your face in beast form. The way it's raised and how none of your fur covers it. But... when you are yourself and it's across your face? It's handsome and unique."

Olen's head dropped. "I would be blushing if I could."

I laughed and laid back on the floor, staring at the moon from the top of the window. My eyes closed while I imagined the sun through this window and bright white clouds above.

"How many passageways are in this palace?" I asked.

"Only Ulrich knows the answer to that," Olen replied.

I sat up once more. "He's awful."

Olen's teeth peeked above his lips. "So am I."

"Yes you are." I frowned and pulled my feet away forcefully. The beast jumped to his feet, scowling at me.

"Leave me," I said coldly.

His massive head shook in response. "No."

"You are not my keeper, Olen. I am not escaping. I only wish for solitude."

We held our glares for a moment before his head dipped to the ground, startling me with the show of respect.

"As you wish, princess. The king expects you to be in bed soon."

I waved the beast away. "Tell your king I will do as I'm told."

Olen stalked away silently, allowing me more time alone.

I took it in. The silence of the palace with the lack of wall-trembling music. The red light, warming the hall and my heart. I appreciated the beauty of the city below with the water at its edge and the black mist barely visible in the distance. It was a hidden world of monsters and secrets, but surprisingly beautiful despite the chaos of it all.

When my body began to ache from laying on the ground for so long, I pulled myself up and left the hall. I made my way back down the hall to the stairs, winding through the Unseelie palace with ease as though it were actually becoming my home.

When I found myself before the bedroom doors, my hands trembled as I reached for the handles. They slammed open and Ulrich's cold wrapped around my lungs.

"I've been waiting for you."

"Shouldn't old men be sleeping?" I snapped.

His chuckle rang out through the dark and I lifted my hands, finding the wall to guide me into the room.

"I need light to change."

"No, you do not," Ulrich replied.

"Ulrich."

"Get into the bed, Brenna. I am tired," he replied.

I reached the end of the wall and shuffled through the dark. Making a scene with my stumbling feet despite having learned the room weeks before.

"I grow older by the minute," Ulrich groaned.

"Perhaps you will wither into dust by the time I reach the bed and I'll be free of this madness."

His chest hit mine, taking my breath and his hand landed on my lower-back.

"Is that what you want?" he whispered. "For me to wither away?"

My words stuck in my throat at the heat of his hand on me.

"Brenna," he groaned. "Have you ever laid with someone you loathe?"

"Is that not what we do each night?" I forced out.

He laughed and pressed his hand against my back. "*Ursa*, you know what I'm asking."

My body was too close to him. Suffocating my ability to think straight.

"Let me go," I whispered.

His thumb circled my back. "You were taking too long to get into bed. I had to fetch you."

"Stop doing that," I squeaked.

"That noise." He pressed my body against his. "Do it again."

"Unhand me," I replied.

His palm left a burning brand on my skin when he pulled away. "One day, Brenna, you will ask—no—you will *beg* for my touch."

"Ulrich," I laughed. "I would have to go mad for that day to come."

His hand brushed my cheek. "I'm patient."

The bed groaned and I blinked, realizing he'd been leading us across the room. Quietly, I slipped off my gown, allowing myself to sleep in only my chemise.

"You should sleep like that more often," Ulrich sneered in the dark.

I climbed under the covers quickly, lining the pillows between our bodies.

"Do not touch me," I demanded.

His body shifted toward mine and his voice drew closer. "Fucking someone you hate can be addictive. It fuels the body and your blood with a need for more. The passion, *Ursa*, it's as maddening as faerie wine."

"Then go fuck someone you hate," I replied. "I'm sure there's plenty of people who fit that requirement.

"None as close to me as you."

I shoved against the pillows and my hand connected with a hard muscle. "Unfortunately for you, that's not an option."

"What, will you cut me from *my balls to my head* if I do?"

I froze at his words.

"Olen and I are the closest of friends. We tell each other everything."

"I hate you," I replied.

"He didn't fail to mention the little ink you have on your hip."

My shocked gasp echoed in the room. "What?"

"When he removed your clothing so you wouldn't stink up his bed, he said he found ink on your skin. A little bird on your hip."

"Olen took advantage of me in a vulnerable state and removed my clothing without my permission," I replied.

"Avoiding the conversation like a perfectly trained princess." Ulrich laughed.

I grabbed the pillow under my head and threw it. His shocked grunt filled me with satisfaction.

"A bird," his voice coiled around me. "I would think a bear is more fitting. But a bird... I wonder what that looks like."

"Gods," I groaned, pulling the covers over my head. "Silence yourself," I begged.

"Princess skin is not supposed to be inked. Has no one told you that?"

I sat up, glaring in the dark. "It's my body. I can do whatever I please."

"Show it to me," he replied.

"No!" I yelled.

The pillows just barely below my arm were gone and his body was against mine before I could move.

"I'll show you mine if you show me yours," he whispered.

"Stop it."

"It wouldn't take much for that chemise to rise, *Ursa*. Just a little peek?"

I turned on my side, holding the edges of my chemise between my legs. Glaring at him in the dark, hoping he could see the hate in my eyes.

"I've seen yours," I bit back. "Fitting for you to have monsters on your skin."

He laughed. "You haven't seen *all* of mine. There are some in more *intimate* places."

"Get away from me," I seethed.

His hand brushed my cheek, bringing a startled gasp from me. "Maybe one day."

Then the heat of him was gone and the pillows were back under my arm.

"Again, Ulrich, I would have to go mad to allow that to happen."

"Whatever you say, princess," he laughed.

I pressed the back of my head into the pillow while his breaths slowed. Not able to prevent my mind from wondering what other places he could actually be hiding ink on his skin.

And that one insane part of my mind considered, only briefly, if I really did want to see it all.

Chapter 20

"We'll start at the kitchens," Ulrich stated while I struggled with the small easel strapped around my neck.

The pouch around my waist clattered together with my koal—far more than I ever needed to map out a palace.

"Why the kitchens?" I enquired.

Ulrich smiled at me. "Because they lead *everywhere*. They are the veins of my palace."

"Who uses them?"

Ulrich led the way through the palace, toward the kitchens I had surprisingly not yet visited.

"Myself and my *troll*," he replied. "Olen as well. Those who need to get around quickly."

I pondered his words while we talked, noting down on my parchment the path we took from the library. Down stairs I hadn't known existed just beyond the table I'd come to claim.

The stone staircase spiraled down with small windows providing red light as we descended.

Every few feet a door would appear, jutting off from the stairs but Ulrich ignored each one.

I, however, did not.

I scribbled the stairs and each door we passed, making sure to note the size of each one and the strange markings carved into their surfaces. I wanted to ask what they all meant, where they all led, but somehow I knew I would find out eventually.

Ulrich's cold filled the staircase while we walked, making it hard to take in a full breath. And so, by the time we reached the door he stopped at, I was struggling and huffing loudly.

"Do you need to begin training your body, Brenna?" Ulrich laughed.

I threw him an irritated glance, bending at my waist to catch my breath. "No." I gasped in more air. "I need you to control yourself and not take all the available air."

He laughed then shoved against the door before him.

Scattering echoed just beyond the threshold, and I followed close behind, watching *troll* dip down in respect. My eyes took in the kitchen, marveling at the grey stone and copper pans lined across the wall. The hearth, massive and taking up one wall, had a roaring fire lit with a copper pot hanging on a hook before it.

And the smells—making my tongue salivate instantly.

"These are the kitchens," Ulrich spoke.

"I'm aware," I replied.

A *troll* appeared, slightly taller than the rest, bending at its waist. "Your grace," it said softly, its voice deeper than I had expected for such a small creature. "My people do not make deals."

Ulrich's eyes met mine and he smiled. "Gard, my *wraith* is not here to help me claim a soul."

My blood boiled at the word.

"She is here to map for me. I am showing her the passages."

Gard stood, its red eyes studying mine. "Am I required to allow it to assist in my kitchens?"

Its voice was nearly frantic as it asked its question.

Ulrich laughed. "No, Gard, *she* is assisting me with a personal project. You all can return to your duties. She will not return to your kitchens after today."

Gard nodded its head then dipped away. The noises of the kitchen resumed with spoons clattering against pots and pans and shuffling feet echoing around.

Ulrich snapped his fingers, pointing to his side.

"I am not an animal," I said, standing beside him.

"I'm aware," he winked.

I stared at his eyes through his favored black mask. The green, brighter than usual behind the dark color.

"Why the masks?" I slammed my mouth shut as the question left my lips.

Ulrich smiled. "Why not? It's been a long-standing tradition in the Unseelie Court. One I am not inclined to end for your comfort."

My hand instinctively went to the ribbon around my head and the silver mask resting on the bridge of my nose.

Ulrich turned on his heel, leading the way through the kitchens. When we'd crossed the surprisingly large space, he stopped before four separate doors.

"This one—" He pointed to the left. "That goes directly to the ballroom. A set of stairs going up two stories right to the left-hand corner of the room."

His hand pointed to the door beside it. "This one leads to the *troll* personal quarters, of which I cannot show you yet without Gard's permission."

I stared, unmoving and listening intently.

"Are you not going to record this?" Ulrich asked.

I shook my head, pulled from my intense focus.

"Oh yes," I muttered, pulling up the easel and marking down a few rough sketches with notes beside them.

When I lifted my head once more, Ulrich continued.

"This one—" he pointed to the door on the far-right, "leads straight down to the docks and city street."

"For provisions," I whispered.

"Correct," Ulrich replied. "And this one—" He pointed to the door near the middle. The third-one from the left. "This one holds *all* the secrets."

My pulse picked up while the words left his lips. The chance to explore secret passages in an ancient palace was enough to make my head swim with ecstasy. An experience I'd dreamed of having throughout my long life. A longing I had each time father and I visited Aesir.

"Would you like to go first?" Ulrich asked.

My hands trembled, making the koal in my hand shake against the parchment. "You lead the way," I managed to reply.

Despite how enamored I was with the exploration, I would not place myself in a position that would allow him to be at my back. I wasn't a total fool.

Ulrich nodded with amusement in his eyes, and he pushed the door open, stepping through with his hand waving for me to follow.

I gripped the easel and the koal in my hand as I stepped through then gasped at what I saw.

Before me was indeed a passageway, all lit by bright, unmelting candles but above was a brilliant unending skylight with the moon like a painting above.

"How is this possible?" I asked, spinning in place with my head craned up.

"Excellent builders who knew how to execute my vision," Ulrich replied.

I pulled my eyes from the beauty above me and stared at the king. "How old are you?"

He stopped his steps, turning slowly to meet my eyes.

"There is no number in existence to recount the years I've lived."

"That's impossible," I replied.

Ulrich smiled, stepping back and motioning to his body. "Look at me, Brenna. How old would you say my *body* appears to be?"

My blood rushed through me, and I turned my head. But his shadows had gripped my chin before I could fully cast my gaze away, forcing me to look upon him once more.

"Answer the question," he commanded.

I shoved away the shadows, my fingers going through them eerily. I studied his features. Only I could barely study a single one beside the youth in his hands and body with his beard and mask covering his face.

"Well," I sighed, "if you didn't hide behind that mask, I would be able to tell you."

His smile crept across his lips. "How old is Oberon?"

My mouth opened then closed suddenly. Shock ran through me. I hadn't considered Oberon's age. He was older, that much I knew with the white to his hair and wrinkles at the corners of his eyes, but I hadn't ever stopped to wonder just how old he was.

I rubbed my temples. "I do not know," I admitted.

"You are nearly one-hundred and fifty years old," Ulrich stated. "Your father is, what, eighty years your senior? Perhaps a little more with his fae blood?"

I nodded.

"And your grandmother? Is she half or full fae?"

"She is half," I replied.

"Explain that to me," Ulrich steered the conversation. "That makes your father half-fae as well."

"There is always half-fae blood within my bloodline. My father married a mortal making me still half, but I was expected to marry a full-fae man to continue the half-fae tradition."

"That did not work out."

My stomach dropped and I stared in both rage and shock. "I am aware."

"You wouldn't have outlived him."

"Are you intent on reminding me of my mortality and ticking lifespan, your grace?" I snapped.

Ulrich leaned against the wall. "No. You were the one questioning ages."

"I only wanted to understand how long you've been terrorizing our world, your grace."

"Your world," he winked and shoved away from the wall.

Leaving me to catch up behind him with my tools clanging together as though I were nothing more than a mare saddled with provisions.

"Why do you have no magic?" he asked, staring down at me.

My brow crumpled. "What?"

"Your father has abilities."

"I—" My head shook. "Yes, the water calls to him."

"Not you?" Ulrich stopped his steps.

"No, your *grace*. Nothing. I'm as close to a mere mortal. As defenseless as one as well," I snapped.

"That's unlikely," he replied.

I scowled. "Will you stop your questioning and resume showing me whatever it was you were intent on showing me?"

His grin was wide and he turned back on his heel, continuing his trek down the hall. His hand ran down the stone walls. "When you leave my kitchens, you walk a while before any entrances appear to the rest of the palace."

My hand began to move while he walked, scribbling and noting his words. We stopped every so often while Ulrich allowed me to roughly sketch the long hall. Making sure I was recording the passage as accurately as I could.

We rounded a corner, and I let out a gasp.

We were standing in what appeared to be a foyer with entrances to candle-lit hallways surrounding us.

I stepped to the middle of the room, spinning in place, realizing it was circular.

"This is magnificent," I whispered in amazement.

"I know," Ulrich replied.

I didn't turn to meet his eyes. Not with the beauty before me. It was a labyrinth and a puzzle all at the same time. I counted each passageway, stopping when I'd completed my observation.

"Twelve?" I questioned. "Like..."

"A clock," Ulrich interrupted. "Running a palace is like clockwork. Something you'll learn when you take over from your father."

I dropped my head, unwilling to hear those words when I wasn't sure I would claim my own birthright.

"The building of the palace started here," Ulrich muttered, and I looked up, watching him run his hand around the walls, waving his hand through each open hallway as he passed them. "I had to have a place to access every point of my home if need be. While also having a place to retreat to if a threat came upon it and my people."

My hand stopped noting his words and I lifted a brow.

"There's nothing in our world more dangerous than you."

Ulrich's hand dropped. "I am not the most dangerous being in your world, Brenna. I would advise you not to forget that."

"Impossible," I objected. "No one else in the world terrorizes as you do. I have never in my life seen so much violence and death since arriving here."

"The most dangerous monsters are the ones who lurk in plain sight, undetected, trusted, and knowing," Ulrich replied coldly.

My body shivered at the cold now layering over the circular room. The koal in my hands trembled and I stepped back. Ulrich was tense where he stood, his shoulders heaving and fear coursed through me in response.

Had I awoken that monster that had appeared on the beach once more? Had I unintentionally sparked his hidden rage?

He stood, running his hand through his hair before shaking his head.

"We'll start at twelve," he said as though nothing had happened.

"Twelve?" I questioned.

"On the clock?" his hand rose pointing across the room. "I told you the room is mimicking clockwork. I will take you down this hallway first."

I nodded nervously, adjusting the easel on my neck and quickly marking the room before following behind him.

The hallway was like the other, with candles lining the walls, only there was no skylight. Ulrich followed the winding path, stopping at the first door.

He pushed it open, allowing me to peek into the room.

"A closet," he laughed.

I scoffed, thumping him on the chest as I backed out.

His laugh stopped abruptly, and his head snapped down in my direction. My hand went to my chest in response.

"Sorry," I muttered.

"That was a playful gesture," he said blankly.

I stepped back. "It won't happen again."

His gaze met mine and he blinked then nodded before heading back down the hall. Too stunned to speak, I met his pace, marking the winding turns of the hallway and the lack of additional doors.

We walked for too long, causing me to worry I had truly been a fool to follow him when he stopped, and my face slammed into his back.

The contents of my pouch clattered to the ground and sticks of koal scattered along with the other contents of the pouch.

"Fuck the Gods," I groaned lowering to gather my supplies.

I reached the koal closest to me when his palm wrapped around mine, pulling my eyes away from the floor.

"It's just koal," he said, handing me a handful I hadn't seen him gather.

I nodded, placing it into the pouch before standing.

"I was startled," I whispered.

Ulrich nodded his head, an odd distant stare in his eyes as he turned away from me and shoved on a door I hadn't yet noticed.

"Twelve is my favorite hallway," he said quietly.

"Why?"

"Watch."

Cold air hit me right in the chest as he shoved the door open and then I smelled it—the sea.

The easel and pouch were on the ground before I could consider my next move, and my feet were moving at an unnatural speed.

The sand crunched beneath my shoes, and I kicked them off, gasping at the cold from the winter air. I threw my hands out, spinning under the moonlight, breathing in the smell of home.

"Gods," I cried, placing my hand on my heart. "Oh Gods."

The cries were unstoppable and surprising when I'd gone to the secluded beach just earlier in the day, relishing in my hour of solitude in the water. Only, I hadn't realized another, possibly even more secluded beach was closer to me than the one across the city.

I lowered, sinking my knees into the sand, throwing my mask to the side before I dug fingers as deep as they would go.

"What is this?"

I pulled my eyes to the king, finding him unmoving and staring at me. His body rigid, his hands softly trembling at his side.

"My beach," he muttered.

"I do not understand how your home is built," I replied, laying back into the sand.

"You're going to get filthy," Ulrich said above me.

I closed my eyes, allowing my body to sink into the miniscule fragments. "I do not care."

I wasn't sure how long I laid on the beach. My hands were splayed out above my head and my legs out at the sides, turning my body into the same shape as the creatures lurking deep in the sea lapping at the shores a short distance from me.

Despite being lost in my peace and comfort, I was still aware of the towering body near me. Watching me. Silently.

A predator watching his prey.

Eventually I broke, not able to ignore his presence any longer.

Sand stuck to my dress and hair while I sat up, cocking my head to the side. "Why two private beaches?"

Ulrich's gaze went to the water behind me. "Reminds me of somewhere."

"Where?"

His response was a whisper, too quiet for me to hear. But his shoulders slumped in defeat while his mouth barely moved.

I pulled my knees to my chin, observing the king now lost in his own thoughts and memories. Wondering if perhaps I should leave to allow him privacy.

His body suddenly relaxed, his tight shoulders loosened and he offered me a smile.

"Care for a swim?" he asked.

My neck twisted while I glanced back at the sea. I wanted to, so badly my bones ached, but I did not want to be alone in the water with him. I most definitely did not want to enter the frigid surface with only the winter gown I had on my body.

"I do not have my suit," I replied.

"And?"

I stood, brushing as much sand as I could from my dress and shaking out my hair. "I'll freeze."

"I'll warm you," he replied.

"No." I stepped back toward the open door. "I would rather not."

Ulrich's eyes gleamed under the moonlight. "Perhaps another night?"

I didn't answer. Instead, I continued my retreat back to the palace, picking up my supplies as I went.

The door shut loudly behind me, but I held my head high. Cursing myself for allowing him to walk behind me.

By the grace of the Gods, my scribbles and notes allowed me to reach the foyers of Ulrich's passages but once we'd arrived, I could not understand which way to return.

Ulrich approached by my side, pointing a few hallways down.

"Hallway three leads to the floors with the bedrooms."

"Thank you," I replied, ignoring the sand still falling from my dress as I walked.

"You are welcome to use twelve for your daily swims," he said quietly.

"I do not think that is necessary."

Ulrich grasped my wrist, stopping me in my place. "I would prefer you to stay close, Brenna. Use these passages to my beach."

I pulled away. "No, I will use the tunnel I found on my own to go to a beach far from you."

His eyes widened. "And if I command it?"

"Try and stop me," I challenged.

The same hum that had coiled around us on the beach picked up, lifting my hair. The sound of sand falling filled the space alongside the hum.

"You will use my beach," Ulrich said slowly.

My body buzzed with his words, and I shook my head. "No."

His grin went wide.

A deal.

The words infiltrated my mind, blocking out my thoughts. Then it was gone, as quickly as it came, and I glared at the king.

"No," I repeated.

He blinked at me, taking a step back.

"Fine," he scoffed. "I can't save you should the need arise."

"I only need saving from you, your grace," I bit back.

"Words to regret, *Ursa,*" Ulrich muttered.

Chapter 21

Six months.

One hundred and sixty-eight days.

I was almost half-way through my service. Impossible when I considered the fact. Almost as impossible as my father having not replied to a single letter I'd sent him since my arrangement with Ulrich.

My hands trembled at the desk in the library while I wrote out my hate-filled words. Accusing my own blood of not caring. Begging him to come for me.

My tears hit the ink, making it run down the page and I did not care. I wanted him to see the pain he put my heart through. I wanted him to understand his daughter's growing hatred for his cowardice.

My lips were shaking, my chest heaving when I laid my quill down. The tears blinded my vision, and I jumped when rough fur brushed against the tips of my fingers.

"Princess," Olen's beast voice was soft, softer than I had yet to hear it. "Are you well?"

I wiped my eyes, crying out from the sting of ink. "Fuck!" I cried, picking up the skirt of my dress and dabbing away the pain.

When I'd done my best, I found Olen's black eyes staring at me with his brow crumpled.

"I'm writing to my *father.*" I choked on the word.

"That's quite a lot of tears," Olen said softly.

I pushed him away. “Please leave me be.”

Olen shook his head. “It’s dinner time.”

I threw my head back with frustration. Somehow forgetting my nightly routine with Ulrich. An uncomfortable dinner of silence.

“I can’t,” I admitted, holding my hand to my chest. “I need to rest.”

Olen shook his head. “You made an arrangement with him. He won’t allow that to be broken.”

My eyes went out across the library and the new seating that had been placed in the room in recent weeks.

“I don’t want to eat in a suffocating room, Olen.”

Olen nodded his head and then turned away.

“Go change, princess.”

I stood in the circular room, twisting my hands nervously. Unsure of which pathway to take. I’d only received a note when I’d exited the bathing room. It was placed on top of a long-sleeved sparkling black gown that was not my own.

The clock.

I’d known what it meant instantly, having spent every day for the last month with Ulrich in that room. With him pointing out the hallways.

So far we’d come from hallway six, the kitchens. Gone down hallway twelve, the beach. Also, hallway seven, leading right out to the city. Many times, we went down three, the bedroom hallway. And lastly, hallway two, leading up to the main hall where the front entrance to the palace resided.

I stood in the silent room, waiting for Olen or Ulrich to approach. Unsure of what to expect when a familiar rattling of an ear full of golden earrings came down a hallway.

I turned from where I was staring at twelve, finding Olen leaning against the doorframe of four.

"This way," he said, motioning.

I picked up the heavy gown. My fingers rubbed the velvet fabric together, grateful for the warmth with the temperatures that continued to drop with the winter.

Olen was silent while I followed him, realizing we were walking at an incline in a perfectly spiraled walkway.

The candles lit the way and the higher we climbed, the colder it became.

I was close to cursing myself for not bringing my cloak when Olen stopped and pointed to a wall beside him. I turned my head, finding cloaks hanging on hooks and fur-lined hand covers on a shelf beside them.

"What is this?" I asked, wrapping the cloak around me and placing the hood on my head.

Olen was silent while he did the same. Irritating me instantly.

He turned, continuing our trek upward. My hands wrung against each other in the cover while I bit back my questions.

My feet ached and I was close to curses once more when Olen stopped again, shoving open a towering stone door.

"Enjoy dinner, princess." He grinned with a maniacal glimmer in his eyes as his hands connected with my shoulders and he pushed me out the door, slamming it loudly behind me.

I pulled one hand out of the warmth of the fur, turning on my heel while my fists hit the barrier, sure he had just tricked me when a voice cleared behind me.

I twisted back and gasped, dropping my cover into the brilliant snow on the ground.

It was hard to take it all in. The light from the stars, illuminating the cobbled path lined with snow. The table a distance away with candles lit. The fire behind it, roaring and so full of heat I could feel its call from where I stood.

But most shocking of it all was the king standing before the table with a fur-lined cloak over his shoulder.

"I—"

I was speechless. I was terrified.

I was absolutely enamored.

And I was livid.

My shocked yell echoed around us, moving with the wind that had caught it when Ulrich suddenly dipped his head.

A royal acknowledgement of who I was.

I stepped back, my hands searching for the handle of the door I'd been shoved through.

"Brenna," Ulrich said softly.

"No." I shook my head in disbelief. "I am not doing this."

Ulrich approached and I picked up my backward retreat. "No." I cried. "No."

We will eat under the stars, my Enaid. Just the two of us. Allowing the Gods to wash us with their approval of our love.

Leif's words, even if they had been feigned, ran through my mind. The letter that had meant the most out of all that he'd sent me. The one when he'd asked *me* for my hand. When he'd proclaimed his intention for only my eyes to see.

My back hit the stone door while my tears fell, but I could not find a handle and the monster before me continued his approach.

I glanced at the ground, finding the cover, and I threw with all my might. It hit him in the face as I intended, and my scream made even my own ears ring.

"I hate you!" I sobbed while I sank to the ground, using the door to guide me. "I hate you!"

Ulrich threw the cover at my feet, forcing my eyes to meet his.

"It's only dinner," he replied.

"You *knew*. You knew what he wrote. You guided it all. You are mocking me."

My tears grew cold on my cheeks while my cries continued.

"I can't—" My chest tightened and my eyes widened. My heart pulsed quickly, and I was sure I was going to die.

Panicked, I slammed my hands against the cold ground. I couldn't catch the breath my lungs desperately needed. I couldn't clear my mind from the overwhelming thoughts and hate taking control.

Ulrich was before me, grasping my face tightly.

I met his eyes, finding his mouth moving but I couldn't hear a word. I could only hear the blood in my veins, pulsing frantically inside of me. About to explode from the pressure in my chest.

My tears fell faster, and I turned my head out of Ulrich's touch, wanting the demon's hands to remove his hold on my skin. But I didn't have the strength, and my vision blurred while my hands continued to hit the earth in a panic.

I was going to die. Yes, I was sure I was going to die from the inability to find the air my lungs were searching for. I stared at Ulrich, tears running down my cheeks while my panic grew.

Then he slapped me—right across the face.

I gasped from the shock as air barreled down my throat. My vision cleared, and the ringing ceased in my ears.

"Breathe!" Ulrich was shouting, shaking my shoulders.

I shoved him away then leaned my head against the door. "Keep your hands off me."

He stood, brushing the snow from his pants. "I will not have tantrums," he said coldly.

I glared at him. "You are mocking me."

"Get off the ground, Brenna."

"No."

His body crouched and he met my eyes. "Do as I say."

"No," I repeated.

"Fine. Starve for all I care."

His cloak whipped me in the face when he turned on his heel and sauntered to the table.

My back pressed further into the door behind me while I begged it to give way and allow me back to the palace.

Ulrich pulled out his chair, flipping his coat in a show of triumph behind him while he sat, picking up a cup steaming in the cold air.

"This fire feels fantastic," he yelled over the wind, sipping from his silver mug.

I scowled and picked up my cover, placing my hands into it for warmth.

Ulrich set his drink down and opened the tray before him. I could not see the meal but the steam blocked his masked face and the smell—it instantly hit my nose.

"Gods dammit," I muttered, knocking my head back against the door.

To my surprise, it sprang open, and Olen's head popped out. "Just go eat, princess," he laughed.

I scrambled to my feet, trying to get my body through the threshold but Olen slammed it back in my face. Almost hitting my nose in the process.

I screamed, throwing the cover back onto the ground. I turned on my heel, heading right for my target.

My finger was raised, shaking in his direction while I readied my words of war. When I arrived right before him he smiled at me, unphased and emotionless.

"Hungry?" he asked, pointing to the covered plate on the other end of the table.

"I hate you," I whispered.

"You really enjoy repeating that," he sighed and picked up his cup. "It's as though you believe I don't know this fact."

"I wouldn't want you to ever forget it in your old age, your grace," I replied.

He snorted and his dark drink splattered over his plate.

Relishing in my victory, I turned on my heel and placed myself in the chair across from him. Crossing my legs while I sipped from my own mug. Finding a delicious, mulled wine with slices of citrus floating on the top.

Ulrich patted the surface before him with a napkin and shook his head.

"About that court jester."

"I have a knife," I interrupted.

His hand stopped and he glanced up. "I have a pulse." He cocked his head, pointing to his neck. "Want to give it a try? You did fail last time."

I continued sipping on my drink, allowing the wine to warm the inside of my body while the fire warmed the outside.

I hated how beautiful this place was, with the bright stars glittering above us and the red moon muted on the other side of the sky.

Ulrich's utensils scraped across his plate, but I did not lift my tray. Instead, I finished my wine and reached for the silver flute in the middle of the table. He grinned at me while I leaned back, continuing to watch as he ate his meal.

"How's your drink?" he asked, slowly placing his fork on his tongue.

"I wish it were faerie wine," I grumbled.

His hand thumped the table, startling me. "That is *poison.*"

"It's a drink," I countered with a scowl.

"It alters every one of your senses. Leaving you defenseless and at the whim of others."

"Personal experience?" I asked with a laugh, not expecting the snarl that ripped from his throat.

"I suggest you hold your tongue, Brenna."

I blinked and set my cup down. "How is faerie wine any worse than this?" I lifted my drink again. "Give me a few more glasses, and I am just as likely to remove my dress and roll in the snow nude."

Ulrich's grin was mocking and hungry.

I hated it.

"I could certainly call for more if you feel so inclined to give me that show," he taunted.

I shoved away from the table, wrapping my hands around the mug, attempting to heat my cold fingers. As I approached the fire, I allowed its warmth to work while I gazed at the stars once more.

They sparkled, magically and so much brighter than I had seen them before.

"They are magnificent," Ulrich said beside me.

I chose to ignore his successful, silent approach.

"Some say the Gods themselves shape the stars and planets above. I say it's Fate."

"There is no such thing as fate," I replied.

"Fate controls all, Brenna. Even me."

I turned to watch him admiring the sky. His eyes searched. For what? I wasn't sure. But it was a look I didn't recognize in the green. A hope and desperation, scanning the vast star-scape above.

"Where are we?" I asked.

Ulrich glanced at me. "On top of the mountain."

I gasped and observed our surroundings. The trees, covered in snow. The rocky grey ground, also covered in the powder. I stepped forward, stretching my neck to find the light of the city far below.

"How on earth did we get up here so quickly?" I wondered aloud.

"An old trick a friend once taught me," Ulrich replied, motioning back to the table.

The chill picked up around me and I pulled the cloak against my face. "When is your winter festival?"

Ulrich paused his retreating steps. "Two weeks."

"What happens?"

My mind went to home. The fires and the singing in the town circle. The feast where everyone would gather in our large hall, warming the space to a suffocating heat.

The ball. Not anywhere near as grand as the parties Ulrich threw. But full of joy and laughter. Full of carefree fun.

"Things happen at the Winter Rite," Ulrich said bluntly.

"*Things?* What in the Gods does that mean?"

Ulrich's hand thumped the table. "Why does it matter, Brenna?"

"Because I'm trying to learn about this stupid fucking city," I yelled. "Is there anything I can look forward to? Anything your people do that brings joy to this cycle of death and debauchery?"

"You are not to attend the Winter Rite," Ulrich replied.

"Rite? What does that mean?"

Ulrich's hand hit the table again and the contents of his plate splattered across his black shirt. "You are not to attend the Winter Rite!" he yelled. "Do I always have to repeat myself with you?"

I shrank back, tears lining my eyes. "I'm not a child."

His shadows grabbed my wrists, pulling me toward him. He stared up at me from his seat.

"I have lived millennia, Brenna. You have lived barely over a century. You are a child. An insignificant infant refusing to behave."

I tugged against his power on me, my tears falling once more.

"Did you like my setting tonight? Leif did have a rather active imagination."

My lip trembled at the callus way he spoke. "Stop."

Ulrich's shadows held me tighter. "I rather admired the suggestion to eat under the stars. I must admit I've never done this with anyone before."

"Why must you always make everything vile?" I sobbed.

He stood, throwing his chair toward a tree. The crack of it splintered from the force, echoing around us.

"I'm a monster," he breathed out. "When will you accept that?"

"I have accepted it," I replied.

"No, I do not think you have."

He dropped his hold on me and the door across the path swung open. Olen stepped out, eyes widening at the food across the table and the destroyed chair in the distance.

"My king," he whispered, dropping his head with a bow.

"We're done. Escort her back to the bedroom," Ulrich replied.

Olen nodded, reaching for me but I pulled away. "I know the way."

"I would expect nothing less," Ulrich snapped as I passed him.

When I reached the hook for the cloaks, I refused to hang mine back up. I kept walking, allowing my hate to fuel my descent, until I'd reached the clock room. I turned toward three, running up the stairs with all my might.

When I reached the great hall, I pumped my legs, running not for Ulrich's bedroom, but the one I'd briefly been given weeks before.

Olen let out a shout behind me, but I kept running until I found the bedroom. I slammed the door open as I rushed to the fire I had somehow known would be waiting for me.

Then I stripped. Ripping my cloak from my body, throwing it and the cover into the flames.

Burning it all to ashes.

Watching it catch flame with my hate.

Olen caught me right as I pulled the dress from my body and threw it into the fire. He yelled out his shock.

"Princess! What the fuck?"

I held up my hand, silencing him.

I watched those flames, with the shimmer of the dress I now realized glistened like starlight catching fire and filling the room with its smoke.

Chapter 22

Ulrich was silent while I sat in the middle of the clock room, meticulously drawing the skylight above and the hallways circling around me.

We'd barely spoken in the days since that ill-fated dinner on the top of the mountain. Our daily meals were silent, the bed quiet and cold each night. Exactly how I preferred it.

His feet shuffled loudly, and I glanced up, finding him watching me.

"Yes?" I asked, rolling my eyes.

"Are you finished?" he replied.

With a sigh, I set my parchment down and held his gaze. "*You* requested that I map these passages. Do you want them to be accurate or rough sketches?"

"Does it have to take so long?"

I admired the room and my hand ran against the stone floor beneath me.

"Your stone has markings," I said absent-mindedly.

"What?

I pulled my eyes to my hand, drawing the tip of my finger across the marking. A line down, then one at the bottom jutting upwards, with another jutting down. Then at the top of the line, two similar lines as the bottom going opposite directions.

"What does it mean?" I asked, noting the floor covered in the barely visible marking.

Urich stared at my hand drawing against the stone.

"Nothing that concerns you."

"Why won't you let me go down that hallway?" I asked, pointing to hallway nine.

Ulrich's body went rigid, and his hands landed at his side while he blocked the hallway from my view.

"So full of questions today," he replied.

"And you're lacking answers."

A thump from the music several stories above us rattled the walls of the circular room and Ulrich smiled.

"All done."

"I am not," I protested.

Ulrich leaned down, ripping my easel from my hands. "I said you're done."

He walked away, my supplies bumping against his back and I glared. My head turned back to the hallway he'd still refused to show me, and then I stood.

"I need entertainment tonight," Ulrich called over his shoulder. "You're to join my side."

"I'd rather not," I yelled and he whipped around, his eyes wide when he found me at the threshold of the ninth hallway.

"Brenna," he warned.

"Ulrich," I challenged.

"Do not—"

I didn't let him finish his warning before I'd turned my body and ran down the hall. The candles around me went from brilliant warm light to an unsettling red the further I ran. Like an omen, warning me to turn back.

Only I refused to heed the warning, and I continued down my path, rounding the corner while the hallway became more narrow.

My body slammed into the wall and Ulrich's hair brushed against my neck.

"What are you doing?" he demanded.

I struggled against his hold on my arms that pinned me to the wall. "I just want answers!"

"Not here," he snapped.

I stared into his masked eyes, my chest heaving with my breaths. "Why?"

"Brenna, enough."

His hands released me while he walked away. I stared at him, insulted he believed I would follow him back so willingly.

A pull from the darker end of the hall wrapped around my body. It was quiet. A whisper. A warning.

I ran to it again, ignoring his shout of irritation.

His cold bit at my heels but he did not grasp for me. As though he were allowing me to see a glimpse of the mystery.

The candles went bright red when my running stopped, and I stood before a wooden door the color of blood. My fingers trailed the wood, tracing the grotesque carving on its surface.

It was a face, and based on the carved lines of hair, I assumed it was a woman. Only half of this face was carved in, while the other half appeared skeletal—corpse-like. And tears fell from the corpse side, dark red of the wood carved to mimic lament.

Ulrich's cold was wrapping around me, and I turned to face him. "What is this?"

He was utterly silent with his shadows crawling around his body like a blanket of protection.

"Get upstairs," he muttered.

I didn't protest when his hand wrapped around my wrist, pulling me away from the door. My feet stumbled while I kept my gaze on the entrance with the strange carving. Wondering what it was. What it meant.

Why Ulrich appeared terrified of it.

We made it to the circular room and he picked up my tools without addressing me. He grasped my wrist again, guiding me through hallway three and up the stairs to the bedroom.

My chest was frantic by the time he threw his bedroom door open, tossing my things to the side.

"You don't listen," he whispered. "You do not listen."

He led me to the bed then knelt before me, shocking and terrifying me all at the same time.

"You cannot go back to that hallway, do you understand?" he asked.

I blinked at him.

"Brenna?" he snapped his fingers in my face.

"You are kneeling before me," I muttered.

He glanced down, then met my eyes. "Yes, Brenna, I am. The Unseelie King is on his knees, asking you to do as he says. Can you do that?"

My hands trembled on the bed. "Where does that door lead?"

Ulrich stood, lifting his hands with frustration. "Fate fuck it all! Are you not listening?"

"You don't listen to me!" I yelled back. "You have yet to hear a single thing I've said."

His hands gripped my face, pulling me toward him. "Tell me then, *Ursa*. What have I not *heard?*"

The green eyes behind his silver mask were alive with a burn behind them as he stared at me. He shook my head softly, his hands on my face tightening but not painful.

"Tell me. Tell me and I will hear," he whispered.

His breathing was slow, as slow as my own then I blinked myself back to reality.

"Unhand me," I demanded.

He stood, releasing my face and taking a step away.

"Stop putting your hands on me."

He nodded once.

"Stop jesting that you will use *my* body to *your* pleasure."

Another nod.

My feet were moving me upward and I approached him, one finger raised and pointed in his face. "Never, and I mean *never,* call me a whore again."

Ulrich's blank expression broke with a slight smile while I waved my finger. But he nodded once more.

"Take off your mask," I said.

His smile dropped and he stepped back. "That I cannot do."

I let out a huff, turning back to the bed. "It was worth a try."

The room went quiet, and I gazed around the space.

"Why do you have three separate entrances to your room? I would assume that to be a risk for the king."

"Who's going to try and kill the Unseelie King?" He met my eyes and grinned. "Other than a foolish half-fae woman?"

I dropped my eyes.

"Tell me something about yourself, Brenna," he said, sitting beside me. "We spend so much time in each other's company either fighting or in silence."

I shifted away from him. "I do not have much to tell."

"Why the bird?"

My cheeks warmed. "Men always want to talk about one topic and one topic only."

"I'm not asking because I want to see. I'm asking because it appears to mean something to you."

I turned to him, staring into his eyes. "What do yours mean?"

He was standing suddenly, pulling his shirt from his body. My breath stopped while I watched the fabric fall to the floor and he bared his torso to me.

I rose to my feet, hands trembling while he motioned for me to come toward him. His shoulders rose slowly with his breaths while I circled him.

The beasts—they did not meet in the middle in the way I had originally assumed. No, one had the neck of the other in its throat, but there was no inking of blood or gore. Neither creature appeared in conflict, at least not angry with one another. Instead, their eyes were so full of sorrow it made my heart ache.

I continued circling, finding the beasts' two different sizes on his back. One slightly larger than the other. Surprisingly, the smaller one was the one holding the other in the death bite.

I followed where the limbs wrapped around the front of him and the tails, twisting from his back, over the bodies, down the edges of the shoulders and coiling down his forearms.

I studied the markings.

Running up the tails were miniscule symbols, reminding me of the ones carved into the stone in the clock room.

I appeared before him again and jumped when his hand grasped my wrist, placing my palm against his chest.

"What are they?" I asked, tracing the tear-lined eyes of the one whose mouth grasped the neck of the other.

"There is no word in the fae language for them," his voice whispered above me.

"What are they?" I repeated.

"*Dreki,*" he muttered, stopping my hand from tracing the ink any further.

My eyes snapped up to his, finding that same burn from before. I opened my mouth but he shook his head.

"These symbols?"

"Death, Fate, Freedom, Friendship, and Battle," he muttered, staring into my eyes.

"What?"

"No more questions," he replied, removing my hand from his chest.

I stepped away. Then a creature, a foolish, wild creature, took control of me. I made my retreat, keeping my eyes on the king until my knees hit the edge of the bed.

I was sure he'd stopped his breaths when I pulled at the hem of my gown and slid it over my head. Leaving me in only my thin chemise.

I motioned to him, as he had to me while I laid back on the bed, lifting my thin skirt, revealing everything most intimate.

He was before me in an instant, dropping to his knees as I bared myself to him, revealing the ink on my skin.

His eyes didn't once venture below my hip while his fingers traced my smallest, most insignificant secret.

"A bluebird," he whispered.

I jumped at his touch, my body shaking with fear while my mind cursed me for allowing myself to be so vulnerable in his presence.

"You asked me what it meant to me," I whispered, my voice shaking while his finger continued to trace the outline of the ink.

"Yes," he muttered.

"Freedom, hope, peace, and love." My tears fell while I voiced my own list. "A chance to be who *I* want to be."

"Why hide it?"

His hand pulled away and my breath loosened in my chest.

I sat up, pulling my chemise back down.

"Because I'm destined to be a queen, Ulrich. I'm a princess of an island the majority of our world believes should not exist. My blood is *tainted*, unclean, and unwanted. I cannot have a marking on my skin that anyone can see."

"Do you wish to be a queen?"

His question was an attack on my soul, digging into my darkest secrets. I pulled my knees to my chin, refusing to meet his eyes.

"I want to be myself. Whether that ends in my queenhood, or me doing whatever it is the Gods have planned for me."

"What about Fate?" he asked.

I laughed and shook my head. "There you are with that word again. *Fate*. What does that mean to you?"

The king let out a breath. "Everything, Brenna. It means everything."

My words stuck in my throat as the lights in the room went out and a clatter sounded on the bedside table. The sound I'd come to recognize as him removing his mask in the dark.

"What are you doing?" I questioned.

"I'm going to sleep. Would you like to join me?" he replied.

The bed shifted with his weight and the comforter lifted beneath me. My body shook while I contemplated what had just happened between the two of us.

I turned back, hoping to see an outline of his features in the dark.

"You cannot look upon my face," he whispered.

"Nearly six and a half months, your grace," I replied.

"Until what?" he laughed.

I climbed up the bed, finding his bare torso while I ran my fingers where I believed his *Dreki* to be.

"Until I'm going to force you to remove that mask."

His hand laid against mine, flattening my palm to his chest.

"Perhaps Fate will allow such a thing," he whispered.

I pulled my hand back, laying against the pillows.

"Whatever or whomever Fate is, I wonder if perhaps you are right," I replied.

Then the strangest thing in the months since I'd been in his bed occurred—I fell asleep, peacefully. With the giant hand of the Unseelie King wrapped around my own.

Chapter 23

Six and a half months.

One hundred and eighty-two days.

The day of the Winter Rite.

I stared in the bathing room mirror while Adie combed my wet hair. The young girl chattered about some boy down at the docks who her uncle disapproved of. A scandal given her family's standing beside the king.

I told her I loved a good scandal and listened contently while she recounted her forbidden romance.

The bedroom door slammed open, startling us both.

Ulrich appeared with his menacing presence layering over us. I startled in my chair at the mask fitted across his face. Another death mask made of bones, but this one was also horned like his others. The object terrifying, painting the king like the beast he was to fear.

"Your grace," Adie whispered, ducking her chin down before she scurried out of the room.

"You just interrupted a rather entertaining conversation," I said coldly.

I kept my eyes on him while I returned to the mirror, running the comb through my hair myself while he leaned against the door frame.

"Why are you readying yourself?" he asked.

I twisted around. "For the Winter Rite?"

He grinned. "You are not attending that. Do you not remember?"

"That's not fair," I countered. "We've been getting along for the last week. Why would you deny me some fun?"

The stool by the tub clattered before me. The sound echoed across the room.

"You will not attend the Rite. Do you understand?"

I glared at him, sitting back in my seat while I crossed my arms over my chest.

"Tell me why."

"I'm not required to. I am the king," he replied, standing.

I stared up at him, my eyes tracking the velvet black suit cut tight against his body.

"What am I supposed to do while the rest of you enjoy your evening?"

Ulrich glanced around the room. "You're supposed to stay here and not move. I'll have *troll* bring you dinner and some of that mulled wine you enjoyed."

I scoffed at the wink he gave as he sauntered out of the room.

I followed him. "Wait!" I called out as he reached the bedroom door.

He turned around with a smile.

Gods, I'm a fool.

I dropped the towel around my body, exposing myself to him.

He blinked then his smile grew wide. "If I knew all I had to do was ban you from a party to have you offer yourself so brazenly, I would have done it *months* ago."

Regret settled over me and I bent down, reaching for the towel. Only he got to it first and held it before my face, waving it mockingly.

"My Brenna," he put emphasis on my name, "there was much more hidden behind those undergarments than I'd realized."

I covered myself with my arms and scowled. "Give me that towel."

He flipped it over his shoulder. "Promise you won't attend the Rite."

"That's not a fair bargain," I protested.

His eyes tracked up and down my body. "I would agree. I'm certainly receiving the better end of this agreement."

"Ulrich!" I shouted.

He laughed. "I did not force you to bare your body to me. Yet you're shouting at me as though I were Lokii's trickster determined to best you."

His free hand reached around me, hovering just over my skin, but not touching me. "It is tempting, though," he whispered. "To lock this door and stay in this room with you knowing you are so willing."

I gulped. "I am not willing."

"So, you are a tease?" he taunted.

"Do not," I warned.

"I did not use that *word.* You are now the one implying it," he replied.

The towel hit my face, blocking my vision while the sound of his footsteps retreated.

"Ulrich!" I yelled after him, wrapping the fabric around my body once more. I had almost reached him when the door slammed in my face.

"Enjoy an evening of solitude!" he yelled from the other side.

I gripped the towel, rushing to the hidden door, only to find it also locked. As well as the third exit down to the docks.

I sank onto the bed, cursing his jests and taunting while the music began to thump throughout the palace. Different though, wilder and heavier than it had been so far. More alluring, igniting a need inside of my body.

The hidden door opened, and I jumped to my feet when Adie appeared, pushing a cart of food.

"Your highness," she whispered, closing the door behind her.

"Let me out, Adie," I ordered.

The girl glanced back at the door nervously. "I cannot, your highness."

I stood before her. "What happens at this Rite?"

She gulped.

"Adie?"

"I cannot, your highness."

"If I eat this meal and drink that wine? Will you tell me?"

Adie glanced at the door again with apprehension. "Your highness."

"Adie, your boy? Is he at the Rite?"

The handmaid met my eyes.

"Did you want to spend this festival with him?" I asked.

She nodded.

"Help me dress, Adie. Help me fix my hair and tie a mask upon my head and you can slip out to him. You can tell everyone I beat the keys from your hands. I'm sure the court wouldn't question that story."

Adie looked back at the door then met my eyes again. "You're going to have to hit me as hard as you can."

Startled, I stepped back before letting out a nervous chuckle. "What?"

"My uncle is right hand to the king, your highness. I have been trained to fight. It has to be believable that I was unable to fight off a partially mortal woman."

"Adie?" I questioned. "Why?"

She shrugged. "You're kept in the dark, your highness. I believe you should be allowed to see the light every once in a while."

"Will he hurt you?"

Adie grinned. "*Uncle* Ulrich would never harm a hair on my head. I believe he'd rather sink himself into the bottom of the sea before doing so."

I quelled the hate in my heart responding to her words. Not one ounce of me believed Ulrich was fully capable of gentle love. Of caring so deeply for someone that they would never meet his wrath.

Then a darker, more cynically insane part of my heart wondered if I were possibly jealous of this statement. If I perhaps wanted to see this side of the monster that had tormented me for months.

Even with just a week of light-hearted conversation, I was still weary of him. Not accepting our brief moment of vulnerability was enough to unlock this hidden kindness Adie spoke of.

Silently, Adie and I worked together. Her hands moved at an unnatural speed, twisting my red hair into a half-bun with loose ringlets running down my back. Sshe covered my eyes in dark koal and an even darker lipstick. The color of the red moon.

When she'd completed painting me like her own personal canvas, I stared in the mirror. I was like a Goddess. An image of a being representing the moon of her blood.

I stood quickly, rushing to the closet, knowing just what to put on my body.

When I returned, Adie cocked her head then yelled out when I began ripping the inner layer of the dress.

"Your highness!"

I smiled. "Adie, this is what I want to wear. Do not question me."

Adie stepped back, nodding her head with a mischievous smile similar to my own. Then she helped me slip from my towel and slide the gown over my head.

I stared in the mirror, my eyes going to the sheer red gown draped over my body. It was striking with the color of my lips and hair. Making me the blood moon personified. Appearing to drip in the substance. The only object on my body that was not red was the black mask Adie had tied behind my hair.

"Gods this is perfect for the Rite," Adie whispered.

My hands ran over the gown and my curves, softly brushing against my skin just beneath the fabric.

"He's going to kill you," Adie muttered.

I did not look at her. Not when my body was on full display. The red gown I had been forced to wear my first night here now turned into a gown more suited for Ulrich's court.

A gown of sensual need.

With only a thin band across my hips after I'd ripped out the majority of the inner lining, it exposed nearly every surface of my bare skin. My breasts were now the most focal point of the gown, with the cowl neck accentuating the curves and the fabric doing nothing to cover my nipples.

"He can't kill me," I muttered. "I have not broken our deal."

Adie shook her head. "He'll kill anyone who may put their hands on you tonight."

I turned to meet her eyes. "What is this Rite? My winter festivals at home are a family affair."

"Your highness," Adie laughed. "This Rite is to bring in a new year. It is full of carnal pleasure, of indulging, of allowing our most basic needs and desires to take control."

"So, I am dressed the part?"

"Yes, your highness, very much so."

I twisted back to the mirror. "Perfect."

Adie cleared her throat, pulling my eyes away from my reflection. "Do not mark me too severely. I do want to allure my *boy*, not scare him."

"I'm sorry, Adie," I whispered.

"Oh, it's been an honor, your highness," she replied.

She held her chin high while I lifted my arm, reeling back my elbow. My fist collided with her jaw, throwing her backward. She stumbled, not making a sound but her eyes were full of mischief and delight when she straightened.

Her hand went into the pocket of her gown and keys rattled in her grasp.

"These keys will reveal the doors you cannot see in that hallway. The third key opens the hallway to the throne room. It is a few minutes' trek to get there," she instructed.

"Will the keys reveal all of the doors?"

She shook her head, rubbing her bruising jaw. "Just hold the third key and the magic will do its job."

I nodded, heading toward the hidden door.

"Your highness?" Adie called after me.

"Yes?"

Adie offered me a wide grin. "Have fun."

I did not process her disappearing through the main door to the bedroom. But suddenly she was gone, and I was alone in the room, my trembling hands holding the keys.

Light appeared behind the hidden door and I gulped down my nerves.

I could do this. I could confidently walk into that ballroom and participate in whatever festival it was that Ulrich was hosting.

My terms did not require me to obey and sit idly while the rest of the palace enjoyed themselves.

I gripped the third key and opened the hidden door, eyes scanning the hallway. Nothing happened and I stared at the keys, rattling them with frustration. The movement appeared to be what was required when a creaking sound caught my attention and I watched a wooden threshold appear a few steps away.

I glanced back at the bedroom nervously. There was the chance Ulrich would kill me for disobeying. Possibly even the chance he'd publicly humiliate me again.

But igniting his rage was worth more than the fear.

I unlocked the door that had appeared, pushing it open as quietly as I could before leaving the keychain behind. As there was nowhere on my body I could carry them.

The walls thumped with the blaring music of the party a floor below and I held my skirts in my hand. The cold in the hallway wrapped around my body and perked the piques of my breasts without my permission.

When I reached a set of descending stairs, I twisted my body back to the hallway. It would have been easy to return to the room, wash my face, and crawl into bed as though I had made no plan. Gods, there was even the chance that Ulrich would become wrapped up in his own carnal desires and I would get the bed alone.

The music coiled up the stairs, inviting me to take part and I turned toward it. The beat was welcoming, sensual, clawing at my skin. Creating a buzz throughout my body as though I had little control to follow.

I walked to it, my hands running along the dark hidden passage. The thump of the beat grew stronger the closer I came. I could hear it—screams, moans, and laughter.

So much louder than any other evening I'd heard in this palace.

And the current in the air? Gods, it was intoxicating.

My hand brushed against a circled pull, and I stared down. I made it. I had bravely made my descent and Ulrich's *Rite* was just beyond this threshold.

Before I could second-guess myself, I pushed the door open. The music came at me with force, hitting me in the chest with its strength.

When I stepped through, I realized Adie had directed me to a passageway that did not open to the dais. No—this opened in the corner of the room. Hidden in the shadows.

My pulse calmed at her unspoken kindness.

No heads turned my way when I closed the door quietly and slipped into the room. Likely due to where I'd arrived and the utter lack of people around me.

A voice cleared near my knees and I glanced down, finding the *troll* from the kitchen—Gard.

"Princess," his rough voice spoke.

"Gard." I nodded my head.

The creature's eyes scanned my body and it grinned. "I see we should anticipate a show this Rite."

I scowled. "Is that a problem?"

Gard turned its head and I followed their gaze, finding Ulrich sitting atop his throne. His horned mask of death was fitted tightly across his face while his eyes scanned the room. Olen stood at his side, unmoving with his hands behind his back but his body was bent as though he were addressing his king quietly.

"His grace will not be thrilled," Gard sang. "Oh my. Oh my. He will not be thrilled."

I lowered myself, meeting the creature's eyes. "Will you get in the way?"

Gard smiled at me, its dark teeth sharp and jagged. "My *princess,* absolutely not. This palace has needed a proper Rite for centuries."

I stared after Gard while it scurried away, opening a smaller door near the one I'd appeared through. My gaze went back to Ulrich.

His hands thrummed the arm of his throne while his crossed leg gave him an appearance of boredom and distaste.

While my ears were barely becoming used to the sounds of people lost in ecstasy, I could not decipher how this celebration was different from any other night. Yes, the music had that addictive beat to it, a noise that rattled my soul and bones. But there was laughter, food splayed across countless tables, and more wine than I'd ever seen in my life.

The only difference was the roaring fire in the middle of the room. Warming the space to a suffocating heat.

My hands wrung the skirts of my sheer gown, and I held my shoulders tight while I stepped out from the shadows.

At first, no one batted an eye at me. I was as invisible as I felt in Ulrich's court. The whispers started.

Wraith.

Whore.

Harbinger.

Fingers pointed at me while hungry eyes licked up my body. But their mutters were still too quiet for the king to notice. Not one whisper grew louder than my ears to pick up.

I made my way through the ballroom, my eyes watching the king. Hoping he'd find me in the crowd. Wanting to see the rage light in his eyes at my disobedience.

I ignored the whispers while I slinked through the bodies like a serpent. A hand gripped my wrist, and I gasped, meeting the eyes of the man who had threatened me by the palace entrance weeks before.

Bjorn grinned at me with desire.

"Ulrich let his pet out," he taunted.

I could not respond when the beat of the music was suddenly silent and a cold presence stood at my back.

"What the fuck are you doing?" Ulrich sneered above me.

Chapter 24

Scowling at the fae that had grasped me, I turned my attention to the king, offering him a sweet and tempting smile.

"I am enjoying your festivities, your grace."

Ulrich's eyes widened when my body was before him. His gaze went right to my barely covered breasts.

"Go back to the room. Now," he ordered.

I glared. "No, your grace."

"Who let you out?"

"I did."

Ulrich stepped back and his fists balled at his side. His rage was evident, but I had become aware enough to know he was considering his next steps before his court.

"Your grace," Bjorn hissed. "Each member of your court and home are required to participate in the Rite. Do not tell me you were to give this mortal leniency?"

"She is a half-fae princess, Bjorn. Address her as such," Ulrich growled.

Bjorn smiled a wicked grin. "She's dressed for the Rite. I'll give her that much."

Ulrich snapped his fingers and the man before us went still.

"Return to your fantasies, Bjorn. The Rite will begin shortly."

The man turned on his heel, glaring at me while he left.

Ulrich returned his attention to me. "What are you wearing?"

"Don't recognize it?" I spun in my place. "You gifted it to me."

A low whistle came from behind Ulrich, and I stepped to the side, finding Olen with a bright grin on his face.

The right hand was dressed in a dark gray suit, cut to his body in the same way as Ulrich's. Accentuating every muscle on the towering man's body.

"Princess," he whistled again. "Gods."

Ulrich's head turned to his right hand. "You keep an eye on her."

Olen nodded, reaching for me, but I stepped back.

"I want to enjoy myself," I stated. "You will both leave me be."

"*Ursa*," Ulrich warned. "Not tonight."

The music picked up again and I placed my hand on the king's chest. Right where I knew his ink hid beneath his dark shirt. I circled him, my fingers tapping his dress coat.

"It's been nearly four years," I whispered. "I am a woman with needs."

The king was unmoving while I continued my circling. His right hand was as equally unmoving a few steps away.

"This is not the day," Ulrich growled.

"I say it is," I bit back, pulling my hand against my chest.

My hips moved with the music, and I turned my attention to Olen, trailing my fingers across his arm. In the same teasing motions I'd done to Ulrich's chest.

"Princess," Olen whispered. "Do not test him."

"Dance with me, *beast*."

Olen's eyes moved from mine. I raised my hand, brushing his sharp jaw, softly caressing the edge of his mask.

"Do not look at him," I muttered.

Ulrich's cold ran a chill up my back. "Keep an eye on her," he said again, leaving me in the arms of his right hand.

I grinned at Olen, puffing out my chest. Hoping the man would stare in the way I wanted him to. Instead, he gripped my hand and dragged me back to the shadows I'd come from.

"What are you thinking?" he whispered, shaking my shoulders.

I shoved him away.

"I'm thinking I'm not bound to obey every single thing Ulrich tells me to do." I stepped away, observing the party resuming in the light of the blood moon. "What is so different about this festival that Ulrich banned me from attending? Other than the naked bodies, very little is different from my island's winter celebrations."

Olen blocked my view of the grand room. "Princess, you are so foolishly wrong in your observations, but it's too late now. Bjorn has made his public challenge."

"Who is he?" I asked, finding the tall and slender man slinking around the room, his eyes meeting mine.

"Someone you do not want to find yourself alone with," Olen sneered.

Olen held out his palm, and I met his gaze.

"You've already made an entrance, but do you care to make another?"

I smiled at him. "Please."

He guided me back to the middle of the room while the whispers picked up again. Starved eyes tracked my steps. Tongues lapped at their lips.

I was the visual meal in a room full of starving monsters.

Olen spun me in place and my sheer gown spun around my body. It wrapped me in red with the crimson light of the moon shining down on me in approval.

My chest slammed into his and his hand landed on my back while I swayed my hips.

"I will get us drinks," he whispered into my ear.

I nodded, allowing him to leave me briefly. The music rose the hairs on my body, and I spun in place. The energy was overwhelming, intimate, and thrilling.

I laid my eyes on the king, his eyes stared at me with the same hunger of those bodies swaying alongside me.

My feet moved before I'd decided my next choice. Guiding me to the king. Determined to win this battle I'd started.

When I reached the dais, I dipped low, allowing the cowl of my gown to reveal my already visible chest.

"You're fitting in," Ulrich said coldly.

I lifted the gown, stepped on the dais, and placed myself on the seat beside his throne.

His head turned toward me and he cocked his head. "Willingly?" he asked with a grin.

My chest heaved while I watched the twisting bodies before us. The view from the dais was different. Heavier. More tempting.

"I needed to rest my feet," I replied, not meeting his eyes.

His shadows trailed from his fingers, gripping the legs of the small seat, dragging me until I was between his now open legs.

"That dress," he hissed.

I leaned back, revealing my chest to him. "It's rather comfortable."

His shadows coiled around my legs, traveling up my body until the tendrils gripped my chin.

"I wonder how much more comfortable it is when it's removed."

Heat grew between my legs and my hands gripped the seat. He grinned, leaning back in his chair while his shadows dropped their hold.

"Have you chosen your partner for the evening?" he asked.

"Your grace?"

Ulrich laughed, throwing his head back. "The Rite, *Ursa*. It requires each body present to have a partner."

My blood went cold. "For what?"

"You should have asked that before," Ulrich grinned. "You'll have to find out for yourself."

Olen appeared before us with two glasses of dark liquor. I pointed to him.

"I choose him."

Olen laughed. "Too late. My partner picked me out the moment I stepped into this room."

Fuck the Gods.

I turned slowly, meeting Ulrich's inquiring eyes. He shook his head. "Not me. I have been claimed."

"That's one way to put it," Olen taunted.

I stood, ripping the drink from Olen's hand and threw it back. Choking from the burn, I glared at the king.

"What in the Gods does that mean?"

"Ulrich will be a *very* busy man tonight," Olen replied.

My hands balled at my sides. "I don't want his hands on me anyway."

Ulrich leaned back in his throne, setting his feet on the seat I'd risen from. "You may regret that statement by the end of the night. You may be begging for my touch when you find yourself in the hands of someone who does not know how to make all of those delicious noises come from your lips."

"I hate you," I grumbled.

"I'm very aware," Ulrich replied then clapped his hand, calling forth a *troll* with a tray topped with a glass.

He picked it up, eyeing me over the rim before waving his hand. "Go, Brenna. You have an hour."

My stomach dropped. "Until what?"

"Until someone will *claim* you."

The sounds of the party drowned out with the pulse ringing in my ears while the words left Ulrich's lips.

"Olen said you would never allow a man in your court to defile a woman."

Ulrich stood from his throne. His cold wrapped around my body once more.

"The Rite is a different night. It is required by the Gods to give tribute with our bodies. Our blood."

"You don't believe in the Gods," I protested.

Ulrich smiled at me. "I do one night a year, Brenna. When we fuck, bleed, and sacrifice to pay tribute."

His hands lightly brushed my shoulder as he passed me. "One hour," he whispered.

He left me on the dais, practically naked and realizing I really was a potential feast for the starving monsters surrounding me.

I set my glass on the table. My fourth in just a short span of time. My head was hazy from the liquor while my stomach knotted with nerves.

My eyes went to Ulrich on the throne, finding his hands down the skirts of a topless, gray-skinned woman. He smiled at me while his hands moved faster under her skirts.

He was taunting me. Knowing I hadn't done any work to determine the *partner* he claimed I was required to find.

Gods, how I hated him.

Gaining a stupid confidence from the liquor, I stood, swaying on my feet.

The Unseelie surrounding me sneered with glee.

"The *wraith* is unsteady," one shrill voice laughed.

"Easier to hump," a gravelly voice replied.

I snapped my attention to them, scowling.

"Do either of you have *deals?*" I asked with a smile.

They both shrank back, hissing at me while they retreated.

Triumphant in my victory, I stumbled again. Right into the open arms of a man. My head moved upward, pausing when I found Bjorn grinning at me.

"My prize for the evening has found its way to me," he chuckled.

I moved to rip away from him, but he held tighter. "Do not run, princess. I will not harm you."

There was a hum in his words, a calming command that took root inside of my mind.

"I believe we find ourselves without a partner," he whispered while his eyes went to my chest.

I was too intoxicated to cover myself. Instead, I nodded confidently.

"It appears so."

Bjorn stepped back, holding out his arms as though he intended for me to admire him. So I did.

I stared at his dark skin and the dark hair atop his head. The tall, slender build of his body. Significantly different from Ulrich and Olen's muscular frames.

Then there was the black mask covering half of his face, ending at the bridge of the left-side of his nose. Behind the mask two dark brown stared at me.

Gods, were they hungry.

My eyes went to Ulrich who was unmoving on his throne with the woman on his lap gone. His rage was palpable even across the room.

"Your king said I must find someone or else I'd be claimed," I said to Bjorn, keeping my gaze on Ulrich.

Bjorn's hand lifted mine, bringing it to his lips. "The Rite has its rules and customs, princess."

I was disgusted by his touch, immediately wishing I could scrub my skin clean. I fluttered my eyelashes instead, allowing him to kiss up my arms.

"Explain the Rite to me. Please, sir."

"My lord," he whispered.

I snapped my eyes to him. "What?"

"*Lord*, my title."

"I apologize," I cleared my throat. "I did not know."

Bjorn waved his hand without a care. "My little plot of land *graciously* gifted to me by the king is not one to worry about. I'm rarely there."

He stood, placing his hand against my back. "Have you had enough to drink, princess?" he whispered.

My shoulders grew stiff, and I turned my eyes to Ulrich. My hour was close to ending. This much I knew and by the evident hate in his eyes, I knew I'd picked the best partner for whatever this night would entail.

I turned back to Bjorn. "I believe I could do with one more." My stomach rolled in protest while the words left my lips, but I remained calm. I had to dull my senses further to allow my body to lose itself in lust with the Unseelie before me.

Bjorn dropped my hand, bowing his head. "I will return shortly."

I sat back in my chair, my head spinning with the moving bodies around me.

"What the fuck are you doing?" Olen snarled above me.

I glanced up then shrugged. "Found a partner."

"You're intoxicated," Olen stated. "You can't."

"Ulrich did not say I couldn't be filled with liquor. He said I had to find a partner."

Olen's body turned toward the dais, and I followed his gaze, finding a line of naked bodies circling around Ulrich.

"What is that?" I asked.

"The Rite requires nine deals to be made. One of peace, lust, gluttony, greed, wrath, heresy, violence, fraud, and treachery."

I stared at the bodies, counting exactly nine. A group of both men and women.

"How does he complete these deals? What does any of that mean?"

Olen sighed. "He fucks them, Brenna. Before us all while they yell out their deals and intentions."

"That's disgusting."

"That's the Rite," Olen replied blankly. "We all do the same, declaring our intentions."

"Ulrich mentioned *sacrifice* and blood."

Olen laughed. "Each person before him will offer him blood and he will offer his own before he takes them. And then, the one declaring a deal of *treachery,* will be sacrificed."

His hand wrapped around my mouth, muffling my shocked yell.

I wiggled away, shoving him from me. "He can't do that!"

"He can and he will."

"Do they know they're going to be sacrificed?"

Olen's eyes went back to the dais and the bodies kneeling before their king.

"Not one of them realizes what deals their hearts long to make until his blood hits their tongue. Sacrifice is an honor they all wish to have, but even their own treachery will shock them."

"He..." I paused, raising my brow. "*All* of them?"

"Not to completion, princess. If that's your question. He only goes long enough for them to yell their deal. *Or* I guess until he—"

I shrieked and covered my ears. "Oh my Gods, I need to get to my bed."

I stood to leave, but Olen gripped my arm. "Too late. You must allow yourself to exchange blood with your partner. You both must declare your intentions and you both must remain, watching until the traitor is killed."

"I can't participate in this," I whispered.

Olen stared at me. "This is exactly why Ulrich banned your attendance. This is the consequences of your own choices, princess."

I opened my mouth to protest when a voice cleared behind Olen. The beast-man stepped aside, a scowl now tight across his face.

"Bjorn," he said coldly.

Bjorn held up two flutes of wine. "Olen."

"It appears you are not on friendly terms," I spoke, reaching for one of the flutes.

Bjorn handed me the glass then turned back to Olen.

"I believe myself and my partner are in need of a few moments to acquaint ourselves better before the festivities begin."

Olen gave me a worried glance then nodded his head.

"Call for me if you need," he said softly.

"That's unneeded," Bjorn cut in. "She is *safe* in my arms."

There was a hiss to his words, like a serpent waiting to attack in the shadows and my blood went cold. I'd made a mistake. I'd allowed my own stubbornness to potentially put me in harm's way.

Bjorn clinked his glass against mine, pulling me from my fear.

"Do not fret. I will be gentle."

I put the wine to my lips, drinking heavily.

"I'm not fragile," I replied when I'd drained my glass.

Bjorn's eyes lit with amusement. "Yes, it would appear you are not."

The fire in the middle of the room climbed higher and a drum began to beat in repetition. The sound thumped throughout the room. Like a heartbeat, connecting us all together.

"It's beginning," Bjorn said calmly.

My hands went numb at my side as he gripped my wrist, dragging me through the room. He placed me right before the dais where I had a clear view of Ulrich and his nine partners.

Bjorn's hand brushed my neck and traveled down my arm while I held the king's hate-filled gaze.

"He likes to watch," the man whispered into my ear. "I figured I'd allow him a delicious view of his *pet.*"

My head went foggy with the wine mixing with the liquor while the drumbeat picked up. My chest heaved with the rhythm. Uncontrollable. Terrifying.

Bjorn's breath was hot on my neck when his hand grasped my breast. "Do you know how this Rite is completed?" he whispered.

My words stuck in my throat. I couldn't respond. The wine. It was—

My eyes widened. I attempted to turn to face the monster holding my body, but he held me in place.

"Just because Ulrich has it banned, does not mean I cannot get it onto this Island," Bjorn whispered.

Faerie wine. A substance and drink I had only experienced a handful of times in my life. Never more than a sip or two and I had foolishly downed an entire glass.

Ulrich's eyes were still on mine while his shadow blade tore the wrist of the woman before him. Her blood hit the dais, and I could hear it with the wine altering my senses.

The drops were ringing, mocking, laughing at the woman now poisoned and defenseless.

Bjorn ripped the back of my gown while the woman before Ulrich dropped her blood in his mouth.

"Watch that throne, princess," Bjorn muttered against my ear. "Because you will be chained beside it when I claim it."

Screams filled the room when Ulrich suddenly lunged, his blade slicing my cheek as it rammed into the shoulder of my assailant.

I forced my body through the haze, watching in horror while black blood splattered over Ulrich's body.

"Treachery!" voices screamed, pointing at the twitching hand on the floor.

"Run, Brenna." Olen's voice was breaking me through the poisoned haze. "Get back to the bedroom, *now*."

My eyes went back to Ulrich, finding his body encompassed by shadows again. His skin became translucent, his bones shining and white beneath his flesh.

Then I ran, right through the door behind the dais, a victim of my own foolish choices.

Chapter 25

The palace shook as I ran and echoing screams of rage filled the halls, seeping through every stone.

My feet moved me forward and to my relief, I found the hallway leading to a door that opened right beside the door Adie had directed me to. With the keys still laying on the ground.

I picked up the ring and ran to the door to Ulrich's room. When I slammed it open, my hand went to my heart, touching something wet.

Blood—Bjorn's blood was covering my sheer gown.

I shook when I lifted my hand, finding the black liquid staining my fingers.

My body trembled at the image while the palace continued to shake so violently I wondered if Ulrich would bring it down upon us all.

I made my way across the room, almost reaching the bathing room when the main doors slammed open and Ulrich stalked in. Blood dripped from his hands.

"Brenna." His voice was cold and low.

I backed up, lifting my hands. "I didn't know."

My feet stumbled with the faerie wine still poisoning my blood. I'd almost fallen back, when his hands landed against my body, holding me up.

"You are foolish," he muttered.

"I'm sorry," I whispered.

He pressed my body against the wall, his eyes scanning my face.

"Are you harmed?" he asked.

I shook my head. "Not physically."

"You fool," he repeated. "You stupid, stupid fool."

"What did you do to him?"

He shook his head. "We will not speak of him. Not now."

My hands trembled while he held me against the wall, his chest heaving with my own. His hand rose and I flinched as he tucked a piece of my hair behind my ear. His finger brushed my cheek, causing me to gasp at the sting of his skin touching the cut from his blade.

"This outfit," he muttered.

"I made a mistake," I replied, attempting to shuffle away from him.

His hand landed on the wall beside me as he ground his hips against mine. "Do not move," he demanded.

I froze, unable to come up with the words to battle with him.

The loud *swoosh* of the curtains blocking out the moon startled me. The candles extinguished and the familiar sound of Ulrich's mask dropping rang out across the room.

To my shock, he was lifting my hand, allowing me to brush it along his bearded jaw.

"There is a problem," he whispered.

I continued to cup his face, wishing my eyes could see in the dark. Damning the wine for altering my senses in the most inconvenient ways.

"A problem?" I asked.

"I cannot rid myself of you," he groaned, pressing his hips against me. "I cannot rid my senses of your skin, your voice, your smell."

I gulped. "Smell?"

He pulled my hand away from his jaw.

"It's a tempting scent. Like aged whiskey before the first sip. Like the smell of the earth right after rain. You smell like sin, Brenna."

"Like sin?" I whispered, wishing there was light in the room so I could see some of him, any part of him.

His voice dropped, sending shivers down my spine. "Yes, sin, Brenna, and I want a taste."

My heart thundered in my chest. The promise in his tone was enough to send me over the edge. I swallowed nervously and placed my hand on his chest.

His hands slammed against the wall once more. The heat of his body pressed against mine had my senses running rampant. The low, near feral groan rumbling from the back of his throat caught my breath and my hand pulled at his bloodied shirt. One hand slowly moved from the wall, caressing the side of my cheek before stopping at my throat.

Breathing in, he leaned down, placing a soft kiss at the base of my neck. "I am fucking starving," he whispered.

Words choked in my throat when his lips went higher, shocking me when his tongue ran up my cheek, lapping up the blood coming from the small cut.

It was all too much, making my hands shake, but my hold tightened on the fabric of his shirt. I had to hold onto something to keep myself from falling into the maddening oblivion he was tempting me with.

"I want to see you," I whispered back, knowing what his response would be.

His fingers softly twirled against my skin and my eyes rolled at the touch. "You do not need to see me for what I'm hungry for."

I lifted myself onto the tips of my toes and my hand rose again, reaching to brush his lips. But his hand stopped me, holding my wrist in the air.

"I did not get to complete the Rite," he muttered.

I froze. "No, you did not."

"I do not fuck women poisoned on faerie wine," he whispered, pushing away from me.

The cold of the room was a shock to my senses when his body lifted away. Tears lined my eyes while I scanned the dark room.

I couldn't feel him. His presence. That cold that was unexplainable.

Hands grasped mine and I yelled out, twisting around.

His laugh was like a tempting melody. "Clothing and bed."

"Your Rite?" I asked.

"It is a long-standing tradition. Not one that will leave my island or kingdom in dire threat of the Gods. Besides—" his voice went low, "I found my traitor."

Soft clothes were placed in my hand, and I blinked as the red light of the moon returned to the room and I found him with his mask secured on his face once more. The clothing however, he'd changed into loose trousers and an even looser, low-cut shirt. Revealing his inked skin to me.

"Stop staring and get out of that gown." He pointed to me. "Even if I do appreciate every bare bit of your skin I can see."

My skin went cold with his words and the piques of my breasts went rigid.

"Fuck," he groaned. "Get clothes on now before I regret my decisions."

I left him sitting on the bed while I entered the bathing room. When I found my reflection in the mirror, I did not recognize myself. Instead of seeing the woman, powerful and in charge of her choices that I had seen earlier in the evening, I found a scared creature. A woman with smudged koal running down her face from her tears, and a dress—now torn at the back, revealing my scarred skin.

I looked as much as one of the monsters as I'd come to live amongst, and I wondered if I were turning into one of them?

I'd willingly walked into a court I knew ran on debauchery. I walked side-by-side with the Unseelie King each day. I ate across from him each night. I laid in his Godsdamn bed, stopping my attacks to end his life.

No—instead I'd taken the life of a man that was likely as innocent as I was the day Olen had ripped me from my home.

Was I any better than the rest of them?

I certainly wasn't the woman who had left my isolated island. I was but a shell of her. A ghost walking the halls of the monster my world feared.

My hand went to the ink on my hip while my mind traveled to the gentle way he'd traced that ink. How he'd kept his eyes only on the secret I revealed to him.

How he refused to allow me to warm his bed just now because I was not sound of mind.

I turned, staring past the open doors of the bathing room, imagining him in the bed outside of my sight. Waiting for me like he did each night.

Then I remembered Adie's words. The fondness in her voice. The smile that had cracked across her face when she'd spoken of her *Uncle* Ulrich.

The thought settled over me. Brief and a quiet ponder in my mind. I kept it inside while I washed my face and changed quickly. I left my tattered excuse of a gown in the corner of the bathing room.

When my foot hit the stone floors of the bedroom, the curtains snapped away the moonlight and the candles went out.

Without trouble, I made my way through the room, settling beside Ulrich.

I trembled while I moved my body closer, pulling away the wall of pillows he had placed down the middle of the bed.

"What are you—"

"Ssh," I cut him off. "Quiet."

I moved until my body was touching his, turning to settle on my side. As though it were a life-time long ritual, Ulrich turned as well, his body wrapping around mine.

I was a stupid fool for this. A stupid, unthinking fool.

His hand wrapped around me, pulling me closer to him.

"You should fear me," he whispered against my neck.

My body went stiff with the words, but I shook my head. "I don't."

"You lie," he muttered. "You are a *very* bad liar."

"I don't fear you," I repeated, trying to force myself to believe my own words.

He pressed himself against me. "Why?" he asked.

My body shook with the fear he'd trained into me. A reaction I'd come to realize he wanted me to have.

"Because," I breathed out.

I jumped when his fingers pressed into my thigh, lifting my chemise upward with his touch.

"Why?" he demanded.

"I believe you wear that mask for show. You hide who you are, wanting all of us to believe only a monster lives behind it. But there's more. I'm sure there's more."

The pressure of his fingers on my thigh pulled away and he chuckled while he shifted from me, pulling his body from mine.

"The wine still has its grasp on you."

Tension lingered in the air with the mattress groaning from his large frame settling in for the night.

"Goodnight," he whispered before silence enveloped us once more.

"Get up," a voice growled beside me.

I covered my eyes, shocked by the bright sunlight filling the bedroom. When I glanced down, I found Olen in beast form at the side of the bed.

"What is the urgency?" I groaned.

"Penance," he snarled.

I sat up, shaking my head. "I didn't know! I didn't know what this Rite was!"

Olen's shoulders shook with his unsettling laugh. "Not for you. Get up. Ulrich is waiting in the palace courtyard."

I jumped from the bed, dressing quickly and not caring that Olen remained in the room. He was unmoving as I stripped my clothes from my body before redressing.

I grabbed my cloak from the closet and turned to the beast, huffing with heavy breaths.

"That was fast," he laughed.

"Ulrich is waiting," I replied.

Olen bumped my calves with his snout, nudging me through the door. My hands twisted around the clasp of my cloak. When my feet entered the hall, I glanced back at the bed.

I'd slept peacefully again, even after the chaos of the night before. The sound of Ulrich's deep breathing had lulled me into rest rather than irritated my mind.

Was I truly going mad?

Olen grunted beside me, and we picked up our pace, silently making our way through the palace.

Even with my nerves, I could not ignore the air layering over everything. It was heavy and charged with warning. Raising the hair on my body in alarm.

Olen stood on his hind-legs, shoving the grand entrance doors open and I stopped in my tracks.

The courtyard was full of bodies. Every pair of eyes went to me while whispers and hisses filtered into the palace.

And in the middle of the courtyard was Ulrich, with Bjorn shackled on his knees.

I pulled my hand to my mouth. "What is this?" I whispered, shocked to find my assailant breathing.

Olen snarled.

"Traitors receive punishment from those they betrayed."

Olen grabbed the hem of my gown, pulling me into the courtyard. His feet dragged through the gravel, but I could not fight him. Not when my legs shook beneath me, barely holding my body upright.

He dropped my gown when we arrived before Ulrich.

I stared at the king, my stomach twisting at the rage in his eyes and the same death mask he'd worn the night before tight across his face.

He smiled at me before pointing to the man on the ground.

"He betrayed your trust."

I turned my gaze to Bjorn, finding the man staring at me with hate.

"What trust?" I asked.

Ulrich's voice echoed across the courtyard. "The Rite is bloody. It is ancient. It is our tribute to never forget. But it is all based on *trust.*"

The king turned back to me. "This creature broke yours. He poisoned you for his own pleasure."

Bjorn spat at the ground. "She's a *whore*, cousin. Whores do not deserve anything more than a good humping."

The sound of Ulrich's fist connecting with Bjorn's jaw echoed over the shocked gasps of those watching, myself included.

Bjorn's black blood dripped from his mouth as his head lifted. His teeth dragged across his lips and his finger touched the blood.

"Interesting," he muttered.

Ulrich's shadows appeared, pulling Bjorn upward. The shackles rattled and Bjorn let out a groan while his arms stretched back behind him.

I stepped back, bumping into Olen while Ulrich whispered something into the man's ear.

"Cousin," I dropped my voice to Olen. "That is Ulrich's kin?"

Olen snarled. "Distant. Very. Very distant."

Bjorn let out a shrill laugh when Ulrich dropped him to the ground.

"Brenna, a decision," the king snapped.

I startled, meeting his gaze. "I don't understand."

"Death," voices chanted around us.

"Death."

I watched while feet stomped the earth, creating a beat similar to the one that had started the Rite. The gravel lifted with the force of it all, shaking the very dirt of the earth.

"What do we do with him?" Ulrich asked, approaching me.

"I thought you killed the traitor?" I whispered.

Ulrich's hand brushed my cheek, the touch drowned out the beastly chants filling the courtyard.

"The Rite requires a sacrifice. After a deal based on treason is uttered." He turned back to the man staring at us. "This beast betrayed *you.*"

"He said he was going to claim your throne!"

My words came out in a shout and the chants stopped.

Ulrich's jaw clenched, but he kept my gaze. "Decide his punishment."

I pulled away from him, stepping back against the wall of fur that was Olen.

"I can't."

"Coward!" a loud voice yelled from the crowd.

My hands shook as I clasped them together and my tears fell. "I can't."

"Princess," Olen growled.

I shook my head. "I can't be responsible for another death."

Ulrich's eyes lit with amusement. "He would have killed you."

I met Bjorn's eyes, finding him grinning like a madman.

"But he did not."

"Do you have no regard for your own well-being?" Ulrich inquired. "Not surprising to learn about a beast that has tried to end my own life with her bare hands."

Hisses filled the courtyard, and I glanced briefly, finding burning eyes of hate all gazing back at me.

"You decide," I pleaded.

Ulrich was silent. He turned on his heel, picking up his cousin by the bloodied shirt still on his body.

"She's pathetic," Bjorn laughed.

Ulrich's fist slammed into Bjorn's stomach, causing the man to cough up black blood.

"She'll know. When the time is right."

The king turned back to me, waving Bjorn's sagging body as though he were merely a towel.

"You will choose between death or banishment, Brenna."

"I—"

The sound of Bjorn's body hitting the earth cut off my words and Ulrich raised his voice over the whispers of the crowd.

"The princess has two months to decide. If she does not—" he met my eyes, "then the punishment will be death, by her hands."

"Ulrich!" I cried out.

Olen bit the sleeve of my gown, silencing me instantly.

Ulrich smiled.

"Traitors must always be punished. And you must learn how to be a queen."

I fell to the ground, frozen in my shock while the courtyard emptied. Ulrich lifted Bjorn's unconscious body, stalking past me while he returned to the palace. When he was but a few steps away he spoke, forcing my gaze to him.

"This beast will be in the dungeon. I suggest you start to behave, Brenna. I wouldn't want to provide him with a cellmate."

My wine-hazed thoughts that the king was more than a monster ran from my mind while I watched him walk away.

There could be no good intentions within a monster determined to break me.

Chapter 26

Seven months.

Two weeks since the Rite.

Two weeks of constant torment for my soul with the whispers following me wherever I now went. The fingers, pointing, calling me a coward.

The demands for justice and death.

So. Much. Death.

I leaned back against the sand of Ulrich's private beach, allowing the sun to warm my skin. My fingers dug into the surface, wriggling under the grains. Reminding me of home.

My eyes went out across the water and the peace of the lapping against the shore.

Gods, how I missed home.

Winter was beginning to end with the snow across the island melting. And while the earth grew warmer, the melting ice meant my water was colder.

Just how I liked it.

I stood from the sand, jumping into the water like a child. Letting out a scream, hoping to release some of the angst in my heart.

My back floated upward, and my hands splayed up while I closed my eyes.

I'd been waking earlier since the Rite. Opening my eyes to find the bed empty and Ulrich gone but the sun high in the sky. The afternoon sun acted like my morning now.

But the few hours of sleep wasn't troublesome. Not with disappearing to the water each day. Turning my one hour of freedom to two.

Without Ulrich's approval.

Yet, he hadn't mentioned it during our meals or wandering through his palace.

No, we'd barely spoken beyond my lessons on his fortress. Followed by silent meals. Well, silent unless Olen joined us. Those meals were usually louder with the man indulging in his liquors and meats.

My hands wove through the water, turning me to a weightless being on its surface when my head bumped something wet and large.

I jolted up, finding dark, soaked fur before me.

Olen's head lifted from the water, his black eyes filled with glee.

"Princess," his voice rumbled.

"Oh my Gods," I exclaimed. "How will you ever become dry?"

His paw came out, splashing me. I shrieked, swimming backward but was unable to miss his attack and the water collided with my face.

"The water is freezing," he growled. "What is wrong with you?"

My covered arms continued to move. "I would think thick fur like yours would keep you warm."

His teeth dragged over his thin, black lips. "Observant."

I shrugged and returned to my back. "We have white bears wandering our hills. Their physiques reminds me of yours. Your face is more beastly though."

His paws pressed on my stomach, pulling me up and almost under the water.

"Hey!" I shouted.

"What do white bears have to do with anything?" he growled. The noise should have scared me, but I picked up on the amusement hidden within it.

"They swim in water colder than this. Their fur keeps them warm. Gods, they even prefer the cold."

Olen pulled his paw away. "I agree with the bears."

I laughed then turned back to the shore, heading toward the beach.

"Are you done?" he asked.

I nodded. "I'm not sure how long I've been out here. Ulrich will be waiting for me."

"How many hallways have you explored?"

Standing on the beach, I wrapped my cloak around me. "Every single one. Some more than others. We've started on the bedroom floors now with the passages I ran down that night."

Olen growled. "And you are not yet closer to a decision."

The sentence was a question as much as it was a statement.

"I will not send someone to their grave," I replied.

The beast jumped before me, splattering wet sand across my cloak. "You already have. That sniveling prince is dead by your hands and Bjorn will die anyway if you do not make your decision."

"I do not believe Ulrich wouldn't kill him if I choose banishment."

Olen's eyes held my gaze, and his shoulders moved with his breaths. "Why?"

I skirted past him, holding my cloak closer to my body. "He is not someone I trust."

"I don't believe you," Olen countered behind me.

I twisted back to meet his eyes. "There was a *brief*, insane moment when I thought perhaps he wasn't a monster. But it also happened to cross my mind when I was intoxicated with faerie wine. The substance likely made the insane thought pass through me."

"Why do you think people come to him for deals?"

I groaned. "You told me it was because the Gods stopped listening."

Olen nodded his large head. "Yes, but it's because they trust he will do his end."

"Please enlighten me, Olen. Explain how *he* holds up his end of the bargain."

"Did your ancestor not live a long life with his wife and receive the chance to settle a new kingdom?"

"Yes but—"

"Was that not centuries ago?" Olen interrupted me. "Ulrich gained no upper hand at that moment. Yet he held up his end of the bargain."

I blinked. "He offered an insane deal."

"Yes, but that doesn't mean he isn't to be trusted."

My mouth hung open while I considered his words. "Alright, well what about Sigrun?"

Olen snarled.

"What was her bargain? She had her life ripped from her."

"Sigrun was a changeling. He was well aware she'd never hold up her end."

"But that's my point!" I replied. "He makes these deals with those he *knows* cannot complete them."

"Princess," Olen said blankly. "Follow me."

Shocked, I trailed behind Olen while he led me through hallway twelve then down hallway eight; the one I'd learned led right out to the city docks.

The walk was quiet and long. A hidden tunnel under the city of Muspell. When he pushed the hidden door open that led to the docks, the afternoon sun was shifting slowly in the sky.

Olen pointed his snout and I gasped when I found Adalie in the arms of a young man.

"That child," Olen breathed out. "She was not supposed to come here. Nature should have left her in the rubble of fire and death, but I made a deal."

My head snapped to the beast beside me. "Ulrich allowed me to keep her with me. To raise her in honor of my sister and her wife as long as I fulfilled my deal."

"What was the deal?" I asked while tears filled my eyes.

Olen only shook his head. "I am duty bound to keep that to myself. But he is not the monster you think he is."

"He's the monster he wants me to believe he is," I countered.

"Precisely," Olen replied, closing the hidden door once again while he turned back toward the palace.

The conversation with Olen ran through my mind throughout the entirety of the day. Words I could not ignore while Ulrich opened hidden passageway after another, pointing me to the veins of his palace. Showing me every possible escape route I should have never been told of.

My hands dragged my koal over the easel while he spoke, but I barely heard his words. Instead, I studied *him*. The light in his eyes when he opened a door leading to the *looking glass* hallway. The laugh he let out when he unintentionally startled a *troll* cleaning the library.

How his hands ran across the newly dusted books when we entered the library and how he admired it all, stepping back with his hands over his broad chest.

The rumble of his voice, addictive and smooth.

The kindness in his eyes when we returned to the room and Adie was there waiting. The smile, subtle and barely cracking across his lips, when I asked Adie about her love interest.

Gods, was Olen right?

Ulrich left me with Adie, tilting his head with respect before telling me he'd see me at dinner.

I turned to my attendant.

"Adie, can I dress alone this evening?"

Adie shook her head with confusion. "What, your highness?"

"I'm suddenly feeling unwell. I would just like a quiet bath before I head to dinner. I promise you have done nothing wrong."

Adie eyed me. "Your highness?"

"I promise, Adie. I just need a bath."

She tucked her head down. "Yes, your highness."

She ran the bath for me before leaving and closing the bedroom doors behind her.

I stared at the water, my hands twisting together.

I couldn't see it—the good in the monster.

Gods, no I could not see it. I would not allow myself.

After shutting off the tap, I left the bathing room, turning to the doors Olen had guided me through my first day of captivity.

Because that's what this was. I was his prisoner. I was a pawn in the game he played.

I was his opponent in our battle.

And he was the monster.

I returned to the bathing room, pulling my gown off. My tears lined my eyes, and I stood before the mirror, twisting my body slowly.

I hadn't taken a look, not once in these months. Even after Frode had confirmed I was healed.

I turned my head, staring at the scars on my back.

My tears poured from my eyes, hitting the floor. Falling until no tears were left. Until I was sure my body had run dry.

I pulled my gown back over my body before I cleared my throat and returned to the bedroom. My eyes went to the doors leading out to the main hall. Knowing the king waited for his dinner companion.

His irritation likely growing the longer I took.

Then they went to the hidden door and the hallway that led to the room of the mysteriously frustrating right hand.

The other monster in my life.

Finally, my gaze went to the last door out of the room.

I stepped forward and my feet landed on something firm.

My gaze snapped down and my eyes widened.

A key—a key was at my feet.

I picked up it, holding it to my chest as I crossed the room. I shoved the metal into the lock and threw open the door that had led me to my prison.

The cold air from the stairwell wrapped around my lungs.

I glanced back at the bedroom, regret heavy in my heart, then I stepped over the threshold. A strong part of me wanted to run, like so many times before. But another part of me was in a trance; my own despair numbing me from any logical thoughts.

The staircase spiraled downward, and the smell of the sea called for me. My hands trembled against the stone walls while I descended and prayed Ulrich would not return anytime soon.

That I would somehow find a boat to take me off this island long before he came ripping the door of the hinges.

It was a foolish thought, I knew.

I arrived at another door and threw it open, finding the docks below.

"Thank the Gods," I sobbed, rushing toward the water.

When my foot hit the wood, I was sure I'd made my escape. Until the light of the moon was replaced with shadows. Followed by a cold so frigid my tears froze on my face.

I stopped my steps, pulling my gaze up.

"Where are you going?" the Unseelie King asked with a wicked grin.

I stepped to the side, eyeing the docks behind him.

"I'm leaving."

"You're going nowhere," he replied.

I fell to my knees. "Please, Ulrich. Please let me go."

"I thought we had gotten past this battle," he groaned. "Get up."

I shook my head. "Please."

"Brenna, get on your feet now."

"I can't!" My shoulders rose with my sobs. "I cannot do this. I cannot live this madness."

"You've been living it, *Ursa*. For months now."

My eyes met his and I glared. "I *hate* when you call me that."

To my surprise, his eyes widened with shock. "I don't understand."

"Stop calling me a *bear.* Like I'm a beast you're determined to keep caged. Stop using a pet name that claims me as an object you own."

One nod. That's all I received in response.

His hand reached toward me, but I flinched, turning my body away.

"I will not harm you." His voice was soft.

"You're a liar, Ulrich. You're a monster. You've done nothing but harm me."

"I will not harm you," he repeated.

My tears blurred my vision, and I shook my head. "I don't know what I'm supposed to do."

"Do not run."

"Lay in your bed and never look upon your face," I muttered my rules. My spell, entrapping me in this Hel.

"Look at me, Brenna."

My name left his lips, and I wiped away my tears.

"You have taken over, Ulrich. You have infected my mind with a dangerous poison. One I cannot rid my body of."

He was silent but his hands trembled at his sides.

"I want to be *rid* of this poison," I sobbed. "I want to be *free.*"

"Six months," he replied.

Two words, hitting me in the heart.

His hands reached for me again, but I stood on my own, brushing off my skirts. Heading back toward my comfortable cell. Obeying my new master.

Betraying myself and my desire to have a sliver of control.

Chapter 27

Days went in a blur. My heart grew more tormented with each passing hour. Watching the Unseelie King's odd, hidden behaviors. Longing to know the softer side of him, while also hating everything he was and stood for.

I laid on the new couch before the library window, scribbling with my koal. Smudging the edges, blending the lines and curves together.

Lost in my hate-fueled movements with the silent room as my companion.

"Let me see."

My shoulders went tense at the sound of Ulrich's voice above me.

"No," I replied.

"Now," he commanded.

I lifted my eyes, challenging the king before me. "Tell me something truthful and then I will let you see."

He stepped back.

"What do you want to know?"

"Anything."

His eyes appeared frantic behind his mask. I was sure he would deny my bargain when he surprised me and sat beside me.

"This ink on my skin," he muttered, pointing to his chest. "Would you like to know what it means?"

I nodded my head.

"It's a symbol of sorrow. Of remembrance. For me to never forget where I come from and what has made me who I am today. Everything good and vile that lives in my veins."

"I doubt there is any good," I whispered.

His laugh shook the couch beneath us. "I doubt it most days as well. But then I remind myself of where it lives."

I lifted my eyes, finding him staring out across the library.

"It's in moments when I allow my heart to care for the stories that made this city live." His eyes met mine. "When I allowed a little bird to remind me I was being careless."

"Oh." I dropped my gaze.

"Or when I walk the streets, listening to the small babes and youth in their joy. The noise reminds me of a simpler time, lost in my memories and heart."

"Ulrich," I muttered.

"Or perhaps when I allow a bizarre woman to screech at me before my court and I do not remove her head." He winked.

"You ruined it," I groaned, standing.

He laughed. "I get to see now."

With a scowl, I passed him my parchment. His eyes scanned the paper while his fingers traced my work.

"This is beautiful," he whispered.

I took it back, admiring what my hands had created. The map, a perfect replica of the clock room with intricate details of each individual hallway evident in my depictions.

"You labeled each one," he stated.

"Yes, to the best of my ability."

He took the parchment from me again. "*Forbidden?*"

His smile was bright when we met eyes again while his finger pointed to hallway nine.

"It is," I nodded. "I had no other word to use."

"It's fitting," he replied, then stood from the couch. "It is time for our dinner."

I let out a breath and set my parchment back on my workstation. He was still waiting for me when I turned around. His expression behind his mask was soft.

"I decided I would like to have our meal brought to the bedroom tonight. If that is alright with you."

"No, that is not alright with me," I replied.

He smiled. "The red moon is especially bright tonight. I wanted the view from the bedroom windows to accompany my meal. Olen will be joining us, if that makes you feel any better."

"Olen is as much trouble as you are."

Ulrich's laugh followed at my back while I passed him. "I'm very aware of that."

We walked side-by-side, and I noticed—once again—there was no music humming throughout the palace.

"What happened to your nightly parties?"

He let out a breath. "I have grown tired of them."

"Why?"

"Because there is something more interesting to take up my attention," he replied bluntly.

I snapped my gaze forward, refusing to acknowledge his words. Deciding instead to continue our silent approach.

He opened the bedroom door for me when we arrived, positioning his body in an invitation for me to enter first. I hadn't expected what I would find when I crossed the threshold.

My hand went to my chest, tears lined my eyes in awe.

The red moon was so bright, so close in the sky, it was as though it were right outside the window.

"How is this possible?" I asked.

"It happens every blood moon," Ulrich whispered. "Before the cycle ends, and on the first day of spring that year, the moon lowers in the sky."

"I've never seen this."

"That's because the blood moon has been in the sky as long as you've lived. My bedroom was carved in this exact spot to admire this phenomenon during the rare times it occurs."

I stepped back, sitting myself on the bed wiping away the tears threatening to fall.

"I feel called to it," I admitted.

"What?" Ulrich whispered.

"The moon. Like—" My words caught in my throat, but I cleared it. "Like it's part of me. A force controlling my body and my destiny."

"I thought you did not believe in Fate."

I rolled my eyes, turning to him. "Those are two entirely different things."

"I disagree," he countered with a grin.

We held our challenging gazes until *troll* entered the room rolling a round table and pushing carts loaded with food. Three of them went to the plush chairs that sat by the window, dragging them to the table.

The plates and utensils clattered while Ulrich's staff set our places, but we didn't pull our eyes away from each other.

I was sure our gazes would melt one another in place when the hidden door slammed open and Olen sauntered into the room.

I broke first, twisting toward the beast-man.

He grinned at me. "Did I interrupt something?"

Ulrich cleared his throat. "Perfect timing."

The *troll* left us, closing the bedroom as they went and Ulrich pulled a chair out, motioning for me to sit.

I approached the table, pulling out my own seat and placing myself atop it. Ulrich smiled at me before setting himself in the chair he'd intended for me.

Olen eyed us both nervously.

"I can come back..." His voice trailed off.

"No need," Ulrich replied, pouring his wine into his glass.

My heart paused at the liquid and my hands gripped the skirts of my gown.

"Just wine," he whispered, taking a sip to calm my fears.

Olen moved to pour me a glass, but I held up my hand.

"I would prefer to get my own drinks from now on."

"Yes, princess," he replied, handing me the decanter full of the dark-red liquid.

Our meal began, silent, tense, and a continued challenge between me and the king. Olen chattered endlessly, words I barely picked up while my eyes held Ulrich's gaze. But I drank at the same frequency as his right hand. Consuming glass after glass of wine with my meal.

Using the alcohol to wash down each bite I took.

Ulrich did the same.

The red moon continued to light the room. A guest to our dinner, invading us all with its sensual light.

When I was sure my head would sink from the intoxication, I stood. Then immediately, I swayed in my spot. Ulrich and Olen rose to their feet, both grabbing one of my arms to hold me up.

"I drank too much," I admitted.

Olen groaned, gripping my arm tighter. "I did as well."

"Am I a coward to admit the same?" Ulrich muttered.

We all laughed together. A sound I was certain echoed down the halls of the palace. An omen in the wind.

The men guided us all to the bed. Ulrich climbed onto the mattress first, reaching for my arms and pulling me next to him. Olen laughed loudly, laying at my side. Pressing me between both of them.

"I may be sick," I whispered, holding my hand to my head.

"You will not be the only one," Olen muttered.

I stared up at the ceiling while my stomach knotted with my consequences. The bodies beside me settled further into the mattress and I glanced at them both.

"Have you two really—?" My mouth slammed shut, stopping the words.

Olen was the first to sit up, leaning on his palm while he offered me a grin. "Have we what, princess?"

I shook my head, pinching my lips together.

"No, what were you asking?" Olen pried.

"Forget my words," I pleaded.

The wine was taking over. Making me insanely more curious than I ever should have been.

Olen leaned forward, his braids tickling my face while he whispered in my ear, "The king likes to watch."

My head snapped to Ulrich. He didn't meet my eyes, but the smile under his mask— Gods was it maddening.

Olen gripped my chin, pulling my face to his.

"I like to give him a show."

My legs trembled.

"We shouldn't." Ulrich's voice broke the silence. "We are all too seduced by the wine."

Olen kept his hold on my chin. "I think the fact we're *all* intoxicated is the best reason why we should."

I ripped my chin away and sat up, groaning with the room spinning around me. "Don't I have a say in this?"

Ulrich leaned upward. "You're the one in charge."

His eyes held my gaze, and I'd expected him to use that damned pet name. Only, he didn't. He'd made his statement, remaining silent while he awaited my reply.

Heat ached between my thighs, and I held my legs together. Trying to ignore the need and growing pressure low in my belly.

"I'm not sure if Brenna could handle the two of us," Ulrich smiled.

"I could."

Stupid fool.

Ulrich's eyes went wide, and he brushed my hair from my face. "Always surprising me."

The heat of them beside me was too much. I rose to my knees before sliding off the bed.

"Excuse me," I muttered, rushing to the bathing room and slamming the door behind me.

Their laughs were filled with the slurs of their wine-riddled minds, and I laid my head against the frame. My hand went to my heart, and I breathed out.

I needed to calm down. I needed to find logic.

I had consumed too much. Allowed myself to once again become too vulnerable.

But the need...

Gods, did I want it. No—I needed it. The release my body ached for. The thrill of them both admiring my body.

Doing everything I could barely beg for.

I went to the mirror, gripping the sides of the vanity while I stared into the glass. The reflection was of a temptress—a woman with heat burning in her eyes.

I glanced back to the door.

I could admit they were both monsters. Beings and creatures who were used to getting their way. Men who fucked their lives into oblivion.

But Ulrich told me *I* would be in charge.

The decision was made before I could regret it and I turned back to the bathing room door. Pausing for only a moment before I slammed it open and returned to the bedroom.

Their laughing stopped immediately.

Ulrich was on his feet in an instant, his eyes wide. "Brenna, your clothes."

I walked further into the room, allowing the light of the moon to cover my naked body.

"Show me," I whispered.

Olen stood next, joining Ulrich's side.

"Princess."

I held up my hand. "You said I would be in charge." I pointed to Ulrich.

He nodded.

"You will only do what I say?" I asked.

Olen nodded.

"If I do not want to fully..." My cheeks warmed with my embarrassment.

"Fuck?" Olen asked, then grunted when Ulrich elbowed him in the chest.

"Yes," I whispered. "That."

"Brenna you are naked before two men. You should have no shame discussing your needs or wants," Ulrich laughed.

"Don't ruin this with your stupid jests," Olen snapped.

I smiled and glanced at the floor, biting my lip.

Ulrich approached, his body pressed against mine. "What do you want?"

I tilted my head up, meeting his eyes behind his mask. "Release and control. A brief reprieve and pause in our war."

A nod.

The king stepped back and Olen approached, gently brushing his hand over my jaw. His hands ran down my neck, stopping between my breasts.

"Who?" he whispered.

I stared up into his dark eyes then turned my head to Ulrich silently watching behind him. Need ached across my body, but fear was there as well.

I didn't know. I was terrified to allow Ulrich to touch me. To fall further into the poison of him that I could not rid myself of. But I wanted it. I wanted it more than I wanted my next breath.

Ulrich cleared his throat and passed us, pulling up one of the plush chairs around the table to the edge of the bed.

He sat silently with a wicked smirk across his lips, crossing his legs casually.

"I told you he likes to watch," Olen laughed.

His hands gripped my wrist while he led me to the bed. He sat with his feet planted onto the floor and his knees bent.

"Sit, princess," the right hand hissed.

Chills went through my body at the image. The red light, bathing them both in desire. A king in his own make-shift throne and the lap of a man intended to be *my* throne.

Ulrich's eyes went to Olen, and he motioned his hands.

"You are in charge," he whispered.

I nodded. Once. As he was prone to do.

I approached Olen, my hands trembling. My back was turned from Ulrich while I looked into the eyes of my first captor.

His hands grabbed my wrists, and he spun me, forcing me to face the king. His monstrous palms ran over my body, gripping my breasts while he lowered me onto his lap.

"Look at him," Olen whispered. "Keep your eyes on our king."

My knees shook while he lifted my legs, spreading them and myself. Exposing me to Ulrich completely.

Ulrich's expression was blank, but his hands gripped the arms of the chair he sat upon. While his eyes burned.

Olen continued to caress my body, forcing whimpers from my throat.

"Gods," he groaned against my neck. "More."

I laid my head back against his chest as his hands continued their descent, landing on the inside of my thigh. I startled then, jumping slightly and he paused.

"I can stop."

"No," I moaned. "Please don't."

"Look at me, Brenna," Ulrich said, pulling my eyes from the ceiling while Olen teased closer. "I want to watch the moment he touches you."

I bit my lip, lifting my head, bolstered by the desire in Ulrich's eyes.

My hand gripped Olen's thigh when his fingers brushed against my clit, forcing a loud gasp.

"Oh Gods," I cried out.

Olen's fingers circled me, giving me just enough pressure right above the most sensitive part of my body. Expertly bringing forward that tight ache inside of me. His free hand rose, brushing up my body to the base of my neck.

He gripped me, softly, but just enough pressure to make my pulse race with anticipation.

"Such a good girl," Olen whispered, nipping at my ear.

I moaned again, grinding my hips in his lap. Moving them in circles while his fingers continued his teasing.

"Yes." Ulrich's voice broke me from my daze. "She is."

I realized I'd closed my eyes and returned my gaze to the king. Finding him still unmoved from his spot. But his eyes were staring with intent.

"What do you want?" Olen asked, releasing my neck while his hands traveled to my breast.

I watched Ulrich and my body ached. My hands shook while I gripped Olen's thigh harder. I could not utter the words. Not with the intensity of Ulrich's stare holding my soul in place.

"Princess," Olen whispered, tugging on one nipple.

I cried out and bucked my hips while his fingers continued to circle me but not enter me.

Ulrich did not move. I swear he did not blink once. His chest was still, as though he were holding his breath.

Olen continued his teasing, driving me mad. Yet, I could not close my eyes from the pleasure. I could not break my contact with Ulrich's burning gaze.

"Princess," Olen repeated.

"Him," I moaned.

Ulrich's chair clattered and he was kneeling before me in an instant. Olen's hand gripped my thigh, spreading my legs further while Ulrich continued to hold our eye contact.

"You are in charge," the king reminded me.

I nodded.

"Release," I begged. "Please."

Ulrich's mouth claimed me, sucking on my clit with force and I yelled out my screams. The lights in the room went dark. The curtains pulled shut, blocking out the moon. It was pitch black and the sound of Ulrich's mask hitting the floor was as much ecstasy as the way his tongue moved against me.

My head went back against Olen again and his hands moved to my breasts. Circling my nipples and flesh while Ulrich's mouth sucked on me. Their separate movements were somehow in sync, causing my knees to tremble against Olen.

"More," I groaned. "Please, more."

"Such manners," Ulrich whispered while he pulled away and kissed my thigh.

My scream echoed across the room when his fingers entered me, curling upward.

Olen's fingers returned to my clit, resuming his maddening circles from before.

"Let go," he whispered into my ear. "Let go, princess."

I tightened around Ulrich's fingers while he moved faster, curling upward each time he pulled them out. Bringing noises from my lips I had never made before.

I pressed my back into Olen's chest while my muscles went tight. The pressure was building so much more quickly than I had anticipated.

My head tilted back but a hand grasped my neck, and my cheek brushed against a rough beard.

"Let go," Ulrich whispered.

My hand shot out, grasping his shirt and pulling his chest against me.

His and Olen's fingers moved faster, and I held the king in my grip.

"Let go," Ulrich repeated.

"I cannot," I whispered.

"Yes, Brenna, yes you can."

The command and knowing in his words sent me over the edge. Hitting my heart and soul in just the right way and my limbs went rigid with my orgasm.

Both men let out intoxicating groans while I convulsed on Olen's lap. Whimpering with my release and pulling at Ulrich's shirt with all of my might.

Neither of them stopped. Even when I begged. Even when I promised I was done.

They were determined to send me over the edge again, and they succeeded.

The next orgasm was as intense, fogging my mind with bliss and peace.

I couldn't move when they finally stopped, allowing my body relief after forcing yet another orgasm from me. When Olen picked me up I realized his shirt was drenched in sweat from my back.

"Sleep," Olen ordered.

"But what about you both?" I protested with little energy.

Ulrich's arms were pulling me to the bed, right against his chest while Olen climbed in beside me.

"You were in charge tonight," Ulrich spoke softly. "And it is time for sleep."

I couldn't fight his logic as my eyes grew heavy and Olen's muscled arm draped over my waist.

"Sleep, Brenna," Ulrich whispered once more.

I allowed myself to nestle further against his chest, my hand resting against his fast-beating heart. It made me wonder if he was contemplating the fever dream we'd just experienced. Or if perhaps it were beating in sync with my own while sleep claimed me. Convincing me I was safe in the arms of the two monsters wrapped around me.

Chapter 28

When I woke, Ulrich was gone but Olen was snoring beside me, his fur sticking to my bare back.

I shoved him away, pulling the comforters over my body.

He let out a snarl and his eyes opened slowly. “What?” his voice rumbled.

“Did you shift in your sleep?”

“That happens after a good night.” His dark eyes glistened with mischief.

My cheeks warmed and I pulled the blanket over my head.

“No need to be shy,” he laughed. “Orgasms are very natural.”

I kicked him as hard as I could.

“That was rude,” he laughed again.

“So was your jest,” I replied.

He pulled the blanket back with his teeth as he slid off the bed.

Tucking my knees under my chin, I watched the beast walk around the room.

“You want him,” he growled.

My eyes went wide. “What?”

Olen turned back to me. “Don’t deny it.”

“I can’t want him,” I replied.

Olen’s chin laid on the bed and he stared at me. The image of him brought a smile to my lips. When he was a beast, he was more like the canines my father had at home. Snoring, sleeping, and looking for caresses.

My hand patted his head, and I stared out the open window, letting the sun warm my face.

"It's not wrong to want him," Olen muttered.

"Yes it is. It's possibly the most evil desire my heart could have."

Olen was silent and I continued to pat his head.

"You begged for him last night."

My hand stopped moving.

"I did not."

"Princess," he laughed. "You begged for him."

I pushed him away and stood, not caring about my lack of clothing now that the man before me had touched me so intimately.

"Wanting someone's touch is different from *wanting* them."

Olen's brow rose. "How?"

"Did I want Ulrich to be the one to fulfill my desires? Yes. Do I want Ulrich to be the one to hold my heart? To be the one I trust and run to?"

Olen sat on the ground, as silent as the room we stood in.

I stared at the city beyond and the misted sea in the distance.

I released a breath. "I had someone I thought loved me. Someone whom I confided in. Who I allowed to know my most private thoughts and *he* took him."

I turned away from the beast, heading toward the bathing room.

"Ulrich is incapable of love, Olen. He is incapable of being anything more than the monster he has proven himself to be."

Olen let out a rough snarl while I closed the door. His claws scraped across the stone on the other end, but I refused to allow him in. I needed a moment to sit with my choices. To ponder my insanity. To live in silence and penance for my body wanting more.

Of the beast outside.

And the monster I could not rid my mind of.

Olen was gone when I exited the bathing room. The curtains were still open, and I was surprised to see the late evening sun already setting.

I approached the disheveled bed and sank into the mattress, wrapping my towel around me. In front of me the plush chair still sat tipped over, a reminder of my foolish choices.

"You should feel no shame for last night."

Ulrich's voice came from the hidden door, and I turned around. The mask on his face was different. A light cream color, a stark contrast from his usual dark choices.

"I don't feel shame," I replied. "Perhaps regret."

He leaned against the door frame. "Why regret?"

"Why would I not feel regret? I haven't allowed any hands, besides my own, to touch me in nearly four years. One night of wine and suddenly my morals disappeared."

"Why wait for so long?" Ulrich crossed the room. He was silent as he bent, pulling up the chair from the floor and sitting before me.

My breath hitched in my chest at the sight of him.

He gave me a sly smile as he leaned back, crossing his legs.

"I was waiting for him," I replied.

Ulrich sat straight, ending his taunting position. "Why?"

I laughed then shook my head. "Because I wanted to. Because despite him knowing I would never be a virgin bride, I wanted him to know I had waited for him."

"But it was all fake," Ulrich replied with a blank expression.

My hands fisted the blanket beneath me. "It was not for me."

"Would you like to know what he wanted?" Ulrich asked.

I held my towel in place and crawled up to the head of the bed, laying my cheek against my knee. Allowing silence to fill the space.

My heart ached while I stared at the king, unable to respond. Unable to move.

A part of me wanted to know. Wanted to understand how I had been fooled. But the heartbroken part of me that could barely breathe begged for the continued lack of knowledge. To allow me to remain in my ignorance.

"He wasn't supposed to develop feelings for you," Ulrich continued without my response.

"He was supposed to write to you. To gather information."

"Why?" I whispered.

"Because I needed to understand what to expect. Because I knew eventually I had to claim my end of my ancient bargain." Ulrich leaned back in the chair, thrumming his fingers on the arm. "He was supposed to find out if you were a threat to me. Not write intimate, romantic letters. Not profess love."

"You said it was fake," I sniffled.

"Leif was a fool. A hungry and greed-filled being, interested only in his self-preservation. I cannot explain to you why his mind changed, and he allowed you into his heart."

"So, you lied." I glared.

"I have not."

"You said it was fake! That *he* didn't love me. Yet you're claiming he did."

Ulrich was silent but his fingers continued to tap his chair.

"Did you want him?"

I was enraged by the question. "Of course I did!"

"Have you mourned him?"

"Excuse me?" My eyes went wide at the accusation.

Ulrich leaned forward, placing his elbows on his knees while his eyes studied me. "I think he was as much of an escape and a self-preservation plan for you as you were for him."

"Stop it," I whimpered.

The chair fell, just as it had the night before while Ulrich stood and crossed the room. Too fast for me to track.

My head pressed against the headboard while he pushed against me. His hands laid above my head and his green eyes held mine.

"Admit it, Brenna," he whispered. "Admit that while you *believe* you loved him, you actually loved the *idea* of him. The escape he provided."

"No."

Ulrich pressed his hips into mine and I bit my lip at the hardness between us.

"Admit it."

"*I will never harm you, Bren,*" I whispered. "*I will never cause pain or torment to your mind, heart, or body.*"

Ulrich pulled away, blinking with confusion. "What are you saying?"

"I will hold your soul as tenderly as a babe, cradling your kindness with the love it deserves," I continued while my tears fell. "*I will fight for you every hour of every day. Never allowing harm to come your way.*"

"Are you reciting a spell?" Ulrich snapped.

My head turned to him. "Those were his words, Ulrich. His promises. Was I hopeful to have control over myself with him? Of course. But the promises he wrote me, even if they were a ploy in *your* game, meant the world to me."

"But the man?" Ulrich countered. "Did you truly love him?"

My frustrated tears fell, and I leaned my head back. "Does it fulfill your sick fantasies and delights to know that you are right? That I loved the *idea* of him? That I loved the route he gave me toward a life of my own making? That there was a brief, maddening moment of relief when I realized I would not be a bride?"

My lips quivered with my admissions while shame settled over me. It had been there all along; my hidden secret. The apprehension I'd had that day on the dock, waiting to be *claimed* by a man. Ironic, considering that was exactly what happened.

Gods I was a monster when the relief had washed over me when I realized Leif was dead and would never claim to me.

"How does that feel?" Ulrich whispered.

I glanced up, finding him at the side of the bed, kneeling.

"What?"

"Admitting that."

I hated his observation. Gods, did I hate how cutting and accurate his words were. I hated my tears that fell even more.

"Like freedom," I whispered.

Ulrich stood, making his way to the edge of the bed. To my shock, he unbuttoned his shirt, pulling the fabric from his skin.

It fell to the floor. The sound rushing through my blood.

"You let go," he said quietly.

I gripped the towel around me when his hands went to the ties of his trousers, loosening them with one tug.

"Ulrich."

"It does not take much to let go, Brenna. Yet you hold onto it all, constantly. Regret." His trousers hit the ground, and I forced myself to stare only into his eyes. "Hate," he whispered. His hands landed on the mattress, and he crawled forward. "Shame." His palms ran up my legs, stopping at the edge of my towel.

"Need."

I yelled out when the towel was ripped from my body, exposing me to him.

He continued his trek toward me, stopping when he reached my hip. His fingers traced my ink.

"Peace, love, hope, and freedom," he muttered.

My body was trembling, stealing the words from my lips.

"I am still starving, Brenna," he whispered, placing his mouth onto my ink. "Last night did nothing but increase my appetite."

He lifted from me, and I let out a breath of relief mingled with disappointment when suddenly his hands gripped my ankles. My shriek pulled a laugh from his chest, and he dragged my body down until I was laying flat.

I threw my head against the pillow, grasping the sheets under me.

"I'm starving, Brenna," he whispered.

I couldn't look at him. I couldn't. Gods I wanted to. Gods—

I pulled my eyes up, finding him staring at me. His gaze hungry.

"Let go."

His words, once again cut into me. Seeing parts of myself I did not want him to know.

"Please," I whimpered. "Please."

"Yes or no," he replied. "I need an answer."

My legs shook along with my hands. My eyes went to the ceiling.

"What is this?" I muttered.

"Release. Freedom. *Control.*"

I met his eyes again at the last word. "Control?"

"In this room." He crawled toward me once more. His palm landed on my hip, pressing my back against the bed. "You are fully in control."

"What does that even mean?" I groaned.

"Command me." His cold came from him, a release of power and need. "Take control, Brenna."

"I hate my name on your lips."

"Brenna," he whispered, holding me tighter. "Brenna." His head dipped and he kissed my hip once more. "Brenna."

"Oh my Gods."

His free hand trailed up my thigh, stopping when he reached the top. "Do you remember what I said about bedding someone you hate?"

I shook. "It's addictive."

"Addictive," he breathed out. "So fucking addictive."

"Yes."

His eyes snapped away from my hip. "You can always change your mind."

"Yes," I repeated.

"Thank the fucking Gods," he muttered.

His head dipped and his mouth claimed me like it had the night before. My hips shot upward with the shock of the pleasure. My fingers gripped the sheets tighter, pulling them while his mouth moved with precision.

"Oh my Gods," I cried.

His fingers continued trailing along my thigh while his mouth moved on me. His tongue circling my clit was followed by hard, unbearable sucking.

"Oh my Gods!" I yelled out again.

"I am the only God in this room, Brenna," he whispered as his fingers entered me.

Any rational thought, begging me to reconsider my choices, was gone in an instant. Fleeing from my mind while his fingers worked inside of me. Pulling at my need. Calling forth my hidden desires.

"So fucking wet," he growled before claiming me with his mouth again.

My entire being was shaking the more he worked. Moving his tongue and fingers in sync together. Tugging at my body's desire to let go.

But I could not.

"Brenna," he muttered against me. "Control, Brenna."

"I can't," I whimpered, shaking my head.

He rose, pulling his lips from me but his fingers remained. His thumb replaced his mouth while he leaned over me. A giant overpowering me, holding me in place.

"Let go." He circled his thumb.

"I can't," I muttered again.

He added another finger, forcing a scream I could not hold back.

"Control," he whispered again.

He leaned closer, his chest pressing against mine. His long hair brushed my face while I stared past the mask still fitted across his face. His lips grazed my neck, across my jaw, stopping just above my own.

"Control."

The word again while his lips lightly brushed mine. Not a kiss, but just as tempting as one.

"Control," I whispered back.

One nod.

His fingers moved faster.

"Let." His thumb pressed down. "Go."

My orgasm took over, claiming me. My back arched with it while my hands pulled the sheets up. Yet he did not stop, he moved faster.

"Yes," he groaned. "Fuck yes."

I was shaking. My vision was blurring with not just release but tears of relief. Tears I could not fully understand why they fell.

When my body had stopped convulsing and my breathing had steadied, he finally stopped. Removing his fingers from me then lying down next to me on the bed.

I stared up at the ceiling for a moment then let out a breath of confidence, sitting up to gaze upon his body. Understanding what he had meant when he'd previously spoken of the hidden ink I had yet to see.

My eyes went to the two pieces on his legs, both taking up the entirety of the fronts of his thigh.

The ink on his left thigh was a replica of the carving on the forbidden door, but more intricate, the details fascinating. My hands traced the ink, finding the woman's face oddly familiar. Features I recognized but could not trace. I moved my touch over the full half of her, the hate in her eyes, the way her hair whipped around her head as though it were caught in the wind. I moved toward the skeletal side, finding sorrow in her other eye.

I lifted my hand, being sure to keep my gaze on his right thigh and I found a door. Odd when its companion was the woman on the other thigh. It appeared to be wood, with spheres. What I believed to be planets, carved into the surface. Connecting each planet were leaf-covered vines. Appearing like a tether between each world. The crack of the door, along the top of the frame, was lighter ink, as though it were mimicking light.

"What are they?" I asked, tracing the planets on the door.

"Places I've been and wish to forget," he replied.

"Why have it inked onto your skin if you wish to forget?"

His hand grasped my wrist, and I met his eyes. "Because they have marked my soul for eternity."

He released my wrist, and I pulled my hand against my chest. I bit my lip as I forced myself to finally glance below his waist.

My breath caught when I looked upon him and his cock pulsed in response. I moved forward, reaching for him, but he gripped me once more.

"No," he said.

"Why?" I asked, meeting his eyes.

He pulled my wrist up, forcing my body toward him while he nestled me under his arm.

"This was about your control. Your release."

"But—"

"No," he cut me off. "No."

I held my hand against me, breathing heavily. "You do not want me."

"Brenna," he whispered.

I sat up. "Am I not worthy of you when you have a *sea* of bodies ready and willing whenever you wish?"

"Stop," he replied.

I stood, throwing my hands up into the air. "This is not about *my* control. This is about you and your ability to manipulate me." I turned from him, pacing the room. "I am such a stupid, fucking fool."

"Brenna." His voice once again held that low, warning tone.

I twisted to face him. "Your cock obviously wants release, Ulrich." I pointed to him. "Go and find someone to give it to you."

Cold wrapped around my feet. I snapped my gaze down, finding his shadows lifting me from the floor, dragging me back to the bed. I slammed against the mattress, the shock rattling me to my core. He crawled over me, lifting my arms over my head with his magic.

"Would you like to know something?" he whispered against my cheek.

"Unhand me," I cried, fighting against him.

The shadows gripped tighter, and he held my gaze, gripping my face with his hand.

"I have not fucked or bedded a single body since you arrived on this fucking island," he sneered. "I have not thought about burying myself into anyone but you from the moment those defiant eyes glared at me."

"Let me go!" I yelled.

"Do not question my decisions to *respect* your body as me not wanting to destroy and claim you with my bare hands," he growled.

I glared at him.

"You're a coward."

His shadows pulled my legs open, forcing me to scream out in shock.

"Is this what you want?" he whispered, brushing his hand along my jaw. "To be claimed?"

"You're a coward," I repeated.

His hand gripped my hip, and his nails dug into my skin. "You like that word."

I breathed out, holding my angry gaze.

"You are a coward," I said slowly.

His eyes lit.

He'd finally caught on.

"What an interesting game," he muttered.

I bit back my smile.

"Oh, what an interesting game," he repeated while his shadows spread my arms and legs further apart. Holding me completely at his will.

My chest rose in anticipation while he stared at me. His eyes scanning up and down with so much hunger I was sure my body would give out from just his gaze.

"Yes or no," he whispered.

I glanced down, finding a bead of moisture forming at his tip, then I met his gaze again.

A smile cracked across his lips. He leaned down again, whispering against my ear, "I recall you claiming this cock would be covered in boils."

I jumped, tugging against his shadow shackles.

"While I can confirm that is not the case," he reached upward and the sound of the side table drawer opening rattled above me, "I believe a sheath will help calm whatever fears you may have."

I threw my head back, instantly aroused by the words.

"Scream for me," he whispered, and I snapped my eyes up. "Let the world know of your control."

His shadows flipped me to my stomach, lifting my hips into the air. His hand ran down my spine, pausing briefly. His thumb pressed against one of my scars, brushing it with such softness I could not breathe or demand him to remove the hands that had created the mark.

He pulled away and both hands landed on my hips. His finger gently brushed where my ink sat outside of his sight.

"Yes or no," he repeated.

I pulled against the shadows, knowing I had started this all. I had allowed this.

But I had control.

"Yes," I whispered.

His hand grabbed a fistful of my hair, and I screamed out while he plunged into me, the sensation sending my body into a fit of shock.

He moved, keeping hold of me, pulling in and out while his shadows held my limbs down.

I was completely and totally at his mercy.

Gods, did I love it.

Our breaths filled the room, while the moon began to bathe us in its red light. Drowning us in its sensual approval.

My body moved against his while the sting of his grasp on my hair continued to force whimpers from my lips.

"Yes," he grunted, pulling away and then slamming back into me. "Gods, fucking yes."

He released my hair, and the cold of his shadows let go of my wrists. I pulled myself up, lifting my body slightly. Creating an angle that had my legs shaking.

His hand went to my neck, and he pulled me closer while his hips went faster.

My eyes blurred with ecstasy. "I—" The words became stuck and my eyes widened. I wasn't sure I could utter them. It was wrong when I was filled with so much pleasure.

"Tell me," he whispered, tightening his grip on my neck while his other hand reached around me, circling my clit.

My body shook with anticipation, and I reached back with a hand, clawing the skin on his thigh.

"I hate you," I whispered.

He groaned louder, pumping faster and harder. "So fucking addictive."

My orgasm was mind-altering, consuming everything that I was. Turning me into a monster that relished in the hate and conquest of controlling the most despicable creature our world knew.

Making him my own personal beast of lust and rage.

I was becoming just like him.

Chapter 29

There was a new kind of respect following me now. The eyes of Ulrich's court no longer looked at me with disdain. No longer pointed with sneering comments or mocked my presence.

No, the Unseelie fae were just as superstitious as their hated brethren on the Northern Island. Bowing to Ulrich's mysterious princess when I walked beside him or joined Olen's deal claiming.

Every one of them silently acknowledging the princess now regularly warming their king's bed.

I would be deceiving if I did not admit it thrilled me.

My eyes caught the bowing heads while Ulrich and I walked down the docks under the red moon. My easel was strung around my neck, but I had not noted or drawn a thing in hours. Even the weight of it did not bother me while we walked silently.

This change was not one of romance or love. Not of a desire and need to learn everything about him and become enamored with his presence. If anything, it was a change in our war. Each side lifting their flags in defeat. Pausing the bloodshed.

"It's been another month," Ulrich spoke, breaking our silence.

I craned my neck to meet his eyes. "Yes."

"Bjorn still sits in my dungeons."

My stomach dropped. "He does."

"You have mere weeks to make your decision, Brenna."

"You do it." I turned my gaze away, staring out at the water.

He stopped and stood before me, his eyes hot with an emotion I couldn't interpret.

"There are laws and customs of my people. Millennia-long rules I cannot cast aside for the woman warming my bed."

"Stop it," I demanded while heat rose on my cheeks.

"You must make a decision. Does the traitor die or is he banished?"

"What happens if he is banished?"

"I reclaim his title and gift it to the one he tried to betray, and he is sent out to sea on a boat where he can only pray to your silent Gods that he makes it through my mist."

I stepped back.

"There is so much you just said that I can hardly fathom."

Ulrich stepped closer. "You become a *lady* of my court and remain a princess of yours."

"No," I shook my head. "I do not want that."

"Which one?" He smiled.

"Enough," I demanded, avoiding his outstretched hand. "You're alluding that he will not make it past the mist. Meaning I would be sending him to his death even with banishment."

"He will make it if you desire," Ulrich replied blankly, his eyes behind his mask emotionless.

"Why?"

"Because you wish it."

"What are you gaining?" I questioned, stepping back again.

"A woman still willing to warm my bed." His smile crept across his lips.

I threw the koal in my hand right at his head.

A quiet gasp came from behind me, and I glanced to find a young child staring with their eyes wide. Ulrich took advantage of my distraction, grabbing my wrist and pulling me toward him.

"Do not frighten the poor being," he sneered.

"I am not the only one doing the frightening," I replied, yanking my arm to loosen his grip.

"You terrify them. The princess who has their king leashed by her—"

My knee went right into his groin, and he fell to the ground.

My fists clenched together while I glared at him and the child behind me let out an amused yell, running away from us.

Ulrich's shadows appeared around him as he leaned up on his hands.

"What the fuck was that?" he spit out.

"You will not humiliate me." I stood over him, glaring. "I can choose to stop your access to my body at any point. You will not treat me like a conquest you have control over."

His hair fell across his mask, and he smiled at me. "I apologize."

He groaned as he stood, the sound filling me with victory. The smile on his face was still bright and teasing, but it dropped as quickly as it had appeared.

His shoulders went rigid, and his body turned from me, facing the sea beyond the dock.

"Ulrich?" I questioned.

He held up his hand, not twisting to meet my gaze. "Quiet," he sneered.

A hum filled the air. Hot and breathtaking. Terrifying.

Familiar.

"Ulrich," I begged.

"Silence, princess."

I startled, twisting to find Olen at my side. With his hands on two curved blades.

"When in the Gods did you get here?" I questioned, my brow scrunching with confusion.

Olen only shook his head, lifting one of those curved blades toward his face while he held one finger to his lips.

"Olen," Ulrich said quietly, snapping his fingers at his side.

Olen left me, joining Ulrich. Both men kept their backs to me. Almost as though they were protecting me.

"What the fuck, Ulrich?" Olen whispered, just loud enough for me to hear.

"You grab her and run if I give the sign. Do you understand?" Ulrich turned to his right hand, but his eyes glanced at me.

Olen nodded once.

The current in the air grew thicker. Gods, I knew what that was. The warmth.

I'd felt it.

I'd bowed to it.

I stepped to the side, my eyes wide when I watched the mist part for the brilliant white ship cutting across the water.

"Oberon," I whispered. My hands moved without my control, pulling my easel from my neck. Throwing it and my supplies onto the dock with a loud *clatter*.

Ulrich's body rotated to me, and he gripped my shoulders. "Brenna, I need you to be silent. Do you understand?"

"They've come for me," I muttered.

Ulrich's expression dropped. "We do not know that."

I shook my head, hope rising in my chest. "Oh my Gods, they've come for me."

"Brenna," Ulrich's voice sent a chill through my body. "If they take you it is an act of war. One that I *will* take seriously."

My gaze held his while silence enveloped the dock.

"You can't."

He gripped my chin, tilting it upward. "I will, *Ursa*. You. Are. *Mine*."

His hand removed his hold while my blood ignited with hate once more. I had been so foolish. Allowing nights of naked embrace to cloud my judgement.

Olen stepped back, his arm out as though he intended to grab hold of me. I pulled my arms to my chest, refusing him.

"Don't move," he demanded.

The ship moved so much slower than Ulrich's black vessel docked below the palace. But it was just as much of a statement in the water. Bright and a beacon of hope.

Ulrich's fists were shaking at his side by the time the ship arrived at the dock, throwing down pure white ropes while Seelie fae slid down them, tying the ship in place.

One young one, a female, met my eyes and a look of genuine confusion went across her face. She glanced at Ulrich and Olen then back at me, but the slammed gangplank pulled her gaze from mine and she clamored back up before glancing in my direction once more.

"Don't move," Olen repeated.

"I'm not a child," I sneered. "Or an animal to be kept in place."

"You are right now."

I held my tongue when a tall fae came into view. His copper hair was combed to the side while his turquoise blue uniform of Oberon's guard caught my eye.

"Your grace," the fae addressed Ulrich, bowing low but with a mocking grin in his eyes.

Ulrich's power unleashed, filling the air with cold and shadows.

A look of disgust went across the fae's face before he was snapping his fingers.

My eyes glanced around the dock for just a moment, finding every single surface filled with people. Possibly every citizen of Muspell was watching their king.

Part of me had expected Oberon to step on the gangplank. Or possibly one of his wives.

Nothing in me, however, expected the heads that hit the dock or the shrieks of rage that rang out behind me.

"Your spies, *King*," the fae sneered.

"Oh my Gods," I whispered.

"Do not look away," Olen whispered. "Look at the truth, Brenna. Watch."

Ulrich stepped forward with shadows licking at his fingertips. I bit my lip, noticing his skin becoming translucent.

"What is this?" he demanded.

The fae grinned again. "Did you not hear me? Are you too clouded by all of that fucking you and your monsters do?"

Ulrich was on him, pulling the fool up by the throat, lifting him for us all to see. Fear filled the arrogant fae's eyes. The expression brought me sickening delight.

"The king found them all!" the invader squeaked. "Removed each of their heads when he was presented with them."

"He had no right," Ulrich snarled.

"He is the king," the fae spat.

"He is as much of a pawn in this game as you are."

A scream of agony rang down my spine and I twisted, watching an older Unseelie fae woman with grey skin and horns on her head pick up the head before her.

"No," she sobbed. "No. She was only to be a handmaid. Only to listen to the whisperings. No."

More people began to bend, picking up their heads. More screams echoed around me. Families finding their loved ones. Lovers discovering their partners.

It was horrifying.

"Olen," I whispered.

"Quiet, princess," he replied, grasping his palm around my hand.

I held his grip, my knees trembling while more heads came from the deck of the ship. My eyes moved to Ulrich and my heart clenched with fear.

"Death," Olen whispered beside me.

I was frozen in my terror at the image before me. A creature of shadows, bone, and wrath had replaced the king. His hand still gripped the fae, but it was a hand of only bone with wisps of shadows wrapping around his limb.

"These were *my* people," the king's voice rumbled.

Another head hit the dock.

The fae laughed despite the feral fear in his eyes. His head turned to me. "Why do you have *that* in your presence?"

Ulrich gripped the man's neck. "You do not look at her."

"Oh, *she* will not be pleased to learn you have a guest," the fae let out a shrill laugh. The nearly identical sound all Seelie fae made.

The sound unleashed the beast.

Ulrich's hand barely twitched and the fae's head exploded, bursting from the strength of his grip.

My responding scream was muffled by Olen's palm. But the other screams—the Unseelie Fae on the dock—those sounds could not be silenced.

Ulrich moved like a ghost in the wind, his shadows propelling him to the deck of the ship. The magic created an outer skin on the king, masking him from the continued splattering of blood. Blood, so much blood, seeped from the wood of the ship as though the vessel itself were losing the iron substance and not the crew Ulrich was slaughtering.

I didn't think I could handle it. Despite how my eyes could not pull away, my heart was freezing. The sight making me realize he truly was a monster.

Uncontrollable.

Ready to enact death and violence at any moment.

More screams hit my ears. Terror—Gods, they were all full of fear.

I stepped back, bumping into Olen.

"Please get me away," I begged.

Olen's arms gripped mine. "Watch, princess."

My tears fell while headless bodies hit the earth and blood continued to run down the white ship. The liquid staining the wood and pooling into the water lit by the blood moon above us.

I held my hand to my heart.

Everything, every reason why I was here was because of that moon. Because of *blood.* A substance I was seemingly baptized in. The Gods themselves dunking my soul in its waters.

A loud bird cry came from high above and I glanced up, finding a white dove in the air, flying away from the vessel. An oddly comforting image with so much bloodshed; the stench of it now filling the air.

I turned my eyes, finding Ulrich approaching, his shadows alive and wrapping around him.

The darkness opened, and his translucent hand grasped mine, pulling me into his magic. I screamed while he enveloped me in it all, sure he would punish me for my hope of rescue.

"They did not come for you," the beast snarled at me.

I stared into his eyes, now as black as his very soul.

"You. Are. Mine," he whispered.

My tears fell. My fear gripped my heart. My words, they became unreachable in my mind. I let out a breath and gave the only response I could think of—a nod.

As he was prone to do.

Chapter 30

Eight months.

Two hundred and twenty-four days.

My head laid on Ulrich's chest while his deep breaths rumbled against my ear. His hand brushed my arm. A touch too intimate for the arrangement we were both most comfortable with.

I sat up, glancing around the room. My eyes found our clothes discarded to the side. Then the blankets, thrown to the ground. Reminders of the lust we'd fallen into after our meal.

"Pondering something?" he asked.

I turned to him, the cream mask he was preferring in recent days illuminated his green eyes.

"What is this?" I asked.

He rose, leaning against the bed.

"A bedroom?" he replied.

I scoffed and slid off the mattress, stepping away from his reach. "We do this nearly every night. Gods, I don't even know how I can let you touch me when your hands bring so much death each day. Death I'm forced to watch."

I fell to the ground, covering my face, trying to process this insanity and how easily I was slipping into it. A desperate, foolish attempt on my part to try and piece together this game I was part of—this game I could not fight. Not that I wanted it.

Not when I wanted *him*.

"Brenna," he spoke softly, breaking me free from the darkness my thoughts were pulling me down toward.

I lifted my head. "Please."

"Please what?"

"Stop it all. Please."

He stared at me, his expression unshifting. The mask of the king slipping over his face.

"That!" I cried. "That! Stop it! Show me something real. Please. I am begging you."

He didn't move. His eyes did not even blink.

My chest grew heavy. So heavy I was sure my heart was turning to stone inside of me. My hand landed on my skin. I wanted to understand. There was nothing more that I wanted than to understand why he was who he was. Why his darkness claimed him—and why I was beginning to accept that darkness, rather than run from it.

"Please," I muttered. "Please."

I had grown too numb, trying to process all in my heart, to react when he knelt before me. His hand cupped my face; one of those moments of softness that he was prone to show. The moments when I wondered if I could accept him for... *him*.

"Show me something real," I cried again.

He shook his head. "Brenna."

Despite how gently he held my face, his expression was still emotionless. Almost as though he were doing this on purpose—another play in his game.

I pulled away, trying to mask my hurt with rage.

"Two weeks until I must make my decision," I said coldly, reminding him of my inaction with Bjorn's sentence.

His expressionless gaze finally broke. Irritation burned in his eyes.

"Yes."

"And if I do not you will force me to kill this man."

A nod.

"And if I do not kill him?"

His mouth opened then closed.

"You have no answer."

Silence.

"You do not want to utter it."

A nod.

I moved away from him, crawling back in an attempt to put distance between our bodies.

"If I kill you?"

His cream mask was replaced by his shadows. They crawled upward, creating those damned horns he always wore.

"Do not," he warned.

"If I kill you then you destroy my family and everyone that I love. Only..." My heart broke in two. "They have not come for me. They have not cared. Even when I have given them every *detailed* depiction of the torment you have put me through."

I bit back my cry when he moved to his knees, slowly pulling his body toward me. No—*crawling* toward me.

"I have told them that you have marked me. Branded me as yours even when I leave this island," I whispered. My hands went back, moving me away from his approach.

"Brenna," his voice cracked.

"I hate you," I cried. "I hate this poison of you. The scars *from* you." I stopped, standing quickly, and my hand went to my back. "I will never be whole again because of you."

His approach ceased and he suddenly turned around, baring his back to me.

"What are you doing?" I exclaimed.

Shadows wrapped around my wrist, cradling it while a thick line ran down to the sand. A whip—a whip of his own making.

He pointed to his back and the inked monsters on his skin.

"I have violated a princess of royal standing," he began.

"Stop," I replied, trying to shake the whip from my hand, but it only tightened around my wrist.

"I have made her question her sanity." His shoulders lifted with his breaths. "I have killed before her eyes. I have used her body for my satisfaction."

"Ulrich."

He twisted, his eyes burning. "My court has laws for those of us who do these crimes. I have marked you, Brenna. It is your right to do the same in return."

The shadows pulled my arm upward without my control and I cried out.

"Ulrich! Stop!"

It came down onto his skin with a sickening *crack*. The noise echoed around us, bouncing off the stone walls of his bedroom.

He didn't flinch. Didn't move.

The shadows pulled my arm up again.

"Ulrich!" I begged. "I will never forgive you if you make me do this."

My arm froze in the air and he turned his head to meet my gaze. His hair hung over his eyes, another mask, blocking me from ever seeing who the man truly was.

"I will never forgive you," I cried. "Do not force me to become the monster that you are."

His body shook with my words and I stepped back, covering my lips with my hand as a tear ran down the edge of his mask.

"I have marked you," he muttered.

I nodded. "Yes, Ulrich. Yes you have."

The whip was gone as quickly as it had appeared. He remained unmoving in his spot, with his black blood running down his back. My hands balled at my sides. I wanted to feel disgust, or to feel *nothing* at all, but I could not shake my heart's need to understand.

It was too much—too overwhelming.

So, I turned on my heel, walking right out of the bedroom door. Leaving him startled and naked on his knees. I could have run, like so many times before. The motion was becoming as part of myself as my skin and breath.

Instead, I walked slowly through the halls, allowing this cold darkness to wrap around myself and my senses. Knowing he was not going to follow, at least not immediately.

No, he was sitting in his penance; this much I knew.

After months of learning every secret passage of this palace, I was grateful for my knowledge while I avoided any eyes or hands that may have tried to reach out to my unclothed body.

If I were truly slipping into madness, if I were truly allowing his depravity and hate to spoil my soul, then I would move through his court like the whore they all believed me to be.

I rounded the corner, passing Olen who let out a startled yell, removing his hands from the man kissing his neck.

"Brenna!" he yelled after me, but I kept walking, not acknowledging him.

His shouts continued, but they were not close. Of course they weren't, Olen was bound to check on his *king*. Not the woman warming the ruler's bed. Soon his words became distant, and my hands shoved open the doorway leading to hallway three.

I walked down the stairs and my tears built until I was standing in the clock room, spinning in place like a nymph that had lost her mind.

Naked in all of her glory.

"Brenna!" Ulrich's voice echoed around me.

I refused to find him, to acknowledge his choice to follow me. I turned to hallway twelve, needing to cleanse this all from my mind, body, and soul.

His voice repeated my name as I walked away, but I would not respond. I could not respond.

The door to the beach slammed open and my steps grew even slower against the heavy sand. I was mere feet from the water when his hands wrapped around my waist, pulling me against him.

"Let me go!" I begged. "Let me go!"

To my surprise, he released me, and I continued my determined path, flinging my body into the water. I gasped and the cold liquid flooded into my lungs.

I fell, allowing it to envelope me. Begging the Gods of the sea to cleanse me of my sins.

My body grew weightless around me. My sins lifted away from me.

The sins I welcomed—him—he was the sin. He was the poison. The tonic I consumed daily. The green eyes that held me captive. The inked skin that hypnotized me in his bed. The smooth voice—terrifying me and calming me at the same time.

I opened my eyes, barely able to see under the dark surface even with the bright moon above us.

Until he was before me. I pulled my head from the water, gasping in my breaths while he rose slowly.

His shadows were still wrapped around his face, a mask of his own making. Still blocking me from seeing his features, but it was different.

Alive.

"I have hurt you," he said quietly.

I nodded.

"I do not know how to reckon any of this, Ulrich," I replied. "I do not know how I can ever return to who I was before I met you."

He was silent. Just like before. No emotion. No sound.

Until a brief flash of what appeared to be a genuine emotion went across his gaze. A moment of vulnerability.

Despite the weight the expression forced against my lungs, I could not reply. I could not acknowledge it. There was no empathy in my heart for whatever it was he had felt in that moment. Not when he had done all that he could to beat my former empathy, and who I was before out of me.

Not when I was unsure of when the vulnerability would change.

Or even more terrifying: that I did not know if I wanted anything inside of him to change.

"Banishment," I whispered, voicing my choice for Bjorn's consequence. "I choose banishment."

Ulrich remained quiet while I backed away, swimming through the water until my feet were in the sand once more. I only looked back once, finding him staring at me with the moon high above him.

He was a magnificent image at that moment; almost godlike, perhaps something *more* than a God stared at me.

I let out a shaky breath, retreating back to the safety of my prison, leaving him in the frigid water.

When I reached the clock room, Olen was there, holding a cloak out for me. I fell into the strength of his embrace as he wrapped it around my shoulders.

I stared up at him, tears running down my cheeks.

"I chose banishment," I cried.

He nodded his head, patting my shoulder. "Yes, princess."

"Olen," I whispered.

He bent, scooping me into his arms. Cradling me gently.

"Yes?" he asked as I laid my head on his chest.

"He has poisoned me," I cried. "He has gotten into my veins." I met the beast-man's eyes. "Why do I want more?" I asked.

Olen's expression strained with unrecognizable emotion, and his head glanced up toward one of the hallways then back to me.

"I do not know princess."

"I cannot stop it," I cried. "And I do not always know if I want to."

Olen turned toward hallway three and I looked up, finding Ulrich at the end of the hallway I'd come from. His hands trembled at his side while he met my eyes.

Then I was carried away, watching the Unseelie King disappear in his shadows while a rage-filled shout, one that I wondered may have been regret, followed me and the man who carried me. Reminding me why I could not fall completely into the madness.

Even when my heart wanted nothing more.

Chapter 31

Two weeks.

It had been two weeks since I told Ulrich my decision.

He had done nothing.

I laid on the bench in the *looking glass* while my hands stroked Olen's fur. His snoring lulled my anxious mind when Adie appeared before me. I smiled at her, cocking my head at the wild grin on her face.

"Is there something you'd like to tell me?" I asked, sitting up while Olen yawned.

Adie glanced at him nervously before nodding her head. "There is a gift waiting for you on your bed."

I froze.

"For tonight," she continued.

"Tonight?" I asked, glancing at Olen.

"The party," he replied with another yawn.

"I thought Ulrich was done with parties," I responded.

"He can't stop us from throwing a birthday celebration," Olen said.

I stood. "Birthday?"

"A birthday ball," Adie squealed. "It is a *big* event, one he has not allowed to happen in *years.*"

I eyed her. "How big?"

Olen laughed loudly. "It is not a Rite, princess. It is a party. While there will be plenty of moving bodies, this will be nothing like the Rite."

"Your gown is waiting." Adie smiled. "You only have a couple of hours."

"Why wasn't I told about this?" I questioned Olen.

His head pulled up from the floor. "Because Ulrich realized you spent your birthday in a cell in his dungeons and he wasn't about to have that argument with you."

I startled, stepping back.

"I didn't think it would cross his mind."

Olen's snout bumped my calves. "We had not realized the day of. Gods, even in the months after."

I brushed him away. "As long as I get to go home by my birthday this year."

"It's the last day of the blood moon," Olen replied. "That's the last day of your service."

I raised my hand, stopping his words. "I'm very aware of that."

I left the beast in the hall while I followed Adie back to the bedroom. My hate kept its deep root inside of me that the men had known. Had realized I'd spent the day of my birth laying on that rotted floor months ago.

I fisted my hands at the memory.

Of the tears I had shed. The screams I had let out.

Adie pushed open the bedroom door and I walked in, staring at the light of the moon on the bed. It made me hate Ulrich once more. Even though we had found ourselves lost in a hate-fueled fuck on that bed the night before.

Adie cleared her throat.

"The gown, your highness."

My eyes went to it, and I gasped.

"That mask!" I exclaimed.

"Both hand-picked by his grace," Adie replied.

I picked it up, my hands trembling while I studied it. It was metal, possibly silver, the fitting over the eyes dainty, simple. But to the sides were bones, skeletal fingers wrapping around the simple bottom layer, barely touching. Designed to encompass the wearer's face in death.

"I can't wear this," I gasped.

"You have to, your highness," Adie replied. "His grace demands it."

I turned to the bedroom door, wishing the King would burst through them as he was prone to do. Hoping he would appear, ready for the battle of words I had building in my heart.

I set the mask back on the bed, then picked up the gown. It was beautiful. A shimmering silver with translucent sleeves.

I lifted it and somehow the red of the moon caught the fabric, making it glisten in its light.

"I'm going to look like a corpse," I whispered.

Adie said nothing while I marveled at the gown in my hands.

I returned to the bed, placing the fabric down gently.

"I guess I'm to be readied then. I wouldn't want to deny the king the gift I'm expected to be."

Adie's eyes widened briefly, then she nodded. "Yes, your highness."

Olen greeted me at the bedroom door when Adie had finished readying me, having painted me like the omen of death I was now known to be in this court of demons.

The right hand stepped back, his eyes traveling over my body.

"He is going to love this," he whispered.

I took the man in, admiring his towering figure. The muscles in his chest and the deep V shirt he wore, open slightly to expose his muscles. His skin free from ink, vastly different from Ulrich's, but beautiful just the same. My hand rose while I laid my palm on his chest, admiring the rich tones of his skin and how it glistened with the light of the moon behind me.

His shoulders flexed and I met his eyes once more.

"Enjoying yourself?" He grinned behind his pitch black, horned mask.

I blushed, casting my eyes down and pulling my hand back to myself.

"There's a party," I whispered.

Olen took my hand, pulling me to follow him. "Yes, there is."

I wanted to go through the hidden door in the bedroom, to slip into the ballroom under the safety of shadows, but Olen had other plans. He led us through the open hallways, passing partygoers as he went.

The Unseelie fae, adorned in their best suits and gowns. There was more clothing on the bodies of Ulrich's court and palace than I had seen in the eight months I'd been captive.

Olen stopped when we reached the open ballroom doors. He blocked the room from my sight and stared into my eyes.

"You realize everything could change in a moment," he whispered.

I stepped back. "I'm not sure what you mean."

Olen glanced behind him then met my gaze again. "Brenna, there is *so* much you do not know. So much I am duty bound from telling you."

He turned on his heel, leaving me bewildered in my spot. I moved to follow when the cold arrived, ripping me from my confusion. Stealing the breath from my lungs. Calling to me and my sin-stained soul.

I lifted my gaze, finding Ulrich before me.

Dressed as Death.

His outfit startled me. A dark, black suit and the death mask on his face. One of bones, one I had not seen before. One that emanated sorrow.

Along the bones were the same symbols inked onto his arms.

He said nothing, grasping my wrist gently while he pulled me into the ballroom. His people all bowed to both of us as he guided me through.

"I hate this," I whispered.

He stopped and pulled me against his chest, resting his hand at my back.

"I thought you only wanted respect. I thought it was all you begged for," he muttered.

My knees grew weak while I stared into his green eyes.

"I do not want respect because I have suddenly allowed you access to me."

He held me closer.

"I can promise that is not the case."

"Then I am respected because they fear me. The *wraith* of the king. The woman now dressed like one of the corpses you force her to claim."

Ulrich smiled, his teeth bright in the sensual light of the room.

"You do no claiming."

"I stand by and do nothing while I allow Olen to claim your deals and innocent souls," I replied.

"Have you seen a soul?" he asked, lifting my chin, forcing me to meet his gaze.

The metal of my mask bit into my cheeks but I remained silent. I did not want to offer him the satisfaction of a response.

He pulled his hand from my back, then brushed it down my arm while his eyes pulled away. His smile crept up, lifting his lips slightly.

"It's a shimmering silver leaving the body. Illuminated under the sun and moon. A barely visible wisp in the wind before it's claimed." His hold on my chin tightened. "You are not dressed like a corpse."

My breaths grew heavy while his voice lowered.

"You are dressed like a *soul.*"

I was entranced by his gaze and unable to pull away from his poison. My body trembled, begging for more of the man it had become addicted to.

"Claimed souls are merely payments of my deals," he whispered.

I snapped from my daze, shoving him away. "I am not a payment."

His eyes glistened with amusement. "You are, Brenna. You are mine. Do not forget that."

I stared at him, challenging his words with my gaze.

"Each time I think you could possibly receive redemption, you do something awful," I muttered. "You force me to remember the pain you've caused me."

His gaze went blank, the fire in his eyes extinguishing.

"Why?" I pleaded. "Why?"

His mouth opened and hope sparked in my chest. Was he going to be vulnerable? Like the few times he had spoken of that ink on his skin? Would he allow me to see past the monster?

His hands clapped instead, and the music stopped around us. He turned away from me, leaving me in my misery while he approached the dais.

"I know you've all been impatiently awaiting the princess's decision," his voice boomed out.

Yet again, our battle had resumed.

I glared at him and the wicked smile on his lips.

"Brenna, come here."

He pointed to the seat beside him, publicly claiming me as the object they all believed me to be.

I held my chin high, ignoring the sneering smiles while I crossed the room.

Ulrich's other hand was trembling against the arm of the throne when I approached and he snapped his other fingers, pointing to the settee again.

I laid my hand on the trembling palm, stopping it instantly. I leaned into him, raising my legs and straddling him before them all.

"You will not win," I whispered into his ear.

His hand wrapped around me, pressing my body against his. The gasps and shocked laughs behind us drowned out with the blood rushing through my veins. It pumped my heart with a speed I was sure would burst it from my chest.

"What are you doing?" he whispered against my cheek.

I ground my hips into him, letting his court watch me control their master.

"You will not win," I repeated.

His hand pulled my hair back, forcing me to meet his eyes.

"What a good *beast*," he muttered.

"Happy birthday, your *grace*," I replied.

His smile was somehow even more wicked while he stared up at me. His hand pressed further into my back, and he pressed me closer to him.

"No, Brenna. Happy birthday to *you*," he whispered. "It's belated, but this is all for you."

My face twisted with unexpected emotions and my mouth opened but no words left my lips. I was unable to respond through my shock. His lips claimed mine and every muscle in my body became rigid from shock.

We hadn't kissed. Not once in all the nights we allowed ourselves to enjoy each other's touches. It was always that thing we both refused to allow. A touch of intimacy neither of us wanted.

His lips were frantic against mine and his hand held my head still while his other pressed against my back, forcing my hips to grind further into his lap.

My Gods did I love it.

The fullness of his lips.

Knowing every pair of eyes in the room was watching us.

I needed more.

I moved my lips with his, my hands lifted from his shoulder, and my fingers went to his hair. Gripping it and tugging the locks like he did my own. He groaned, biting my lower lip softly.

My hips moved, rocking on him, needing the release he knew how to give.

"Not here," he whispered, pulling away from me. "No."

It was over as quickly as it had started and arms lifted me from his lap, placing me on my feet. My body swayed with my hazed thoughts, and I glanced up to find Olen smiling at me.

"They await to hear the punishment, your grace." He addressed Ulrich, but his eyes were bright, still holding my gaze.

Ulrich's responding voice broke me from my spell.

"Banishment."

My judgement boomed out across the room, and I finally turned, allowing myself to watch his court.

Hate—hate stared back at me.

"Bring him," Ulrich demanded.

The bodies parted in a straight line and a shrill, damning laugh echoed around us.

Those same deadly creatures that had dragged Harold's body from the ship pulled Bjorn into the room.

The man's hair had grown some in the months since his imprisonment. A thick beard accompanied his face now as well.

His head was hanging down while he allowed the creatures to pull him through the crowd. But he laughed the entire way, sending sickening horror through my body.

They threw him not at Ulrich's feet, but at mine.

Bjorn glanced up, smiling like a creature made of evil.

"Princess," he hissed. "Getting fucked now, it appears."

Olen's fist collided into his head and Bjorn dropped onto the stone below the dais. Ulrich stood next, shadows crawling across the floor with his rage.

"She's given you *mercy*," the king announced. "And you choose to mock her."

Bjorn rose, holding a hand to his head. "I am the one doing the mocking?" He laughed. "Tell me, Ulrich. Does she *know*?"

Ulrich's shadows rammed down Bjorn's throat, cutting off his words.

Know?

My eyes went to Olen who nodded just once before placing his finger at his lips.

What was I supposed to know?

The beating started. Ulrich and Olen connecting their fists with every soft part of Bjorn's flesh. But the monster did not cry out.

No, to my dismay he kept his eyes on me. Even when they began to swell shut. Even when I was sure he could no longer see through them.

Yet, I didn't stop it. I took glee from it. Breathing in the triumph of watching the men before me take out their rage on the one who had intended to harm me.

Bjorn fell to the ground, spitting out black blood and I lifted my hand.

"Send him away," I said loudly.

Ulrich lifted his kin's head, forcing the man to look at me.

"I am bound to do as she wishes," he stated. "If only she would allow me to kill you on the spot."

I did not understand why the words ignited a fire of need inside of me, but Gods, my blood felt aflame.

Bjorn sneered at me while his long canines peeked through the blood. "I bet you are delicious," he laughed. "I bet when the time comes, and he is fully without control, that he will *feast* upon your soul."

My breaths slowed.

Ulrich punched the man again, but he did not stop.

"I bet he will bow at her feet like the caged pet that he is."

Another hit.

"And I *know* he will destroy you without a moment of regret."

Olen's fist threw the final blow, knocking Bjorn unconscious.

The room was silent. Tense. Waiting.

I met Ulrich's eyes, finding his skin going translucent under his mask. His hands convulsed at his sides.

I stepped forward, wrapping my palms around his blood-covered wrists.

"Ulrich," I whispered, trying to pull him from the thoughts tormenting his mind. "Ulrich," I repeated.

His eyes snapped to mine.

Pure black.

A void staring back at me.

There was a *thud,* and footsteps retreated, but I did not pull my focus from the man before me. I held firm, gripping his wrists.

His shoulders lifted with his breaths and then slowly, his skin returned to its normal appearance. His eyes cleared and the green gaze that constantly held me in a trance stared back at me.

"I did not kill him," he muttered.

My palms tightened around his wrist. "Thank you."

The music picked up around us and the bodies began to move. Nervously at first but slowly, the sensual beating of the drums cleansed the room of the violence we'd all witnessed.

I led Ulrich back to the throne, helping him sit and then placed myself right onto his lap. I allowed his palm to wrap around the front of me, appearing before his court like the being they believed he controlled.

Yet I knew the truth while I watched them all and his fingers tapped against my lower stomach; I was the one in control.

The bodies continued to dance, and I remained on Ulrich's lap, gripping his thigh to steady myself.

"Should we retire?" he whispered into my ear.

I kept my eyes forward, watching as Olen entered the room again. He was followed by a *troll* offering the right hand what appeared to be a damp cloth.

"You need to clean yourself," I replied.

Olen approached and I stood, allowing Ulrich to be passed his own cloth.

They were both silent, their eyes holding an unspoken conversation between them while they cleansed their hands and wrists of the blood of the man I'd banished.

"What did you do with him?" I asked.

Olen turned to me. "He's in the dungeons until Frode can heal him a bit. Can't banish a man that can't see out of his swollen eyes."

"I could," Ulrich countered.

I laughed.

Olen rolled his eyes with a smile. "He will be brought out to the docks and banished publicly. He'll have to manage rowing a little boat to Oberon to beg for shelter, or the mortals. But I doubt he'd willingly step foot on Middgard."

I nodded my head.

Ulrich pulled me back toward him, pressing my body to his.

"Should we retire?"

I stared at him then my eyes went to Olen. He offered me a mischievous grin.

"Should *we* retire?" he asked.

Ulrich's hand around my body went flat and he cleared his throat, pulling my gaze from his right hand.

"Brenna?" he asked with a smile.

"I think we should *all* retire," I whispered.

Ulrich ran his finger along my lips while fire burned in his eyes.

"Lead the way."

I pulled from him, grasping not just his wrist, but Olen's too and I turned toward the door behind the dais. The captain of our adventure, leading us all into a storm I should have been terrified to venture toward.

Chapter 32

Sounds of the party echoed behind us while we all shoved the hidden door open, stumbling into the bedroom. I released their wrists, and turned toward them, my chest rising with nerves.

Olen's hand gripped mine and I met Ulrich's eyes.

How were we doing this once more? How was I considering this after I'd just watched the two men before me brutally beat and banish a man?

Ulrich's eyes were hot while we held our gazes. My body became tight the longer he stared. He was turning me to liquid where I stood, using his power to win this battle.

He approached, forcing me to press against Olen's chest. His right hand wrapped his arms around me in response.

"Gods, princess," Olen whispered in my ear. "Here we are again."

The desire in his voice shook my knees. I moaned, leaning into him, closing my eyes from the maddening heat of his body against mine.

Ulrich's hand brushed my jaw. "What do you want?"

My eyes fluttered open and I met his gaze. It was full of hunger like each time we found ourselves falling into our lust.

"Both of you," I whispered.

"Like before?" Olen muttered into my ear, stroking a hand across the neckline of my soul-colored gown.

I kept my eyes on Ulrich, biting my lip.

He grinned. "She's too shy to ask."

Olen laughed while he pressed himself into my backside. A moan left my lips from the heat of his erection pushing against the fabric of my gown.

"We will be gentle," Olen whispered.

"She prefers rough," Ulrich replied.

My irritation rose at the knowing in his words, but he shook his head.

"Don't deny it. You and I both know the truth."

Ulrich ran his hand over my jaw, brushing his finger across my lips. "Tell us what you want."

I couldn't utter the words. Not out loud with them both listening intently. I glanced at Olen then pulled away, reaching on my toes to whisper in Ulrich's ear.

The king's eyes went wide with a feral heat. He smiled before turning on his heel and leaving me and Olen standing together while he crossed the room.

"Where is he going?" Olen asked.

I kept my eyes on the king, watching him pull the plush chair by the window back to the bed. When he was before us again, Olen's hand wrapped around my neck, pulling me against him once more.

"He likes to watch," I whispered.

"Thank the Gods for you, princess," Olen whispered, kissing my neck.

Ulrich motioned to the bed, a quiet order for me and Olen to follow. They both went to sit, but I held up my hands.

"I am still clothed."

The words unlocked both of their restraints.

Four hands gripped my body. Two at my chest and two around my waist, pulling at my clothing. Their lips kissed my neck while they tugged at my gown. Ripping it from my body.

"That was expensive," Ulrich hissed when Olen threw the scraps to the ground.

Olen laughed. "I think Brenna can forgive us for ruining her birthday present."

My chest went tight with the words, and I met both of their eyes. They stared back at me, heat burning in their gazes.

"This gift may be better," I whispered.

Ulrich's eyes grew wide, and he moved them down my body, taking all of me in.

"Fuck," Ulrich muttered. "I will never tire of that sight."

Olen was on me first, his lips claiming my own while his hands rose. His fingers pulled at the ribbons of my mask, loosening it from its tight fit against my face. Slowly, he pulled it away from me, tossing it to the ground.

My legs began to tremble as his fingers moved to my hair, pulling the pins and releasing the locks to allow them to brush my back. He moved to my neck, brushing my collarbone until his hands were both cupping a breast.

"Gods," he groaned, leaning down and taking one into his mouth.

My moan was quiet, a whimper of pleasure and my head went back, landing on Ulrich's chest as he approached me from behind.

I reached up, running my palm over the king's shoulder while Olen continued his teasing.

Ulrich grasped my hand, holding it tightly, saying not one word.

"Oh," I cried when Olen bit down on my nipple and pulled softly.

"Do not call for your Gods, tonight," Ulrich whispered into my ear while his hand rose and caressed my other breast. "They are banned from this sacred ceremony."

"Fuck the Gods," I moaned at his words.

"That's it," he laughed, placing a kiss behind my ear.

Olen laughed against my skin, and I lifted my head, watching him lower to his knees. I jolted when his breath hovered over me.

"Ulrich has had a taste," Olen smiled at me. "I believe I get one too."

"Oh my—"

My words were cut off when Ulrich's finger went into my mouth, shocking me with the force of it.

"Ssh," he whispered.

His hands cupped the back of my thighs, and he lifted me into the air, positioning me before Olen.

"Perfect," Olen whispered as his mouth claimed me.

I threw my head against Ulrich's neck, crying out while Olen's tongue worked on me. His movements were different from Ulrich's. Not better. But his own techniques, pulling that low pressure from within me. Rising my need for more to the surface.

Ulrich's hands on my thighs gripped me tighter.

"Does his mouth feel good on your clit?" he muttered, biting my ear.

"Yes," I breathed out.

"Would you like to learn what his cock is like, Brenna?"

I was lost in ecstasy, unable to find a way to respond to his brazen words.

Olen's mouth sucked on me while his tongue moved up and down. I jolted when his fingers entered me, moving slowly, not giving me enough of what my body desired.

"Ask for it," Ulrich whispered. "Beg for it."

My hands shook, but I could not force the words out.

"Beg for it, Brenna," Ulrich repeated. "*You are in control.*"

That damned word. He used it with precision.

"I want it." I groaned. "Gods, please I want it."

Olen stood claiming my mouth against his. The taste of me on his tongue was intoxicating. He pulled away, smiling at me while his fingers moved back to me, entering me slowly.

Ulrich held me closer, his hands gripping my thighs and I was sure he was going to carry me to the bed when suddenly he and Olen were kissing.

I jumped in his hands, staring in shock.

When they pulled away, Olen grinned at me. "You mixed with him is the best taste I've come across."

"Fucking Gods," I breathed out.

"If you say that word again," Ulrich whispered, "we will fuck you so hard you will lose the ability to speak."

My mouth slammed shut and he carried me to the bed, setting me down while he placed himself on his chair.

I trembled in my spot, watching Olen undress before me. His muscled body was on full display as his clothes hit the ground, and I bit my lip.

"What do you want?" Ulrich asked from his seat.

"Control," I replied, dropping to my knees.

Olen's eyes went wide when my mouth wrapped around him. One hand went to the back of my head while the other gripped Ulrich's shoulder.

I moved my lips against him, holding my fingers at his base while I worked.

"Fuck," Olen groaned, thrusting his hips, forcing his cock down my throat.

I smiled around him, triumphant in his pleasure. When I pulled away, I met Ulrich's eyes. He was unmoving. His gaze widened. His cock was rigid, pressing against his trousers.

I moved to him, my hands running across the fabric keeping him from me.

"You haven't let me do this yet," I muttered.

He said nothing.

"I have dreamt about it," I continued. "Of your taste. Gods, have I thought about it."

Ulrich's eyes snapped to Olen, and I yelled out when the right hand rushed behind me, lifting my hips.

"You were warned," Olen laughed, slapping my bare skin.

My eyes went wide, and I met Ulrich's wild smile. His hand ran along my jaw.

"You want this?" he asked.

I turned my gaze to the prize I was determined to claim, wanting the pulse of him in my hands and mouth.

I nodded.

"Open your legs for him," Ulrich demanded.

I did as he told me, and Olen lifted my hips higher letting out a groan when I was exposed to him.

"Fuck her," Ulrich demanded, not pulling his eyes from me.

My body went tight at the sound of Olen slipping on a sheath, but I held onto Ulrich's gaze. Determined to win this battle.

Olen's hands returned to my body, lifting my hips into the air in his monstrously, strong arms.

"Scream for him," Ulrich said as his eyes flared.

I nodded.

Olen slammed into me with Ulrich's order, and I screamed out, gripping Ulrich's thighs.

"Oh Gods," I cried, then my eyes widened as the word left my lips.

Both men laughed and Olen picked up his pace. Slamming into me until I could no longer focus on my desire to have Ulrich in my mouth.

My head went limp against Ulrich's thigh while Olen continued thrusting. The pleasure was so much I could barely breathe. I could only hold onto Ulrich with all my might, terrified I would fall into oblivion.

Then, Olen was pulling away, only he wasn't done. His hands wrapped around my waist, lifting while he settled on to the bed.

He spread me again, just like he had the first time we'd allowed ourselves this sin and Ulrich's eyes went dark.

Olen's hand went to my neck, grasping softly. "He likes to watch, Brenna. Do you know what that means?"

I shook my head while my body trembled.

"He wants to watch me fill you," Olen licked my neck. "He wants to watch you come around my cock. He will not give you what you want until he gets what *he* wants."

I stared at Ulrich while Olen's fingers went to my clit. The king watched, his eyes moving along with Olen's circling. Like he was trapped in a spell.

"Fuck me," I whispered to Olen. "More."

Olen lifted me up and Ulrich's chest rose slower.

"Fill me," I said loudly, holding the king's gaze.

Olen's hip went upward while he held me by my thighs, lifting me up and down on him. Giving Ulrich the perfect view of us joining together.

"Touch yourself," Ulrich said breathlessly.

One hand went to a breast and the other went lower, running along my most sensitive spot. I jolted at my own touch while Olen's hip thrusted into me.

"Fuck," I cried.

Ulrich smiled.

"More."

Olen went faster, his groans now right behind my ear. My legs shook on him while I continued touching, helping my body enjoy the man inside of me and the man watching it all.

My fingers went faster, without my control, while Olen picked up his pace.

"Come for me," Ulrich said.

The demand—Gods, I could not deny it if I had wanted.

My legs spasmed in Olen's hands and my head went back against his chest while I released around him.

He bit down on my neck as I trembled in his hands. By the way his body shook beneath me, I was sure he was finding his own release along with my own.

My body could barely move when a hand ran along my jaw again and I found an unclothed Ulrich before me.

"Open your mouth."

Olen shifted slightly, moving us closer to the floor with him still deep inside of me, providing a better angle to access the man before me. I did as I was told and to my shock, Olen resumed his thrusting.

My eyes went to Ulrich and my hands rose, wrapping around him. Relishing in my conquest.

I claimed my prize, wrapping my lips around him.

They both moaned as I did. Ulrich's hand went to my head, and he pushed down my throat while Olen thrusted up into me.

Tears came from my eyes the faster Ulrich moved his hips. But I did not want either of them to stop.

Ulrich pulled away, brushing his finger over my lips.

"There is one thing we enjoy," he whispered. "But only if you want it."

Olen stopped his thrusting.

My chest rose slowly, and Ulrich's hand cupped my flesh.

"Both of us," Ulrich whispered.

At first I did not understand. I had them both already. I blinked at him, unable to respond when Olen thrusted softly in response.

"*Both* of us," Ulrich repeated.

My eyes went wide, and I pulled my hand from him, holding it against my chest.

"I've never..."

Olen kissed my neck. "You are not required to."

"Control," Ulrich muttered. "We will force nothing."

Olen continued his soft thrusts while his hand held my thigh.

I closed my eyes for just a moment before nodding.

Once.

Just as they did.

Ulrich lifted me from Olen softly. He helped me to my feet, spinning me around to watch his right hand crawl up the bed slowly.

"How?" I asked nervously.

"However you'd like," Ulrich replied, holding me close against him.

"Where?"

He laughed. "There are two choices." His hand gripped my backside.

I spun around, my mouth open in shock. "I will not do *that.*"

"That's a damned shame," Olen laughed from the bed.

"Then there's the second choice." Ulrich brushed my cheek. "It is my favorite anyway."

His hand went to the front of me, brushing my sensitive flesh softly. "Both of us," he whispered.

"Will it hurt?"

"We will stop if it does."

For some damned reason, I trusted him. I trusted both of them. Not questioning that I was safe in their arms. That no harm would come to me at that moment.

Even though they both had caused me harm already.

Ulrich spun me to face Olen again while he retrieved his own sheath.

Olen motioned to me with his finger, calling me to him.

I followed, crawling up the bed and straddling over him. Not lowering but teasing him just enough.

He sat up, gripping my face.

"You are a rare woman indeed," he whispered.

I trembled at his words, shaking further when Ulrich's weight shifted the mattress. I moved, twisting to look at Ulrich. He smiled at me, running his hand down my back. Pausing, as he always did, at the scars on my back.

"Olen, switch with me," Ulrich whispered.

Olen offered me a wink and lifted me away. Ulrich laid in his spot, motioning me to him.

I straddled him, like I had Olen, and paused for a moment with panic rising in my chest.

"We can stop," he said quietly.

"No." I shook my head. "I don't want to."

I lowered onto him, gripping his inked skin until I was fully seated.

"Fuck," Olen groaned behind me.

Ulrich grinned and lifted his hips, thrusting into me. I leaned forward while his hands gripped my backside, giving Olen a clear view of him and me.

"Fuck," Olen groaned again.

Ulrich kissed my neck.

"I cannot," he thrusted again, and I cried out, "explain what it is like to watch that."

He thrusted again.

"The beauty of watching you get filled and fucked."

I lifted my head, staring into the eyes behind his skeletal mask.

"You are perfect," he muttered, claiming my lips like he had on the throne.

My hands gripped his chest while he moved his hips, pounding into me, making me lose myself. When I could no longer stand it, I laid my head against his chest while he continued, wondering when Olen would join us. Wanting to experience something that should have terrified me to the core.

"Just say when," Olen said, slapping my backside as Ulrich thrusted into me again.

"Yes," I cried out. "Please."

"Such manners," Ulrich smiled.

His movements stopped and he gripped my chin, pulling my face to his.

"You need to tell us if this is too much," he said softly.

I nodded.

"No, I am serious."

"I know," I replied. "I will."

Olen approached and Ulrich shifted slightly with me still seated on him, giving Olen more room.

I laid back again, keeping my cheek on Ulrich's chest, gripping his shoulder while Olen slowly slipped into me alongside his king.

I bit down on Ulrich's chest from the pressure of them both together.

"Are you alright?" he asked, wrapping his arms around my waist.

"Yes," I groaned. "Yes."

Ulrich stayed unmoving while Olen began to thrust softly. The sensation was so much. Too much and not enough all at once. Tight at first, but then pure ecstasy within moments of Olen's movements starting.

"More," I begged, gripping Ulrich's shoulder.

Olen's hands pulled my arms from Ulrich, holding them at the base of my lower back. Lifting me so my breasts were bared to the king.

"You want more?" Ulrich said, his eyes burning with passion.

"Please," I cried. "Please."

Olen kept his grip on me, his hands restraining my arms, and together they moved. In sync. In mind-numbing thrusts that took the breath from my lungs.

I could not find the air to let out my screams of pleasure the faster they moved together. My mind wandered, allowing myself to realize they were rubbing against each other inside of me, their bodies touching.

Gods, I could barely stand it.

Olen's grip went tighter while his moans grew louder and soon Ulrich followed. Their hips went faster, forcing more screams from my lips with the sharp inhale that I took.

"Fuck," Ulrich cried out, thrusting upward while Olen's hips did the same.

I jolted with the pressure of them both fully inside of me as they shook below and behind me.

It was a prize feeling them both lose themselves in their release, and knowing my body had brought that for them.

Olen let out a sigh, pulling away first while I remained on Ulrich's chest. Ulrich's hands ran down my body.

"Brenna?" he asked.

I could not move.

"Princess?" Olen whispered.

I sat up, staring at them both.

"That was amazing," I muttered while my cheeks warmed.

Olen grinned, leaning forward and kissing me. His hands ran down my body, stopping at my belly.

"You're not done," Ulrich said, pulling me from the kiss.

Olen gripped me, forcing me to lay between them both. They each grabbed an arm, splaying me out while their bodies laid on my limbs, holding me in place.

"Scream for us," Ulrich whispered while his fingers entered me.

"Let go," Olen added, circling my clit.

I jolted, trying to fight the pressure they were forcing me to release.

"I have already—" My protest stopped when Ulrich began to curl his fingers up.

"You are not done," he whispered.

My head went against the pillow as they worked. Both of them let out moans of appreciation while they played with my body. Putting me completely at their mercy.

Forcing me to scream out with my orgasm.

It was as maddening as before. Consuming my mind and soul.

My body shook, violently, causing the bed to tremble while my legs convulsed with my release. Each time I thought I was done, a wave came over me, drowning me in pleasure and ecstasy. My body happily accepting their insistence for me to lose myself.

To let go.

When I could no longer move, they both pulled from me. Each offering my neck a kiss on either side. Ulrich's arm pulled me onto his chest while Olen's body lifted from the bed. His footsteps retreated to the bathing room and water turned on before I finally met Ulrich's eyes again.

He stared back while his hand ran down my back.

"I think you're going to destroy me, Brenna," he whispered. "No—I'm certain you will."

I did not know what he meant, I only knew he likely was not wrong. Because I was already destroyed and claimed by him.

I was fully at his mercy.

Chapter 33

Another two weeks passed before Ulrich had called us all to the dock for Bjorn's public banishment.

I stood behind him, refusing to step forward while the citizens of his city and island gathered. Despite this banishment being called by my own words, I could not bring myself to watch.

Olen appeared at my side, his clattering earrings giving away his approach. I glanced up at him and he gave me a sly smile.

"Princess," he whispered.

"Olen," I replied, turning my eyes to Ulrich's back once more.

"The prisoner is being brought from the dungeons. Has Ulrich not explained your part in this?"

I met Olen's eyes, stumbling a step backward.

"What? My part?"

Olen grinned further. "Brenna, this is *your* banishment. Ulrich will require your part in it all. You will cut the rope that sends the small ship away and out toward the mist."

I turned my head right as Ulrich twisted his body in my direction. His smile was wide, manic, and wild.

"Olen, thank you for explaining. I wasn't looking forward to another argument today," he laughed.

I clamped my mouth shut. It wasn't worth refuting his decision. Not publicly. Not with something that I could feel was too important for Ulrich and his people.

Ulrich and Olen turned at the clanking ring of chains dragging down the docks. I, however, kept my eyes forward while I took a step toward Ulrich.

The king didn't glance my way when I arrived at his side. His hand ran down my arm and he leaned down, whispering for only mine and Olen's ears to hear.

"Good girl."

My blood went hot.

I turned my eyes to Olen who had a fire in his gaze. Heat that made my knees weak.

Ulrich's hand went to my wrist, holding it tightly. A subtle show of his control and ownership of me.

One I did not turn away from.

Bjorn's smile was sickening when Ulrich's dark monsters deposited him at the king's feet. His beard was still thick, but his face was no longer swollen.

Bruised, yes, but you could see his features once more.

"My king," Bjorn sneered. His eyes went to mine and I held back my recoil. Instead, I held my head high, staring back at him.

"She's confident today," he snarled.

"I suggest you hold your tongue," Ulrich replied. "She can change your punishment at any time, *cousin*, do not forget that."

Bjorn's smile turned to a mischievous, sweet expression. One I hated instantly.

"Princess," he hissed. "Would you give me another chance?"

Ulrich released his hold on me, and I stepped forward, then crouched to meet Bjorn's eyes.

"What was your intention with me?" I whispered.

Bjorn's eyes went wide with glee. "What do you think, princess? My cock needed someone to bury into. It prefers women who do not fight back."

My hand connected with his cheek and I stood, returning to my place between Ulrich and Olen.

Bjorn took several moments to lift his head before he laughed, that annoying, shrill sound.

"Do you not remember what I told you, princess? He will ruin you. He will rip you to pieces with little to no remorse. You are setting yourself up to be destroyed."

I remained quiet while I inhaled deep breaths, trying to ground myself and my anger.

Ulrich leaned down, his beard and the edge of his dark mask brushed my neck.

"Remember that rage Harold ignited inside of you? Remember the thickness of his blood on your skin?"

I snapped my head up, meeting the king's eyes.

Olen leaned in, brushing my arm. "It's just another life, Brenna. Claim it."

The heat of them pressing me between their bodies and the waiting eyes of Ulrich's people was too much. I shook my head, stepping back slightly.

"This fool deserves his banishment," I announced. "Death is the easy way out of facing his crimes."

Ulrich's eyes glassed over with amusement, but he titled his chin in acknowledgement of my words.

My breaths trembled with relief. He was upholding our agreement.

Bjorn would not die at my hands.

Ulrich lifted his kin by the neck of his thread-bare shirt and tossed him into the air. I jumped back in surprise, watching the man fly until his body crashed into the small boat tied to the dock.

Olen approached me again, dropping his voice.

"Ulrich will give you a knife and you will cut that rope. Do you understand?"

I nodded.

Ulrich turned, as though he was aware of my agreement and his hand flicked out, revealing one of his shadow knives.

"My *Lady*," he whispered.

My hands did not tremble when I grasped the end of the knife, wrapping my palm around the shadow handle.

Bjorn stared at me with hate in his eyes while I crouched down.

"You stupid *whore,*" he sneered from the boat.

"I may be Ulrich's whore," I replied, "but at least *I* made the choice to be so."

I ripped the knife across the rope, watching while the threads split. Bjorn's boat did not move, and I wondered what I had done wrong, when Ulrich's cold was beside me. His shadow knife was gone from my hands, and I stared while the shadows crawled across the docks, shoving against the boat and sending it out to the water.

"Banishment!" Ulrich's voice shouted. "You will never return to these shores."

Bjorn didn't reply, but he kept his eyes on me. I steadied my breath while I watched him float away until the mist opened for the boat and he disappeared off in the distance.

My shoulders relaxed once the mist fell again, allowing Bjorn to turn into a distant memory.

"How did that feel?" Ulrich whispered beside me.

I met his eyes, finding intrigue in his gaze.

I lifted my shoulders. "I do not know," I admitted.

Olen's jingling earrings rattled behind me and I turned on my heel, meeting his eyes.

"You didn't cut his throat for calling you a whore," he laughed.

Ulrich's responding laugh instantly irritated me, and I threw my hands up in defeat.

"You both ruin everything with your jests."

"Or we make your life more entertaining," Olen replied.

"Irritating," I replied with a smile.

Ulrich pressed his chest against my back, and he pulled me against him. His hand brushed my cheek, causing me to tremble. My vision blurred slightly from his touch, clouding the faces of his sneering citizens watching us.

"I will take the irritation," he muttered. "It's better than the rage."

"I thought you approved of my hate," I replied.

He pressed further against me and his hand landed against my lower stomach. "I said nothing about the hate."

I gulped and my hand went to his. Then, like a madwoman, I held it against me, pressing my palm against the top of his hand.

"That hate is addictive, remember?" he whispered into my ear.

I nodded my head in agreement, unsure how we had gotten here and why it was so strangely comfortable.

I left Ulrich and Olen on the dock while I made my way back to the bedroom, exhausted from the high emotions of sending Bjorn away.

When I opened the door, my eyes went to the closet. Where my trunks were tucked away at the back.

My gaze went back to the hallway, and I prayed neither man had followed me. I closed the bedroom door slowly and slipped into the closet. My breaths were heavy while I lifted the lid of my deepest chest and peered inside.

To those unknowing, it appeared to be full of dresses I had not yet pulled out. But to the woman who knew this trunk intimately, my eyes found the hidden compartment easily.

My hands trembled while I lifted the gowns and then pulled on the clasp at the bottom. As quickly as I could, I lifted the papers, a handful of letters I had penned to Titania in moments of panic months before.

Words that I knew would change everything if Ulrich were to find them.

I stared at my ink. At the hate that still lived in my heart. The hate that was slowly unraveling to something different. Something I could not fully understand.

I leaned against the trunk, holding the papers out, contemplating my next move.

The door opened, startling me and they slipped from my grasp.

“No!” I whispered, but I was too late.

Olen’s head appeared at my gasps and his eyes went right to the evidence of my deception.

“Letters for your father?” he asked with a grin.

I scrambled to my feet and Ulrich’s head appeared behind Olen’s. My stomach dropped. I was dead. I would be murdered right where I stood.

Ulrich's eyes went to the papers, grasping one before I could stop him. Olen's gaze turned menacing while I watched his eyes scan the words Ulrich was intently reading.

"*My dearest queen, I write, begging for your aid...*" Ulrich's eyes met mine and his chest moved with his slowed breaths. "*Your court's most terrified monster has me locked within his walls.*"

"Brenna, you fucking fool," Olen sighed.

"Ulrich," I whispered.

Ulrich stepped into the closet, shoving Olen aside while his hands gripped the letter, and he continued reading aloud.

"*He has branded me, my queen. Scarring my body and soul. . .*" His words stopped and he pulled his gaze from my words. "Interesting," he hissed.

"Ulrich," I said again.

His shadows came toward me, slamming me into the trunk behind me. He approached, his body a towering omen. His eyes, determined to claim my soul.

"What is this?" he demanded.

My tears built in my eyes while I tried to force myself to reply. To explain myself.

"Brenna," his voice was a warning, "what is this?"

"Nothing," I responded. "Nothing, I was about to get rid of them. I was going to burn them!"

His hand gripped my neck and his eyes went dark.

"You have betrayed me, princess," he whispered.

I shook my head. "I have not! I have not sent one single letter. I wrote them when I was tortured in my mind. When I needed to release the hate in my heart. Ulrich, I promise I was going to destroy them!"

He held the parchment before my face mockingly.

"Tell me what your request was going to be."

I blinked. "What?"

My eyes went to Olen who pulled his gaze away from mine.

"Ulrich," I sobbed. "Please."

"What was your request going to be in just a few months' time, Brenna? Was it to send these? I see no dates on this one. Were you hoping Titania would come to your aid? To enact war on your behalf?"

"Ulrich," I croaked, struggling against his tightening hold.

"Brenna, tell me what your request was going to be!" he shouted.

He dropped me while his voice echoed around us and I fell to the ground, gasping and gripping my throat.

"Fine!" I shouted back. "Fine! Yes! I *was* going to beg for her aid. I was going to request her to come to your shores and help me. But my desire for that ended weeks ago."

He was at my level in an instant, his eyes barreling into mine. "When?" he demanded.

"When Oberon sent that ship," I cried. "I swear it, Ulrich. I swear on my soul that I was going to destroy these."

Ulrich stood, turning his head to Olen while he *tsked* his tongue. "She has been disobedient."

My stomach knotted at the smile on Olen's face.

"It appears she has," he hissed.

Ulrich turned back to me, pulling up my chin to stare into his eyes.

"I could send her to the dungeons," he whispered.

I shook my head. "Please."

"Please what?" he replied.

"Please do not make me go down there."

"Betrayal deserves punishment, Brenna," Ulrich replied, gripping my chin tighter.

"I know," I cried.

Olen let out a loud breath and Ulrich stepped away. My eyes dragged upward, finding them with their arms crossed while they grinned at each other.

They were both absolutely insane.

"How many days?" I asked, pulling myself to my feet.

"For what?" Ulrich replied.

"The dungeons?" I responded, glancing past their shoulders to the bedroom behind them. "How many days will you force me down there?"

Olen grinned and stepped back into the room. Ulrich did the same. I followed them both apprehensively, until I was in the middle of the room.

The fire in both of their eyes ignited a burn inside of me. One of intrigue and fear I could not shake.

"I will not force you to the dungeons, princess," Ulrich replied, circling me. His hand brushed my neck, and I trembled.

"What are you talking about?" I whispered.

His body slammed against mine and his palm gripped my throat, forcing me to stare at Olen.

"Betrayal deserves punishment," he muttered against my ear. "I will choose your punishment."

"Ulrich…" I began my protests and yelled out when my knees buckled under me, sending me to the ground.

He stayed pressed against me, holding my throat tightly, but gently.

"You will accept this punishment, do you understand?"

I did not understand until the sound of a buckle unclasping came from above. My eyes widened when my gaze turned upward, finding Olen undressing before me.

Ulrich held me tighter.

"This is a punishment," he whispered again. "But you are in control. Do you understand?"

"No," I admitted.

"You will take what we give you. Every moment of it. Every bit of pain and ecstasy. If you do not wish for it, then yes, I will lock you in the dungeon for as long as I see fit."

My body trembled against his while I considered his words.

"I need an answer." He bit my ear with his whisper.

My eyes went up again, finding Olen with a full erection standing so close to my face it would have taken little effort to claim him with my mouth.

"What is my punishment?" I replied, trying to understand what I was agreeing to.

"Whatever we deem appropriate," Olen responded above. "Whatever our *king* demands of you."

Ulrich's body pressed into mine and my body went hot at the heat of his arousal under the fabric of my dress.

"Pain?" I muttered.

Ulrich laughed behind me. "And pleasure. Both, at the same time. We cannot allow you to forget you are being punished. You will have to tell us your limits though."

"How?" I whispered, unsure how my voice had managed to speak with the nerves fluttering in my belly.

"Yell out the name of your island if it is too much. If you relent or the pain has broken you to your limit."

Nóatún

The word rang in my head as my hand went back, gripping Ulrich's thigh without my control. His breath hitched against my ear and his hand held my throat tighter.

"It's about trust," he whispered. "Do you trust us, Brenna?"

Trust. The word was hot in my mind. A fire determined to burn through me.

"Do you accept your punishment?" Ulrich's voice was a growl, low and full of need.

I met Olen's eyes and the shimmer of mischief in them. My hand held Ulrich tighter while I considered my choices: accept this punishment and send my sin-stained soul further into the darkest depths, or take the easy choice, the comfortable one of being thrown back into those rotted dungeons.

The woman who had arrived on this island would have chosen the second, easier option. She would have recoiled knowing the fire these men now put through her body and blood. She likely would have died where she stood if she knew that I did trust these creatures, even if it were only that they would not truly harm my body in this way.

I gulped and Ulrich held me tighter.

I was no longer that woman.

"I accept," I whispered.

"What a good *beast*," Ulrich sneered. "Open your mouth."

I hesitated for a moment, my body's attempt to stop me and Ulrich's hand went to my jaw, forcing it to open.

"You will do as you're told, tonight. Do you understand?"

I nodded, trying to ignore the pain of his grip while Olen approached.

"Olen," Ulrich's beard brushed my cheek while he gazed up at his right hand, "fuck her face."

I leaned back, a reaction I had no control over, and Ulrich's free hand gripped my hair. His palm flattened against my head, shoving me toward Olen. My body went hot and tight at the sensation of Olen's shaft sliding down my throat. Gently at first, like the giant wanted to remind me of my control, but then the beast in him took over.

Ulrich's hand gripped my head still while Olen pushed into me, filling my throat with him. Not allowing me a moment to catch my breath when he pulled out then thrusted down again.

My body trembled on my knees and my eyes watered. I wanted to beg for their release. For them both to allow me a moment to pause, but a darker part of me accepted this punishment. Accepted the heavy breaths both men let out and the heat of their desire wrapping around my body.

Slickness grew between my thighs, and I let out a groan as Olen went deeper, forcing me to gag on him and pull away. I leaned down, my hands gripping the stone floor while I tried to steady my breaths.

Ulrich's hand pulled my hair up again, yanking me away from the ground.

"I did not say you were done," he seethed in my ear.

He pressed his palm against my back, keeping me on all fours. His hands threw the skirts of my gown over my hips, and I trembled as he ripped my undergarments from my body, exposing me to him.

"Olen," he demanded.

His hand on my head kept me from being able to glance up to see what he was demanding but then my screams echoed across the room when something cold and hard slapped against my backside.

"Fuck the fucking Gods!" I yelled out.

Olen was on his knees in an instant, his hand cupping my chin.

"You and those Gods, princess," he laughed. "Hold still."

I shook my head, suddenly regretting my choice with the sting of whatever Ulrich had struck me with bringing back memories of my lashes.

"Please," I whispered. "I can't."

Olen's mischievous smile grew serious, and he held me tighter. "You know what to say if you are truly done. The dungeons will welcome you. Are you done, Brenna?"

I stared into his dark eyes. My lips wanted to utter the word. My mind wanted me to end this insanity.

But my soul could not allow it to stop.

I shook my head and Olen nodded with an appreciative grin.

Ulrich's hand brushed against the sensitive skin he'd struck moments before. I held Olen's gaze, my legs trembling at the sound of Ulrich's clothing being removed behind me.

He pressed against me, his hard cock just brushing my entrance.

"Stay here," he whispered as he shoved away.

Olen smiled at me, brushing his thumb across my lower lip. "It's a miracle, princess. You're doing what you're told."

My lower belly ached with need while he continued to circle his teasing and maddening touch.

I began to wonder what Ulrich had disappeared for when his hand appeared in my peripheral, passing Olen a sheath. Olen winked, pulling his thumb away while he rolled it down over himself. Then Ulrich was behind me again, rubbing himself against my slickness once more.

"Olen," he muttered, "our whore is wet for us."

My body froze at his words.

Olen grinned at me. "Is she?"

Ulrich's hand reached around me, stroking between my thighs. He groaned while he moved against me.

"She is so wet for us," he moaned. "Like the good whore she is."

I hated how much I loved his use of the word in that moment. How it sent my legs trembling with desire, clouding my mind's attempt to protest.

Olen stood, leaving me to stare at the bed while he went to my backside. My body was shaking while I waited for what was to come when Ulrich's body pulled from mine and he took the spot Olen had been in moments before.

My eyes went right to the tattoos on his thighs then traveled to his hard cock.

He smiled, brushing my lips as Olen had and I let out a gasp when Olen's fingers entered me suddenly.

"Tell me what you are, Brenna," Ulrich said with his eyes flaring.

I shook my head and Olen added another finger, pumping in and out of me quickly. Stealing my ability to respond.

Ulrich gripped my chin, preventing my head from dropping from the pleasure.

"Look at me," he ordered.

I met his eyes.

"What are you?" he asked.

I wanted to say it. Gods, I wanted nothing more than to fall into his depravities. To accept this punishment for what it was. To accept the consequences of my own foolish actions.

Olen went faster and I cried out again when the same cold sting hit my backside once again.

"What are you?" Ulrich repeated.

I bit my lip and shook my head again. I couldn't do it.

Olen's fingers pulled away. I let out a breath of relief then yelled when he roughly slammed into me, jolting my body forward with his thrust.

"Oh Gods," I cried, trying to gather my breath.

Olens hand pulled at my hair, forcing me to stare into Ulrich's waiting gaze. The king smiled at me. An expression that forced my muscles to tighten around Olen in response.

The right hand groaned, thrusting harder. "Whatever you just did," he panted, "make her do it again."

Olen lifted me higher with his hold on my hair and Ulrich gripped my neck.

"Brenna," his voice was full of need, "you are not doing what you're told."

I gasped out in shock when Olen pulled from me and Ulrich threw me over his shoulder. He set me at the end of the bed, and I turned around, finding them both staring at me with wicked smiles.

"Undress," Olen ordered.

Ulrich smiled.

My hands did as I was told, pulling the strings at the back of my dress, releasing the barrier that kept the fabric on my shoulders. It fell from the front of me, exposing my breasts as it crumpled to the ground.

They both stared at me with hunger. It sent hot need coursing through my body.

"Sit on the bed," Ulrich muttered while his hand went to his cock, and he stroked himself slowly.

My chest was moving at an agonizing speed while I watched him.

"Now, Brenna."

I obeyed once more, backing up until my knees hit the edge of the bed and I sat down.

"Open your legs," Ulrich's voice was so full of heat my body warmed as though it would melt in my spot.

Olen crossed the room, and my eyes went to him, watching as he settled onto the bed beside my head. His hand went to my breast, cupping my flesh while his thumb circled my nipple.

His other hand forced my thighs open, and I cried out in shock.

"Obey, Brenna," Olen ordered.

I was sure my mind was outside of my body when Ulrich slowly approached the bed. In the corner of my eye, I could see Olen stroking himself while his other hand held my legs open.

"How much can you handle?" Ulrich asked.

My legs trembled but Olen held his grip, not allowing one thigh to meet the other.

Ulrich stared down at me, then licked his lip and I was sure I would die from the arousal it sent through me.

"I think she can handle more than she realizes," Olen replied for me.

Ulrich grinned and his hand flicked. My eyes went to his wrist where I found a small black shadow whip in his grasp.

"No!" I tried to clammer away, but Olen held me tighter.

"Say the word, Brenna and I will allow you to dress and be carried to the dungeons," Ulrich replied.

My hands shook at my sides while my mind begged me to yell out the name of my home. I was so fucking foolish for not doing it. For not uttering the words that could have saved me from what would happen next.

I was even more foolish for how much I loved it.

I shook my head, refusing to give him the satisfaction of my concession.

"Good girl," Olen's hand returned to my breast, and he tugged upward on my nipple. "I suggest you hold onto something, princess."

I didn't understand what he meant until the sting of Ulrich's small whip collided with my skin. Right onto my clit, sending shocks of pain and pleasure through my body.

My hands gripped the sheets when his whip hit again. I turned my head, searching for a pillow or sheet to bite into. Olen's hand stopped me, forcing my mouth open while he slid himself back down my throat.

My eyes watered and I stared up at him while he thrusted down. "Do not bite me," he warned, tugging on my flesh again.

"How many letters?" Ulrich asked.

Olen thrusted again, preventing me from being able to respond.

"I believe there were five, your grace," he groaned.

Another lash hit me, and my eyes watered. I expected more pain, and it was there, but even more maddening was the pleasure.

Olen pulled away, allowing me to inhale and his hand went lower, pulling against my skin, revealing more of me to Ulrich.

Giving the insane king more access to my sensitive flesh.

"Two more," the right hand whispered before he sucked on my clit forcefully.

I cried out in shock and my nails dragged down Olen's thigh. My unintentional attack did not stop him from sucking harder.

He pulled away, keeping his hold on me and my exposure to Ulrich.

The next whip was just as overwhelming as the other three. Forcing indecent cries and whimpers from my lips.

Ulrich's voice broke through my noises while Olen started circling my skin, tugging at the tightness aching within me.

"Come for us," Ulrich ordered. "Come for us, Brenna and then you will get your last punishment."

My trembling was outside of my control. I shouldn't have wanted any of this. I shouldn't have needed either of their touches.

But fuck the Gods, I did.

I threw my head back, lifting my hips while Olen pressed against me. My mind went numb with the release and my body shook the bed beneath us.

"Fuck, yes," Olen hissed, not stopping his unrelenting circling on my sensitive skin.

"More," Ulrich demanded.

I wanted to lift my head to meet his eyes, but my body did not allow me to while my next release washed over me with Olen's touch.

"Gods," I cried. "Gods!"

"They will not answer," Olen whispered, "but we will."

I braced for Ulrich's next whip, but nothing happened. My head snapped up and I met his eyes.

"Tell us what you are, Brenna."

This game. Fuck, it was addicting. It was consuming everything that I was, but I no longer cared.

I threw my head back. "I'm your whore," I cried.

"Fuck," Olen groaned. His hands stopped and I inhaled to catch my breath then screamed out my exhale as Ulrich's whip hit me for the last time.

The pain brought an unexpected orgasm to the surface. One so strong it forced tears to fall from my eyes. Olen's hands held me down while my muscles spasmed. My body went tight and hot, stealing my ability to release a breath from my lungs. So much ecstasy, I was sure I would die from the never-ending pleasure.

When my release had finally ended, my vision was blurry and I blinked as Ulrich crawled over me, pressing his chest against mine.

"Do you see what happens when you listen, Brenna?" he whispered. "Ecstasy so sinful, your soul wonders why you want more."

I nodded in response.

"Turn around," Olen ordered.

I did as he instructed, twisting my body and placing my head at the end of the bed with my legs pointed toward the top by Olen. Ulrich's chest bumped my head, and I glanced up.

"Lean on me," he said quietly.

Not caring to understand why, I did what I was told again. I lifted myself onto my elbows, leaning back against his chest. His cold whip licked at my skin, coiling around my arm like a tempting serpent.

Before I could release a breath, Olen was on me again, lifting my legs into the air. My yelp was loud, echoing across the room when his lips touched my clit.

Ulrich's hand went over my mouth. His teeth dragged across my ear. "I will never get over watching you experience pleasure."

My eyes rolled while Olen's mouth and tongue moved against me. Everything was so sensitive, almost too sensitive. But I did not want him to stop.

"Our whore deserves some care after taking her punishment," Olen muttered against me.

I gripped the sheets, trembling against Ulrich as Olen consumed me. It was ecstasy I had never experienced before, pleasure my body could barely believe existed.

My next orgasm was tamer, not as intense, but pure bliss all the same. It was a rush of heat, flowing across my skin and deep inside of me, Ulrich held me against his chest while I shook with my release.

Olen's hands on my thighs gripped me tighter, but he did not pull his mouth from me.

"Yes," Ulrich groaned into my ear. "Come for him."

I groaned back and Olen laughed against me, licking me slowly while my shaking slowed.

When my orgasm had finished, Olen sat back, settling near the headboard and Ulrich smiled down at me.

"Your reward for taking your punishment," he whispered, brushing his finger against my lips. "Two cocks to fill you."

I nodded again, unsure if my body could move. Ulrich gripped my wrists, pulling me upward. He flipped me to face him then helped me crawl back toward Olen. When I had reached the right hand, Ulrich lifted me, keeping my eye contact while Olen slipped himself into me.

I trembled at the pressure of him inside.

"Lie back," Ulrich ordered.

I did as he said, opening my legs for him while I laid against Olen's chest. My hand found Olen's open palm and I wrapped mine around his.

He held me tight while Ulrich slipped inside, pausing for a moment to allow me to catch my breath.

They both began to move after a subtle nod of approval from me. To my surprise, Ulrich's hand found mine and Olen's, gripping us while they both thrusted into me. Their groans sent chills down my body, and I held them both tighter.

Wondering how in the Gods I was falling so far into the darkness, and why I wanted more to consume my soul.

CHAPTER 34

Ten months.

Two hundred and eighty days.

Two weeks since Bjorn's banishment and that night of sin-filled lust with Olen and Ulrich.

I leaned back on my hands, staring out at the water from Ulrich's beach under the palace while my mind pondered it all.

There was a new peace settling into my soul. A possibility of acceptance for the remaining months of my service. An understanding that perhaps the next four months would not be met with brutality and that mine and Ulrich's war had finally ceased.

Neither of us claiming full victory, but both sides conceding our battles.

The sun began to set, and I breathed in the sea air, watching the red-moon rise above me.

"I wonder some days if I prefer to see you under the sun or the red of this moon."

I moved my eyes upward, finding Ulrich standing beside me. His mask was white, one I had not seen yet.

He settled into the sand at my side, digging his fingers into the grains.

I was silent.

"What were you thinking about?" he asked quietly.

My lips trembled and I met his gaze.

"I wonder if it's worth uttering," I admitted. "I do not want to tempt Lokii to pull his jesting strings and ruin it all."

Ulrich laughed.

My hands gripped the sand in response. The sound was so rare, but when he did allow it to grace his lips, it set my body on fire.

"Can I ask you a question?" I turned to meet his gaze again.

His eyes flared for a moment with what appeared to be panic before he nodded.

"Why the masks?"

"Not this again," he groaned.

I shook my head. "I don't mean the physical masks. Well, I do, but I mean the other ones."

He was silent.

I turned to stare at him, studying the white barrier on his face.

"The masks of cruelty, of insanity. The face of a man determined to allow the world to hate him."

"It appears you've made assumptions about me."

I tried not to flinch at the bite in his response.

"I'm not wrong."

He turned to me, his eyes burning with an emotion I could not place.

"Why does it matter, Brenna? What good will it do you if I admitted to what you've come to believe?"

"It would help me understand the conflict in my heart," I whispered.

I waited for his response and yelped when he stood suddenly, heading right for the water. I held my breath while I watched him sink into the red-painted surface. His hair floated for a moment before he dunked his head under.

I sat, shaking, waiting for him to lift for air. Yet he didn't and I rose to my feet, moving across the sand.

When my body was fully enveloped by the frigid liquid, he lifted with his shadows masking his features.

"What happened to your mask?" I asked, trying to keep my teeth from chattering from the cold.

His smile was wicked.

"It's white, Brenna, and made of fabric. I would be breaking my own rule if I did not mask myself."

"You're a conundrum," I sighed.

I swam away from him, directing my body back to the shore, but his hand grasped one wrist.

"Tell me one thing that has made you believe I am not the cruel being you have seen." His voice was a whisper, almost a plea.

I stared into his shadow-masked green eyes. The words were right on my tongue, but they would not come out.

"You're hesitating," he sneered.

"You're not holding me painfully," I replied.

He blinked. "What?"

I glanced at the water, unable to see his hand wrapped around my wrist under the surface.

"You haven't touched me cruelly in months, Ulrich. Since the day we showed each other our ink for the first time. Have you grabbed me? Yes, constantly."

He grinned and I rolled my eyes.

"But you have not grabbed me cruelly. You haven't marked my body. You *heard* me."

"You're wrong," he replied.

"No," I countered.

His gaze was on fire when he smiled back at me. "The night of your *punishment*. I attacked you."

My body stiffened at the memory. "I had made a mistake," I whispered. "You caught me in my betrayal."

"I called you a whore." He grinned. "Multiple times."

"I called myself one first. To Bjorn," I replied, biting the inside of my cheek to prevent my own outburst of irritation.

His eyes squinted for a moment before he spoke again.

"I think you will come to regret your observations," he muttered.

I pulled myself toward him, allowing my body to press against his.

"Why?" I asked, needing to understand his hesitancy.

He stared back at me, not releasing his hold on my wrist.

"Because, Brenna," his gaze went dark, instantly terrifying me, "I am the monster you believe me to be."

"No," I protested. "I don't think I believe that."

His shoulders rose with his breaths and the same chilling grin he'd given me countless times before he lifted his lips.

"You don't *think*. You did not say you *know*."

His grip went tight, forcing a cry from my lips and he dragged me through the water. I stumbled when our feet hit the sand, holding back my protests while he seemed determined to change my mind.

He slammed the door to hallway twelve open, continuing to pull me behind him, holding my wrist with that painful grip.

We crossed the clock room, and my footsteps grew heavy when I saw him heading toward hallway nine.

"What are you doing?" I cried. I tugged at his hold, sniffling back my tears from his sudden outburst.

"You are so uncertain about so many things, Brenna." His voice rose and he continued to pull me toward the hallway. "You *think* I am not a monster. You *think* you could be happy in my home. You *think* you enjoy my touches." He turned around, grinning wide. "And Olen's, like the whore you *think* you may be."

My shock from his shift in mood quickly turned to rage.

"Unhand me!" I demanded.

"I will show you I am the monster your heart tells you I am."

My cries of protests echoed down the hall while he continued his dragging. His grip on my wrist was so tight I knew I would have a mark from it. A bruise that would linger for weeks to come.

My eyes frantically whipped around, staring at the red-flame candles until the cold of the hallway grew unbearable and his footsteps finally stopped.

"Look at it, Brenna," he ordered as he released my wrist.

I sniffled, holding back my tears and stepped forward. My hands shook while I raised them, tracing the carving of the woman on the door. The face similar to his ink, but different.

My chin hit the door when his body slammed into mine from behind. His hand went to my throat.

"You are a foolish woman," he breathed into my ear.

"I am." My voice shook.

His hands hit above my head and his hips ground into my backside.

"You do not do what you're told," he whispered.

My face pressed against the door and my body trembled under his. I couldn't separate reality from this insane fantasy Ulrich was determined to live. The one where he was welcoming and warm in one moment, but deranged and violent in the next.

"So quiet," he muttered.

I let out a breath. "I am not a caged pet."

His laugh rumbled against my back while his hips pressed me harder into the door. His hands removed their stance from above my head, then they were on my hips, flipping me to face him once more.

"The little bird, alone with the beast."

My hand went to his shirt, pulling at him.

"Please, Ulrich, stop."

His eyes were glazed over, distant. An expression of his mind lost in some memory I had no knowledge of.

"Do you want to know what's behind this door?" he asked, not meeting my gaze.

My heart tightened and I moved to shove away, but his hands on my hips pressed me back against the wood.

"Answer me," he demanded.

"No," I admitted. "No, Ulrich, I don't."

"You *think* I am not a monster," he breathed out. "I *think* I should prove you wrong."

The room grew cold, and Ulrich's shadows appeared behind him, trailing up the walls like a poison leaching from the stone of the palace.

"Ulrich," I begged.

"This door only opens with my blood," he continued, removing a hand from my hip. My eyes went wide when a tendril of shadows sliced across his wrist and his black blood trailed from the wound.

"Ulrich." I tugged on his shirt again, but was stopped by the shadows. The cold bite of them slammed my arms to my side, preventing me from being able to fight.

"I *think* you want to know what's in this room," he whispered. "I *think* you want to see the *horrors* I have locked away." His bloodied wrist lifted, and he slammed it above my head. The sound was deafening with only the two of us standing in the quiet hallway.

I suddenly regretted each choice I had made that led me to this moment.

"I don't," I replied.

Click.

The door under me shifted slightly with his blood seeping into the surface. His shadows moved to my face, pulling me toward him while the red-flame candles began to dim.

"I cannot let you see, but I can let you *feel.* I can subject you to all that makes me, *me.*"

He shoved my shoulders, sending me stumbling through the door and in the room. His shadows stayed around me, blocking my vision.

I was sure my blood had frozen in my veins. My tears fell without my control while I tried to see through his darkness. But I could not, and I could not ignore the overwhelming evil of the room he'd forced me into.

It was awful.

My chest grew tight, and the heavy air of the room filled my lungs.

The sorrow. The hate. The pain.

So. Much. Pain.

Death—Gods—death permeated this space. Infiltrating the air.

"Please," I cried, falling to my knees. "Please stop."

His hand lifted my chin, and I gasped, not realizing he had been so close.

"Feel it all, Brenna. Every part of what makes me the monster you have branded me as."

"Ulrich, please," I begged.

"Enjoy your cell," he whispered, running his finger across my cheek.

"What did I do wrong?" I sobbed.

He was silent, unrelenting, and as much of the beast he loved to be.

I stood, yelling out my fear in the dark as the door slammed shut. "I hate you!" I screamed louder. "I hate you!"

There was silence on the other side. Or perhaps he could not hear me. I did not know. Not with his shadows blocking everything.

My legs gave out from me while I fell to the ground.

"I hate you," I whispered, pulling my knees upward.

"I hate you."

I repeated my words, cradling myself while I rocked in place, and I was unsure if they were directed at my captor or myself.

Death

Judgement

Pain

Wrath

Treachery

My back laid against the cold surface of my prison while words from voices I did not know whispered in my head. Vile, grotesque voices. Tones meant to cause fear.

My body had not stopped shaking, for possibly hours, and my tears had long dried. I had no concept of how long Ulrich had left me in the room. Allowing whatever horrors that filled this space to infiltrate my mind and soul.

I began to wonder if this was a new war in our game. If I had been a fool to believe our battles were ending.

If every possible soft touch and gaze he'd given me in recent weeks had been a ploy to manipulate me. To trap me into becoming comfortable. To allow him the conquest of my body and mind.

There were shouts on the other side of the wall—raised, angry voices—but I could not make out who they belonged to.

My body continued shaking. From fear, exhaustion, or cold, I did not know.

Click.

Hands gripped my arms, pulling me back into the hallway. My eyes closed with relief.

"What is the purpose?"

It was Frode.

"Why your grace?"

I did not look up. I did not want to gaze upon his face.

Ulrich's presence was muted compared to the presence in the room I'd been trapped in. Feet touched my arm, and I knew it was him.

Silent and watching above me.

"She has to understand," he replied.

I did not respond or open my eyes when his arms were lifting me into the air. The smell of him was one I had grown too close to. An earthy, smoky scent with a hint of floral. Like the soap in the bathing room. One that brought me comfort when I'd slept in his arms the night before. Or nights before? I was not sure. I only knew the smell now made my stomach turn with hate.

I refused to lay my head on his chest while he carried me away from the torment he had forced upon me. Instead, I allowed it to hang back, my hair a curtain of fire. My body went limp in his grip, my determination to make his trek difficult with my weight.

I kept my eyes closed while he continued to carry me. My mind tried to map our path, tried to pick up on which hallway he took, but I was too exhausted to fully understand.

A door slammed open and scurried feet echoed behind us.

Was it Frode? A *troll*? I could not tell.

Ulrich dropped me, forcing a yelp from my lips and my eyes sprang open.

We were in the library.

I stood, glaring at him but then my eyes went to the table in the corner. My workspace was now completely empty of my drawings and maps. All of my parchment gone. Every piece of koal nowhere to be seen. Even the easel was gone, no longer leaned against the table where I'd last left it.

"What!" I cried out, running to the table, searching around it. Pulling books off the bookshelves in the back.

My tears began to build.

Months of work.

Months of dedication.

Gone.

Where had it gone?

I turned on my heel, my finger pointing in his face, but I found that cruel smile across his lips.

"Why?" I cried. "What did I possibly do?"

A voice cleared and I turned my gaze to find Olen behind Ulrich. He shook his head, trying to demand I stop. I glared back.

Ulrich had unleashed the monster he'd molded me to become with his cruelty.

His unjustified torment on me.

"Why?" I demanded again. "Why?"

Ulrich's hand wrapped around my wrist, stopping my hand from shaking.

"Because I can, Brenna. Because I am the monster you should fear. When will you learn?"

He dropped my wrist and turned on his heel, waving his hand with indifference.

"I've grown bored. Olen, have fun."

I fell against the new couch by the window, covering my tears. All of that hard work taken from me in an instant. In one deranged tantrum. What had I done? What had I possibly said to justify this new outburst?

Olen settled beside me, and I sniffled, meeting his eyes.

"What happened?" he asked.

I shook my head.

"Nine," I whispered. "Nine."

Olen's hand pulled mine from my eyes and I yelped at his tight hold. "What?" he asked.

"Nine," I continued to mutter.

"Fuck," Olen groaned.

His hands landed on my shoulders, shaking me from my spell.

"Brenna, I need you to tell me what happened."

"That fucking monster is the only one who knows," I snapped.

"Brenna," he warned.

I struggled in his grip, twisting until he released me.

"Both of you need to stop putting your fucking hands on me!" I screamed.

My feet lifted me, and I began to pace, my heart racing in my chest. I scanned the library and my empty table. My tears fell heavier.

It had all been for nothing.

All of it.

"I hate him," I cried.

"No, you don't," Olen grunted, standing from his seat.

I snapped up, glaring, gritting my teeth. "Yes I do."

Olen grinned. "You didn't hate him when you laid on his chest, completely unaware I was in the room. Or when you *begged* for his punishment."

"Stop."

"You didn't hate him when he was the only one you would whisper what you wanted to. When you openly called yourself his *whore*. Or when you straddled him before everyone, sitting upon his lap, claiming your seat on his throne."

"Olen, stop it." I pushed my body away, trying to gain distance between us.

"You haven't hated him each time you have allowed him inside of you. Each time you have followed him throughout this palace, listening to his words while he told you of his intricate home."

"Olen, stop it!" I shouted.

Olen pressed his body into mine. "No, Brenna. You do not hate *him*. You hate what he does. You hate what makes him cause the torment he so easily comes up with."

My eyes went wide when Olen claimed my lips, kissing me as he ground his hips into mine. His hands went to my hair, gripping and tugging.

He pulled away grinning like a madman.

"Tell me, princess. How were those kisses compared to *his*?"

I stared at him in shock, hating his observation. I shoved him further away and made my way to the couch once more, sinking into the plush cushions.

"Why does he do these things?"

Olen was silent.

I turned my head up, finding his eyes staring out at the water beyond the city. He approached, dropping to his knees while his hands gripped my shoulders.

"Brenna." His voice dropped.

My breaths grew heavy while I waited for his next words, but he was cut off when the library door slammed open.

Ulrich stared at us both, a smile across his face.

"Wasted no time," he laughed.

"Get away!" I shouted, shoving Olen away while I tried to make it to the hidden door in the back of the library.

Ulrich's arms wrapped around me, pulling me against his chest.

"I grew jealous, Brenna. Wondering how deeply Olen was buried in you."

"Get off me!" I shouted again, slamming my head against his chest.

He held me tighter.

"How is that mind doing?"

His mockery of my own torment only fueled my rage. I kicked him, trying to get his arms to release me.

"I hate both of you!" I cried. "I hate you!"

"Stop making love proclamations, princess," Olen grunted.

I snapped my head in the direction of the king's right hand, glaring while he stood from his crouched position.

Ulrich held me closer, running his hand along the neck of my gown.

"Brenna, nothing is done personally."

My knees weakened with my fit and I sobbed while I went limp in his arms.

"Please let me go," I cried. "Please stop this all. Please."

Ulrich lowered to the ground while my body continued to fall, and my words spilled from my heart.

"Each moment I believe you could stop, you commit another awful act. End me, Ulrich. Please. If killing me is how this ends, do it now."

His arms went taut around me.

"Please," I cried. "Please."

"I cannot, princess." he whispered into my ear. "I cannot. There is no other way."

I hated myself for welcoming his lips softly laying against my neck. I hated the maddening comfort it brought even when my heart felt as though it would explode.

I went lax against him. The darkness of sleep wrapped around me. My mind's inability to fight the exhaustion caused from that dark room hidden beneath the palace.

Ulrich held me closer, and my tears fell from my cheeks. He was my living nightmare. My worst tormentor. Yet, I could not understand why my heart was so determined to prove my logic wrong. To find the light hidden within his darkness.

"There is no other way," he muttered again while sleep fully claimed me.

I fell into it, betraying my mind as I welcomed the comfort of his grip wrapped around me.

Chapter 35

I did not allow Ulrich to touch me after my newest torment and he did not ask.

In just a few months we'd gone from regular lust filled nights to returning to our silent sleeping habits. A wall of pillows between us once more and my hands laid across my chest in protection.

The parties had also started again. A maddening thumping each and every night. Weeks of being forced to sit silently on his whore-seat, watching his court fuck their lives away.

My supplies were still gone as well. Nowhere to be seen. No more walks through the palace. No more secluded swims.

I was a prisoner once more.

"It's been eleven months," Ulrich whispered beside me.

I startled, pulling my eyes from the dark ceiling.

"Yes, your grace."

Silence once more.

A tear ran down my face and I turned my body away from him, wrapping myself in the comforters.

Eleven months. I was so close to the end of this all. Freedom from this torture.

His body lifted from the bed and the sound of the bedroom door closing rang across the room. Leaving me alone.

But I did not care. Instead, I welcomed my sleep. Grateful for a night without him beside me.

"Your highness?"

My eyes opened and I looked up to find Frode standing beside the bed. I jolted upward, holding the comforter to my chest.

He sat upon the stool from the bathing room and gave me an odd smile.

"I apologize for disrupting your sleep." His eyes went distant for a moment. "His grace said I would be better to provide you with this update."

My stomach sank.

"What, Frode?"

The healer grasped my hand, pulling it from the blanket.

"Hilde."

I stood, pulling my hand away from him. "What about my grandmother?" I sobbed.

"She is ill, your highness."

My feet were out of the bedroom door before Frode could finish whatever he had been instructed to tell me.

I passed a *troll* cleaning the wall.

"Where is he?" I shouted.

The creature dropped its water bucket and pointed down the hall with trembling fingers.

"Courtyard, princess," it croaked.

I ran down the hall, sure my auburn hair was like a fire blazing from my head. As I passed people of Ulrich's court, waking for the day, I was met with amused grins.

I was the princess in her nightgown, running through a palace. Ulrich's whore running to find her master.

Likely a sight they would gossip about for years to come.

I ran down the stairs, my feet moving faster than they had thrown me before. My hands slammed the towering palace doors open, and my feet hit the gravel.

Across the courtyard, too far away was Ulrich, stepping into a carriage I had never seen with only his shadows at the front acting as his stallions or mares to pull him away. I stared at him, unsure of where he was going, why he was leaving.

"Ulrich!" I screamed. "Ulrich!"

I moved across the gravel, desperate to reach him. A rock sliced into my foot, and I cried out, but did not stop running. My blood made it more difficult and painful to move across the uneven surface, but I had to get to him.

"Ulrich!" I cried, watching while he pulled the carriage door closed.

"Ulrich!" My scream ripped from my throat.

These emotions, this fear—I was sure it would infiltrate my lungs and drown me where I was.

I fell, gripping my chest while my sobs tumbled from me. Why was I running to him? What did I need from him? Help? Comfort?

His presence hit me in the chest and my eyes snapped up, watching him slowly climb out of the carriage. His black horned mask tight and terrifying.

His shadows lifted him as the omen of death that he was, sending him across the gravel without his feet touching the ground.

He landed before me, his eyes scanning me from head to toe.

"Frode has told you."

I sobbed, holding my bleeding foot. "Yes."

"Go home, Brenna," Ulrich replied, his eyes blank while he stared into mine. "Go home and never return to this island."

I stared in shock and my tears fell faster. "What?"

He was sending me... *home*? Why? Was this another ploy? Another trick to confuse me?

"Go. Home." He replied as he turned from me, slowly returning to his carriage.

"Why?" I sobbed, slamming my hands against the gravel. "Why? What about my rules? The deal?"

"A deal once made," was all he said, leaving me with my wound.

Heavy breaths approached behind me, but I did not pull my eyes from the retreating king. I did not look away when he climbed back into his carriage. I did not blink while that carriage pulled him away and toward the city.

Calloused hands wrapped around my arms, pulling me upward.

"Come, your highness," Frode whispered. "We must prepare your departure."

"He's sending me home," I cried. "*Home.*"

Frode grunted his acknowledgement of my words. He led me away, limping from my wound, but I kept my head turned, watching the king until we were back in the palace and the doors slammed in my face.

Frode's arms around me grew tight.

"We have to be quick, your highness. Hilde does not have much time."

I was in a haze while Frode led me through the palace. One I could not pull myself from. One I did not want to allow to lift from my mind.

Even with the pain of my bleeding foot, I could not focus on anything other than Ulrich.

He was sending me home.

Without my request.

Did this mean our deal was done? Was I no longer bound by his ancient oath?

Frode helped me to the bedroom, setting me gently onto the mattress.

"I will return with Adalie," he said softly.

I nodded—once—as Ulrich would.

A sad smile graced Frode's expression, and then he left me in the room.

Within minutes claws were clinking across the stone, and I glanced up to find Olen in beast form, staring at me.

"You're leaving," he mumbled.

I nodded.

"Your grandmother."

I nodded.

His body approached mine and I did not refuse him when his beastly head laid in my lap.

"What am I supposed to do without a screeching princess to irritate?" he grumbled.

I could not stop my responding laugh at the jest and his laugh mixed with my own. A sound that had once terrified me, now brought me comfort.

"What is *he* going to do without you?" This question was quieter, his voice lower.

I shoved the beast away.

"He is the one who is sending me home."

"Do you want to go?"

I turned my head, staring out at the city. "She is my mother in every sense of the word," I cried. "She is brash and often cold, but she raised me. She ignited the fire that is in my soul. She took me, a motherless babe, long after her years of infant-raising had ended, and she shaped me."

My tears fell. "She may not have written to me in all this time. In her own way, I believe it was her attempt of forcing me to grow, but I must go to her, Olen. I must say goodbye. I would never forgive myself if I did not."

I turned back to the beast, finding his gaze soft. His paw landed on my lap.

"It has been an honor, princess." To my shock, his voice cracked. "It has been an honor to become your friend and to have been your protector these last several months."

"Do not make me cry further, you beast," I sniffled.

"One more hump for goodbye?"

My fist went right into his snout, and he shouted.

"I guess not," he laughed, shaking his head.

The bedroom door opened, and Adie ran in, her eyes wide with emotions. I limped to her, embracing the young girl in my arms.

"Thank you for your friendship," I whispered.

"Will I never see you again?" she replied, sniffling.

I pulled from our embrace, grasping her face and smiling at her.

"I'm not sure, Adie. Perhaps I'll come back some day, with my newfound freedom. Bringing you stories of the other Islands. Trinkets for you to keep. Stories to tell you."

Adie sniffled again.

"Perhaps I will convince this brute uncle of yours to allow you to travel with me for even just a moment."

Olen snarled.

"I'm going to miss your birthday," Adie cried. "I'm going to miss seeing you turn another year older, like the old woman you are."

I laughed loudly. "I am going to miss your spirit Adie. Gods, will I miss it."

"And we will miss you," Olen said solemnly.

Adie pulled away, returning to her tasks as my handmaiden, filling my trunks. I should have helped her, offered an extra hand, but my feet moved me to the window.

I wrapped my arms around my body, scanning the city streets, trying to find the black carriage amongst the buildings. Wondering if the king would send me off himself or if that had been our goodbye.

One of tears, hate, and blood.

Fitting really, when I considered it.

Chapter 36

Ulrich did not send me off. He did not arrive at the docks. He did not walk me up the plank or order my trunks to be carried.

Olen, however, was tasked to ensure the black vessel went to my island home and my island home only.

I laid in the cot of the ship, my stomach rolling with the waves, watching the sun high in the sky. My eyes went heavy, now used to sleeping during the day, knowing this hour was well past my usual hours of sleep.

The cabin door creaked open, and I turned to find Olen in beast-form staring at me.

"How are you feeling?" his voice rumbled.

"Like I'm going to be sick," I laughed. "I'm not sure how I'm going to travel in my life if I can barely handle the sea."

Olen's canines came over his lip with his smile.

"May I sleep in here? The crew quarters are disgusting."

"Olen you have been inside of me. Yes, you can sleep beside me."

His eyebrows rose with amusement and his laugh rumbled throughout the cabin. "Gods, will I miss you."

I shifted on the cot, patting next to me.

"I won't fit there," he laughed.

"We can fit," I replied. "Please, I have grown accustomed to someone sleeping next to me."

Olen dropped his eyes but nodded and his massive body climbed onto the cot, pressing me against the wall with the small window.

"Will you be able to sleep?" he asked.

I shifted, turning my back against his, facing the window.

"Yes, actually. I will."

His breathing slowed quickly, and his light snores picked up, filling the cabin with the sounds. I held my hand to my chest, listening to him. Appreciating his comfort, but wishing I was back in a large bed, in a room in a stone palace, lying beside the man I shouldn't want.

"Princess."

I glanced up from the book I'd pulled from the small shelf in the cabin and found Olen at the door. My hand went to my barely aching foot, thanks to Frode's salves and care instructions.

"Yes?" I asked.

"You're home," he whispered.

I threw the book, rising from the cot. I ran through the cabin door and out to the deck of the ship. Wincing at the pressure on my scarred sole.

The sun was bright above the deck and then I saw it, my beloved fjord. The end of the small neck of water we traveled down, opening to the blue my home faced.

I ran to the edge of the ship, leaning over, and watching my village appear.

"Gods," I sobbed. "Oh my Gods."

Olen's paws clinked against the wooden deck. His warm body brushed my leg, and my hand went to his fur.

"Olen," I sobbed. "What if she is not...?"

Olen's shoulders shook. "Do not, princess. This ship has been moving at its highest speed. It has only been days since Frode received word and we left Muspell. Do not lose hope."

I gripped the edge of the ship, unable to accept that I was at the helm of the vessel that had taken me nearly a year before. That *I* was the one approaching, likely terrifying my people in the distance.

Rain and clouds did not follow us while we made our approach, and instead of screams of fear, my ears pricked at shouts.

Cheering.

Proclamations of excitement.

"They're waiting for you," Olen whispered, nipping at my fingers.

My tears were heavy and thick when the gangplank hit the dock. Olen butted his snout to my knees, trying to push me to descend into the echoing screams.

I turned around. "You are coming with me, correct?" I asked.

He shook his head.

"I was tasked with returning you to the dock I took you from, princess. This is goodbye."

"No," I cried. "Please at least walk me to my home. Please."

Olen shook his head once more. "Princess, I would terrify them all. Go home, Brenna. Go *home.*"

He backed away and I ran to him, dropping to my knees, wrapping my arms around his thick neck.

"Don't let it claim him," I muttered through my sobs. "Whatever it is that he fights. Do not let it claim him."

Olen was stiff in my arms, his body heaving with his breaths.

"I will do my best," he growled.

I wiped my tears and stood, watching *troll* carry my trunks away. Followed by startled shouts below.

I chuckled then shook my head, allowing my expression to shift to my mask of my home's dutiful princess.

"I will miss you, Bren," Olen said when my foot hit the gangplank.

I twisted to him, my eyes wide. "What did you just call me?"

He winked then backed away, motioning me forward with his snout.

My hands trembled at my sides when I turned again, making my descent. Into the arms of my joyous people and their relieved sobs.

"My grandmother," I called out to them. "Please, I must get to her."

"I will take you."

Relief, mingled with hate, rose in my chest when I found my father before me with his own tears running down his face.

I said nothing, refusing to argue with the king before his people.

"We must hurry," he whispered.

I allowed him to take my hand, pulling me through the crowd. But my eyes did not follow him. No, I turned my head, watching the black vessel sail away. Finding the dark creature at its helm.

"She has little time," my father whispered when we made it back to my childhood home. "She has waited for you."

I ripped my hand from his grip. "I know where her rooms are."

He stared at me with shock. "Brenna?"

"I will not discuss the words in my heart right now. I need to say my goodbyes. I need to hold her hand until the Gods claim her.

Only after we have burned her body at sea, and said our farewells, will we speak. Do you understand?"

I didn't allow him the chance to reply before I was rushing through the palace. More like a small home in my eyes after having explored and lived in Ulrich's stone fortress.

When I arrived at my grandmother's room, my heart was racing. With fear and sorrow. Anger and regret.

I pushed it open, welcoming the familiar scent of her. Of the sweet cakes she always had on her table. The fresh tea, hot and waiting for a visitor.

"My child." Her voice was a welcome sound.

I rushed through the room, falling onto the bed and into her open, frail arms.

"My child," she whispered, raising her arms to stroke my hair.

I cried, releasing every broken part of myself into her embrace. Sobbing until her nightgown was soaked, until my sobs could no longer come from my chest.

"You did not come for me," I cried.

She held me as tight as her weakening limbs could.

"Do you think *I* could have?" she laughed.

The sound—oh Gods—it broke me in two. A noise I knew like a piece of my soul, but it rattled now. Evidence of her illness.

I sat up, staring into her blue eyes and the wrinkles painting her face. Her hand held mine and I shook my head.

"Why?" I cried. "Why leave me? Why not fight?"

"Did you fight?" she asked before coughing.

I stood, pulling the shoulders of the gown from my body and turned for her to find the scars not covered by my chemise.

"Bren," she gasped. "What in the Gods?"

"The Gods are silent, cruel beings," I replied, settling beside her. "I tried. Each day for the first month and several days after. Even when I was thrown in the dungeon to lay on rot and death, I still tried. So, he punished me."

I met her eyes, finding them burning with pride.

"Yet you live. Does he?"

My gaze dropped.

"Brenna?" she pried.

"He lives. He released me, three months early."

"Three months?" she coughed again. "No, two months."

I smiled, like a fool. "He added a month to my service. After the murder attempts."

Her laughing put her into a coughing fit and I startled. I leaned toward her, helping her sit up to clear her lungs.

"You've changed, my child." She coughed. "A woman stands before me."

I left the bed, slipping my gown back over my shoulders and turned to her once more.

"I was a woman when I left home."

She shook her head. "No, you were an obedient daughter in a woman's body. A quiet shell of a woman. Doing what she was told. Waiting on that dock like a prize to be claimed. You return with scars of torment, a head high in confidence, and something else I cannot quite place."

"He tortured me," I replied. "Yet..." My voice went quiet.

"What, child?"

I went to the window, staring at the hills beyond, searching for the bears in the distance. The ones that would not yet come close to our village with heat still in the air.

"I wonder what he is doing now. I imagine him walking through that stone palace with his creatures at his side. Barking orders, claiming deals he started."

My heart tightened. "I wonder why he left me there in that courtyard and if we were supposed to end this all with the spilling of my blood."

"Tea and cakes," my grandmother's demand pulled me from my spiral.

I obeyed, gathering her sweets before climbing onto her bed and setting a small tray on her lap. Her hands rose to pour the tea like she had every day of my life, but her arms shook. A clear indication of her quickly losing her strength. My hands wrapped around her wrist, stopping her.

Her eyes were full of sorrow when she met my gaze, but I nodded my chin, letting her know she was okay to give up this sacred rite we'd shared for the last one-hundred and fifty years. Reluctantly, her hands passed me the pot and I poured our tea, making sure to leave hers with less liquid so she could lift her cup. I laid beside her, leaning my head on her shoulder while she brought her drink to her lips.

My heart grew heavy at the familiarity and comfort of it all. A new painful reminder that soon I would have more mornings without our tea and whispers. Mornings without the sound of her harsh laugh. Her stern lectures. Her loving advice.

My tears fell again. Quiet, barely falling onto her frail shoulder.

"Is he handsome?" she whispered.

I laughed at the question. "Grandmother," I scolded.

"Entertain a dying woman, Brenna. I need to know. The curiosity may take me to my grave the longer you refuse to answer."

I scoffed at her jests and sat up. “He has handsome features. Thick hair, a groomed beard, inked skin that is—” I paused, finding her eyes wide. I shook my head.

“I cannot have this conversation with you.”

She sipped from her teacup slowly. “I entirely disagree.”

Biting my lip, I chuckled. “His inked skin is like a spell to the eyes. Pieces of art that are beautiful, sorrowful, and horrifying.”

“Go on,” she whispered, picking up a small cake.

“But I have yet to see his face.”

She choked on her treat.

“What?”

“He wears *masks*, grandmother. Every single day. Blocking me from seeing nothing more than a small bit of skin on his nose and his eyes behind them. I have never seen the upper half of his features. Besides the few times I’ve seen the top of his forehead, I have no idea what his brow looks like or his nose. Or how his jaw, hidden by his beard, fits with the rest of his face.”

“My Gods,” she whispered. “How exciting.”

I laughed. “There is no light that breaks through his darkness. When we climbed into our bed each night, the lights were gone, and I could not see him.”

“Our bed?” she asked, raising her brow.

“My service was to sleep beside him each night. An odd request.”

She coughed and pointed to the mantle on her hearth.

“Bring me that.”

I turned my head, following her direction to a long box. Glancing back at her, I cocked my head. “What is it?”

“Get off this bed and go and grab it, child. I cannot.”

I bit my lip at her sternness, my body flooding with love at the familiarity to it.

Once again I was climbing off the bed, fetching her something. When I returned, I held the box out to her. She stared at it, not reaching for it.

"Open it."

"What?" I asked.

"Open it, Brenna."

I did as I was told, lifting the lid and finding one black candle and a glint of gold beneath it. I lifted the candle from the velvet fabric, finding a gold coin underneath.

"What are these?" I asked.

She held out her hands, finally asking for her items. "I've kept our family's most hidden secret. Every woman in our lineage has."

"What?"

She hushed me, holding up the black candle with her frail hands, studying it.

"There is a woman's mark on these. A kind of magic I have never experienced. A knowing, the only kind that comes from a woman's mind. And this coin?" She held it up. "Gods, do I wish to know where it came from. The weight of it, the markings. Again, a woman's marking on it as well."

I sat on the bed once more, holding out my hands.

"My secret," she paused, "the secret of the women, the one I was to give to Frey before that cursed night."

I choked at the mention of my mother.

"An ancient, mortal woman in our family was given these. A gift to honor her new marriage to a fae king. The gifter has been lost to history, but she was told to hold them until the time was right. That the women of our family would know that moment; when a warmth and buzz of a deal being completed would settle over them."

"Grandmother," I whispered.

"A deal once made," she muttered. "Brenna, take them."

I shook my head. "What am I supposed to do with them?"

She shrugged, "I do not know. I only know that warmth is around me now, my child. Confirming my years of keeping it secret are done. That no other woman in our family will need to carry this burden."

I gripped the candlestick and the coin, noticing a warm hum from the gold. Not knowing what it meant but understanding the finality of this moment. That it was this stern, quiet woman's goodbye. Passing yet another thing to me, marking another part of my soul with a part of her.

"Tell me more," she patted her shoulder. "Tell me of how *you* have changed."

I returned to my spot by her, placing the candle and coin on the table before wrapping my hands around her cold grip.

I told her everything.

I told her of the dungeons, the clock room, the hallways. I told her of the parties and the openly, moving bodies.

She had gasped, begging for more details.

I told her of the Rite, of that horrible night when I had been a fool. Of the sacrifice I had unintentionally stopped.

I told her of Olen, my beastly, irritating companion.

But I told her no more of Ulrich. Not of his smile or his laugh. Not of his secluded beach or the maps I had drawn for him.

I did not tell her how he had brought his library back to life at my request, even if he had not admitted it. Even if he had only allowed me to silently notice the changes in the room I worked in each day.

No, I kept him locked inside of me while I attempted to wash those soft feelings I had with the hate still in my heart. I tried to re-write my memories of the man, reminding myself of the pain he inflicted for his own pleasure and gain.

When my voice had grown raw, and I was unable to speak any longer, we both fell asleep. With my head on her shoulder and her hand in mine.

The only mother I knew, repairing my broken heart with her touch. When I woke, hours later, her grip was no longer tight. Her hand, while cold when I'd fallen asleep, was now a temperature I could not describe.

A new kind of cold.

A lifeless one.

My wail echoed throughout my home. Adding to the cracks of the walls. Shattering through the air like the pain shattered through my heart.

She was gone, and I was left alone. With only memories, a candle, and an odd gold coin to accompany me.

Chapter 37

I walked through the halls of my home like a Ghost. Ulrich's *Wraith* surrounded by a sea of people who did not understand what that title meant.

Gliding through life while the preparations for my grandmother's final departure commenced. Busy work. Things to keep us all occupied while we mourned the loss of a great woman.

I entered my father's great hall, finding the tables and chairs set with her favorite colors. Crimson red, her reminder of the daughter she'd lost and the daughter she'd gained. And white, the color of the white bears she adored.

I saw only blood.

"How many guests?" I asked, turning to the handmaid beside me.

She startled, then cleared her throat. "For the final journey or the dinner after?"

"The dinner," I replied.

"Your father, your mother's parents, the king."

I whipped around. "What?"

She stepped back. "The *king*, princess, and his wives."

My heart dropped. "Oh."

She eyed me nervously, continuing to list other names I did not take the energy to recognize. I waved my hand in approval of their decorations then turned away to ready myself for the farewell.

It was melancholy and surprisingly cold, while we watched the burning boat head across the Fjord. Grandmother's trip to the Gods. A wishful hope the wind would pick up her ashes, taking her to their island in the sky. Where they would joyously return her to her younger body, and she would live out her afterlife in peace.

The village had gathered for her, to no surprise, and distant relatives arrived. I'd greeted no one, keeping myself tucked away with my black veil covering my face.

The people of the village dispersed, and the familial group returned to our palace where our meal awaited.

When I entered the great-hall, I found the seat furthest away from it all, tucked in the shadows. Refusing to sit beside my father or the family members pretending to mourn.

They had not known her. They had not understood who the woman was. The hold she had on us all. The impact she'd had on *me.*

I thrummed my fingers against the table when footsteps approached. Rolling my eyes, I glanced up, pausing when I found a queen before me.

I jumped to my feet. "Titania," I whispered, bowing to her.

Oberon's quietest wife nodded at me. I stared at her, realizing I had forgotten she would attend this meal. Her dark golden hair was tied up into loose curls with the ends falling against the high neck of her black gown. Her still youthful brown eyes burned with golden embers.

"Brenna," she said softly. "Are you well?"

"Yes, your grace," I whispered.

She eyed me, stepping back while her face went solemn.

"Hilde was a great woman."

"Yes, your grace."

"She always knew when to offer respect."

I nodded.

"She also knew when to speak her mind," the queen continued.

I smiled and met her eyes. "Yes, your grace. She did."

"I liked that about her."

"I did as well."

Titania held out her hand and I grasped it, thankful for her familiar kindness. Her head turned to my father, whispering with King Oberon.

"Isn't my husband handsome?" she whispered.

I startled, allowing myself to turn to the king. His long white hair was shining in the candlelight. A metal crown of branches sat atop his head while his hand grasped the hand of another woman—Mab, his other wife.

"Your grace," I replied. "I cannot comment on your husband's features. Is that not disrespectful?

Titania laughed. "I guess it could be considered as such." She turned back to face me, offering me a smile. "Are you celebrating your birthday with me this year? It's the end of the blood moon. A rather exciting event."

My chest rose with a twinge of pain while my thoughts went to Ulrich, but I nodded.

"Oh good," she whispered. "Aesir will be so ready for nights without that ghastly red. Please let your father know you are to arrive a full month before the harvest."

My brow crumpled. "Your grace?"

She smiled. "The whole of Aesir lives in a month-long celebration. It's rather spectacular. It is a command, Brenna." Her voice became stern.

I nodded. "Yes, your grace. I look forward to it."

She squeezed my hand tightly. With more strength than I thought her small frame had. Then she left me.

A voice cleared beside me, and I glanced over, finding my father.

"Bren?"

"Not now," I snapped.

I walked away, ready to leave this dinner that was quickly turning to a party with Oberon's presence. His hand came out, wrapping around my wrist, stopping me.

"Unhand me!" I shouted.

Every head turned our direction. Glasses clattered against the tables and Oberon gave me an odd smile.

I hated it. Having to keep my mouth shut when I knew that the king being paraded and admired had murdered all of those people. Sending their heads to Ulrich's shores.

Shattering all of those Unseelie faes' hearts.

"Brenna." My father's voice was quiet. The same commanding tone Ulrich used when addressing his court.

I dropped my head. "I apologize, my king."

"Brenna, stop. I am your father."

"You are no better than the beast who hurt me," I replied.

His hand lifted my chin, and I found sorrow in his eyes.

"What?" his voice cracked.

I stepped away from him.

"Why did you not come for me?"

"Brenna, what are you talking about?"

My eyes went to Oberon and his wives, and I dropped my voice to a whisper. "Why did you not reply to a single letter I sent you? The ones where I told you about my pain and scars. About my torment."

I met his eyes, my tears running down my cheeks. "Why, Papa? Why?"

He blinked and a tear rolled from his eye. "Brenna, he did not mention this. What letters?"

"*He*? What do you mean *he?*"

My father said nothing, he only turned on his heel, motioning for me to follow.

At first I did not want to, but the regret in his eyes, I could not allow our relationship to fracture. The chatter began again as we exited the room. Leaving our guests to mourn grandmother alone.

When we made it to his study, he slammed the doors open, and I was sure my heart stopped at the sight.

Along every single wall, on every surface, were my maps and drawings. My scribbles, my notes.

The work Ulrich had led me to believe he'd disposed of.

"What in the Gods?" I sobbed.

My father passed me, heading straight for his desk and pulling the drawer open, laying down pile after pile of letters.

"The first one," he held it up. "The king apologized for the death of your betrothed and the fear his ship's arrival caused. He promised to take care of you."

My father slammed the paper down. "Then a month of silence. Nothing. No letters. No updates and I was about to go straight to Oberon when another one came. And more. Every single day. An update of what you were doing. If you were well."

"You're lying," I cried.

"Then your letters came, and they were so full of pain," my father cried. "Gods, I almost went to Oberon again, but the king always sent one at the same time, calming my fears."

"Threatening you," I replied.

"No, Bren, never."

He picked a parchment. "*King Enok, I know her recent letter is filled with lament and sorrow. Caused by my own hand. I cannot beg for your forgiveness more than I am now. If I were in your presence, I would drop to my knees. I promise she is well. She will return to you by the eleventh month. I am ending her servitude early.*"

I let out a shout. "Stop! What is this?"

"This is why we all knew you were coming home. Ulrich was told your grandmother had taken a turn for the worse. Gods, we were even surprised, but we were already preparing to welcome you."

"Why did you not write back?" I cried. "Why, Papa?"

My father's expression was blank, and he pointed to the walls around him.

"He sent them to me. The notes and scribbles at first. Telling me he was sure you wouldn't miss them, but I saw you in them. The quiet thoughts you always keep inside of your heart."

He turned his gaze back to mine.

"I saw something else too."

I stepped back.

"I saw love."

"Stop it."

I leaned against the wall behind me, holding my hand to my heart, unable to understand what was happening.

"Do you?" my father whispered.

"Do I what?" I snapped.

"Love him?"

"No!" I shouted. "Gods no!"

I fell to the ground, sobbing heavily. "I can't. Papa, you do not understand."

He approached, dropping to my level. "Explain it to me."

"My heart is conflicted. I cannot care for them. I cannot want to know what they are doing. If he is well."

"They?" his brow rose.

I sighed. "Ulrich and the beast who claimed me, Olen. They have both caused me torment."

"Two?"

I laughed. "Olen is like the friend my soul has longed for. He is rough but as soft as your smallest canine. He is brash in all the wrong ways, but he has protected me. Ulrich—" I sobbed again. "He is the cold and heat my body longs for. The poison I cannot stop myself from ingesting. He is everything I should not want, yet I yearn for him."

"Do you want two men?" My father cleared his throat.

"I want the friendship of one and possibly the very soul of the other," I admitted.

My father's hand rose, passing the letter he held.

"Read his words, Brenna. Understand why I did not come."

I ripped the letter from his hands as my legs found their strength again and I pushed myself up off the floor, pointing at him. "Were another *man's* words more important than your daughter's pain?"

Guilt flashed across his face, and I continued.

"Why? Why did you allow *him* to persuade you to stay away? Why was my begging, my pleading, and rage not enough for you to come for me? Are another king's words really so much more significant than those from the daughter of your own blood?"

His shoulders slumped with shame. "Brenna, please understand."

"I cannot understand," I sobbed. "I cannot understand why after so many years of my unquestioning duty and obedience, you could not gain the confidence to come to me when I needed you most."

He took a step back. "I see I have made a grave, foolish error. One I will now spend my days to beg your forgiveness for. But please, try to understand."

"I understand you are a coward. I understand no matter what I do for you, you will always choose what *you* believe is best for me. I've fulfilled my duty, father. I'm leaving you and this island. I am never coming back," I snapped.

His voice cleared and I met the same stoic, unmoving expression that was burned into my memory. A ruler stood before me. Not my father. Not the man who had raised the daughter born in a bath of his wife's blood.

No, he was a king who had done what he believed to be best for his subjects. Not what he'd believed best for his child.

He left me in the study, surrounded by my own works of art and the lingering hate of his inaction in my heart. My hands shook in my lap while one fist crumpled the parchment.

Did I want to read the words? Did I want to discover whatever lies my captor had sent to quell my foolish father's fears?

I raised my fist, releasing the paper and smoothing it out, refusing to flip it over and read the words until my heart was sure I was ready.

I was not ready for what I found.

King Enok. . .

My eyes snapped up.

I jumped to my feet, propelling myself down the long hall until I reached my bedroom door. My hands threw it open, and I went to my vanity, ripping open the drawer. Papers spilled out, unleashed from their hidden place.

I was frantic while I grabbed as many as I could, splaying them out across the top of the vanity. My eyes searched the ink, the words I had committed to memory.

There had been a change in the lettering, subtle in the beginning. One I had brushed off as him being more intentional with his writing.

I flipped through the pages, trying to find what I searched for.

I found one, lifting it with shaking hands while I read the words.

My enaid,

I dream of you, Bren. Every night my mind wishes to know what your voice is like. For I'm sure it will be a sound my soul has longed for. Perhaps it will be similar to the music that floats through the palace, calling for you to join me by my side.

I *knew* this handwriting.

Chapter 38

My mare flew through the village, kicking dirt and mud from the pouring rain while I steered her to my destination.

I knew that handwriting.

Gods, what was this?

What had he done?

The rain grew thicker, almost blinding me when I arrived. I dug my feet into the mare's side, alerting her to stop and I jumped from her, tying her to the post outside the small building I'd run to.

I opened the door, finding the little cottage empty and dusty.

The only thing my mother had left me. The seaside home her parents built when she first met my father. A place just for her on a strange new island.

I moved around the space, my heart racing while I lit the fire and threw my cloak onto a dusty chair at the table.

When the heat had warmed the building some, I turned back to the front door. Walking right out into the rain.

It only took a few steps before I was stopping at the crossroads. The only one I knew to exist outside of our village.

I reached into my gown's pocket, my finger brushing the gold coin and the knife I had hidden. I lifted the blade, trembling while I breathed out and sliced it across my wrist.

"Ulrich!" I screamed, allowing my blood to hit the dirt. "I know you can hear me!"

I was not in Vaneer. I was not burying my blood as he had instructed me. But he had already lied so much.

And my soul was the one guiding me in this moment.

Calling him to me.

"Face me you coward!" I shouted.

The lightning cracked with my words like it had filled the sky the day his black ship and right hand had claimed me. I peered over the hill sloping down toward the sea the cottage overlooked.

Mist came from the water as thick, dark shadows.

He was coming.

Hands wrapped around me, pulling me back.

"I cannot rid myself of you, *Ursa,"* he whispered into my ear. He flipped me around, forcing me to meet his eyes hidden behind the death mask tight across his face.

"You liar," I said calmly.

"So, you do not have to bury the blood. It still makes quite a tale," he laughed.

I slapped him.

His eyes went dark, and he gripped my wrist. "Did you call me to slap me?"

"I *know,*" I seethed.

His expression turned to one of panic.

"Brenna." His tone dropped.

My hand went to my gown, pulling two letters out, throwing them at his face.

"Is it Ulrich or Leif? I'm not sure anymore."

The papers fell to the ground at his feet, but he did not pull his eyes up. The lightning cracked in the sky again while the rain grew thicker. Plastering my hair to my head.

Soaking us both.

"I demand answers."

His eyes rose upward.

"Now."

He was silent.

"Ulrich! Do not make me hate you further than I already do!"

"You—" He paused, and his chest lifted with his breaths. "Are maddening."

More lightning.

I scoffed. "I am maddening?"

He rushed toward me, pulling me into his arms. Pressing my body to his.

"What is it that you *know?*" he whispered. "Tell me, Brenna."

I gulped.

"Tell me," he demanded.

"You fooled me," I cried.

"*When I gaze out in the night, I can't help but marvel at the land. In the dark, its beauty is of another world—an old, distant world, but in the day is when it shines. The brilliant blue skies captivate the mind, forcing you to forget any hardships in your heart. I imagine your blue eyes will do the same for me.*"

My pulse skipped as he recited one of the letters. Not the ones I'd thrown at his feet, but one I had left at home.

"I was not wrong," he whispered. "They captivate the mind. Blue so bright I wonder if they could cleanse my dark soul."

"I hate you," I sobbed.

His hand brushed my cheek. "I hate you as well. Fuck, I hate what you do to me."

I leaned into his touch, unable to accept the insanity of his skin against mine.

He breathed out. "I did not intend for this to go this way."

"You're insane," I muttered. "You have played me a fool."

I fell to the ground, sinking into the mud. He fell with me, gripping my face in his palms.

"What did you do?" I whispered, shaking my head. "What did you do?"

"Leif wrote at first. Gathering the information I needed. Doing what I demanded of him. But then he started to fall for you, disobeying my instructions."

His grip on my face tightened while he breathed out slowly.

"I took over, writing to understand what *beast* I was claiming. To know what triggers I could use to make you hate me and ensure you would never want to show me kindness." He let go, releasing a rageful yell.

"Fuck!"

The sound cracked with the lightning in the sky.

"Fuck, Breanna!" he shouted. "You made it so fucking hard to not be intrigued—to not want more. It was all a game, a jest to play you as the foolish woman I believed you to be." His gaze held mine and I was sure he would melt me into the earth.

"Then you walked into that fucking ballroom, wearing that fucking *red* dress, with hair to match the fire of your hate and Fate fuck it all, it made me hate you instantly."

I sniffled. "Hate?"

He gripped my face again, pulling me to him. "Because I suddenly realized there was *nothing* I could do to stop myself from actually falling in love with you. Which only made my hate for all that you make me feel turn deeper, all-consuming."

I shoved him away.

"I hate you," I said again.

"I know, Bren. I know," he whispered.

My name being uttered like that on his lips was my undoing. Cracking open the madness I did not want.

"I hate you," I repeated.

"I know," he replied.

"I may never forgive you," I muttered.

"I know," he repeated.

I looked into his eyes, barely able to see through the rain. His lips claimed mine in an instant. Our kiss was a fire, burning through my body while he lifted me from the ground. My legs went around his hips, and he held me in place, moving his lips against mine.

Hungry.

Gods, was he hungry.

He pulled away.

"Where?" he asked breathlessly.

I pointed to the cottage and the smoke disappearing with the rising red moon. We were before the threshold in seconds, moving at a speed I could not understand.

He kicked the door down, keeping his hold on me around his waist.

"What do you need, Bren?" he asked, kissing me again.

"You," I sobbed. "Ulrich, I need you."

We fell onto the bed with the light from the fire warming the space. Our wet bodies instantly soaked the blankets, but neither of us cared. All that mattered was he and I.

Us—together.

My hands went to his mask, but his hands stopped me.

"No."

"Ulrich," I begged. "Please, please do not do this."

"I am not supposed to be here," he muttered. "This is not supposed to happen."

"You started this all," I replied. "You made me a pawn in this game."

"Brenna," he sighed.

"How did you get here so quickly?"

"I never left you *my Enaid*," he replied. "I have hidden myself and my ship in the shadows."

"Say that again," I whispered.

"*My Enaid*."

"Again."

"*My Enaid*," he repeated himself, allowing the words to leave his lips with a slow, sensual tone.

The fire went out and his shadows grew around us, blocking my sight like so many nights before.

"I cannot yet show you my face," he whispered. "But I can allow you to touch me."

The mask landed beside me and my hand rose, trembling. His hand stopped me, guiding me to the right-side of his face, allowing me to brush against his cheek.

"Oh my Gods," I sobbed at the touch of his skin.

He grunted at my touch, gripping my fingers in his palm, holding me to him. My tears fell while I brushed his cheek with the end of my palm laying against his beard.

"*My Enaid*," he whispered again. "You have destroyed me."

His kiss claimed my soul. Ripping a part of me away with its movements. Guiding me into the void of his shadows encompassing us. But the darkness did not bother me. Not when I could feel his nose against mine. The softness of it with no hard mask hitting my skin.

I did not want to remove my hand from him, but I pulled away, wrapping my arms around his neck.

He lifted my hips with his, keeping his hands on my waist.

"I need you," I whispered. "I need *you.*"

"I am at your mercy," he replied.

His hands gripped me, and he moved as though he were going to flip me onto my stomach, but I grabbed his hands.

"No, not like that. Ulrich, I need you to make love to me."

He paused.

"Please."

"You do not know what you're requesting."

"I do," I replied. "Please."

The darkness was too much for me to see through now that he had layered the entire room with it. Blocking out the windows and every possible crack of light that could slip through.

"Ulrich," I repeated. "Make love to me."

He was silent, unmoving. I regretted my words. Wondered if I had been asking for too much too soon. When we had yet to even speak about what he had done. When he hadn't even tried to explain himself to me.

"Brenna." His voice was soft, barely audible, as his lips brushed my neck.

I jolted.

"Bren."

His mouth went lower while his hands pulled up the hem of my gown. He lifted it over my head, undressing me completely.

My body shook from the cold of the room and the sounds of wet fabric hitting the floor raised the hair on my arms.

His hands ran up my legs, rough, large, strong. Gripping my thighs.

"My *Enaid,*" he whispered as his mouth claimed me.

I cried, jolting with the heat of his tongue on my clit. Flicking back and forth while his fingers entered me.

It was all insanity.

Gods, I needed more of it.

His mouth moved faster, sucking on me while his fingers moved slowly. In and out. Curling with precision each time he left my warmth.

"*Enaid,*" he muttered around me, sucking once more.

"Ulrich," I cried, gripping his hair. Allowing myself to touch him. To actually feel him when he gave me pleasure.

He grunted when I tugged the tie from his hair, releasing the bun he had it wrapped in.

"More of that," he groaned.

My legs trembled around his head while I kept my fingers in the thick strands. Tugging and pulling. Forcing indecent noises from his lips.

He rose, keeping his fingers inside, pressing his chest against mine.

"The taste of you," he groaned. "I could live on it for eternity."

"Ulrich," I gasped his name again.

He leaned into me, claiming my lips. Shocking me in the dark. His fingers curled more, moving slightly faster.

"What do you want?" he whispered against my lips.

"More," I cried. "More. I will never have enough of you."

"Yes," he moaned.

"Please."

He removed his fingers but continued to brush my sensitive flesh.

"You came for me," I cried while he continued his caresses.

"I did not leave," he replied.

I didn't understand the words. But I did not want to understand them. Not now. I wanted to let go; I wanted to continue to fall into oblivion with him.

He leaned over me, kissing me softly and I moved my hand down. My fingers brushed him, and he jolted.

"Bren," he muttered. "I am fine."

I kissed him back, wrapping my hands around his shaft. "You do not allow me to give you the pleasure you give me."

His hand gripped my hair. "Brenna."

"Say my name, Ulrich," I whispered. "Call out to whatever Gods you worship."

I pressed against his chest, forcing his back against the mattress, trailing my hands down his broad chest. Moving them along where I knew his ink to be.

I moved upward, reaching for his face but he stopped me, only allowing my palm on his jaw.

"Brenna," he whispered again.

I kissed him, cutting off his words. Wanting his fears to die with the heat of my lips. Like mine were melting away from me.

He was shaking when I pulled away. His hands trembling against my back, pressing into the scars created by his own hand.

I removed his palm from me and laid it gently on the bed.

"Call my name, Ulrich," I muttered while I made my descent. "Call my name."

My tongue licked his tip, taking in the small bead of moisture coming from him. His fingers wrapped in my hair.

"Brenna," he gasped as my lips wrapped around him. "Oh fuck."

I smiled around him, loving the pleasure I was giving back to him. Returning the release he was always so willing to give me.

His hips moved while my head lifted up and down and my hands gripped the base of his shaft. I tightened my hold on him, wanting him to feel my desire for his release. Wanting him to know I needed him.

His sounds—they were addicting.

A hand removed from the tangle of my hair, coming down and holding my chin while he continued to thrust down my throat. Bringing tears to my eyes from the force of it.

He stopped and pulled my chin up. As though he were gazing into my eyes in the dark.

"You wanted to make love," he whispered.

I nodded.

"Do you love me?"

My tears fell—unexplainably. I couldn't answer. The response was at the tip of my tongue, but I could not do it.

His thumb stroked my lips. "I will make love to you, my *Enaid*."

His hands wrapped around my hips, pressing me into the bed. With one hand, he held my arms above my head. Trapping me in my spot.

"I want to touch you," I protested.

He said nothing, he only gripped me tighter and I yelled out when he pressed into me.

"Oh Gods," I cried.

He leaned forward, releasing his hold on me, allowing my arms to wrap around his neck.

He thrusted into me, making my lip quiver from the pleasure.

"I have told you about those Gods," he whispered, then thrusted again. "They are not welcome."

I brought my legs up, enveloping his body in them while I held onto his neck. I tugged on his hair, pressing my lips against his while he continued to move.

Holding him so close was an addiction, a poison I never wanted to leave my body. The heat of his chest on mine. His breath on my lips. His hair brushing my fingers at his neck.

He was mine and I was his.

He pulled away from me, kissing hard before he was lifting my legs up, placing them in my own hands.

"Hold on," he whispered, kissing my calf.

My head hit the dusty pillow on the bed when he entered me, pressing in forcefully but not hard like all the times before.

This was firm, controlled.

Him and I.

His thumb began its maddening circles on me, and I held onto my legs, using them to ground myself while he moved. Pulling the tight need within me to the surface.

"Let go," he grunted, thrusting into me. "Let go."

I shook.

"Why?" my mouth uttered without my control. "Why?"

My tears fell but he did not stop moving. The emotions between us were hot, a blanket over the room.

"Why?" I repeated.

He thrusted again, circling his thumb.

"There was no other way," he whispered.

My head went back against the pillows while the pleasure of his movements took over.

"There was no other way, my *Enaid*," he whispered again, slamming into me with his release.

He shook against me and his fingers moved faster, forcing my own release without my control. My legs shook in my hands, and I bit my lip, holding in my cries.

Our breaths were the only sounds in the room when he finally pulled from me and laid at my side, pulling me against his chest.

I looked up, hoping to see anything through his shadows but I was blocked from him. Like all of those times before.

My hand rose to stroke his face and he gripped it, placing my palm on his right cheek. My gasp was quiet, but my startled jump shook the bed when I felt the wetness on his skin.

Tears.

"There was no other way," he repeated, holding me tighter.

I remained quiet and unmoving until his arms went lax against me.

When his breaths had finally shifted to that deep sleeping sound I'd learned to recognize, I slipped from his grasp. The bed shifted with him turning to his side and I laid on my back, staring at the dark ceiling.

I had a choice. A choice I knew to be foolish. My eyes went to where I believed my cloak still hung on the back of the chair and I stood slowly.

My feet moved with apprehension with his darkness still wrapped around the space. I held my hands out, guiding the way until my toe hit the legs of the chair.

I reached down, grasping my cloak, pulling it toward me, reaching into the deep pockets.

My hand wrapped around it. The black candle and the piece of flint I'd grabbed before rushing out of my room in a mad dash. My fingers trembled as I lit the flint and quickly stuck it to the candle wick before Ulrich's shadows could extinguish the flames.

To my shock the candle became bright. Red—just like those candles on the walls in hallway nine.

I turned to the bed, the light illuminating his figure before me and I froze.

What was I doing?

What was I starting?

I shuffled across the floor, my hands shaking until I was before him.

My gasp was quiet, almost a sob when I found his hair laid over his face, covering his features. It was startling, how he appeared as normal as a simple man in the bed. Sleeping off the high of our shared ecstasy.

I leaned forward, lifting his hair as softly as I could while tears fell from my eyes.

The emotions were overwhelming me as I stared down at him. Trying to map the lines of the face I had been forbidden to see for all this time. Trying to force my mind to remember every last detail.

Gods, he was beautiful.

His nose was sharp, his brow thick. Surprisingly, a scar ran down his face. From his right brow, right across his nose, to the end of his left cheek, disappearing into his beard. I admired it, realizing each and every one of his masks were fitting perfectly to disguise the scar. It was old by the color, but deep enough it had marked his face for eternity.

I held back my desire to stroke his cheek, not wanting to wake him from his peace. Instead, I sat on the floor, admiring him. Imagining that face with his eyes open and his emerald green gaze bright and alive, staring back at me.

I wondered what his cheeks looked like with the lift of his smile. Whether or not the skin around his eyes wrinkled with the movement.

My mind wandered.

Could I love him?

Did I want to?

He was a monster. A madman—always unpredictable. Always seeming to snap at a moment's notice. Gods, he'd locked me in that dark room. Allowed the torment to torture my mind. He'd laid his hands on me countless times. He'd embarrassed me before his court. He'd encouraged *me* to commit murder.

My body was forever marked by his hand. Scars I would never be able to rid myself of. Reminders of his cruelty.

My heart ached while I considered the last eleven months. The hours of his brutality but also the hours of his softness. Even if it were subtle. Even if the creature that lurked within him usually took control.

I thought about those damned letters. For at least half of those long three years, he had been the one writing to me. It was halfway through the courtship when the lettering had changed. When the words were more elongated and appearing to come from a steady hand. And I, like a love-sick adolescent, chose to ignore the change. Not thinking twice on whether or not the words were being written by another's hand.

Words that were not Leif's, a fool I now realized who was as much of a pawn in the king's game as I had been. No, it had been Ulrich.

I leaned back, staring at him. In his sleep he was peaceful. Still terrifying with the harsh features of a towering man, but he was beautiful. Someone I could see who had kindness in his heart.

Someone that had written that kindness in ink, addressed only to me.

I stared until I could no longer keep my eyes open. Until I could barely believe I had seen the face of the beast.

Who I realized was the man who also held my heart.

I stood, leaning over him with the candle in my hand, kissing the scar at the top of his right brow.

"I love you, Urich," I whispered. "I may also hate you and what you do." My voice shook. "But Gods, I do love you."

He smiled at my words and my heart cracked at the peace on his face.

I stood again then heat ran down my fingers and I jumped in pain as wax fell from the candle. Wax that had not melted since I'd lit it.

It hit his cheek and his eyes sprang open, staring into mine.

"What have you done?" he shouted, jumping to his feet. "What have you done?"

A shrill laugh filled the air, and I screamed out in shock. I stumbled, trying to get away from the rage—no fear, in Ulrich's eyes. His hand reached for me, but it snapped back, grotesquely, unnaturally.

I let out another shocked shout, retreating further. My feet slipped on the wax, still falling from the candle, and my legs went out from under me. Causing me to slam my head into the wooden floor, knocking myself unconscious with the sound of an enraged roar guiding me into darkness.

Chapter 39

Sunlight and the smell of a smoking, extinguished fire woke me. I groaned, sitting up and holding a hand to the back of my head. My eyes scanned the room, and I tried to remember where I was and why I was naked.

It all flooded back.

Letters.

Lies.

Love making.

I stood quickly finding myself alone, but Ulrich's clothes were still piled where he'd discarded them when we'd entered the cottage the night before. I turned in place, trying to decipher what could have happened when I found his mask laying on the table near the smoking fire.

Something was wrong.

I threw my gown on quickly. Metal clattered onto the ground with the movement, and I watched the gold coin roll toward the hearth. I did not know why I brought it. What prompted me to pull it from grandmother's box, but it had come with the candle, and so it came with me.

For a moment I considered picking it up. Then a more cynical part of me stared with contempt. That damned candle had burned him. That damned candle had been tempting enough for me to be foolish.

I didn't need the omen that would come with the coin.

I turned on my heel, leaving it by the hearth and I threw my cloak around my shoulders. When I ran out of the cottage, I found my mare no longer tied to her post. But a trail of blood led away from the cabin.

"Fuck the Gods," I sobbed, running down the mud road where my village lay in the distance.

Where had he gone? What had happened?

His rage when we'd make eye contact—I thought he was going to kill me on the spot. His hand... Why had his hand snapped back so grotesquely?

I kept running until my sides ached and my lungs burned. When I made it up the hill the white bears usually crested, I let out a sigh when I saw it on the horizon: the tip of his ship, barely peeking past the neck of the fjord leading out to the sea. Hiding. Waiting for me.

A bird circled above me, squawking annoyingly but I threw my hands up, trying to shoo it away. The movement caused me to trip on my gown, sending me tumbling down the hill. Covering myself and my body in mud and debris.

"Princess!" a startled man yelled from his garden I had landed beside.

I popped to my feet, brushing him away. "I am fine," I groaned.

I kept running. Perhaps he was with father. Perhaps everything was fine, and I had not ruined anything. His ship was still there. Still waiting for me. Never leaving me.

The bird followed me while I ran through town, even ducking so low I thought it would attempt to peck at my head.

"Get away!" I shouted at it again, picking up a pebble and throwing it, trying not to hit the animal but startle it.

It appeared to work. The pebble flew over the bird's head, and it squawked angrily then flew off.

When I was almost to the palace, I noticed Oberon's ship still in the harbor and my heart sank.

Ulrich would not be in the palace if Oberon were there. Or—

Hope rose in my chest. Would he?

Would he request both of my kings' permission?

Not for my hand. I did not believe either of us were ready for that step, but for their approval for us to be—whatever we were.

I approached the palace doors, reaching for them but they flung open before I could grasp the handles. I stepped back, startled by the movement. Even more startled by who waited on the other side.

Titania stared at me with her eyes wild.

"Brenna," she said sweetly.

I let out a breath of relief. Falling to my knees.

"My queen." I lifted my hands, ready to plead for myself and Ulrich.

Titania bent to my level, lifting my chin with her hands. An action that suddenly made me weary. She stroked my knotted hair, then met my eyes.

"You smell of *him*," she sneered.

My eyes widened and I opened my mouth to protest when someone grasped my arms from behind me.

"Vengeance is sweet," their voice whispered.

I snapped my head back, finding Bjorn with his arms wrapped around me.

"Unhand me!" I screamed.

He gripped tighter and that damned bird attacked, pecking at Bjorn's head.

"Grab that beast!" Titania ordered and guards ran out past her, chasing the bird.

"Bring her," the queen snapped.

Bjorn kept his arms on me, dragging me through the palace. An empty palace.

Where was everyone?

Titania threw the great-hall doors open, and I gasped at what I saw. My father was seated on his small throne with our entire staff behind them. His brown eyes were frantic, but when he opened his mouth, no sound came out. My heart raced and I stared at our staff, wondering why none of them moved. My eyes then found it, the thin layer of shadows, holding them all back. I turned my gaze back to my father, finding a thin band of shadows across his lips.

What was Ulrich doing?

I turned my head, trying to find him, but gasped again when I found Olen in the middle of the room in his beast-form.

Titania laughed again.

"This is not what I was expecting when I came to a funeral." She approached Olen, stroking his fur gently.

The fur on his back rippled at her touch and his sorrowful eyes stared at me.

"Olen?" I asked.

Titania's head snapped to the creature then back to me and she grinned. "My Gods, she does not know."

"Know what?" I jerked in Bjorn's hold, but he held firm.

Titania stroked Olen again and the beast snarled.

"Do not bite, king," she purred. "You are *mine* now."

King?

Her guards clambered into the room, two of them holding the bird in their hands. I bit back my amusement that they struggled with such a small animal. Until they threw the bird, and I cried out at its broken wing when it landed at my feet.

"You monsters!" I yelled.

"We are not the monsters," Titania laughed. "These two are the monsters."

I didn't understand who the second person she referred to was until the bird before me was shifting. Its bones transformed from wings and a body covered in feathers to elongating limbs.

I stepped back when the naked man stood before me with one arm dangling from the break Titania's guards had caused.

His dark skin was one I knew too intimately.

His uninked skin.

Olen.

"This isn't possible!" I shouted, staring at Olen in beast-form beside Titania.

The queen laughed again, slapping the beast on the back. "You are an expert in manipulation, Ulrich. I will give you that."

"Brenna," Olen's voice before me was a warning. "Stay quiet."

"No!" I refused

Bjorn released me, retreating away as I stepped around Olen and moved to the beast. I was almost beside him when Titania's guards shoved me away, pressing their swords into my side. I pushed them away, trying to get to the beast. Its eyes were wide with me just an arm's length from it, but the guard's gripped me before I could touch that fur I'd grown to love.

"Let me tell you a story," the queen began. Her guards continued to push me away from the beast staring at me with sorrow in its eyes.

"Millennia ago, a *beast* of shadows appeared in our world. Followed by a court of monsters. Creatures we had never seen before." She stroked the black fur.

"He was terrifying and amazing. A being I had never encountered in my long life. And his inked skin—"

My stomach dropped.

"Gods did I want it."

She gripped the fur on the beast's neck. "He came with a group of them. Monsters and a few who could shift into anything they wanted." She pointed to Olen.

"I was a lonely wife. He was a lonely man. Confiding in me that he had left a kingdom in ruin. In death, betrayal, and bloodshed. Only bringing those he could save. Allowing his own world to fall into the hands of a tyrant."

The beast's eyes dropped in shame.

"I fell for him so quickly, Brenna. Gods did I fall. He was the new breath of air that I needed. But when I confessed that love?" Her gaze turned hateful. "He refused. He refused me. He refused my plan to turn my terrifying lover into our world's new king. Mocking me in every sense of the word."

My stomach twisted; I was going to be sick.

She continued, "I of course told Oberon. Who in a fit of rage, banished Ulrich because we both know my sniveling husband holds no power compared to the man we both love."

She smiled, pulling at the beast's fur again.

"Only I *cursed* him under the blood moon. He hadn't experienced one in our world yet. Having no idea how long they lasted or that *my* power was stronger under its light. I was determined to turn him into as much of a monster as I knew him to be." She stroked his fur again. "He was terrifying, but lived with a mask of stoic royalty.

Only, I saw the monster within. When he was lost in the faerie wine, it would unleash. Random outbursts of rage. Violence so delicious it made my body heat with need."

My head swam the longer the queen talked, trying to piece together all that she said.

Titania glanced at the beast again. "With my curse, he would live life as a beast under the sunlight, shifting under the blood moon. Periods of one hundred and fifty years of beasthood. A creature of my own making that mirrored the creature that lived inside. I made sure to mark him with my blood blade as a reminder as well, branding his skin with my own hate."

She lifted his chin, running her fingers over the red scar his fur did not cover.

My tears fell then. Tears of realization.

"To break the curse, he had to find a woman, any woman who would fall in love with him even after seeing everything horrible that he was. If he did not, then the beast would claim him fully, a *deal* of my own making. Turning him into my personal pet of rage and hate."

"She was only required to follow one rule; never look upon his face before she told him she loved him." Titania laughed. "You *failed*, Brenna. You professed your love to him while gazing upon the beautiful face that always got him what he wanted."

"No," I sobbed. "No."

I didn't believe it. I couldn't believe it.

Titania's hands gripped the beast's fur and she sighed. "Ulrich, shift."

My chest was heavy with shock. My stomach twisted in knots when the beast did as he was told. The fur disappeared around him, slowly, revealing his inked skin. My hands went to my lips as our gazes locked onto one another's.

He towered over us all. The giant that was the Unseelie King, now standing in my childhood home.

Without his mask.

Ulrich's green eyes were so full of sorrow and regret. An expression my heart could barely handle.

Titania whispered to him and his body went rigid.

"Now, Ulrich," she demanded.

Ulrich stepped forward and his shadows wrapped around his skin. Creating a black wisping suit around his body.

He stepped forward, barely a fingers-length from me and I reached for him.

"Ulrich," I pleaded.

He did not look me in the eyes. My tears fell and I was sure he would not acknowledge my presence when a small tendril of his shadows came toward me, licking between my outstretched fingers.

"Ulrich," Titania cleared her throat. "Do not speak to her. Your deal was not honored. Claim your soul."

My pulse froze and I stepped back, watching Ulrich continue his approach. Not to me—no—he was walking straight toward my father. The thin shadows masking him and the members of our household fell, and my cry echoed across the room.

Our staff, my family, they were dead. All of their bodies collapsed as Ulrich's shadows dropped and their clotted blood covered the wood of the dais.

"Oh my Gods," I cried, falling to my knees.

A rough hand grasped my arm, holding me up before I hit the floor, and I leaned into Olen. Unable to process what was happening. Why Ulrich was not fighting back.

"King Enok," Titania said sweetly. "Your daughter took something from me."

My head went to my father, and he let out a gasp. "Brenna," he yelled. "Unhand her!"

His commanding voice did nothing for the queen before him. My chest grew heavy as I watched the fear grow in his eyes when his gaze met mine.

I'm sorry, he mouthed.

Ulrich was silent as he stood before my father. His shadows created shackles, holding my last family member to his throne.

"Ulrich," I pleaded. I moved to shove Olen off me, but the giant kept me still.

"Brenna, I beg of you. Stop," he whispered into my ear.

I fell to the floor with Olen's arm around my waist, bringing my eyes up while Ulrich leaned over the throne.

I could not hear his words, his whispers. But I could see the hate in my father's eyes. The determination of a king ready to go to war with an enemy.

My scream fractured through my body when Ulrich's hand rose with a shadow sword in his grasp. Olen held me tighter, but it was no use. It was no comfort while I watched helplessly as Ulrich stabbed my father straight into his chest, nailing him to his throne.

"No!"

I kept screaming, sure everything inside of me had cracked to nothing. My heart—barely beating with the loss of my grandmother and the revelation of Ulrich's letters—tightened in my chest.

I was going to explode. From either grief or rage.

Or both.

Ulrich's body lit with silver light while he stayed leaning over my father, his shoulders heaving for several seconds before he stood.

And when he twisted back in my direction, I could not stop myself from emptying the contents of my stomach onto the ground. Not with his black eyes staring right through my soul.

He returned to Titania's side, and she stroked his arm lovingly.

"We're leaving," Titania smiled at me.

Olen removed his arm from me and ran forward toward her. His unbroken limb was out, as though he intended to wrap his palm around the queen's neck, but a guard stopped him, holding a sword at his throat.

Titania stared at the right hand.

"I could take you. I could leave this poor woman with questions she'll never have answered, but I am not that *cruel.*" Titania laughed. "I can make you worthless though."

Another guard approached and stabbed its sword into Olen's side. Ulrich did nothing, not even a flinch or shift in emotion on his face.

Those soft feelings I had for him from before began to crumble. Was this all the point? To ruin me fully?

My body shook while they passed me. I could barely glance up at Ulrich with my tears running down my face. He passed where my feet were beneath me as I knelt against the marbled floor. A guard was at his heel almost like a protection for the unkillable Unseelie King.

The hate I had quelled in my heart returned and my rage unleashed. I was on my feet instantly, grabbing the sword of the guard behind Ulrich. The fae stared at me in shock, pulling his weapon back but I pulled harder. We struggled, both of us trying to get the sword. Titania let out an amused laugh, enough to distract the man I struggled with. I took my opportunity, kicking him in the thigh and knocking him to the ground.

Before the guard could reorient himself, I lifted the weapon, gripping it in my palm tightly.

"Ulrich!" I shouted.

Ulrich turned on his heel, his eyes burning with hate.

"Brenna," he warned.

"Fight me!" I screamed, shaking while I held the heavy blade out. "You fucking coward! Fight me!"

Titania's shrill laugh near the door brought instant irritation. I snapped my gaze to her, glaring. Making me distracted enough for Ulrich to attack. The blade cut into his palm and his blood spilled onto the marble. His unbelievable strength pulled on the blade, dragging me toward him.

"You think I'm the coward?" he seethed. The sword clattered to the ground while his hand gripped the neck of my gown. "You think I do not fucking know that, Brenna?"

His eyes burned while he held my gaze.

"I have *never* hated someone as much as I hate *you*," he whispered.

I stared into his black eyes. "I hate you," I sobbed. "You killed him."

Finally, the monster cracked. His expression shifted from nothing to actual pain. Real regret and he brought me closer. I stared at his unmasked face, blinking back my tears, hoping for something that would redeem him. Something to bring clarity to this insanity.

His beard brushed my neck, and his other hand grasped my palm gently. He dropped me, letting out the same laugh he'd done for months. One of amusement. One of mocking.

"Come, my pet," Titania sang from the door. "We must go *home*."

I moved to run after Ulrich, but more guards approached, holding me back.

"Get back here!" I cried, slamming my fists against them. "Face me!"

Ulrich and Titania walked away while I struggled with the guard before. He was stronger than me physically, but my rage had unlocked something inside of me. A feral hate overpowering even the strongest man.

I kicked his feet out from under him and his sword clattered in his surprise. I brought it high into the air, then brought it down, right through his chest. His choked gasp echoed with the sound of the front doors opening. Fueling my vengeance further.

More guards began to approach but Olen twisted, fighting them off. Snapping necks with one arm as though they were nothing more than dolls. Even with his black blood bleeding from his wound and a useless arm dangling at his side.

"Go!" Olen screamed.

I turned, running to Ulrich, determined to catch him. To get answers.

When I reached the palace doors, I slipped, glancing down and finding a trail of black blood.

His blood.

I ran faster, holding the sword in my palm, almost reaching the queen and the man she now called her *pet* when hands gripped the back of my hair, ripping me to the ground.

My head hit the earth, and my back slammed down. Stars formed in my vision and my breath stuck in my lungs. Then he was over me.

That damned monster who had poisoned me.

"Brenna," Bjorn sang. "I love when fate allows destiny to do its job."

His hand gripped my gown, pulling me to his face. "I will have his throne, Brenna. I will take his place in this world as the Unseelie King. Oberon and Titania have promised it."

He dropped me and I cried out from the pain of my body hitting the ground once more.

"Titania loved to learn Ulrich had brought a woman home. That she was forced to sleep beside him. She especially loved your hate for him."

My tears fell.

Bjorn held my shoulders down, keeping me in place. His smile was sick and knowing that he was keeping me from Ulrich. Keeping me from doing anything to catch him.

"Titania has agreed to make you my personal *whore*, Brenna." Bjorn licked my neck. "I will give you everything that coward of a king has failed to give you."

He pulled one hand away, running it down my ribs and I bit my lip.

"Oh yes," he hissed. "You will do—"

His words were cut off and I laid in shock, staring when his head was ripped right off his shoulders. His black blood spewed from his head, covering my body in the gore.

I saw it, what Ulrich had mentioned, a sliver of silver in the sun, lifting upward. I was sure it would disappear in the wind when Olen's head appeared, and he sucked it into his lungs.

What. The. Fuck.

Olen shoved the body down when he'd finished his demented meal and he bent down, offering me his uninjured hand.

I stood, letting out a sob when I found the gangplank lifting on Oberon's ship.

"Olen, you better get me to that ship. Immediately."

Olen threw me over his shoulder, like so many times before and he ran. Just as fast as Ulrich had run to the cottage the night before. I held his shirt, watching the blood from his injury trail alongside Ulrich's black blood.

We reached the dock, and Olen dropped me. His breathing was heavy, his eyes full of pain.

I dove then, like a foolish mad woman, into the frigid water, pumping my arms through the waves. Believing I could catch them.

Oberon's ship, while not nearly as fast as Ulrich's, moved through the water faster than any vessel I had at my disposal.

My arms began to burn with my movements. Begging me to stop. To relent my foolish attempt at catching up.

I stopped, kicking my feet beneath me while I slammed my arms against the surface of the water.

A hand gripped my gown, pulling me back while I screamed, watching the ship sail away. Olen deposited me onto the dock, sopping wet and heaving down my sobs.

He grunted behind me.

"What is happening?" I whispered

"Princess," Olen groaned. "It was a ruse."

The word, *ruse*, it turned me into the monster Ulrich's court liked to claim I was. I jumped to my feet, whirling around and I slapped him.

"Tell me," I demanded.

Olen was silent, for seconds too long. I slapped him again.

He grunted out in shock holding my challenging gaze. Both of us breathing heavily, knowing Ulrich was being taken further and further away.

Olen relented, telling me Ulrich's plan. How he made an ancient deal. How he sent letters. How he unintentionally developed feelings for me. How he had forced Olen to be part of it all. Part of this game of manipulating me.

Turning me into a piece in their fucked up game.

I stopped the right hand, not understanding his words and what Titania had said in the palace.

"You were a beast with me!" I cried, keeping my eyes on the ship.

Olen shook his head, and I jumped when bright light blinded me and Ulrich was standing before me. Then more bright light and the beast I'd spent hours beside was before me. More light, another shifting, and Ulrich before me once more.

No mask, his long hair dangling, his green eyes staring at me with shame and guilt.

Only it wasn't Ulrich. It was Olen.

Evident when he shifted again, back to the face of the man who I'd believed had been my protector this whole time. But he was without that damned scar I now realized was and always had been Ulrich's.

The shock was too much. My mind could hardly fathom what I was being shown. Olen could shift. To anything and *anyone* he wished.

"Oh my Gods," I sobbed. "What is this?"

"Think, Brenna." Olen shook me. "Each time you were ever harmed by Ulrich, who was always at your side?"

I blinked.

"You as a beast."

He shook his head. "Brenna *he* was the beast. The man sauntering around the dais? Murdering and hurting? It was *me.* Always me. The whipping? Me. Sigrun? Me. Harold...?"

My body went hot with hate. Realization rushed through me while Olen paused his words.

The man before me let out his breath, dropping his head in shame.

"Me, Brenna. Harold, claiming that life, I forced you to do that. Ulrich was the beast beside you the whole time."

I fell to my knees. Ulrich had slept by my side when my wounds had healed. Ulrich stayed at my feet when I was lost in myself, drawing my maps.

Ulrich had swum in the sea with me laughing about white bears.

Ulrich had not whipped me.

He always, each time we laid together, paused at my scars, pressing them with rage.

"He didn't leave me in the courtyard."

Olen knelt beside me. "No, Brenna, that was me. He stayed with you on the ship the entire way. He said his goodbyes."

I glanced up, finding Oberon's ship crossing the fjord.

The image of my father's bleeding body in the palace ran through my mind. "He killed him," I gasped.

Olen knelt before me, gripping my face. "Brenna." He shook me again. "That is *not* Ulrich. That is the curse. The one Titania mentioned. She has full control."

I have never hated someone as much as I hate you.

Ulrich's last words rang in my ears.

"He hates me," I gasped out. "Olen, this was all just a game to him."

Olen continued to hold my face. "No, princess, he hates that he *loves* you."

Love.

The word—the foolish phrase I'd uttered that had ruined whatever this all ways. The words on the paper, confessing the same thing.

Was it true? Had he been trying to speak to me this entire time? How long? How long had the madman loved me?

I stared into Olen's black eyes.

I wasn't confident Ulrich knew what love was. But I also wasn't confident that he was lost forever.

"We have to get him," I sobbed.

"Princess," Olen objected.

I stood, pointing to the water. "We have to get him!" I screamed.

Olen said nothing. He was silent while we watched Oberon's ship pass Ulrich's and I cried out when blasts of fire hit the vessel, igniting it in flames instantly. Preventing us from being able to catch up to the king's ship.

"What have I done?" I whispered, falling to my knees, watching the man I hated and loved sail off.

The man who had done everything he could to ensure *he* would not cause me harm.

I had to get him back.

Even if it killed me.

Epilogue
Ulrich

There was a whisper in the air, words my conflicted heart hoped to hear. Words I was too much of a coward to utter myself. Fuck, words I was still unsure if I believed were true within me.

Her words—a proclamation.

Then pain, searing pain and my eyes snapped open.

Brenna's blue eyes stared back at me, full of fear. Fear I had caused her. My eyes went to the red-flame candle.

How the fuck did she get one of those?

"What have you done?" I shouted, jumping to my feet, panic gripping my heart and soul. "What have you done?"

She was all around the room. Her laugh, sickening. A memory I had tried to ignore. A pull my body had fought for millennia.

Brenna *heard* it. She stepped back, possibly from the fear and rage in my gaze. I lunged for her, but my hand snapped back, the curse taking control. She continued to stumble back, slipping on the wax that should not have fallen from the candle, slamming her head against the floor of the small cottage we'd secluded ourselves in.

"Come to me, my pet," my tormentor whispered in my mind, calling upon her curse.

"No!" I shouted while my voice turned to a roar.

"*Come for me,*" Titania coaxed again.

I shifted, without my control, my body changing to the beast I hated. My hands turned to clawed paws while my back arched as fur grew over my body.

My shout of rage rattled the cottage, but Brenna did not move. Was she dead? Oh fuck, was she dead?

A breath, a low breath, lifted her chest and my beastly body relaxed with relief.

"*Ulrich, come to me.*"

Titania's pull tugged at me, forcing me to leave the cottage. My eyes landed on the mare. The animal stared in fear, and I lunged, ripping into its neck.

My attack destroyed the rope Brenna had tied it with and it took off, bleeding from its new gaping wound.

My own predatory instincts begged for me to follow my prey, but I could not. Not with *her* calling to me.

I bounded down the road, with my shadows covering my tracks. I couldn't fight it. Fuck I hated her. I hated this.

Everything was ruined.

I had ruined it all.

My body followed Titania's call, and I growled when I found it leading me to Brenna's family home. The small palace—her place of safety—the place I had stolen her from.

My shoulders slammed into the door, hitting a guard in the process.

"There he is," Titania purred.

My eyes went up, meeting her brown gaze.

"It has been so long." She put emphasis on her words. "You have never come for me, Ulrich. Even when you were cursed during these long blood moons. I have heard you fucked yourself silly. Was that to ignore the desire to warm my bed? To fight the urge to take that black ship across our waters and ravage me like you once did?"

I snarled and moved to lunge, but her hand went up and my body froze.

"I smelled you on her." Titania's eyes went dark. "Gods, Ulrich you were burying yourself in a child. She is nothing compared to the millennia we have lived. *Her?* That obedient little miscreation?"

I snarled again.

Titania laughed again. That annoying, shrill sound these irritating creatures all made.

"I smelled your little pet on her as well." Titania frowned, the expression was like a child's pout. "Why did you never offer him to play with *us*? That is rather rude, Ulrich."

"Olen doesn't hump trash," I growled. "His standards were always higher than mine used to be."

A spear rammed into my side, forcing an echoing shout from my lungs.

"Behave, Ulrich. I could force you to destroy this entire little village."

I met her eyes. "You wouldn't," I warned.

Her eyes went past my head to the palace door behind me. "Oberon and Mab are on that ship. Likely lost in their disgusting lust. Gods, somedays I wonder why I stay. Why I sit on the side allowing them to live their little bubble of love and family with all of their disgusting offspring."

"It's because you're too much of a coward," I replied. "You couldn't even end the man yourself. You had to beg the new monster that entered your world to do it."

Titania was before me in an instant, her hand gripping the fur on my neck.

And I could do nothing. Could not fight this curse she held me in.

"I am a *queen*, Ulrich. I do not get my hands dirty."

"You just have him do it for you," I growled. "Did he enjoy removing my peoples' heads?"

She laughed again. "Gods, yes he did. After the bloodshed was the first time he and I enjoyed each other's beds in decades. It gave him a thrill that I had begged him to put you in your place."

She held her grip tighter while her finger dug into my open wound.

"It's time to actually put you in your place, Ulrich. Once and for all."

I struggled in her grasp, biting my snarls and growls from the pain of her attack.

"Wake them all," Titania ordered, standing and eyeing her guards. "Gather them in the great hall."

"What are you doing?" I demanded.

"She'll never forgive you after this. She'll never come for you." Titania laughed. "Gods, she'll hate you even more than I believe she already does."

I was ordered by my newly claimed master to remain in place while her guards gathered Brenna's father and his staff. Innocents in mourning, rubbing their sleep from their eyes.

"What is this?" King Enok demanded from the throne her guards forced him upon.

Titania laughed and stroked my fur.

"Beast!" Enok yelled. "Where is my daughter? Have you claimed her once more?"

"Do not answer that," Titania whispered.

The words were like a lock on my throat, preventing my words from forming.

I would kill her for this. I would burn her kingdom to the ground.

"King Enok," Titania breathed out. "Your daughter took something from me."

Enok's eyes went wide, and he moved to lift himself from the throne, but her guards held him in place with their spears.

He shook his head in disbelief. "My queen, I can promise she has not."

Titania's laugh echoed in the room while the morning light of the sun began to shine through the windows.

"Oh, she did, Enok. She's warmed his bed for months. She's been his little *whore* at his side."

Enok's rage was unmistakable. His hands trembled and my head went down in shame, unable to stare the man in the eyes.

But the king surprised me with his response.

"My daughter is a woman who can do as she wishes with her body. You will not speak of her that way when the entire court is aware of your constant humping of your own whores, *queen*."

Titania's rage unleashed and she snapped her fingers. The guards dragged Enok's staff forward, forcing them to their knees.

"Do you want them to die, Enok?" she demanded. "Do you want to be responsible for their deaths?"

Enok struggled against the guards. "Where is Oberon?"

Titania laughed. "Poisoned on his faerie wine and likely fucking Mab. Why does it matter?"

"He won't let you do this," Enok spat.

"He lets me do whatever I wish to avoid me leaving him, Enok. Those *whores* I hump? Those are given to me by Oberon. To keep me happy."

Her hand gripped at my fur, forcing me to look into her eyes. "Watch this, Ulrich. Watch the power I have."

Her hand shoved between my shoulder blades, forcing me to lower and watch her bloodshed. Screams echoed around the grand hall while her guards started their slicing. Knives across necks, spears into sides.

A massacre.

Of everyone Brenna loved.

Enok shouted on his throne, screaming out his rage, unable to fight while her guards held him in place. Forcing him to watch the bloodshed.

And when I thought it was done. When I thought she had her fill of horror, she bent to my level.

"Shift, Ulrich."

My body moved again, my bones cracking inside of me. I fell, my paws turning back to hands, gripping the floor of the hall. My hair fell over my face while I heaved from the pain.

"Silence him, Ulrich," Titania ordered. "Keep his disrespectful tongue quiet."

My eyes went up and I met Enok's eyes. My body began to shake, trying to fight her words.

"Now!" she demanded.

I stalked forward and my shadows came out, going straight for the king. I glanced down, watching my skin turn translucent, my ancient power hoping to claim its next meal—the lives that keep me living.

I fought her, the entire walk toward the throne. Watching Enok's eyes burn with hate. He was unmoving, determined.

Fuck, he was exactly like his daughter.

"I thought you would have protected her," Enok snapped at me. "You will break her. You will *ruin* her."

I nodded once.

"Kill me, beast," he demanded. "And send your soul into the darkest depths of torment."

I knew my face had shifted to one of pale bones by the fear in Enok's eyes. It was there, the soul, swimming in his body, reaching toward my power.

"My soul has resided in Hel for eternity," I whispered. "What else do you expect from its king?"

My shadows went down the king's throat, choking his ability to speak, but not taking his breath. Despite the begging in my body for me to do so.

"My good little pet," Titania said behind me, running her hand down my bare back. "Now we wait for her.

Her hand slapped my skin.

"Shield them, Ulrich. Do not let that whore see this until I am ready to reveal it."

I pounced, wrapping my hands around Titania's neck, throttling her into the floor. The crack of her head hitting the ground filled my body with glee.

My power bit inside of me, begging for her soul. Relishing the smell of her fear.

"Unhand me!" she choked.

My stupid, fucking hands released her in an instant.

"Shift, you animal!" she shouted.

My shout echoed again, and my body changed once more, sending me on all fours like the beast that I was.

"Let's wait for her, Ulrich. Let's watch the woman you love fall to her knees and realize what a horrible creature you really are. Doesn't that sound great for such a vile being like yourself?"

My chest heaved while I watched Titania's guards lift the people they'd murdered, staging them behind the king staring at me with hate in his eyes.

My shadows came from me, masking them all. Only showing their faces. Not revealing their wounds or blood. Leaving the king surrounded by the gore of those he likely loved.

Titania's hand went to my fur again.

"I can't wait to take you home with me, my pet." She gripped me. "You do nothing when that whore appears. You do not speak. You do not move. You do not fight."

My breaths went slow, my rage shaking inside of me.

"I own you now. Do not forget that," she whispered.

My head dipped in shame at her words. But my hate went darker.

I imagined Brenna's appearance. The rage that would burn in her eyes. The hate she would throw my way.

Fuck all the Fate created; I hated her as well.

Because she had broken through my walls. She had created soft cracks within the unrelenting Unseelie King. She had made me totally at her mercy. Stirring a new emotion within me that I had never felt in my long life.

I stared out the grand-hall doors. Knowing that wild woman would do all that she could, even if she were fueled by the hate I had beaten into her, she would come for me. It may be to end me, to take my life for what she was about to witness, but I would gladly fall by her hands.

No death would be greater than my life being claimed by the woman I loved. Fitting, for a king whose soul had been damned for eternity.

Author's Note

That was a wild ride. You may be confused (understandably), so let me simplify it for you:
Anytime Brenna was with the "beast", it was Ulrich.
Enjoy your re-read.

If you want to. I won't force you.

Acknowledgements

First, as always, to my husband: thank you for supporting this wild book. Thank you for being there while I spiraled about this story for a year before I was able to finally write it. Thank you for encouraging me to go nuts with this and let out my freaky side.

To Patricia, who helped me write this in 12 days: thanks, boo.

To my coven (you know who you are): thank you for reading this while I wrote it. Thank you for instantly supporting this feral fae f—k court and hyping it up along the way. Thank you for the late-night laughs, and emotional bonding. You're all amazing. I love each of you dearly.

To my editor, Sophie: Thank you for your continued help and support with my insane stories. Thank you for running with my idea to publish this book so quickly, and making sure the editing was done on time. I'm sorry for continuing to shock you with my endings, but thank you for sticking around on this crazy adventure.

And finally, to my readers: you've changed my life. Thank you for supporting my insanity. Thank you for loving these stories. Most importantly, thank you for giving me a chance.

About the Author

Courtney (C.A.) Blooming is an adult fantasy author. She began writing her debut novel, Threads of Fate, in July 2023. As of March 2025, she has three published books, with multiple projects underway.

Outside of the safety of books and stories, she is a wife and mother to three children. She works full-time in client success management. You can generally find her sitting in front of a computer working on her never-ending task list, or in a family snuggle pile with her husband and children.

For updates regarding upcoming publications, or to follow Courtney's author journey, you can find her on the social media platforms below, or through her website:

Website: cablooming.com

Instagram: @cablooming

Tiktok: @cablooming

MORE FROM C.A. BLOOMING

OF FATE SERIES

THREADS OF FATE - BOOK I

GRIEF CAN CAUSE YOU TO MAKE RASH DECISIONS. SHE DIDN'T EXPECT HERS TO TRAP HER IN THE LAND OF GODS.

BINDINGS OF FATE - BOOK II

THE ONLY THING MORE DANGEROUS THAN A DEAL WITH A DEMON IS A DEAL WITH FATE.

FEATHERS, FROST & FATE - NOVELLA

WHAT WOULD YOU DO FOR LOVE?

www.ingramcontent.com/pod-product-compliance
Lightning Source LLC
Chambersburg PA
CBHW020354310726
48979CB00015B/2597/J

* 9 7 8 1 9 6 4 0 8 7 1 0 8 *